KILT
TO ORDER

ALSO BY SUSANNAH NIX

Starstruck Series

Star Bright

Fallen Star

Rising Star

Lucky Star

Chemistry Lessons Series

Remedial Rocket Science

Intermediate Thermodynamics

Advanced Physical Chemistry

Applied Electromagnetism

Experimental Marine Biology

Elementary Romantic Calculus

King Family Series

My Cone and Only

Cream and Punishment

Pint of Contention

KILT TO ORDER

SUSANNAH NIX

Haver Street Press

FIRST EDITION: July 2023

ISBN: 978-1-950087-20-4

Haver Street Press | 448 W. 19th St., Suite 407 | Houston, TX 77008

Edited by Julia Ganis, www.juliaedits.com

Cover designed by Cover Ever After

For every wallflower who wishes Derek Craven
would steal her spectacles.

1

CASEY

I can't believe I'm actually on a date with a real live man.

Me, the girl who never gets asked out on dates.

Okay, yes, technically tonight is a blind date, which means this guy—his name is Tom and he's a vet tech—didn't voluntarily ask me out.

It's still *a date*. Even if I had to get someone else to arrange it.

And since that someone was my friend Kenzie, there's a decent chance intimidation and coercion played a role in said arrangement. Possibly also threats of bodily harm. I wouldn't put it past her.

I don't care. That's how desperate I am to break this losing streak that's been hanging over my head my entire adult life. I don't know what it is about me, but I seem to be invisible to men.

Not literally. They don't walk into me as if I'm not there.

I'm *romantically* invisible. A sexual null space, that's me. I'm everyone's pal Casey. Ozzy's younger sister Casey. Mayor Goodrich's Goody-Two-Shoes daughter Casey. Quiet, helpful, straight-A student Casey. Everybody loves me, but no one's ever fallen *in* love with me.

I've never had a single boyfriend. Not unless you count Seth Bumgarner, who invited me over to watch movies in his rec room in tenth grade, tried to shove my hand down his pants, and never spoke to me again after I said no. He was both my first and my last kiss. That's not a dry spell, that's the freaking Dust Bowl.

It's not as if I've been holding out for anything or anyone in particular. I'm not asking to find true love. I just want someone to like me enough to kiss me. And then take me to bed so I can rid myself of this virginity albatross around my neck.

Is that so much to ask? Everyone else I know is having sex. Why can't I?

I'm half convinced Seth Bumgarner put a curse on me for refusing to touch his penis, and now I'm sexual Kryptonite. As soon as men get near me, their sex drives wither and die.

But maybe tonight's the night I break the curse. Maybe I'll get lucky enough to get lucky finally. I don't want to get my hopes up, but I'm feeling cautiously optimistic.

Across the wooden picnic table from me, Tom's knee bounces up and down, rippling the surfaces of our beers. I think he might be nervous. But so am I. I can't fault him for that.

He's got freckles and short dark hair that's receding before its time. It's an odd combination that makes him look a little like a kid playing dress-up in an old man wig, but I've decided to find it charming. Frankly, I'm relieved he's not *too* handsome. He's not so hot that it's intimidating, which is good.

He likes animals—obviously, since he's a vet tech—which is another check in the pro column that's given us plenty of conversational common ground. He seems nice. Friendly, well-mannered, good hygiene. In my book that pretty much makes him Prince Charming. I would definitely consent to touch his penis if invited.

Canned rock music plays over the Rusty Spoke's outdoor speakers. Up on the small stage at the back of the patio, a sound guy sets up equipment for Shiny Heathens, the local band that'll be playing later tonight. The Spoke is a popular Friday night destination here in Crowder, and it's early enough in what passes for spring in Central Texas that the cool weather is perfect for sitting outside. The tables around us are starting to fill up, but for now it's still quiet enough to have a conversation.

"Kenzie said you work at a gym?" Tom says, giving me a curious look.

I don't exactly look like a gym rat. Not like Kenzie, who can crack a watermelon between her thighs. Seriously. She made me record a video of her doing it for TikTok.

"I'm the office manager," I explain, hoping he wasn't expecting me to look anything like Kenzie. If so, my doughy, not-at-all-fit body will be a disappointment. "I'm not like a trainer or anything."

Tom seems relieved. "I'm not much of a gym person. I can't even bench the bar."

"Me neither. My brother's the athlete in the family. I just sit behind the front desk and take care of all the paperwork and computer stuff."

"Is there a lot of that at a gym?"

"It's a fitness center and physical therapy clinic, so there's a lot of patient and insurance paperwork on top of managing the scheduling system for the trainers and PTs, plus membership renewals, billing, payroll, ordering supplies, that kind of thing. Oh, and I also run the social media accounts and make sure all the equipment is maintained. So there's a lot to keep me busy." My job's so dull, I'm practically putting myself to sleep talking about it.

Tom nods politely and sips his beer.

"You've definitely got me beat in the cool job department," I say with an awkward laugh.

"I don't know, I'll bet you don't have to express anal glands." He smiles. "At least I hope not."

This time my laugh's more natural. "True. Although I do have to mop urine out of the squat rack sometimes. You'd be surprised how many women pee when they squat. Or maybe you wouldn't be surprised. I don't know you that well. You could be a pelvic floor expert."

His ears go pink as he chokes on a laugh. "Is cleaning up human urine better or worse than dog shit, do you think?"

"I'm not sure. We might have to call it a draw."

Lord help me, why are we talking about bodily functions so much?

Tom's gaze drops to my chest. "I like your shirt."

I glance down at the T-shirt I'm wearing under my cardigan that says *I Closed My Book to be Here*. "Thanks!"

"I'm guessing that means you read a lot."

"I do, yeah. I was an English major, I loved it so much. I have a book blog on Instagram where I post all my latest reads."

"That's cool," Tom says politely and sips his beer.

"What about you? Do you like to read?"

He shakes his head. "I only read social media these days. I don't know how my parents passed the time before we had the internet for entertainment. I asked my twenty siblings, and they can't imagine it either."

"Wow."

"That was a joke," he clarifies. "I'm an only child. And not very good at jokes, clearly."

"No, it was good. I liked it." I'm a terrible liar.

Tom smiles awkwardly and takes another drink of beer.

I squirm on the hard wooden bench, fighting the urge to scratch my boobs. The new bra I bought for tonight feels like it's lined with sandpaper. Possibly thumbtacks too. I suspect it's actually a medieval torture device designed by sadistic nuns to punish heretics and promiscuous women. And don't get me started on the matching thong, which is currently lodged so far up my wazoo I think it might be trying to give me a colonoscopy.

It's my first experience with fancy lingerie. Apparently this is the price women are expected to pay for sexy underwear. On top of the *actual* price, which nearly gave me an aneurysm in the store. For that kind of money, it ought to be made of solid gold. I'll be paying off these pretty instruments of torture for the next three months, but it seemed like the least I could do for my first date in over a decade. No one can accuse me of not making an effort.

Except my mom, who'd take one look at my bookworm T-shirt and throw her hands up in despair. She's a politician—the mayor of Crowder, in fact—so she's obsessed with appearances and doesn't think much of my personal style. I'm not a big fan of her style either, so I try not to let her opinions bother me too much.

"Are you hungry?" Tom asks. "You want to share some chili-cheese fries or something?"

"I'd love to," I say, knowing my mom would be appalled.

Eating CHILI on a date??? she'd gasp in horror. *Honestly, Casey, it's like you don't even want men to find you attractive. Why not just douse yourself with gasoline and belch fire in his face?*

Well, too bad. My date offered me chili-cheese fries, and I'm not turning down that kind of ooey-gooey spicy fake plastic cheese deliciousness.

While Tom's inside ordering our fries, I check my phone and find a new text from my roommate Gareth.

How's your date? LMK if you need a rescue.

Gareth's always checking up on me like a protective older brother. Unlike my actual big brother, who couldn't care less what I'm up to unless it provides him with an opportunity to mock or annoy me.

I think it's going okay, I text back, afraid to jinx myself. *No rescue needed so far.*

Glad to hear it, he replies immediately. *Call if you change your mind.*

You're not going out tonight?

Maybe later. You can still call me though.

For a hot jock who's allergic to commitment, Gareth can be a real sweetheart. But no way am I interrupting his plans, which probably involve some gorgeous woman he barely knows. That's how he usually spends his Friday and Saturday nights when he's not on shift at the firehouse.

Although, not so much lately, come to think of it. He's been staying in more often and spending more nights vegging on the couch watching TV with me. I wonder what that's about.

Tom comes back with a heaping basket of the Rusty Spoke's delicious chili-cheese fries, and I put my phone away. I'm hungry enough to eat a whole truckload of fries, but I can't stop hearing my mom's voice in the back of my head insisting that men don't like women who eat too much.

Usually, I try not to give the stuff my mom says too much credence, but I can't help thinking she might be right occasionally. To hear her talk, she was beating men off with a stick before she settled down and married my dad. Maybe if I'd taken more of my mom's advice I wouldn't be a twenty-eight-year-old virgin on her first real date since high school.

So I make myself stop after a few fries, leaving most of them for Tom.

After he finishes off the last of the fries, Tom pushes them away and looks up at me. "Don't move," he says and reaches across the table.

I freeze when he takes my chin in his hand and tips my head up. "What's wrong? Is there a bug on me?"

It's all I can do to hold still and not freak out, so of course my nose decides that's a good time to tickle with an impending sneeze.

"Relax, there's no bug. You've got some chili on your face is all." Tom smiles as he wipes the corner of my mouth with his thumb.

Oh.

Hang on.

Was that flirting? Was Tom trying to flirt with me?

I think he might have been!

His smile fades as his attention shifts to something behind me, so I guess the flirting's over now. Bummer.

"What's wrong?" I ask him when he continues to frown.

"I don't want to alarm you or anything, but there's a scary-looking guy over there who keeps glaring at us."

"Really?"

"Don't look."

Too late. I've already turned around. I spot the scary guy in question and give him a wave. "Ignore him. He's harmless."

Mostly. As long as you don't give him a good reason to use his two hundred and eighty pounds of solid muscle against you. I've seen him put four drunk frat bros on the ground like he was swatting gnats, but they had it coming for escalating an argument over the best Billy Joel song into a bar brawl when the answer is obviously "Captain Jack." Duh.

"That's Darius," I say. "He's one of my roommates."

"You live with that guy?" Tom asks, alarmed.

With his long hair, beard, leather jacket, and perma-scowl, Darius looks more like a Dothraki warlord moonlighting as the front man of a death metal band than the kind of guy you'd expect to be roommates with a straitlaced book nerd like me. Unless you also happen to know that Darius has a degree in quantum physics, a habit of borrowing my romance novels, and a pet rabbit named Mr. Twinkletoes.

The rabbit was a rescue, so he didn't name it himself. But he also didn't change its name when he adopted it.

"I live with my older brother and two of his friends in one of our parents' rental properties," I explain as I twist a strand of hair around my finger. "Mom would only let Ozzy rent the house if I lived with him to keep an eye on the place. Basically, she expects me to be the stick-in-the-mud babysitter who keeps my slob of a brother from turning their investment property into an annex of the town dump, which isn't exactly my first choice of living situation, but at the time I was working at Beaver Burger, and it was either that or move back in with my parents. And since they agreed to let me have the big bedroom with the en suite bathroom, I don't mind all that much."

I snap my mouth shut, realizing I've been rattling on and that's probably way more information about my living situation than Tom ever wanted. I have a tendency to babble sometimes when I'm nervous, which sadly isn't even my most awkward trait.

Tom nods at my overly lengthy explanation, but still appears unsettled as his gaze darts over my shoulder to Darius again. "Why is he lurking over there scowling at me?"

"He's the bouncer here. Lurking and scowling is part of his job." I don't tell Tom that Darius can also be a little protective of me, just like Gareth. Which may have been part of the reason I chose the Rusty Spoke for our date tonight.

Not that Kenzie would set me up with anyone skeevy. Plus, no guy is going to risk pissing her off by pulling anything shitty with one of her friends. Still, I figured it couldn't hurt to have a professional murder puppy on standby if I need one.

Except I didn't fully consider the extent to which Darius's protective instincts might freak out my date. Tom looks like he's ready to cut and run. Or possibly pee his pants. Could go either way.

"I'll be right back." I swing my legs over the bench and stride across the patio toward Darius. Unfortunately, both my butt cheeks have gone numb after sitting on a wooden plank for an hour, so it ends up being more of a lurching Quasimodo stagger than the confident strut I was aiming for.

Darius arches a dark eyebrow at my approach. "Why are you walking like that? What's wrong with your legs?"

"Never you mind." I square my shoulders, which drives the sadistic underwire in my bra deeper into my breast tissue. "Can you please stop glowering at my date? It's harshing the mood."

Darius grunts. "You actually like this guy?"

"Sure. He's okay." Truthfully, I don't feel much of anything about Tom, but that's beside the point. I don't *dis*like him, which is good enough for me. "More importantly, I think he might like me, so I'd appreciate it if you wouldn't scare him off."

"He seems kind of twitchy."

"Maybe because he's worried Khal Drogo is about to challenge him to single combat."

Another grunt. "I'll lay off."

"Thank you." I smile at Darius and spin around, fighting the urge to claw my thong out of my crack. How do people *wear* these things? Do they just get used to walking around with a strip of elastic wedged between their cheeks all day? Insanity.

Tom watches me as I walk back to the table. Fortunately, most of the blood has returned to my butt, and I manage an almost-normal gait.

*Un*fortunately, a blonde hand-talker in a Bowman U sweatshirt chooses the worst possible moment to flail one of her arms out, bumps the tray of a passing server, and I wind up with four styrofoam cups worth of frozen margaritas dumped down the front of my shirt.

Mother *cracker* that's cold!

Also sticky.

And did I mention cold?

"God, I'm so sorry!" The server is mortified, as is the hand-talker who caused the accident. They both grab handfuls of napkins and shove them at me, apologizing profusely while lime-and-tequila slush soaks into my new bra and drips onto my favorite red Converse.

I tell them not to worry about it, since it was an accident that could have happened to anyone. It just had to happen to me on my first date since tenth grade. Figures.

Oh good, here's Tom, who saw the whole thing.

He offers me a sympathetic look and more napkins. "Are you okay?"

"Peachy," I say as I wring out my T-shirt. "Well, limey, actually. And you probably shouldn't light a match near me."

The hand-talker has already gone back to her friends. The poor server offers yet another apology before she scampers off to replace the spilled drinks for the customers still waiting on them.

"At least margaritas don't stain?" Tom offers.

I let go of my soaked T-shirt and shiver as the wet cotton plasters itself to my skin.

Tom stares at my chest and visibly swallows.

I glance down and realize my white shirt's clinging like plastic wrap and is nearly as transparent, which means my new pink bra is plainly visible. Thank god I splurged on a nice one, I guess.

From the way Tom's eyes are glued to my chest, I'm thinking it was money well spent. *So this is what it feels like to have your boobs ogled.* I wouldn't mind if it wasn't for the part where I'm wet, sticky, and freezing.

"You, uh, you must be cold," Tom stammers.

Because yeah, my nipples are standing at full attention, as

everyone including Tom can see quite clearly through my lace bra.

He clears his throat and manages to tear his gaze away from my breasts. "You probably want to go home now, huh?"

Disappointment sinks into my stomach, but it's too chilly to be sitting around in wet clothes after sundown. There's not much else to do but call tonight a loss. "I should probably change out of this wet shirt, yeah."

"I'll walk you to your car."

Darius shoots me a questioning look as we pass him, and I give him a quick head shake. I don't need the bouncer following me out to the parking lot and putting even more of a damper on this date.

"This is me," I say when we reach the Picklemobile, my trusty Honda hatchback that's been with me since high school. So named because of the bright green paint job it was given by the previous owner for reasons that shall forever remain a mystery. My little green car is probably the most notable thing about me. Kind of sad, when you think about it.

"This is *your* car?" Tom says. "I see it around town all the time."

See? The Picklemobile is unforgettable. Unlike me.

"Thanks for tonight," I say glumly. "I had a really nice time."

Tom raises a skeptical eyebrow.

"Well, it was nice until I got doused with forty-eight ounces of lime slush," I amend.

"I had a nice time up until then too. Maybe we could try it again sometime?"

I perk up. "I'd like that."

"Hopefully you won't end up wearing someone else's margaritas again."

"At least they weren't Bloody Marys. Then I'd look like an ax murderer."

He smiles, and I'm suddenly aware of how close he's standing. Close enough that I can smell the mingled scents of beer and chili on his breath as his gaze drops to my mouth.

Wait.

Holy shirtballs, is he going to kiss me?

Oh my god, he's leaning in! He *is* going to kiss me. It's happening! The heavens have opened up to bless me with their quenching rain and put an end to my dry spell.

My heart's pounding, and my mouth has gone dry. It's been ages since I've kissed anyone, and it wasn't all that great the last time. What if I'm terrible at it? I barely even know what I'm supposed to be doing. What if I'm the world's worst kisser?

As soon as the thought flashes through my head, that's when I feel it.

An itchy warning tingle in my nose.

I try to ignore it, but it won't be ignored.

I try to tamp it down, but I can't.

It wants out, and there's no stopping it.

My nose starts to itch.

And then it starts to twitch.

And then—

Ahh-CHOOOO!

My head snaps forward as the sneeze racks my body at the exact same moment Tom goes in for the kiss. He doesn't have time to pull back and save himself.

Not only does he get the contents of my sinuses expelled directly into his open mouth, but my face slams into his with a bone-jarring crack. Pain explodes across my vision, and I hear Tom swear as I stagger backward, clutching my throbbing cheekbone with both hands.

Fiddlesticks.

I don't think I'm getting kissed tonight after all.

2

GARETH

Something unbelievably soft is nuzzling my ear.

Weird.

I must be dreaming because I haven't had a woman in my bed in months. I also didn't go out tonight, so I couldn't have brought anyone home, even if I'd had the urge.

For a sexy dream, it's kind of a rip-off. My earholes rate pretty far down the list of my favorite erogenous zones. Belly button action, on the other hand, now that's the stuff. I know my libido's been starved for attention, but I wish I was having a belly button dream instead of this weird ear shit.

As I drift the rest of the way toward consciousness, the ear nuzzling continues. I'm starting to worry this might not be a dream after all. *What the fuck?*

I lift my hand to fend off the rogue ear-nuzzler, who turns out to be furry.

Which means she's a *he*, and also a rabbit.

"God dammit, Mr. Twinkletoes!"

Darius's pet rabbit scampers down my chest, using my diaphragm as a launchpad to hop to the floor. Since he's one of those big lop ears who weighs a good ten pounds, it's like being punched in the gut.

Mr. Twinkletoes hops a few feet away before he sits up on his big hind legs. The bunny nose that despoiled my ear twitches as he gives me an indignant glare as if *I'm* the rude one.

"How would you like it if I stuck my tongue in *your* ear without consent?" I ask him.

He shivers and galumphs away in a huff.

"That's what I thought," I call after him.

Stupid rabbit.

I sit up on the couch and rub my tired eyes. My laptop's gone into power save mode, which means I've been asleep for at least twenty minutes. Crap, I'm supposed to be working on my English lit essay tonight, not taking a nap. I usually go to the Bowman library to study, but I figured I'd take advantage of the house being empty for once to kick back on the couch and crack the books. Great plan.

When I touch the trackpad to wake the screen up, the Spark-Notes study guide I was reading for *Great Expectations* reappears. I thought it'd be less boring than the actual book, but it put me to sleep just as fast. At this rate I'll never finish this damn essay.

Instead of getting back to work like I should, I pick up my phone. Because procrastination is a hell of a lot more fun than trying to make sense of Dickens.

No new texts from Casey. That's good, I guess. Hopefully it means she's having a good time on her date. I fight the impulse to text her again to get an update. It's a struggle, but I need to keep my mother hen tendencies in check. Casey doesn't need me cramping her style.

It surprised me when she announced she was going on a blind date tonight. In the three years we've been roommates, she's never been on a single date as far as I know. Never had a boyfriend or a girlfriend or a casual hookup. I actually wondered if she might be ace or aromantic until she admitted to having a crush on one of her coworkers last year.

The fact that she's out meeting up with some stranger at a bar has me on edge. I know Casey's smart and can take care of herself, but worrying is sort of my thing.

Rather than bug her again, I decide to text Darius, who's working the door at the Rusty Spoke tonight.

I'm not being paranoid. I'm only trying to gauge how much longer I'll have the house to myself to work on my paper. My curiosity is purely motivated by self-interest. That's my story, and I'm sticking to it.

They left together 30 min ago, Darius replies.

Huh. Her date must be going well if she left with the guy and hasn't come home yet.

It's fine.

Casey's fine.

Kenzie wouldn't set her up with a creep, and Darius wouldn't have let her leave with a dude who was giving off red flags. Casey knows what she's doing. She's a grown adult who doesn't need me playing nanny.

But I have fucking issues, so I'm going to worry anyway until she's safely home.

Sighing mightily, I pick up my laptop and force myself to read about *Great Expectations* some more. I seriously do not get the point of this story or why it's supposed to be so great. As far as I can tell, it's just a bunch of people being mean to this poor dumb kid.

Why do all the characters have such goofy made-up names? Wopsle? Pumblechook? I thought this was supposed to be serious literature, but they sound like animal characters from a children's book. It's a weird choice for such a downer of a story, especially since the characters are almost all unmitigated assholes and not friendly furry companions.

It's only when I hear the garage door opening that I realize I've been staring blankly at the same paragraph for the last five minutes without reading a word. Snapping out of my stupor, I shove my paperback copy of *Great Expectations* under the couch, slam my laptop closed, and lunge for the TV remote. By the time the kitchen door opens, I'm kicked back with my feet up on the coffee table, innocently watching a women's softball game like the slacker my roommates think I am.

I haven't told anyone that I've been taking online community college classes because I don't need them hazing me about it. Except that's not entirely true, because I know Casey would never haze me about going back to school. She'd be nothing but supportive.

But that's the problem. She'll get all excited about it, and I won't be able to face her disappointment if it turns out I can't hack it. Because I have a sinking feeling I can't.

School's never been my strong suit. In high school I only ever put in the minimum effort required to maintain my eligibility for football. After my dad died and my life went to shit, I ended up dropping out my senior year. I had to get my GED a few years later when I decided to apply to the fire academy.

Passing the GED exam was a cinch compared to taking actual college classes, which have been kicking my ass big-time. The courses for my emergency management major haven't been too bad since I've already picked up a lot of it in my four years on the job as a firefighter. It's the core curriculum classes that are killing me. I managed to squeak by with a low C in algebra last term, but this English lit class might be my villain origin story. Fucking Dickens.

"Gareth?" Casey calls from the kitchen behind me.

See? She's perfectly safe. All my worrying was for nothing.

"Hey," I call back. "How was your date?"

"Fine. I thought you were going out tonight."

"I fell asleep on accident. I might go out later though."

It's getting harder to maintain the pretense of a social life around my roommates. I barely go out anymore unless it's to hole up in the local university library to study in secret. Eventually, someone's going to notice I haven't been frequenting my usual haunts and the jig will be up.

I glance over my shoulder as Casey comes out of the kitchen with her attention glued to her phone and her wavy brown hair curtaining her face. It takes me a second to notice her shirt is soaking wet. "What happened to you?"

"An unfortunate collision with someone else's margaritas," she says as she disappears into her room. "I need to wash off and change."

The door slams shut behind her, and I chew on the inside of my cheek as I stare at it. The margarita incident plus Casey's rush to hide away in her room makes me think the date might not have gone so well. I'm tempted to follow her and get the real story, but if she'd wanted to talk, she wouldn't have disappeared so quickly.

But maybe I should check on her anyway?

Except she's in there changing clothes, so maybe not.

Yeah, better to give her time to get cleaned up first. Then I'll go knock on her door to see if she wants to talk.

Right when I turn back to the TV, Casey lets out a blood-curdling scream.

3

CASEY

I hate my brother.

Okay, not really. But I would very much like to throttle him sometimes.

I assume the murder clown lurking in my shower is Ozzy's idea of a joke. Ha ha. So hilarious. I nearly had a heart attack when I saw Pennywise in the mirror behind me.

I'm bent over the sink clutching my chest when the door of my bedroom bursts open, slamming against the wall loud enough to give me a second coronary.

"Casey?" A Gareth-sized shape fills the bathroom doorway. "What's wrong? Are you okay?"

My soul's still trying to leave my body, so I gesture mutely at the life-size cardboard cutout that inspired my scream.

"Jesus," Gareth says, rearing back a little when he sees Pennywise in my shower. "I would have pissed myself if Ozzy had pulled that shit on me."

"I'm going to replace his toothpaste with Monistat," I manage to mutter now that my heart's starting to calm down again. "No jury would convict me."

Gareth's gaze meets mine in the mirror, and the smile drops off his face.

Oh crud.

What with my life flashing before my eyes, I forgot to hide my brand-new shiner.

"What the fuck happened to you?"

The sudden dark rage in his expression sends a shiver over my skin. Gareth almost never gets angry. He's one of the friendliest, most easygoing people I know. But right now he looks ready to go John Wick on someone's ass.

Ducking my head, I cup my hand over my bruised eye. "It was just a dumb accident."

"Let me see." He turns me around and gently pries my fingers away from my face as he tips my head up for a better look.

I can't help my shiver when his thumb skims over my cheekbone. "You should see the other guy," I say in a feeble attempt at a joke.

Gareth's lips press together so hard they're nearly white. "Did it happen on your date? Was it that guy Kenzie set you up with?"

He may not be as big and scary-looking as Darius, but he's a six-foot firefighter with enough muscle on his athletic frame to snap poor Tom like a twig. Easily.

"No one did anything. I told you, it was an accident."

"Casey." He doesn't believe me.

"I swear. I did this to myself."

I squeeze Gareth's thick wrist as his eyes search my face. They're an unreal color of blue that's so striking it still catches me off guard sometimes, despite having lived with him for three years. I wonder how many women have had their heart broken because of those eyes and that way he has of gazing at you with them—attentive, compassionate, aware.

Dozens and dozens of women, is my guess.

That's why I try not to look directly at his face too often. It'd be too easy to forget myself and fall under his spell. Gareth's insanely handsome, even with his light brown hair sticking up in crazy directions from dragging his hands through it too much, which he only does at home and only when he's tired or stressed. That's how well I know him.

Too well to allow myself to feel any kind of way about his perfect face and equally perfect body. I've seen the kind of women who attract his attention, and they don't look like me. If he hadn't been friends with my brother, Gareth wouldn't have noticed I exist. He's so far out of my league, we're not even playing the same game. It's like he's an Olympic swimmer, and I'm flailing around in the kiddie pool yelling "Marco Polo." No matter how nice he is, he's not going to invite me to swim a four-hundred-meter medley with him.

He arches a skeptical eyebrow at me, still not buying my story. "I suppose you dumped a margarita on yourself in addition to punching yourself in the face?"

"They were two completely unrelated accidents, believe it or not, and the margarita wasn't my fault." Maybe one day it will be a funny anecdote I can tell at parties, but right now I feel too much like crying to laugh about it.

"Must have been some date."

"It didn't exactly turn out the way I'd hoped." I'm trying hard to put on a brave face, but my lip has to go and betray me by wobbling.

Gareth folds me into his arms, and I cling shamelessly, gulping down a sob as I rest my uninjured cheek against his big, muscular chest. It's a bit like being hugged by a rock-hard teddy bear, which feels way more amazing than it sounds. Trust me, it seriously rules.

"I'm sorry," he says, rubbing consoling circles between my

shoulder blades like the stand-up guy he is. "Does your face hurt?"

"Not as much as my pride."

Tragically, this isn't the first time a sneeze has spoiled a big moment for me, only the worst and most embarrassing to date. Ever since I was a kid, I've had this nervous tic where I sneeze when I get stressed. My past is littered with inopportune sneezes in the middle of tests, school plays, oral presentations, job interviews, and other high-pressure situations. Most of the time it's not so bad since a stray sneeze isn't usually an unrecoverable faux pas.

Until tonight. This is the first time I've ever caused anyone else bodily injury with one of my stress sneezes. Not having been on any dates in over a decade means I haven't had to deal with the sneezing issue in a romantic situation. Talk about a mood killer.

"Want to tell me what happened?" Gareth asks.

"Someone bumped a waitress and knocked a tray of margaritas into me."

"That's bad luck."

"Yeah," I say to his chest. "The date was actually going well before that."

"And the black eye?" he asks when I don't offer any further details.

I sniffle and burrow harder. "It's humiliating."

His fingers give me a tender squeeze. "I promise not to judge."

"You know how sometimes I sneeze when I get nervous?"

"Yeah." He's only seen me do it once or twice, but my brother loves to tease me about it and has regaled Gareth with plenty of hilarious stories about my most embarrassing sneezes. If Ozzy gets wind of tonight's calamity, I'll never hear the end of it.

"Tom walked me out to my car and was about to kiss me, but right as he leaned in..." I can't even say it.

"You sneezed?" Gareth fills in for me.

"So hard I bashed my face into his and gave him a nosebleed."

There weren't any tissues or napkins in my car, so I'd had to improvise. The memory of Tom glaring at me with two blood-soaked tampons sticking out of his nostrils is one that will haunt me to my grave.

Gareth rubs more consoling circles on my back. "I'm sorry. That really sucks. But it's not your fault."

"Who else's fault would it be?"

"You can't control when you sneeze. It's just bad luck."

"You won't tell Ozzy, will you?"

"If he finds out, it won't be because of me."

"Thank you."

I could easily stand here hugging Gareth for the rest of the night. It's the best hug I've ever had, and who knows when I'll get another one like it. Not only is he warm, strong, and safe, but he smells fantastic.

Me? Not so much. Also, I'm damp and sticky. I should probably let him go.

Reluctantly, I pull out of his arms and wipe my eyes. "Sorry, I'm probably getting margarita on your shirt."

"I don't give a shit about that." Gareth gives my shoulders a squeeze as he bends his head to kiss my forehead. The touch of his lips is so light and barely-there, I might think I imagined it if not for the tingle humming over my skin and down my spine.

It's not exactly the kiss I was hoping to get tonight, but a good forehead kiss is an underappreciated art form and nothing to sneer at. Even if it is purely platonic.

As he lets me go, Gareth's gaze drops to my sticky shirt. He swallows visibly—just like Tom did—and takes a hasty step back.

That's when I remember my T-shirt's still see-through and indecently clingy to boot. Also apparently my nipples didn't get the platonic memo because they're trying their hardest—and I do mean hardest—to drill through my bra.

With an apologetic smile, I grab two fistfuls of my damp shirt and hold it away from my body. "Gross, huh? I smell like limes and alcoholism."

"I'll let you get cleaned up. Want me to take that out of here?" Gareth hooks a thumb at Pennywise, who's still lurking in the shower and definitely would have scared the bejeebus out of me all over again because I'd already forgotten he was there.

"That'd be great. If you feel like burning it, even better."

"I'm thinking I'll hang on to it and spring it on Ozzy when he's least expecting it."

"Excellent idea."

"You should ice that shiner," Gareth adds as he carries the life-size cutout out of the bathroom.

"I will."

On the other side of the doorway, he glances back with Pennywise tucked under his arm. "Are you hungry? Want me to make you a grilled cheese?"

"With grated parmesan toasted onto the bread?" I ask hopefully.

I may not have gotten laid tonight, but Gareth's grilled cheese sandwiches are the next best thing. I can't say from actual experience that they're better than sex, but they're certainly orgasmic.

He smiles. "Just the way you like it."

"Cut diagonally?"

"How else?"

"Yes, please. I'll be your best friend forever."

"Coming right up." He raps his knuckles on the doorframe on his way out.

"You're the best!" I shout after him.

"That's what all the ladies say," he calls back.

Not for the first time, I remind myself how lucky I am to be Gareth's friend. As much as I sometimes wish I was the kind of woman he'd want to sleep with, the women he sleeps with don't get to be part of his life like I am.

He hasn't had a girlfriend since he moved in, and he doesn't seem to date so much as flit from one casual hookup to the next without letting anyone stick around long enough to get to know him.

As far as I know, I'm the only woman Gareth makes his special grilled cheese sandwiches for. All those gorgeous women he hooks up with might get to have him in a way I never will, but it's only temporary. I'm the lucky one because I'm the one who gets to see him every day. The one he hangs out with and actually talks to.

That's better than getting to sleep with him. It's more than enough to make up for the sense of longing I feel sometimes when I look at him.

4

GARETH

Ozzy's voice rings through the house at an ungodly hour for a Saturday morning. "Rise and shine, mothercluckers! It's games day! Time to kilt up and go where glory awaits thee!"

I roll over and bury my head under a pillow. The sun's not even up yet. It's too damn early for this shit. Especially after I was up half the night trying to finish *Great Expectations*.

I've still got to write the damn essay response that's due tomorrow night, but today's the Crowder Scottish Festival, and I'm starting a twenty-four-hour shift at the fire station in the morning, so basically I'm fucked.

My door bursts open and a two-hundred-pound human cocker spaniel cannonballs onto my bed.

"Get up!" Ozzy hollers, bouncing on the mattress like a kid waking his parents on Christmas morning. "Let's go. Move it."

"Asshat," I mumble and whack him with a pillow. "Cut it the fuck out before you break my bed."

I love the guy. I really do. Not only was he the first friend I made when I moved to Crowder four years ago, he was the first real friend I'd had since I left home at eighteen. He kind of saved my life when he forcibly befriended me, and I'll never stop being grateful for that. But sometimes Ozzy's hyperactive muppet energy is a lot to take.

"Aw, come on, princess. Don't be cranky. Today's gonna be an awesome day."

I scrub my hands over my face. "Go jump on Darius's bed. I dare you."

"Fuck no. I'm not dumb enough to piss off the beast."

My kilt hits me in the face. I toss it aside and glare at Ozzy, who's already dressed, his curly brown hair damp from the shower. "So it's only me who has to put up with you climbing into my bed?"

"Yeah, and you should be fucking honored. I don't get into bed with just anyone, you know. Unlike some people, I have standards." He grins and tosses my team T-shirt at me.

It's pink and matches his, with our Highland Games club logo on the front and *Keep Texas Kilted* in big letters on the back. Ozzy was the one who campaigned for pink T-shirts this year, claiming it would make the club more welcoming to women. Which might be true, but I'm pretty sure he also wanted to fuck with the guys who think they're too macho to wear pink.

"Anyway, Darius is already up," Ozzy says. "You're the only lazy ass still lolling around in bed."

I'm impressed, considering Darius didn't get home from work until almost three a.m., which I know because I was still up reading fucking Dickens.

Of the four of us, Casey's the only one in the house with a regular nine-to-five job. I work twenty-four-hour shifts at the firehouse with forty-eight-hour breaks in between. Ozzy operates a residential services company that does pool and gutter cleaning, exterior power washing, and window washing, which means he works whenever he's got a job scheduled. And Darius's bouncer job keeps him at the Rusty Spoke from six to closing Wednesday through Saturday nights, plus he and I sometimes pick up extra work from Ozzy when he's got some for us.

"Where are your shoes?" Ozzy stoops like he's going to look under my bed, which is where I stashed Pennywise last night.

Yes, as a matter of fact, it is deeply unsettling to know there's an evil clown hiding under my bed. But it'll be worth it when I scare the shit out of Ozzy to get him back for giving Casey and me heart attacks last night. But to maximize the scare factor, I need to wait until he's forgotten all about it, which means not letting him find it now.

I jump out of bed and strip off my underwear because it's the fastest way I can think of to get Ozzy out of my room. "I'm up, okay? I can dress myself."

"Dude, put your One-Eyed Willy away." He does an about-face, heading for the door.

"That's what you get for barging into my room first thing in the morning."

"Who's riding with me?" Casey shouts up the stairs.

"Shotgun," Ozzy and I both yell at the same time.

We eye each other. The back seat of Casey's Honda isn't built for guys our size, and Darius always insists on listening to this ear-brutalizing speed metal in his truck. That shit gives me a headache on a good day. I seriously cannot deal with it on this little sleep.

"Rochambeau?"

Ozzy nods and counts us off. "One, two, three, go."

"What the hell is that?" I say when he makes a weird hand signal.

"It's Spider-Man. We're doing Rock, Paper, Scissors, Lizard, Spock, Spider-Man, Batman, Wizard, Glock."

"No way. We're not doing any of those complicated try-hard versions where you need an advanced math degree to figure out what beats what. It's plain old Rock, Paper, Scissors."

"If you want to be boring, I guess."

We go again and both choose rock this time.

I'm so intent on beating Ozzy, I don't notice that Casey's come upstairs.

"The Picklemobile's leaving the station in fifteen minutes," she says from the hallway outside my bedroom.

Because he's a compulsive shit-stirrer, Ozzy oh-so-helpfully steps to the side, giving his sister an unobstructed view of me and my morning wood.

"Oh *god*!" she squeaks as her eyes go cartoon-character round, which looks even more comical because she's wearing a puffin onesie.

"Pretty horrifying, isn't it?" Ozzy cracks.

Casey pins her gaze to the ceiling while I snatch a pillow off the bed to cover my junk. "What's the house rule about leaving doors to common areas open when you're having naked time?"

Ozzy's hand shoots into the air. "Oh! Oh! I know this one. We're not supposed to do it because, and I quote, 'No one should be subjected to anyone's genitals without prior consent.'"

He ought to know since he's been busted for it more than once. Dude loves to walk around naked even more than I do. Hence the rule.

"Sorry," I mutter, shoving Ozzy out the door and slamming it shut. "Ozzy's the one who left the door open."

"Yeah, but he didn't strip naked until after I was in his bedroom!" Ozzy shouts from the hall.

I snatch my Sport Kilt off the floor and secure it around my waist. God bless Velcro. Easy on, easy off. When I fling the door open again, Casey jumps and her gaze drops to my kilt-swathed pelvis.

"NASGA regulations require athletes to wear appropriate

garments under their kilts during competitions," Ozzy says, lifting a brow. "I don't think you're NASGA compliant, G."

"I can be ready in fifteen minutes, and unlike some people, I won't complain about your musical taste," I tell Casey.

Who's still staring at my crotch.

A grin spreads across my face as I lounge against the doorframe. "If you want another show, all you have to do is ask. I'm not shy."

I can't help myself. I like the feel of her eyes on my body. I'm not used to getting that kind of attention from Casey. She's never seemed the least bit impressed by my looks the way other women are.

Or so I thought.

I have the pleasure of watching her face go bright red again, and she shoots me a glare that says she's not afraid to give me a purple nurple. Just in case she decides to go in for the kill, I fold my arms across my chest to cover my defenseless nipples.

Casey pointedly turns her attention to Ozzy. "Are those your eggs cooking on the stove? Because I'm pretty sure they're burning."

"Oh shit!" Ozzy yelps and sprints for the stairs.

"If you ruin my good omelet pan, you're buying me a new one," I yell after him.

"He can ride with Darius," Casey says, shaking her head at her brother's epic lack of kitchen skills. The guy once fell asleep while boiling eggs and woke up two hours later to a scorched, dry pot and eggs exploding all over the kitchen. "Shotgun's all yours if you can be ready in fifteen minutes."

I snag her arm when she turns to go. "Hey, wait. Let me have a look at your eye."

She tilts her head up so I can examine her bruise. "I tried to cover it with concealer. Does it show?"

"No, you did a good job." If I didn't know the contusion was there, I wouldn't have noticed it. More importantly, the eye itself appears okay. "Does it still hurt?"

"Not much."

Casey's got the biggest, most beautiful brown eyes framed by the kind of long, thick lashes most women would kill for. It's not often I get to see them up close like this, and I get distracted staring at them for a second.

The bathroom door opens behind her, and we jump apart as Darius steps out with a towel wrapped around his waist and a polka-dot shower cap on his head. He pauses, lifting his eyebrows slightly, and continues down the hall without a word.

"Does he know?" I mouth as he disappears into his room.

Casey shakes her head.

I figured as much. Darius might be the stoic, silent type, but I suspect he'd lose his shit if he thought someone had hurt Casey.

We all would. Even Ozzy. He and Casey might bicker and torment each other, but when she had the flu last year he drove all the way to Austin to get this particular kind of tea she likes. And then he made me swear not to tell her how hard it was to get. God only knows what he'd do if he ever found out anyone but him was giving his sister grief.

Casey's like the Wendy to our Lost Boys. Or the Snow White to our messy-ass dwarfs. She organizes the cleaning rota, remembers our birthdays, makes the house smell nice with all her candles and girly shit, and just generally keeps the three of us civilized so we don't go completely feral. We'd do almost anything for her. Except pick up our dirty socks because there's only so much you can do to civilize three single male jocks sharing a house.

"Are you going to the Scottish festival dressed as a puffin?" I smile as I pull up the hoodie of Casey's puffin onesie—the one I got her for her birthday last year.

She's obsessed with puffins. She's got a collection of puffin stuffies and figurines in her room, and her head's full of puffin facts from watching endless hours of nature documentaries, most of which she forced me to sit through with her.

It's not that easy to find a puffin onesie, it turns out. I had to order it all the way from Japan. But it was totally worth it because she looks cute as hell.

"I thought it'd be thematically appropriate since Scotland's well-known for its puffin-watching hotspots."

"It looks awesome." I love how enthusiastic she is about the stuff she's into, and that she's not afraid to be exactly who she is. There's no pretense with Casey. What you see is what you get. Not many people can say that. Definitely not me.

"I better go finish packing the cooler. And *you* need to put some underwear on if you want to ride in my car." She pokes my bare chest with her index finger, and warmth spirals outward from the point of contact, making my One-Eyed Willy spring to attention again.

Fortunately, she's already turned away, so she doesn't notice the tent in the front of my kilt.

I grip the doorframe as I watch her walk down the hall. It's pretty much impossible to see her ass inside that baggy onesie, but I find myself wishing I could.

Which isn't the sort of thought I should be having about my roommate.

As soon as I climb out of the Picklemobile at the Crowder Festival Grounds, I'm hit by the smell of fresh-cut grass and funnel cake floating on the breeze. Heaven.

I love festivals. The food, the music, the vendors. So many things to see and do and buy. Is there any better way to spend a spring day than outdoors at a festival?

A few feet away, my brother jumps out of Darius's truck and throws his arms open wide as he breathes in a lungful of air. "Nothing like the smell of cow shit in the morning!"

Yes, there's some of that in the air too, thanks to Wee Hamish. The Highland cow with his thick mop of hair is the star attraction of the petting zoo at the Crowder Scottish Festival and Highland Games every year. There's a Ziploc baggie of apple slices tucked in my pocket for him.

"You should have been a farmer," Gareth tells Ozzy, unfolding himself from the front seat of my car and settling his straw cowboy hat on his head.

The guys grab their gym bags, camp chairs, and the cooler from the back of Darius's truck. The heavy athletics competition starts at ten in the morning and goes until late afternoon, so they'll need to stay hydrated and keep their energy up for the long day ahead. But before it starts, they're helping out with the children's Highland Games camp where kids can try their hand at the events with lighter, play equipment. While they're doing that, I'll be working the athlete check-in table.

Since my brother, roommates, and best friend Kenzie are all part of the local Highland Games club, I've tagged along to enough of their events that I'm basically an honorary member. They keep trying to talk me into throwing with them, but sports are very much not my thing. I've got all the coordination and strength of a newborn foal, so throwing heavy weights around is a hard no from me. I'd much rather sit on the sidelines and watch.

I mean, come on—a chance to go to a festival and watch muscly men in kilts perform feats of strength? Try and keep me away.

I've been to a lot of different Scottish festivals around the state, and tagged along to Highland Games in Austin, San Antonio, Fort Worth, Houston, Decatur, McKinney, Salado, and Waxahachie. The one here in Crowder may not be the biggest or the fanciest, but my hometown festival is still my favorite of all of them.

The sound of bagpipes carries all the way out to the staff parking lot as we set out for the athletic field at the far end of the grounds. The festival gates haven't officially opened to the public yet, but you can smell the food cooking in the food court and hear the musicians warming up on the three stages set up for live Celtic music and dance performances. There's a children's area by the petting zoo, a whisky-tasting tent, and a marketplace full of vendors selling Scottish-themed goods and Celtic jewelry and art.

A gaggle of teenage girls dressed in tartan kilties and ghillies for the Highland dance competition stare and giggle as the guys stroll past in their Sport Kilts and matching pink T-shirts. Ozzy waves at the girls and Gareth flashes a handsome smile that no doubt makes their day. Darius ignores them completely because that's how Darius is.

The bagpipers are at the main stage where a crowd of people mill around in clumps of different colored tartans waiting for the parade of clans to start. I duck my head and quicken my steps when I spot my mother standing by the stage with her assistant, who's juggling a phone, two coffees, and the leashes of Mom's two French bulldogs, who've been dressed in kilts with matching tartan berets on their little doggie heads. My mother's here in her capacity as mayor to officially open the festival, and if she catches sight of me, there's a fifty-fifty chance she'll try to drag me up onstage with her.

Ozzy spots Mom too and picks up his long stride, outstripping me. We manage to make it to the athletic field without being waylaid by the Honorable Jeannette Goodrich and drop our stuff next to the metal bleachers facing the grassy field where the Highland Games will be taking place. A few other people from the local club are already here, helping set up the equipment. They've already erected the crossbar for the height events and painted the boundary lines of the throwing box for the distance events.

"Hey, chicken butt," Ozzy says as we're unfolding our chairs. "Did you pack any food? I'm starving."

"You ate half a dozen eggs before we left the house," I remind him.

Yes, they were burned, and yes, he ate them anyway.

Starving is my brother's default setting. He's constantly eating, yet somehow manages not to have an ounce of excess fat on him. I wish I could say the same, but Ozzy hogged all our mom's statuesque genes while I take after our softer, rounder dad.

"It takes a lot of protein to look this good." Ozzy strikes a bodybuilder pose and flexes his arms.

"Maybe you should have thought to pack some food for yourself, booger breath." But I dig a packet of jerky out of my backpack and toss it to him because I'm nice that way.

Living with three muscle-bound athletes has taught me to always keep protein-rich snacks on hand. You wouldn't believe how whiny big guys can get when their blood sugar starts to dip.

Ozzy shoves a piece of jerky into his mouth and drapes himself around me to poke through my bag. "What other goodies you got in there? Ooh, I'll take one of these."

I let him have a protein bar before I shove him away. "Don't hog all the snacks. These are for Darius and Gareth too."

We'll be out here all day, so I came prepared. My backpack's crammed with jerky, trail mix, protein bars, sunscreen, bug spray, athletic tape, and a first aid kit. Plus, I packed the cooler with bottled water, sports drinks, sandwiches, grapes, apples, and orange slices. I'm a veteran team mom by now. Honestly, I don't know what the boys would do without me since none of them ever think ahead. They're always scrambling around at the last minute trying to find their cleats and kilts, which are usually buried at the bottom of a laundry pile in their rooms.

I leave my backpack with the rest of our stuff and head over to help Ryan McCafferty at the check-in table. Ryan runs the local Highland Games club and also happens to be Gareth's lieutenant at the firehouse. He's easy to spot from a distance since he's a hulking redhead big enough to make Darius seem small by comparison. Ryan's girlfriend Maggie, who's helping him set up, is over six feet tall herself, and the two of them look like a superhero duo descended from a race of giants.

Ryan seems frazzled this morning as he greets me with a relieved smile and thrusts a clipboard into my hands. "Casey, thank god. That's the athletes' roster. I just need to find you a pen so you can start checking people off as they sign in."

While he's patting himself down as if there might be an invisible pocket in his T-shirt hiding a pen, I push back my hood and retrieve the pen I tucked into my ponytail before I left the house this morning. "I've got one."

"Oh good." I get another relieved smile as he scratches his head. "Okay. So. Everyone who checks in gets a registration packet and a T-shirt. We just need to open all these boxes and figure out which size is—" He breaks off when a naked four-year-old with curly black hair streaks past us, screeching like a banshee.

Maggie sucks in her lips to suppress a laugh as Ryan sighs loudly.

"Isabella, where did you leave your clothes?" he shouts after his niece. "And your parents?"

Isabella's answer is to cluck like a chicken as she runs in loop-the-loops around the people standing on the field. You have to admire the kid's zest for life. And her energy.

"We've got all of this handled," Maggie tells Ryan. "Go take care of that."

As he ambles off, I hear someone shout my name and spot my best friend Kenzie marching my way in a mini Sport Kilt and skull-and-crossbones knee socks, with a determined, *I want to talk to you* look on her face.

Uh oh.

She'll want to hear all about my date with Tom, and I really don't want to talk about it here. I'm just glad it's sunny today so I've got an excuse for wearing sunglasses to help hide my black eye.

"Cute onesie," she says as she stops in front of me and props her hands on her hips.

"Thanks." I try to look harried as I gesture at the boxes of T-shirts Maggie and I need to go through. "We're still trying to get everything set up for check-in."

Kenzie squints at me. "How's your eye?"

Oh crud.

That means she talked to Tom. And he told her about the sneeze kiss.

What did he say exactly? And how many other people has he told? Am I going to be the town laughingstock? Am I *already* the town laughingstock, and I just don't know it yet?

"It's fine." I give Kenzie a look meant to telepathically communicate my urgent need for her to *keep her mouth shut* about last night, hoping it translates through my sunglasses. "We'll talk later, okay? You've already got some kids waiting for their throwing lessons." I nod toward the small group of parents who've wandered over with their children in tow and are watching in amusement as Ryan chases his naked niece around the field.

Kenzie's not happy about being put off. But she gives me a nod and marches off with a flounce of her kilt. "All right, ye wee sprogs," she shouts as she seizes a bundle of pool noodles bound together with duct tape. "Who among ye wants to toss a caber?"

"What happened to your eye?" Maggie asks me as the children cluster around Kenzie.

"Poked myself in the eyeball with my mascara wand," I lie. "Don't you hate it when that happens?"

Maggie's a big-time management consultant from New York City who only moved to Crowder last summer to take a job as a top-level executive at King's Creamery, so I don't know her that well. She seems very nice, but I'm intimidated by how stylish and successful she is. She's probably never poked herself in the eye with a mascara wand in her life.

She gives me a smile that I'm pretty sure means she knows I'm lying, but she doesn't press me on it. Thank goodness. Of course, now she probably thinks I'm a battered woman, which isn't great either. But I shouldn't have to describe to everyone in the world how I made a fool of myself on a date.

Ten minutes later, Maggie and I have sorted out the T-shirts, Ryan's niece has been reunited with both her parents and her clothes, athlete check-in is underway, and my cousin Kaylee has taken Maggie's place beside me. I recruited her to help out, not that it took much convincing. She practically jumped at the chance to spend the day surrounded by hot men in kilts.

The children's Highland Games camp has attracted quite the crowd of spectators, many of them seemingly childless and female, who've wandered over to watch the strength athletes work with the kids. Kenzie's surrounded by a fan club of enraptured little girls, Darius is showing some of the older boys how to hold the lightweight Braemar stone, Ryan's got another group of little ones throwing a "hammer" made out of a tennis ball in a tube sock, and Ozzy appears to be playing a game of zombie tag with the attention-challenged kids, which seems about right.

From the thready sighs Kaylee keeps emitting, I assume she's enjoying the spectacle.

Meanwhile, I'm having some regrets about my puffin onesie. I should have double-checked the weather before I left the house this morning. The daytime temps have been in the sixties and low seventies all week, but it totally figures it would spike into the eighties on the day I chose to wear a black fleece onesie outdoors. A onesie that's going to be at least fifty percent sweat by the time the sun peaks overhead.

"Daddy, what zat?" a toddler standing nearby asks, pulling his finger out of his nose to point at me.

The boy's father scratches his head as he peers at me. "An owl, I think."

"That's not an owl," the toddler's mom says. "She's obviously a penguin."

Kaylee snickers as she leans over to elbow me. "See? It's not just me who can't tell what the hell you're supposed to be."

"I'm a puffin," I explain to the family, ignoring my cousin, who wouldn't know a penguin from a duck. Unless you're talking about pro hockey players—then she can talk forever about their respective rosters and game stats.

The little boy gives me a suspicious eyeball. "Wuzza puffin?"

"A kind of seabird that nests along the Scottish coasts," I explain, happy to educate young minds about my favorite animal.

"Basically a penguin," the mother tells her son, and I swallow the urge to correct her.

Penguins and puffins aren't even in the same bird family. And puffins can fly, unlike penguins. Who live exclusively in the southern hemisphere, by the way, nowhere near Scotland. But it's not a nit worth picking since no one but me actually cares.

"Puffins are *way* cooler than penguins," Gareth says, tipping his hat back as he squats in front of the little boy. "Want to know why?"

"Why?" the boy whispers, staring at him like he invented dinosaur-shaped chicken nuggets.

The kid's not the only one sporting an awestruck stare. Squatting like that with his kilt hiked up and his forearms resting on his knees, Gareth looks like a thick-thighed god posing for a kilted stud of the month calendar.

Next to me, Kaylee emits another sigh.

"Puffins are cooler because puffins can fly and penguins can't." Gareth tosses a wink at me before turning back to the little boy. "I'll bet you can fly too if you flap your wings hard enough."

The boy pumps his arms as hard as he can and shrieks with delight when Gareth sweeps him into the air and flies him around the edge of the field like a swooping bird.

"Damn, that man can wear the shit out of a kilt," Kaylee says, fanning herself. "I want him to squeeze me with those thighs until I'm unconscious. Honestly, how do you live with that kind of hotness without swooning 24/7?"

"You wouldn't be swooning if you'd smelled the dirty gym socks he leaves all over the house."

"Gareth Kelly could bury me in his dirty gym socks as long as he promised to walk around the house naked on the reg."

"That's gross," I say. Only now I'm thinking about Gareth naked, which is the opposite of gross. But it's also an image I'd rather not have in my head. It's easier to be friends with someone when you don't know what their semi-erect penis looks like. And honestly, it kind of sucks to be confronted by a sexy male body when you're already depressed over the fact that you may never get to have sex with one.

"If you try to tell me you've never thought about him naked, I'll know you're a lying liar."

I'm thinking about it right now, but I'm not about to admit that out loud.

It's not like I'm unaware of Gareth's attractiveness. Obviously. I've just learned to tune it out. It's like living by an airport—you get so used to the sound of planes flying overhead after a while that you stop hearing it. I'm so used to seeing Gareth that I can look past his magnificent body, ridiculously square jaw, and twinkling blue eyes to the person underneath. I don't see a hot guy anymore. I see someone I'm glad to have as a friend.

Kaylee fans her boobs again and glances over at me. "God, you must be roasting in that getup."

She came to the festival in costume too, as a unicorn, the national animal of Scotland. She looks both adorable *and* sexy in a low-cut white tank top, rainbow tutu, fur leg warmers, and a hood with a unicorn horn and long rainbow mane.

Next to her, I'm a lumpy, sweating sack of potatoes. This could be why I've never attracted a man—instead of dressing as a sexy unicorn, I chose to dress as a shapeless puffin.

"Hey, Casey."

My throat goes dry when I glance up to find Connor Autry in front of me.

I tell everyone I'm immune to the appeal of my brother's jock friends, but Connor's the exception. I've had a crush on him since we had a Spanish class together in high school. Not that he knew I existed back then. He was a senior on the varsity football team, and I was a dorky sophomore nobody. I used to stare at the back of his head every day in fifth period and try to imagine what it would feel like to run my fingers through his silky dark hair, but I never worked up the nerve to talk to him.

When he went off to UT on a football scholarship, I figured I'd never see him and his beautiful silky hair again. Everyone expected him to go pro after college. But then he got injured, and instead of going on to a pro football career, he came back to Crowder and took a job as an athletic trainer.

As luck would have it, at the same gym where I happen to work. Once we became coworkers, Connor actually learned my name and started saying hi to me every day. He even stops by the front desk to chat with me sometimes while he's waiting for one of his clients, so now I know he's more than just good-looking. He's considerate and thoughtful. And he can be funny sometimes. But he's also got this quiet intensity that hints at hidden depths beneath the ruggedly handsome surface.

Basically he's perfect. I could stare at him all day. And I get to do exactly that when I'm at work. It's one of the best things about my job, which is otherwise pretty meh. You'd think I'd get tired of staring at him after a while, but nope. Connor gets better the more I see of him.

But while he might know I'm alive these days, he's still hopelessly unattainable. Just like Gareth and all the other hot guys here today, Connor is way out of my league. If he thinks about me at all, it's only as a friendly acquaintance and nothing more.

"Connor, hey." I hope he can't see the flush in my cheeks as I reach for the clipboard to check his name off the list.

"Hi, Connor." Kaylee pets her unicorn mane as she beams up at him. "Long time no see."

The pen slips out of my clammy hand and bounces under the table.

I forgot to mention that Connor and my cousin Kaylee had a *thing*. A brief one, but still. It smarts. Especially since I'm the one who introduced them. She came by the gym one day to see me, and the next thing I know he's asking her for her number.

Story of my freaking life.

I drop to my knees and grope on the ground for the pen. So does Connor, squatting in his kilt the same way Gareth did a few minutes ago. He plucks my pen out of the grass and holds it out to me beneath the table.

"Here you go."

He's so beautiful it hurts my heart, and when I take the pen my fingers brush against his, and he *smiles* at me, and—

Oh no.

Ah-CHOO!

The back of my head hits the underside of the table.

"Shit, are you okay?" Connor asks.

"Totally fine," I mumble as I back out from under the table and scramble to my feet. Fortunately, it's a plastic folding table, so it didn't hurt that much. Although at this point I might welcome a concussion.

Kaylee gives me a pitying look. "Still doing that sneezing thing, huh?"

"Hay fever season is the worst." I shoot a *don't you dare say another word* glare at her as I drop into my folding chair and check Connor's name off the registration. "Can you grab Connor a large shirt, please?"

"Here's your T-shirt." Kaylee leans over the table to pass it to Connor, conveniently giving him a view of her cleavage.

A shadow falls across me as a heavy hand drops onto my shoulder.

"Autry," Gareth says in a clipped voice an octave deeper than usual.

Gareth isn't a fan of Connor. Not after he found me drowning my sorrows in a pint of Double Double Fudge and Trouble ice cream last year when Connor hooked up with Kaylee. In a moment of weakness, I confessed to my long-standing crush on Connor, and Gareth's been super scowly around him ever since.

"Kelly," Connor replies, frowning slightly.

Gareth puts a bottle of water in my hand. "I thought you might be thirsty."

"Kick ass out there today!" Kaylee chirps at Connor.

"Yeah, good luck," I wish him.

"Thanks." He darts an uneasy look at Gareth before wandering off.

Gareth gives the back of my neck a sympathetic squeeze. "I heard you sneeze. Are you okay?"

"I'm fine," I say with a wince. "You didn't have to do that."

I wish I'd never told him about Connor. Or the sneezing. It's bad enough feeling like this without Gareth *knowing* I feel like this.

I don't want him to feel sorry for me. And I don't need to be babied or protected.

All I want is for a man to want *me* for once.

And that's not a problem Gareth can fix for me.

6

CASEY

T he pipes and drums show up at ten to commemorate the official opening of the Highland Games. By then, it's hot enough that I've unbuttoned the top of my onesie to tie it around my waist, so I'm looking extra cool and fashionable with my weird fur pants and *BOOKS ARE JUST WORD TACOS* T-shirt.

Kaylee claps her hands over her ears as the pipe band marches onto the field. "My god, why does it have to be so freaking loud?"

"I don't think bagpipes have a volume control."

My mother doesn't usually stick around for this part, but I'm on the lookout for her just in case. She's been known to take me by surprise before, so I've learned not to let my guard down. Wherever there's a microphone, there's a chance my mom's not far away.

"I'm getting a beer," Kaylee says. "Wanna come?"

All the athletes have been checked in, which means our volunteer shift is done and we're free to enjoy the festival for the rest of the day. "It's ten o'clock in the morning."

"And?"

"I think I'll stay and watch the pipers."

Kaylee shakes her head like I'm a total weirdo. "Suit yourself."

The stands are barely half full, and I find a primo seat front and center to watch the pipe and drum band play. A minute later, Kenzie plops down beside me.

"I don't understand why people think bagpipes are annoying," I say. "I think they're majestic."

"Yeah, they're cool." She stretches her legs out and slants a look at me. "So last night was a disaster, huh?"

"You talked to Tom."

"He called me as soon as he got home and told me everything. I think he was terrified I was going to think he hit you because he knows I'd peel the skin off his balls."

"He's not going to tell anyone else, is he?"

"I made him promise not to." Her smile turns lethal. "Or else I *will* peel the skin off his balls and fry it like pork skins."

I wrinkle my nose at the unsavory image. "Thank you. No one knows but Gareth, so don't say anything, okay?"

She raises an eyebrow. "Gareth knows?"

"He saw me when I got home last night, unfortunately."

"Did he flip out?"

"A little."

Kenzie lifts my sunglasses to peer at my face. "How bad is the bruise under all that makeup?"

"It's not too bad. Could have been worse."

"What about you? Are you okay?"

I push my sunglasses back down. "I'm terrific. Just trying to make my peace with being a virgin forever."

She pulls me into a crushing hug. "The entire concept of virginity is an artificial construct of the patriarchy used to shame and control women. There's no physical difference between a woman who's had sex and a woman who hasn't. Not to mention how heteronormative it is to frame the act of sex around vaginal penetration."

"I know," I say when she releases me and I can breathe again. "But none of that changes the fact that I'd still like to get laid at some point in my life."

"It'll happen when you find the right guy."

"Yeah, sure." I turn back to the field and see Gareth trotting toward us.

"Did you happen to pack any tacky by any chance?" he asks. "We all forgot to bring it."

"It's in the outermost pocket of my backpack."

"You're the best," he says, breaking into a grin. "What would I do without you?"

Kenzie gets to her feet as the pipe band marches off the field to "Scotland the Brave." "That's my cue. I better go get ready for my first event. I'll come find you when we break for lunch so we can go visit Wee Hamish, okay?"

"Good luck," I call after her as she jogs off across the field to join the other athletes in the women's class.

———

"MEH," the baby goat says.

"I agree," I tell him as I lean on the fence enclosing the petting zoo. "Meh is right."

Wee Hamish the Highland cow watches us through his woolly forelock from the far side of his private pen beside the petting zoo. I think he suspects I have apples for him in my pocket, but he's waiting for proof before he deigns to come near the fence.

"You're depressing the goats," Kenzie says. "Here, have some more cheese."

I stare down at the cube of goat's milk feta she bought from a local farmer's stall on our way over here. "Is it rude to eat this in front of them?" I whisper. "Since it's goat cheese?"

Kenzie squints at me. "You don't think goat cheese is actually made out of goats, do you? Tell me you don't think that."

"Of course not. I just thought since it's made from milk that was meant to be theirs, it might be bad manners."

"Goats have no concept of manners. That one's trying to hump the pig, and that one's eating your shoelaces."

I jerk my slobber-soaked Converse away from the goat sticking his head through the fence. "Shoo! Bad goat."

"I'm sorry your date with Tom sucked," Kenzie says.

"Is that what he told you?"

"What did you expect him to say? You sneezed into his mouth and head-butted him in the face."

A peel of laughter erupts behind us. "Oh my god! That's the funniest *and* the saddest thing I've ever heard."

Kenzie and I spin around to find my cousin Kaylee grinning at us. I swear to god there was no one there a second ago. How the eff did she manage to stealth up behind us like a level fifty rogue?

"Where did you come from?" I ask her.

"The food court." Kaylee holds up her half-eaten sausage on a stick with a *duh* look. "Which Tom was this? Tom with the Corvette or Tom who had to have his finger reattached after he blew it off with a firecracker last Fourth of July?"

"Tom who works at the vet clinic with me," Kenzie says, and I glare at her to *be quiet*.

"Don't worry, I won't tell anyone," Kaylee promises. "As long as you share all the dirty deets. What'd this Tom guy do after you head-butted him?"

I wince. "Bleed, mostly."

"Did you break his nose?"

"No." I frown. "I don't think so, anyway."

How do you know if a nose is broken? God, maybe I did break his nose. What if he has to go to the doctor to get it reset or something? Should I offer to pay his medical bills?

"He said it's not broken," Kenzie offers. "It's probably just bruised, like your eye."

Kaylee takes a bite of sausage and peers at me. "*That's* why you're wearing so much makeup today. I thought you might be trying to impress someone."

"There's no one to impress," I mutter with a sigh.

"You sure? Because earlier it seemed like you might be interested in Connor. It's okay if you are, you know. The two of us didn't really click, so I don't mind if you want to go for it with him."

"That's not happening. Not in a million trillion years."

"Why not?" Kenzie asks. "If you want to go out with the guy, just ask him out."

I make a scoffing sound. "You make it sound so simple."

"It *is* simple."

"Maybe for people with the body and self-confidence of an Amazonian warrior."

"You think that makes it easy for me?" Kenzie says. "Most men are too insecure to date a woman with quads bigger than theirs, which seriously narrows the field of prospects. Not that I'd *want* to date a man with puny quads. But there aren't all that many men in this town with quads bigger than mine, and I already know most of them too well to want to date them."

"You do have *amazing* quads." Kaylee tilts her head to admire Kenzie's thighs. "Seriously hot."

Kenzie appears pleased as she sticks out one of her long, muscular legs, which look extra hot today in her kilt and knee socks. "Thank you. I owe them all to my three-hundred-fifteen-pound squat."

I stare down at my own stumpy legs and vaguely potato-shaped body with another sigh. "Maybe I should give up on dating and join a convent. Wait, are nuns allowed to read romance novels? Because that could be a deal breaker for me. Better idea: I'll go live in the woods and take up sorcery so I can spend my free time haunting terrible men with my harrowing visage."

"Stop being so dramatic," Kenzie says with a fairly dramatic eye roll of her own. "Tom liked you until you gave him a bloody nose. Last night was just a spectacular convergence of bad luck. A once-in-a-lifetime freak accident."

"Yeah, I wouldn't be so sure about that," I say, thinking of how I sneezed over a tiny, innocent finger touch with Connor earlier. "I'm afraid the sneezing is likely to be an ongoing problem."

Kaylee tosses her sausage stick in a nearby trash can and offers me a consoling smile. "If it makes you feel any better, I always thought it was cute."

I groan and rub my forehead. "Maybe when I was a kid. It's not so cute if you're twenty-eight and start sneezing as soon as a guy tries to kiss you."

"You poor thing." Kaylee pats my hair. "I thought you'd grown out of it."

"Sadly no, I've just gotten better at avoiding situations that trigger it."

"Was it something about Tom specifically that made you nervous?" Kenzie asks, tapping her lips thoughtfully. "Or does it happen with every guy you date?"

"I haven't exactly been doing a lot of dating, have I? That's why I asked you to set me up."

Kenzie continues to ponder the problem as she munches on a piece of cheese. "You hang around with guys all the time, so we know you're not nervous about talking to men in general. Is it the prospect of physical intimacy that triggers your anxiety?"

"I don't know," I mumble. "Maybe."

Kaylee's eyes go wide. "How do you have sex? Do you sneeze all the way through it, or does it stop after a minute?"

"Time to feed Wee Hamish," I announce, stalking over to his pen. As soon as he sees me take the baggie of apples out of my pocket, he ambles toward me.

"You're not a virgin, are you?" Kaylee whispers, leaning on the fence beside me. "Oh my god, you are," she says when I ignore her. "Are you serious?"

Kenzie slices a quelling look at Kaylee. "It's not a big deal,"

"No, of course not," Kaylee agrees, even as she's staring at me like I'm some sort of curiosity or rare endangered animal.

Which I kind of am. How many twenty-eight-year-old virgins are walking around in this day and age? I haven't looked up the data because I suspect it will only depress me. I'd guess less than ten percent. Maybe even five. Not many, in other words. And the older I get, the more of an outlier I become.

It'd be one thing if it was a conscious choice, if I was saving myself for marriage or my soul mate or something. But my abstinence isn't my choice. I'm not saving myself for anything or anyone. I want to have sex! I'm not even that picky about who I do it with at this point. There just haven't been any opportunities. Not since I refused Seth Bumgarner's fumbling attempt to pressure me into it in tenth grade. Which I don't regret because he turned out to be a huge jerk, but it's not fair that apparently he was my one and only shot.

"There are a lot of ways to have sex," Kaylee whispers after glancing around to make sure no one's close enough to overhear. "Just because you haven't done P-in-V—"

"I haven't done *anything*." I hold out a slice of apple as Wee Hamish approaches the fence. "Who's a good wee coo? You are."

I thought the sex thing would work itself out when I got to college, that being older would bring more and better opportunities. But the only thing it brought was a sense that sex was something everyone else had already experienced. It was like finding out the kiddie pool had closed over the summer and the deep end was the only place to swim when I hadn't even learned to dog-paddle yet.

"It's really not a big deal," Kenzie repeats.

I hold out another slice of apple for Wee Hamish, who leaves me with a palm full of drool to show his thanks. "It feels like a big deal when you're the one who's never touched a penis."

"Have you ever even *seen* a penis?" Kaylee not-quite whispers.

I try not to think about Gareth, but of course that's the image that immediately pops into my head. "I have access to the internet. I know what penises look like."

"I mean IRL. A 3-D flesh-and-blood penis."

"I have a brother, so yes."

"Ew." Kaylee takes an apple slice and offers it to Wee Hamish. "That doesn't count."

"Need I remind you I live with three men who are used to walking around locker rooms naked and occasionally forget I'm in the house."

"Oh my goddddd," Kaylee breathes, spreading her hands wide as her mouth forms a dramatic O. "Whose penis have you seen? Was it Gareth? Or Darius? Please say both of them."

"Like I was saying," Kenzie intervenes, "there's nothing wrong with having more or less experience than anyone else. It happens at different times for everyone. You shouldn't let it bother you."

"But it *does* bother me," I say as I ruffle Wee Hamish's woolly coat. "It feels like there's something wrong with me, like everyone else has been invited into this secret club and I've been blackballed."

"There's nothing transcendent about having sex. It's just a thing some people do. It's not magic or anything."

"Boy, if that isn't the truth," Kaylee agrees.

"I know it's not magic. But I want to have the experience. I'm tired of waiting for it to happen. I want to get it over with."

A minute ago, when I said I don't regret saying no to Seth Bumgarner? That's not entirely true. Sometimes I do wish I'd gone along with it so it'd be done and over with. It's not like it would have been that much worse than most people's first time, and at least it wouldn't be this Big Thing hanging over me now, making me feel like a freak. And I know I shouldn't let it make me feel that way, but sometimes it does anyway.

"Then that's what you should do," Kaylee says. "Just get it over with. Pick a guy and seduce him. Once you've popped your cherry, you won't feel as much pressure anymore."

I laugh. "If I knew how to seduce a guy I wouldn't be in this situation, would I?"

"Pfft. That's easy. All you do is walk up to one in a bar and tell him you want to have sex with him. Bang. Done."

"What if he says no?" I ask as if I'm actually considering it.

Am I?

Possibly.

I'm not as convinced I can pull it off as Kaylee seems to be, but maybe it's worth a shot? I'm not good at putting myself out there, but I'm starting to feel hopeless enough about this whole situation that I might be willing to try something drastic.

It's not like I need my first time to be special. I'm not holding out for a boyfriend. I've only got limited time to live my one wild and precious life, and I'm not wasting it waiting around for someone to fall in love with me when there's a chance that may never happen. I don't want to miss out on the pleasures of the flesh because I was waiting for my soul mate Powerball numbers to come up. All I'm asking for is a willing sex partner who doesn't make me gag. It shouldn't be that tall of an order.

I mean, sure, I'd love to have a boyfriend, but that's not my most pressing concern. I need to get past this sex block first. Once I've got my first time out of the way, then I can worry about finding love.

"A man turning down no-strings sex?" Kaylee says with a snort. "Not likely. But if he does, you just move on to a different one."

I pull the bag of apples back as Wee Hamish impatiently tries to snuffle it through the fence. "Sorry, buddy," I murmur as I hold out another apple slice. "What happens when the guy finds out I've never had sex before?"

"Who says you have to tell him you're a virgin?"

"Wouldn't he be able to figure it out?"

Kaylee throws her head back and laughs. "You're giving men way too much credit. Most of them wouldn't notice if you transformed into a bear halfway through."

"You've been reading too many shifter romances."

"I'm telling you, the vast majority of guys have no clue what they're doing and even less of a clue what's going on with you while they're doing it. He's gonna be off in his own little world just happy to be getting some."

Part of me wants to ask Kaylee if that's what Connor Autry was like in bed, but another part of me doesn't want to know the answer. It would ruin the fantasy, and my fantasies are all I currently have.

Instead I look to Kenzie for confirmation.

She shrugs. "Sad but tragically true more often than not."

"So go find yourself a one-night stand and don't tell him you're a virgin," Kaylee says as if it's the easiest thing in the world.

Kenzie doesn't seem nearly as confident as Kaylee. "I don't know if that's a good idea."

"She just needs to break the seal. If it sucks the first time, so what? Move on and try again with someone else. It doesn't have to mean anything."

"I'm not sure hooking up with a stranger is the right answer for Casey," Kenzie says. "How is that going to get around the sneezing thing?"

"That's easy," Kaylee says, looking proud of herself. "Get trashed first. If you're drunk enough, you won't feel nervous and you won't sneeze. Problem solved. You're welcome."

"That is a seriously terrible idea." Kenzie gives Kaylee a hard glare before directing a worried look at me. "Please tell me you're not considering it."

"How did I know I'd find you here?" a familiar voice says behind me, and I flinch.

Oh goody. Gareth's arrived. Right in the middle of our embarrassing sex conversation.

Kenzie's deadpan is flawless, but Kaylee has to slap a hand over her mouth to smother a giggle.

"What aren't you considering?" Gareth asks with a teasing twinkle in his eye, as if he knows we were talking about sex.

I pull a lie out of thin air. "Becoming a vegetarian."

"Why would you want to do that when meat is so delicious?" He tosses a wink at the cow. "Isn't that right, Hamish?"

Wee Hamish does not look amused.

"Is it time to get back already?" I ask.

"Nah, we've got another twenty minutes." Gareth hooks his thumb over his shoulder. "I'm gonna go grab a beer. Just thought I'd see if you wanted anything from the food court while I'm there."

"I'm good, but thanks," I say.

He takes off his straw cowboy hat and plonks it on my head.

"Your nose is getting pink. You don't want to get a sunburn with that fair skin." He straightens the hat and smiles. "I'll see you back at the athletic field."

"Bye, Gareth!" Kaylee calls after him as he strolls away. "He is *so* sweet."

"Yeah, he's all right," Kenzie agrees.

"A man that hot who's actually thoughtful? I mean, how often does that happen in real life? He's a total unicorn."

"You know what?" Kenzie says to me. "He'd make a good candidate."

"Candidate for what?" I ask as I feed Wee Hamish the last slice of apple.

Kenzie hands me a disinfectant wipe to clean the cow slobber off my hands. "I'm not convinced 'just get it over with' is the best approach, but if that's what you really want to do, maybe you should look closer to home instead of propositioning a total stranger."

I stare at her. "You're not suggesting I have sex with *Gareth*?"

Kaylee claps, bouncing on her toes. "Oh my god! That's such a great idea! Why didn't I think of that?"

"It is not a great idea." I wave a hand in embarrassed dismissal. "It's the most absurd thing I've ever heard."

"Why?" Kenzie asks, folding her arms across her chest.

"Because Gareth has me shelved so deep in the friend zone he probably doesn't even register me as a woman."

Her eyebrows raise. "I wouldn't be so sure about that."

"What? Why? What do you mean?"

"He's a good guy and he cares about you. If you're deter-mined to do this, asking a friend is a way better option than putting yourself in the hands of some random stranger you know nothing about who could possibly be a serial killer or just really bad at sex."

Kaylee seizes my arm. "You know what this is? It's one of

those stories where the shy wallflower asks a notorious rake to give her sex lessons so she can learn to seduce someone else! It's a Lisa Kleypas novel!"

"Or Sarah MacLean," Kenzie adds.

Kaylee frowns. "Didn't Joanna Shupe write one like that too?"

"They've all written books like that," I say. "It's a popular trope, but my life is not a historical romance and Gareth is no Derek Craven."

"Obviously." Kenzie sniffs. "Derek Craven is the ultimate fantasy. No real-life dude could ever compare."

"Okay, but Gareth is *hot*," Kaylee says. "And it's not like he's picky about who he sleeps with."

"Gee, thanks," I mutter.

"Everyone knows he's a total manslut. I'm sure he'd be up for some casual friends with benefits action. It's win-win for him."

"You really think so?" I ask doubtfully.

"Guys don't turn down sex," Kaylee insists.

I look at Kenzie, who shrugs. "You won't know unless you ask him."

7

CASEY

The longer I sit with Kenzie's suggestion, the more convinced I become that Gareth is my best option for losing my virginity.

I don't know why it didn't occur to me sooner. He's kind, decent, likes me as a friend, and is comfortable treating sex as a casual, no-strings activity. Hopefully that means he won't laugh in my face. Maybe he'll even say yes. Who knows? But I figure it's worth a shot before I try my luck with the rest of the male population.

It takes me all week to work up the courage, but by the time Friday night rolls around I've decided to go for it. Darius and Ozzy are both out tonight, so Gareth and I are alone in the house. Who knows when I'll have a better opportunity?

This is happening.

It's possibly the craziest thing I've ever done. Which is a pretty sad statement on my life, come to think of it. I suspect it means I've played it too safe. Maybe that's why nothing ever happens to me. I don't take enough risks.

Well, that ends now. I'm doing this. Even if it seems totally crazy. Crazy might be exactly what I need more of in my life.

After one final check in the mirror, I head upstairs to proposition my roommate before I can talk myself out of it.

The upstairs part of the house is the boys' domain. In addition to their three bedrooms, there's a single bathroom they all share, plus an open loft area at the top of the stairs that they've turned into their man cave, filling the space with mismatched secondhand furniture arrayed around a big-screen TV where they while away hours playing video games.

That's where I find Gareth now, kicked back on the couch with a controller in his hand. He's got his bare feet propped on the hand-me-down coffee table, and his hair's sticking up all wonky like he just got out of bed. For all I know he might have. His sleep schedule is all kinds of random because of the twenty-four-hour shifts he works at the firehouse.

He's concentrating so hard on the zombies he's blowing to smithereens that he hasn't noticed me, and I stand there for a moment and watch him. I don't tend to look at him much usually. I don't need to look at him. I know what he looks like, but I also know there's a lot more to him than his appearance.

Besides, it'd be weird if I stood around ogling my roommate all the time.

Like I'm doing right now. *This* is weird.

Something tickles my foot, and I glance down to find Darius's rabbit sniffing my toes. I bend down to pet the soft fur between his floppy ears.

"Hey," Gareth says, noticing me and pausing the game. "You look nice. Are you going out tonight?"

"No," I answer, feeling self-conscious about straightening my curly hair and putting on makeup. On the other hand, he thinks I look nice, so maybe it was the right call. "Are you?"

He glances down at his rumpled T-shirt and threadbare sweats, then back up at me with a grin. "Do I look like I'm going anywhere?"

"I guess not, dressed like that."

That's a relief. It would throw a big, awkward wrench in my plan if Gareth already had plans to hook up with someone else tonight. Taking it as a good sign, I cross the room and sit on the couch beside him.

"Did you want to do something?" he asks, setting the game controller aside. "We could watch a movie. Or one of those nature documentaries if that's what you're in the mood for. I'm cool with whatever you want."

I bite my lip. This is my moment.

I just need to say it.

Out loud.

Except when I open my mouth, I blurt out something random instead. "Do you have any tattoos?"

Where did that even come from? Why am I asking him about tattoos?

His lips pull into a smirk. "If I had a tattoo, you'd have seen it already, don't you think?"

Right. Because I walked in on him naked last weekend. Although I did only get a frontal view.

"You could have one on your butt cheek," I say before I can stop myself.

His eyes gleam with mischief. "Do you want to check, is that it? Are you asking to see my butt, Casey?"

"No!"

Only...well...that *is* kind of what I'm here to do, isn't it?

"You can just come out and ask if that's what you want. I don't mind. Here..." He leans forward and twists around, reaching for the back of his sweatpants. Gareth's never been shy about showing off his body, and I'm afraid he might actually moon me.

"Stop that." I shove his hands away from his pants before he can pull them down.

He laughs and slumps back against the couch. "I'm just messing with you. I know you're not after my ass."

But I am though. I *am* after his ass.

Oh god, I don't know if I can do this.

He nudges me with his elbow as he leans forward to grab his water bottle off the coffee table. "Are you thinking of getting a tattoo? I'll go with you if you're scared to go alone."

"Why would you assume I'm scared? Do you think I'm scared to do things?"

"No, of course not." His smile fades as he sinks back against the couch. "Where did that come from?"

"Nothing. Never mind." This isn't at all how this was supposed to go. I should have known I'd mess it up. I should probably cut my losses and give up now before I start sneezing and break one of our faces.

"Hey, talk to me. What's up?" His blue eyes are soft and warm as they search my face. Asking me to trust him. Wanting to understand and make it better. Because he's nice and also my friend.

I tilt my head back and stare up at the ceiling as if I'm going to find the courage I need hiding in the stippled texture. "There's something I want to ask you."

"So ask."

"It's a favor. A big one."

"The answer's yes."

I swivel my head. "You don't even know what I'm going to ask."

"Whatever it is, I'll do it. Assuming it's something in my power to do." He shrugs and takes a swig of water.

"I want you to have sex with me."

He makes a choking sound and launches into a violent coughing fit.

Great. I've killed him. And I didn't even have to sneeze to do it.

"Are you okay?" I try to pat him on the back, but he waves me off.

"Fine," he croaks in between coughs. "Went down the wrong pipe."

I take the bottle from him and set it on the table while I wait for him to pull himself together.

"Sorry." He clears his throat. "Could you say that again? Just to be sure I didn't mishear you?"

Based on his reaction, I'm pretty sure he heard me right the first time. "I want you to have sex with me."

"Yeah, that's what I thought you said." His eyes narrow as he glances around the room. "Is this a prank or one of those TikTok challenges? Are you filming me right now? Did Ozzy put you up to it? Where are you hiding the phone?"

"It's not a prank."

Gareth's brows knit together as he stares at me. "You're serious?"

"Yes."

He takes a deep breath and blows it out in an audible gust. "Casey, you and me...that would be a really...not smart thing for us to do."

"Why?"

"Because we're friends, that's why. And I'd like us to stay that way."

"It'd just be a one-time thing," I tell him. "No strings attached. I'm not asking to be your girlfriend or anything. Nothing has to change."

He looks stricken. Always what a girl likes to see when she's asking a guy to have sex with her. "Why do you want to...you know?"

The knot in my stomach cinches tighter. "Does it matter?"

"Of course it fucking matters. What the hell kind of question is that?"

"You're attractive, and I think it would be nice if we had sex." I attempt to pull off a casual shrug. "That's all there is to it."

"*Nice*?" He snorts in disbelief. "I call bullshit. Where's this really coming from?"

"Nowhere," I say stiffly.

"I'm supposed to believe you woke up this morning and decided completely out of the blue that you want to fuck me?"

The harshness of the word *fuck* hits me like a clap of thunder, making what I'm asking feel a lot more real.

Gareth shakes his head. "Look at you. You can't even stand to hear me say it without cringing."

He's right. This is a terrible idea. What was I thinking? Of course I have to be as weird and awkward as possible. I can't just be normal about this and do it the way everyone else does it.

"Forget I said anything." If I start walking now, I can probably make it to the coast in three or four days and walk into the sea.

"I can't do that," he says with this awful expression of concern and apprehension, like he's afraid I've gone completely off my rocker, and he's trying to decide if I'm in need of professional intervention. "What's going on?"

I need to get away from this conversation. Away from Gareth and the way he's looking at me, and away from all this stupid pent-up stuff inside me that makes me this way. But when I push off the couch, he grabs hold of my hand.

My throat tightens, and I try to tug my hand free, but he won't let go. He's so much stronger than me. Not rough—he's never rough with me. But he holds me fast.

"Gareth, let go." *Please*, I beg him with my eyes. *Please, let's pretend this never happened. Forget I ever asked for that, forget this whole conversation took place, just please forget.*

"No." He stares at me, searching for explanations I don't want to give. "Talk to me."

I shake my head.

I'm not prepared for him to drag me into his lap, and I let out a shocked "Eep!" as I find myself balanced on his thighs with my knees straddling his hips. "What are you doing?"

"I'm not letting you go until we've talked about this."

His thick arms are locked around me, keeping me in place. There's no use struggling against his impossible strength, so I do the opposite—slump forward and hide my face against his chest. At least this way I don't have to look at him.

And I have to admit, the closeness is nice. He smells excellent, like clean laundry and the spicy scented shower gel he uses. Plus, the way his arms are holding me is reassuring, like a seat belt keeping me safe. We're sort of hugging and sort of cuddling. We're cuddle-hugging, and it's awesome.

It makes it easier to forget what an idiot I've made of myself. I can already feel myself calming down. As I close my eyes and breathe his scent, I can't help imagining what it would be like if we did have sex. If it's anything like this, I'll bet it's pretty great.

"I can do this all night," he says.

So can I.

But he's not talking about cuddle-hugging. He's waiting for me to talk to him. And as nice as cuddle-hugging feels, I can't actually do this all night because eventually my legs will fall asleep and I'll need to pee.

I release a shaky breath and tell him the truth. "I've never had sex."

He goes stock-still beneath me. He's not even breathing. Maybe his heart has stopped from shock. Or I've freaked him out so badly he's gone catatonic.

"You're still a virgin?"

Stiffening, I push myself off his chest. "Are you really that surprised? What invisible men do you think I've been having sex with all this time?"

"I don't know. I guess I just assumed—"

"That I'm normal? You should know me better than that."

His hold on me tightens. "You *are* normal. There's nothing wrong with being a virgin."

"Yeah? Exactly how many twenty-eight-year-old virgins do you know?"

"Shit, I have no idea. It's not something I go around asking people. I didn't even know *you* were a virgin, and you're one of my closest friends." His brows draw together as he studies me. "Is there a reason you've never..."

"Fucked anyone?" I supply testily, taking satisfaction in the way it makes him wince. *Who's uncomfortable now?*

"Is there a reason?" he asks again. "Were you waiting on purpose?"

"No! That's the problem. The only thing I've been waiting for is an opportunity. But my life has been one big sex desert, and I have no idea why. Seriously, what's the deal? Level with me, Gareth. Am I repulsive or something? Is that why no one wants me?"

"You're definitely not repulsive."

"Then why? What's wrong with me? Do you think it could be some kind of pheromone thing? Maybe I have a mutation that causes me to give off boner-killing pheromones."

His lips twitch. "I promise you don't."

"How can you be sure?"

He gives me a long look. "How do you think?"

My jaw drops. "Are you saying I've given you a boner before?"

"Well, yeah. You're pretty and I'm not dead, so it's gonna happen sometimes."

I blink in surprise. "You think I'm pretty? Do you have a

boner right now?" I try to look down at his lap, but his stupid T-shirt is hanging down and blocking my view.

"Casey." He hooks a finger under my chin and tilts my face up to look at him. "Of course you're pretty," he says with a troubled frown. "Is that a serious question?"

"If I'm so pretty, why haven't you ever tried to have sex with me?"

"Because we live together, for one thing. For another, you're one of my best friends, and I like you too much to mess that up." His fingers squeeze my waist. "There's nothing wrong with you. I can promise you that."

"There has to be something about me that puts men off. Maybe I have resting anti-sex face. Come to think of it, no one's ever offered me drugs either. Do I give off a killjoy vibe that makes me seem like a no-fun stick-in-the-mud? Is that my problem?"

He grunts in amusement. "No, of course not."

"Well, I've got a complex about it now. I think that's why I sneezed on Tom. How am I supposed to get more sexual experience if I'm so nervous about my lack of sexual experience that I sneeze on anyone who tries to kiss me?"

Gareth rolls his lips together, fighting to hold back a smile.

"Go ahead and laugh. I know it's funny."

"It's not. I'm sorry."

"I sneezed directly into his mouth, Gareth! His mouth!" I cover my face and drop my forehead to his chest. "I can't even blame the poor guy for giving up on me."

"I can." Gareth's hands smooth up and down my back. He's great at this comforting stuff. "If he was good enough for you, he'd know you're worth a little snot and some light facial bruising."

It sounds like he's joking, but when I lift my head his face is serious. The warmth in his gaze makes my insides feel all squishy. Meanwhile, his thumbs are rubbing these little circles on my waist that send sparks of electricity shooting through my whole body.

I'm suddenly conscious that my hands are on his chest. Completely innocently, of course. That's just where I happened to put them when I pushed myself upright.

But now that I'm thinking about the solid firmness of the pectoral muscles under my palms, my fingers can't help twitching with the urge to squeeze them. Just to see what it's like.

I swallow thickly. "I've never even had a boyfriend. Last night was only my second date ever."

Gareth's frown deepens. "But you've been kissed before, right?"

"Once, in tenth grade." I shudder involuntarily at the memory. "It was such a long time ago that I can barely remember what it was like, except it wasn't very good. But for all I know that was my fault. Maybe I'm a terrible kisser."

"I'm sure you're not." Gareth stares at my mouth as though he's giving the matter serious thought. Contemplating what it would be like to kiss me.

"But how would I know?" I whisper and lean a little closer. I don't plan to do it. It happens entirely on its own.

I fully expect him to pull away. But he doesn't.

It almost feels as if he *wants* me to kiss him. Maybe he's as curious as I am to find out if I can do it without sneezing.

Testing the theory, I lean in more.

Our lips are as close as they can be without actually touching. I hold my breath, waiting for the telltale itchy tingle in my nose to start.

Any second now.

It doesn't come. There's nothing. No fear, no nervousness. Only this lovely anticipation fizzing in my stomach like Coke bubbles.

"I'm not sneezing. I can't believe it."

"Casey," Gareth whispers, low and rough. It's somewhere between a warning and a request, like he's not sure which one he wants it to be.

I've never heard him sound like that before, and it makes my pulse race hard enough that I can feel it between my legs. I'm in danger of crumbling away to dust from the tension crackling between us. I want to kiss him so desperately. And I think he might want it too.

This is my chance to change my destiny. To become the kind of person I actually want to be. I have to seize the moment.

Time slows to molasses as I make my move. I'm practically outside my own body watching it happen. Until I press my lips to his. As soon as we touch, it snaps me back inside myself, and everything ceases to exist except this kiss.

Real life is so often disappointing compared to what you read in books. But not this. It's even better than I imagined.

Gareth's lips are unbelievably soft, but somehow also rough? I don't know how to explain it, but it's perfect. There's just a hint of moisture, unlike my vague memories of Seth Bumgarner's wet, sloppy mouth mauling. This feels more like a slow, careful caress.

And it's not just me out here doing this thing. Gareth is definitely participating in the kiss. That much is obvious even before his hands come up to cup my face.

His rough, warm fingers stroke over my cheek as his lips explore mine. He eases off enough to let me catch my breath before he comes back for more, tilting my head to slant our mouths together.

I love the feeling of being handled. That he's arranging me the way he wants me. When his tongue flickers against my lip, I open for him instinctively. I don't have to think about it. It's the most natural thing in the world to invite him inside.

I've never felt anything like the thrill I get when his tongue darts against mine. The sensation unfurls inside me, sending electric ripples down my spine and sparking over my skin.

At some point my hands must have slid from his chest to his arms, because I'm clutching his biceps to steady myself. I don't remember doing it, but I'm squeezing his biceps *and* his triceps, and god, it's the most incredible thing. They're so thick my fingers can't even reach halfway around his arm. I can feel the muscles shifting beneath his skin, which is so soft and smooth I want to touch it forever.

Everything is so new and fascinating. I can't get enough. Is there any such thing as *enough* of something this wonderful?

I'm afraid I might be attacking his face with my mouth. Maybe it's too much? But he doesn't seem to mind. Not if the sound he makes in the back of his throat is any indication. I'm pretty sure that's a good sound.

It makes me greedier. My hands slide up over his lovely, broad shoulders to stroke the thick column of his neck. I press against him and get this intense gush of pleasure when my nipples graze his chest. It makes me moan, which seems to make the movement of his mouth more frantic. That makes me think he likes it, so I press against him even more.

It's not just our mouths grinding together now. Something hard presses between my legs, and *whoa*. It's the most amazing sensation I've ever felt.

A shudder racks Gareth's body, and he tears his mouth away from mine.

The next thing I know, he's moved me off his lap and set me on the couch. I feel a bit whiplashed as he launches to his feet.

He paces across the room and rakes his hands through his hair. "Fuck."

The word splashes over me like ice-cold water, bringing all

that pleasure and happiness of a moment ago to an inglorious end.

And boy, if that hadn't already killed the mood, the expression on Gareth's face when he turns around would have. Because he looks like he's experienced some kind of trauma.

Caused by kissing me.

If it was possible to expire from humiliation, I'd be flatlining right now.

Here I was, slobbering all over his face and actually thinking he liked it. But his face says otherwise. His face says he's horrified by my nightmare kisses.

His next words say it too. "We can't do this."

He doesn't want me. I've disgusted him with my clumsy advances. Who could blame him? I'm disgusting.

No one wants me. Don't I know that by now? Especially not someone as attractive as Gareth. What was I thinking? He can have any woman he wants. Why would he ever settle for me in a hundred million trillion years?

Mortification pins me in place. I'm paralyzed, unable to move or speak or do anything but pray for death. Or for the couch to swallow me up at the very least. If only there was a pocket dimension hiding in its upholstered depths. A nice, dark void where I could hide forever and never have to interact with another human soul again.

No such luck, unfortunately. I'm still sitting on our normal three-dimensional couch staring at Gareth, who probably wishes I'd disappear as much as I do.

The crushing silence is broken by the slam of the front door. We both start at the jarring sound, and Gareth's eyes widen in panic as footsteps pound up the stairs.

"Yo," Ozzy says, pausing at the top when he sees us.

"Hey," Gareth replies, covering his discomposure by stooping to grab his water off the table.

I pull my knees to my chest and pretend to study my fingernail as my brother's gaze bounces back and forth between us.

"What's up?" he asks, clearly sensing something amiss.

"Playing video games." Gareth's already pulled himself together and slipped his poker face back on like a pro. "You're home pathetically early. What's the matter? You strike out already?"

Something that resembles chagrin thins Ozzy's lips for a second before he shrugs it off. "You win some, you lose some, right?"

"I can grab another controller if you want to drown your sorrows by blowing up some zombies."

"Nah, I'm wiped. I think I'll take my sad self to bed for some self-care."

Gareth nods. "Cool, man. Thanks for sharing."

Ozzy grins and salutes us both as he backs down the hall toward his room. "Hasta mañana, iguanas."

As soon as my brother steps out of sight, Gareth's mask drops, his expression shifting to regret.

I can't take it. Not for another second. As soon as I hear Ozzy's door shut, I rocket off the couch and down the stairs to my room, locking the door behind me.

Unnecessarily, as it turns out, because Gareth doesn't try to follow.

8

GARETH

S ometimes it seriously sucks being the good guy.

Casey's been avoiding me all week, and it's making me feel like a toenail fungus. Even though I'm pretty sure I did the right thing by turning her down.

Didn't I?

Deflowering my virgin roommate doesn't seem like the sort of thing a good guy would agree to do. Even if it's what she thinks she wants.

I'm not convinced she knows what's best for her in this particular situation. The odds of her hating me afterward seem awfully fucking high. In my experience, it's safer to keep sex and feelings separate so one doesn't end up ruining the other. Attachment leads to suffering. That's why I don't do girlfriends.

Hooking up with one of my best friends seems like a surefire way to ruin the friendship. Not that the friendship is doing so great at the moment. I may have made the noble choice, but it turns out rejecting a friend's request for sex puts its own kind of strain on the relationship. I'm trapped in a no-win situation here. Damned if I do and just as damned if I don't.

Not that I'm completely blameless. I definitely fucked up by letting Casey kiss me. And fucked up even worse by kissing her back as enthusiastically as I did.

What can I say? I'm not made of stone. The second Casey kissed me, all my good intentions went up in flames. All I could think about was how good it felt.

I shouldn't have let it happen because now I know what she tastes like. I know how soft her lips are, and what her breathy sighs sound like. It's burned into my memory. Every touch of her fingertips, every hot glide of her tongue, every needy, satisfied sound she made.

I want you to have sex with me.

It's all I can think about now. What it would be like to do more than kiss her. To feel her body writhing with pleasure beneath mine.

Fuck.

I shouldn't be thinking about her like that. She's my friend, not some one-night stand. I could barely look Ozzy in the eye all week knowing I'd had my tongue in his sister's mouth.

At least I put a stop to it before I got completely carried away and actually had sex with her. That's got to count for something.

It doesn't do a lot to relieve my conscience though. Casey's hurting, and it's my fault. She came to me with a problem, asked for my help, and not only did I refuse to help her, I led her on and *then* rejected her, when she was already sensitive about being undesirable.

Yeah, I seriously suck.

I made everything a thousand times worse, and I don't have any idea how to fix it.

That's why I'm at the gym on a Saturday night. I need to work off some of this guilt and stress. Or at least exhaust myself into the temporary relief of numbness.

Except it was stupid to think I could forget about the situation with Casey by coming to the gym where she works. Even though she's not here, I can feel her presence. My gaze keeps drifting to the reception desk where she sits during the week, expecting to find her there.

As if this week wasn't already shitty enough, I got my Dickens essay back from my English professor today. Apparently I failed to "engage critically with the material" and express myself "at a level suitable for college work." Whatever the fuck that means.

I bombed so badly, he's giving me a chance to redo it for fifty percent credit. Except I don't know how I'm supposed to do any better when I don't even understand what he wants in the first place.

It might be time to admit that I'm not cut out for this college thing after all. I was fooling myself to think I could hack it. My best asset has always been my body, not my brains. I should have stayed in my lane and stuck to what I'm good at.

Time to cut my losses and move on. It's what I usually do. I don't believe in fighting losing battles. Better to walk away than bang my head against a wall.

But for once, the thought of quitting makes my stomach turn. I wanted to prove that I could do this, that I can be more than just a pretty face. I'm not ready to give up quite yet.

Ignoring my exhaustion, I start another set of squats. The punishment feels better than anything else has in days. At least moving weight is something I can do. It's something I can control.

I drive through my feet, relishing the pain as I battle the crushing weight of the bar on my back. My mind's eye tunnels, forcing everything else out of my head while I focus on my breathing and the mechanics of my form.

Except it doesn't last. As soon as I rack the bar, it all comes flooding back. School stress. My guilty conscience. The memory of Casey's tongue sliding over mine. I shut my eyes against the dizzying assault as I fight to catch my breath.

When my vision clears, the first thing I see is Connor fucking Autry. He's over by the dumbbell rack working with a client. A young, hot, female client who's giving him thirsty looks and checking out his ass whenever he turns his back.

I can't help scowling as I wonder if he's fucked her. She seems like she'd be willing, but he's harder to get a read on. To his credit, he's not touching her more than necessary or overtly flirting like I've seen some trainers do. As far as I can tell, he's taking his job seriously and paying attention to his client's exercise form instead of her tits.

Despite the evidence of my eyes, I have a hard time giving him the benefit of the doubt. On some level, I know I'm not being fair to him, and yet I can't seem to give a fuck.

It's possible he doesn't have any idea that Casey likes him. I sure wouldn't have guessed she had a thing for the guy if she hadn't told me. It's not like she flirts or does the sorts of things women usually do to get a man's attention.

Casey doesn't vie for anybody's attention. She's friendly to everyone, but in a quiet, understated way that's easy to take for granted. Even if Connor does know Casey's got a crush on him, it's not like he's obligated to reciprocate.

I don't care. He made Casey sad, and that pisses me off. Fair or not, I can't forgive him for it.

I add more plates to the bar and do another set of squats. My legs and abs scream in protest, but I keep going, pushing myself until I'm on the verge of muscle failure. Only then do I rack the bar again.

My body hurts all over. It doesn't help that I haven't been sleeping well because I can't stop thinking about Casey. As I reach for my water bottle, I wonder what she's doing tonight. Is she thinking about me at all? Will she ever forgive me? Have I hopelessly fucked up our friendship when all I was trying to do was save it?

I should probably go home before I pull something, but I can't stand the thought of going back to the house. Either Casey will be there giving me the cold shoulder, or she won't be there and I'll spend the rest of the night wondering where she is.

A flash of pink over by the stationary bikes catches my attention as I'm unloading the bar. A busty blonde in a tight workout top is watching me. God knows I'm not above flirting at the gym, but I'm in no mood for it tonight.

I've always been popular with women. Even back in elementary school, giggling girls would vie for my attention on the playground. As I got older, passing me notes in class progressed to making out under the bleachers after school. By the time I made the varsity football team and started to pack on muscle, I was already used to girls throwing themselves at me.

Attracting women is the only thing I've ever really been good at. I definitely wasn't good at school, and I wasn't good enough at football to entertain hopes of a college scholarship. I played because it was fun, and because I liked the attention football players were showered with at my Lubbock high school.

I guess that's why I've always liked flirting so much. I enjoy the heady rush of the game as much as I get off on the ego boost. Truth be told, the flirting's usually more fun than the actual hookups that sometimes follow. It's the challenge of the chase that gets me off.

Don't get me wrong, I love sex. It just doesn't give me the same thrill as that initial sizzle of attraction. Especially lately. My last few hookups have left me feeling strangely empty. No matter how good the sex is, I walk away feeling like I have an itch that still needs scratching.

I don't know what the deal is. Maybe it's just a phase. Or maybe I'm getting old.

Fuck, I hope not. I'm not even thirty.

The woman in pink ducks her head and reaches up to smooth her ponytail, casually thrusting her breasts out with an arch smile of invitation. Sending a clear signal that she's interested. I've seen the same moves a thousand times before, and I know how to play the part expected of me. I could easily take her up on the offer. Follow her home and use her to forget about my problems for a few hours. A year ago I might have.

But right now the thought fills me with a creepy-crawly queasiness.

I don't return her smile, but she makes her way toward me anyway.

Terrific. The last thing I want tonight is company.

No, that's not true.

There's one person whose company I'd kill to have tonight, but she's not currently speaking to me.

"I'm done with the rack," I tell the woman in the pink top as I hurriedly gather my stuff. "All yours."

Before she can say anything, my phone rings in my earbuds, and Kenzie's name lights up the screen. I offer an apologetic shrug as I swipe to answer it and turn my back.

"Hey, Kenzie," I say loudly as I walk away from the rack. "What's up?"

"Are you on shift tonight?" It's hard to hear her over the sound of dogs yapping in the background, which means she must be at the vet clinic still.

"No. Why?" I say, mopping the sweat off my face.

"I think our girl's about to do something stupid, and I need you to go check on her."

My steps falter. "Casey? What's going on?"

"You know that little problem she asked you to help her out with?"

I close my eyes and press my fingertips into my eyelids. "She told you about that?"

"Don't be pissed, but it's possible I was the one who gave her the idea in the first place."

"What the fuck, Kenzie?" My outburst earns me a few odd looks as I stride past the reception desk and step out into the parking lot.

"I'm sorry, okay? I didn't mean to make things awkward for you."

"Well, that's exactly what you did."

"Yeah, she told me you said no."

"What the fuck was I supposed to say?" I snap, bristling at the accusation I can hear in her tone.

"Hey, it's your business and your body, man. You're allowed to say whatever you want. But Casey's still got this bug in her bonnet about losing her virginity. It's like she's on a mission or something. And since you turned her down—which you're completely within your rights to do—she's apparently desperate enough to take advice from her dumbass cousin Kaylee."

"Oh god." I grip the back of my neck as I lean against the fender of my truck. "What does that mean?"

"She let Kaylee drag her out to some party tonight. Apparently her brilliant plan is for Casey to get drunk and throw herself at the first available rando with a penis."

"Jesus tittyfucking Christ. Are you goddamned serious?" A pit opens in my stomach at the thought of Casey letting some crusty sleazeball touch her.

"I wish I wasn't. She sent me a bunch of drunk texts twenty minutes ago while I was with a patient, and now she's not taking my calls. I'd go over there and stage an intervention myself, but I'm working a shift at the emergency vet clinic tonight."

I yank open the door of my truck and climb inside. "Do you have the address?"

"I'm texting it to you now. Just try not to make a scene and embarrass her, okay? I called you instead of Ozzy because I thought you'd handle it more tactfully."

I don't know about tactfully, but I'm going to fucking handle it all right.

9

GARETH

The party is at some townhouse complex up by the Cedar Creek Resort where Kaylee works. I drive around the mazelike property, searching for the unit number Kenzie gave me.

Once I've parked, the sound of blaring hip-hop leads me to the door, which is hanging wide open. The living room is packed with people. I don't recognize many faces, but I spot Kaylee standing over by a keg that's been set up in the dining room.

Her face lights up when she sees me. "Gareth! Holy shit! You're here!"

She throws her arms around my neck, earning me a testy glare from the dude standing next to her. He's welcome to have her back as soon as I get what I came for.

"Where's Casey?" I demand as I peel Kaylee off me. She smells like beer and too much perfume. Based on the glassiness of her eyes, she's already drunk. And definitely not doing a proper job of looking out for Casey.

Kaylee's lips purse smugly, and she jerks her thumb at a set of glass patio doors across the room. "Outside, talking to a cute guy who's totally into her. You had your chance and you missed it, hotshot."

It's tempting to give her an earful about this harebrained plan she talked Casey into, but I clamp my mouth shut and head for the patio instead. Casey's my priority right now, and telling Kaylee off won't accomplish anything.

There aren't many people outside, just a small group of smokers sitting around a patio table and a few couples scattered around talking quietly. I almost don't recognize Casey at first. She's wearing a shit ton of makeup and a low-cut top I've never seen before. It's practically see-through and so tight it hugs her every curve. Jesus, is she wearing a push-up bra? Because her breasts have never looked so big before. They're spilling out of her top and jiggling with every move she makes.

I don't like the look of the dude she's talking to. Not one goddamn bit. I especially don't like the way he's leering at her tits like they're two scoops of ice cream he'd like to lick. He's standing so close he's basically panting on her, and it's all I can do not to lunge at the prick and choke him out.

"Casey," I bark, marching toward them.

She breaks into a smile. "Gareth! What are you doing here?"

It's the first time she's smiled at me since we kissed last weekend, and it hits me like a punch to the chest. That's how I know she's drunk, because she doesn't remember she's supposed to be mad at me.

The prick eyeballs me warily as I approach.

"Meet my new friend Bryce," Casey says, tugging me closer. "Bryce, this is my roommate Gareth."

"Hey, man," Bryce mumbles, giving me a nod.

I'd like to introduce my fist to his fucking teeth, but instead I take the plastic cup out of Casey's hand and give it a sniff. "How much have you had to drink?"

"I don't know. Two or three beers?" She tilts her head and giggles. "Maybe four. I didn't keep count."

That's way too much for her to be making good decisions. Casey doesn't drink a lot, so even two beers is enough to get her buzzed.

"We're leaving," I announce. "Say goodbye to Bryce."

She blinks at me in confusion. "What? Why? I'm having a good time."

"You're drunk, that's why. I'm taking you home."

Bryce puffs his chest up like he's about to say something, but when I turn a lethal glare on him he wisely decides to keep his fucking opinion to himself.

"Let's go." I reach for Casey's hand, but she jerks it away.

"You don't get to tell me what to do. You're not the boss of me."

"No, I'm your fucking friend. And I'm not going to let you do something stupid you'll regret when you sober up."

"It's my stupid decision to make if I want to!"

"Like hell." I'm not having a fight with her about it in front of all these people, so I throw her up onto my shoulders in a fire-man's carry.

"What are you doing? Gareth!" She tries to struggle, but she's not going anywhere with my arm locked around her. All she can do is pound a single, useless fist against my back. "Put me down right now!"

Ignoring her protests and the curious eyes of the outdoor party guests, I carry her across the yard and out the side gate. No one says a word, if you can believe it. Not even fucking Bryce. They're all perfectly content to let me carry a protesting woman off into the night. What a bunch of assholes.

"I can't believe you," Casey complains as I march across the parking lot with her slung over my shoulder like a sack of grain.

"I can't believe you either," I growl back at her. "I thought you were smarter than this."

"You're being a real jerk right now, Gareth Kelly!"

"Since you've already decided I'm a jerk, I'm just living up to expectations." We reach my truck, and I set Casey down beside the passenger door, but keep a hold on her in case she tries to bolt.

Instead of making a break for it, she starts to sway and clutches at my shirt. "Why is the ground so tilty here?"

"It's not."

"Whew." She sags against me and lays her head on my shoulder. "Okay, maybe I am a little drunk."

"You think?" I wrap my arm around her waist to keep her from sliding to the pavement while I dig my keys out of my pocket.

"You smell like sweat."

"That's because I came straight from the gym. I was in the middle of a workout." I swing the passenger door open and gesture her inside. "Are you getting in willingly or do I have to put you in the seat like a tantruming toddler?"

She pushes off me and lurches toward the truck. I stick close enough to make sure she doesn't slip as she steps onto the running board and hoists herself into the bucket seat. Once she's situated, I shut the door and walk around to the other side.

"How did you know where I was?" she asks when I get behind the wheel.

"Kenzie called me. Buckle up."

Her face twists in a scowl. "I never should have texted her."

"She was trying to look out for you, something that fucking cousin of yours couldn't be bothered to do." I take the seat belt from her when she has trouble getting it to buckle. "I can't believe you let Kaylee talk you into this."

"I don't need everyone treating me like a child," she snaps as I clip her seat belt for her.

"You sure about that?" I shoot back.

When she doesn't say anything, I start the engine and throw the truck into reverse.

We pass the entire drive in stony silence.

"I'm sorry she interrupted your workout," Casey finally mumbles when I turn onto our street.

"I'm not." I park in front of the house and cut the engine before glancing over at her. "You weren't really going to let that asswipe sleep with you, were you?"

Her shoulders give a noncommittal twitch. "He wasn't so bad."

"You realize I just threw you over my shoulder against your will, and that dude didn't even try to stop me? For all he knows, some violent psychopath just kidnapped you, and he doesn't give enough of a fuck to raise an alarm. Is that the kind of guy you want your first time to be with? Someone who couldn't care less if you're okay?"

She pins me with a glare. "He's not my first choice, but my first choice said no."

I clench my jaw as guilt slashes through my gut. "You deserve better than either of us."

"Why? What's so great about me? It's not like I'm anyone's idea of a prize. If a guy like Bryce is all I can get, maybe he *is* what I deserve."

Before I can respond to that, she shoves the passenger door open and launches herself out of the truck. Cursing under my breath, I hurry after her. "Casey, wait."

She ignores me as she weaves across the overgrown front yard that Ozzy swore he'd mow last week.

When I catch up to her, I spin her around to face me. Her eyes are shiny with tears, but worse than that is the bleakness in them. Whatever meaningless words of encouragement I was about to offer vanish like a puff of smoke. My tongue feels too thick to speak, and there's a tinny taste in my mouth.

Because I recognize that look in Casey's eyes. That yawning void that threatens to swallow you up because you feel so unwanted and completely alone in the world. I'm acquainted with that void to an extent I'm not prepared to admit.

I pull her into a hug and stroke her hair as she lets out a shuddering breath.

It's only now that I really understand how much my rejection hurt her. How much courage it took for her to ask me to do something like that. How heavily this situation must be weighing on her to drive someone so otherwise level-headed to make such rash, out-of-character decisions.

"Casey..." I don't know what to say. An apology hovers on the tip of my tongue, but I'm still not convinced I did the wrong thing. I want to make this better for her, but I don't know how.

"I'm gonna be sick—" She twists out of my arms and upchucks into a potted plant next to the front porch.

I kneel beside her and hold her hair back while she pukes up all the beer she drank earlier.

"Oh god," she sobs. "I feel like I'm dying."

"You'll feel better once it's all out."

"I'm never drinking again."

The front door opens, and Ozzy fills the doorframe, holding a bag of Nitro Takis and wearing a shirt that says *Body by Nachos*. "What the hell? Is she okay?"

"She's fine," I say as Casey horks into Darius's cherry tomatoes again. "Someone just got a little overserved tonight."

Ozzy's jaw falls open. "You're shitting me. Not *my* sister."

"Fuck off," Casey mumbles in between dry heaves.

His eyes go wide. "Drinking *and* swearing? That can't

possibly be my sister. Clearly she's been body-swapped by an alcoholic potty-mouthed alien life-form."

"Your cousin Kaylee took her to a party," I tell him. "Bad decisions were made."

Ozzy breaks into a grin as he licks spicy chip residue off his fingers. "I'm proud of you, Stinkerbelle. This is a real grown-up right of passage you're experiencing. Fist bump."

"I regret every choice that led me to this moment," Casey moans, leaving him hanging.

"I know," I say, rubbing her back in sympathy.

"Don't worry," Ozzy says. "That feeling will pass, and you'll live to do something stupid again another day."

"I've got her," I tell him pointedly, hoping he'll take the hint. She's having a rough enough time without her older brother enjoying her misery so much.

"You sure?" he asks, cocking an eyebrow at me.

"I'm fine." Casey sits back on her heels and scrubs a hand across her mouth. "I don't need any help."

Ozzy snorts. "You say that now, but when Darius sees what you did to his precious tomato babies..."

She staggers to her feet and glares at her brother as she shoves past him. "Move."

Ozzy and I follow her inside, watching warily as she makes her unsteady way through the house.

"Looks like you've really got this whole walking thing under control," Ozzy says around a mouthful of Takis when she careens off a wall. "Very impressive."

"Yeah, well...your face is stupid," she shoots back, waving off my attempt to assist her. She staggers the rest of the way to her bedroom and slams the door in both our faces.

I give Ozzy an *are you happy now* look.

"Sounds like my work here is done," he says with a shrug and heads back upstairs with his Takis.

My hands clench at my sides as I stare at Casey's door, hating that she's so miserable. But after a minute goes by with no concerning sounds to indicate that she's fallen and hit her head in the bathroom, I head into the kitchen.

Before long, I'm back at Casey's door with Gatorade, Gold-fish crackers, and ibuprofen. "Casey?"

"Go away."

"I'm coming in." I twist the knob and push the door open.

She's sitting up in bed hugging her biggest puffin stuffie against her chest. She's washed off all the makeup that streaked down her face after she puked and looks more like herself again.

"I brought you some Advil. But you should eat something before you take them." I set the Gatorade and ibuprofen on her nightstand. "Hold out your hand."

Without looking at me, she uncurls one of her arms from around the puffin, and I shake a few Goldfish crackers onto her palm.

Sitting on the bed next to her, I swing my legs up as I lean back against the fabric headboard. My calloused man feet look extra big and ugly on the floral patchwork quilt alongside Casey's pretty feet and lilac-painted toes.

"Look, I know you're mad at me for—"

"I'm not mad at you." She holds out her hand for more Goldfish.

I dump more into her palm. "Really? 'Cause it sure seems like you've been avoiding me all week long."

"I was embarrassed." She groans and buries her face in the puffin. "I can't do anything right. What's the matter with me? Why am I like this?"

"Nothing's wrong with you." I put an arm around her and pull her closer. "You're just going through a rough patch. It'll get better."

"You don't know that." She rests her head against my chest,

still hugging the puffin. "What if it doesn't? I don't want to be alone forever."

"Hey. Come on. You won't be." The rawness in her voice makes everything inside my rib cage ache. My lungs, my diaphragm, my heart, even my esophagus. It hurts so much I have to reach up and rub my sternum. Which is so close to Casey's head, it hardly takes any effort at all for my fingers to find their way to her hair and stroke the soft strands out of her face.

"I can't even flirt without making an idiot of myself. I'm going to spend the rest of my life as the plucky spinster friend no one wants to see naked."

"I wouldn't mind seeing you naked."

"Gee, thanks," she says as she crams her hand into the bag of Goldfish. "How reassuring to know you wouldn't run screaming from the room at the horrifying sight of my nakedness. All my self-esteem problems are solved."

Shit, that didn't come out right. It just feels weird and wrong to admit I think about Casey that way, even if it's true.

But it seems like something she needs to hear, so maybe in this case it's okay?

Fuck. I don't know.

"I didn't mean it like that. I'd be thrilled to see you naked. Is that better?"

"Liar," she mumbles around a mouthful of Goldfish crackers. "I offered you the chance and you said no."

"Not because I don't think you're attractive." I tip her chin up to gaze into her face. "You know that, right? I think you're beautiful. Any guy would be lucky to have you. Me included. You don't have to put all that shit on your face or straighten your hair. I like your face the way it is, and I miss your curls."

She squeezes her eyes shut and shakes her head. "You have no idea what it feels like to never be wanted. You can't understand because you're gorgeous and charming and it all comes so easily to you. I'll bet you've never been this hopelessly bad at anything your whole entire life."

A sour taste fills my throat as I think about the English essay I just got back. And all those hours I've spent struggling to understand the kind of basic reading assignments that most eighteen-year-old college freshman can do by pulling an all-nighter after a weekend drinking binge.

"You'd lose that bet," I say. "And you're not hopeless."

A big fat tear rolls down her cheek as her big brown eyes stare up at me. "Then help me, Gareth. I don't want to feel like this anymore."

"All right," I say before I can think better of it. "I'll do it."

10

CASEY

I scramble upright and blink at Gareth. "You mean it?"

Did he really agree to have sex with me? I'm not entirely certain I didn't imagine it. Does alcohol poisoning cause hallucinations? Maybe I'm having a medical crisis and need to go to the hospital.

He looks like he can't believe he said it either. Like maybe he regrets letting the words out and would like to take them back.

But he doesn't.

"I don't want you throwing yourself at random douchebags. Your first time should be with someone you trust. Someone who cares enough to make sure it feels good for you."

"That's why I asked *you*. Because I trust you."

He startles a little and goes still. Like he honestly didn't know I trusted him. It takes him a second to pull himself together before he can respond.

"You really think having more experience will help you get over this sneezing thing?"

"I really, really do."

"If that's what you need, then okay. I can give you some pointers to improve your self-confidence."

"Pointers?" I'm picturing chalkboards and study guides and flash cards instead of the kind of real-world experience I was looking for. I've already read enough books about sex. I need a practical lab, not a lecture.

"Lessons," he clarifies.

"Hands-on lessons? Or like a TED Talk?"

"Hands-on," he says, and my brain overloads as it imagines Gareth's hands *on me.* "By the time I'm done with you, you'll be a certified sexpert."

"You'll teach me how to be good at sex?"

"I'll teach you how to be fucking awesome at sex. As long as you're absolutely positive this is what you want."

"It is. I am. Maybe not tonight though. I still feel sick."

"Definitely not tonight," he agrees. "And I have a few conditions we need to discuss if we're going to do this."

"Okay." I brace myself, wondering what they could be. Maybe he doesn't want to kiss on the mouth. Or we have to keep most of our clothes on, so he doesn't have to see more of me naked than necessary. I can probably work with that.

"First of all, we agree that this won't change anything between us. I need to know that we'll still be friends afterward."

I nod. "Agreed. Absolutely."

"I'm fucking serious, Casey. I'll never forgive myself if you wind up getting hurt somehow and it messes up our friendship." He looks stricken again, but I try not to take it personally.

"I won't get clingy, if that's what you're worried about. It'll be strictly platonic sexual congress."

Gareth winces. "Christ, don't call it that. Let's consider that another one of the conditions."

"Okay. Sorry."

"Also, we're going to take it slow, and check in with each other every step of the way. If at any point either one of us starts to feel uncomfortable, we mutually agree to stop, okay?"

That all sounds extremely sensible. I knew I'd be in good hands with him. "Yes. Good. Totally agree. What else?"

"I don't want anyone else to know about this. It has to stay between us."

"Is it that embarrassing to sleep with me?"

He's taken aback. "God, no. It's not that at all. It's just that everyone thinks I'm such a player, and you're all sweet and innocent. If anyone finds out about this, they'll assume I'm an asshole who takes advantage of defenseless virgins. And Christ, I don't even know what Ozzy'll do. Just thinking about it makes me feel like a fucking monster."

I believe him. Or at least I believe he genuinely thinks that's what people will assume. Maybe he's right. Maybe it is what people will think. Not everyone. But some people. Maybe some of our friends. Maybe even the ones who live in this house. Which could be a problem.

God, but I hope that's not what *he* thinks.

It is though. I can hear it in his voice.

"I'm not innocent and you're not doing anything wrong. I'm a consenting adult who's asking you to do this."

"If you weren't innocent, you wouldn't need to ask me for sex lessons."

He's got me there. No matter how many books I've read, it's not the same as experiencing it. That's why I need his help.

I nod, conceding the point. "We'll keep it a secret."

Honestly, I don't want Ozzy or Darius knowing either. Darius can be as overprotective as Gareth. As for my brother, he's a wild card. I can't predict how he'll react, except that he's sure to be a pain in the ass. I don't need our roommates involving themselves in my personal choices, and I don't want to be the cause of tension between them and Gareth.

He looks relieved. "Good."

"Is that it?"

"There's one other thing." A muscle ticks in his jaw as he hesitates. "I need to ask you for a favor in return."

"Okay." Whatever it is, I'm game. I'll do his laundry for him. I'll wash his car inside and out every week. I'll even trade bedrooms with him if that's what he wants, although it will pain me greatly. But if sharing a bathroom with my disgusting brother is the price I have to pay to remove this virginity curse, so be it. There's not much I wouldn't be willing to do.

Gareth lifts his arm off my shoulders and swings his feet to the floor. But instead of getting up, he just sits there on the edge of the bed with his back to me. "I haven't told anyone about this yet..."

My stomach clenches at his long pause. Whatever it is, it's hard for him to say. Is it bad news? Is he moving out of the house? Or worse—out of town?

He glances over his shoulder but doesn't quite meet my eyes. "I've been taking online college courses."

I release the breath I was holding. That's not bad news at all. It's good news. Isn't it? But why keep it a secret? I bite down on the impulse to congratulate him as I study his expression. "For how long?"

He seems embarrassed, but I don't understand why. "A few months. It's for this emergency management administration degree program."

"Why didn't you say anything?"

He stares at the floor like it's the most fascinating thing he's ever seen. "I've never been much good at school. I guess I didn't want anyone to know in case I couldn't handle it."

It's impossible to imagine Gareth not being able to do anything he applies himself to. The guy fights literal fires and saves lives for a living, knows how to cook, can fix almost anything around the house, and tosses hundred-pound logs around for fun. He's basically Superman.

Tentatively, I lay my hand on his forearm. "You can do this. I know you can."

He makes a dismissive, scoffing sound as if I've just suggested he could build a spaceship and fly to the moon. "I've been doing okay with the technical courses for the major since it's mostly stuff I've already learned on the job. But I have to take these core curriculum classes, and they're kicking my ass. I managed to scrape by in algebra last term with a C-minus, but now I'm in this English literature class, and I'm in way over my head."

I scramble across the bed to plant my butt next to his. "I majored in English literature!"

He grimaces and rubs the back of his neck. "Yeah, I know."

"But did you also know I had a part-time job in the undergraduate writing lab? I can help. Let me help." I'm so eager I'm bouncing on the mattress. Even if I didn't need a favor from him, I'd jump at the chance to help Gareth with his English class. Talking about books is one of my favorite things to do.

I can't believe he's been hiding that he's in school all this time. For *months*. He's been walking around the house pretending everything's peachy while he's been struggling with his classes.

If he'd said something sooner, I could have been helping him all along. It hurts a little that he'd keep it a secret. I thought we were closer than that, that he'd confide in me if there was something wrong.

I have to wonder how many other things he's kept from us. He always acts like such an easygoing, happy person that it's easy to assume nothing ever gets to him. But obviously some things get to him. He's just been keeping them to himself.

"I'm afraid I might be a lost cause."

He sounds so dejected it makes me want to hug him, but I'm not used to initiating hugs. He's usually the hugger, and the way he's hunched over makes him seem closed off, so I end up awkwardly patting his back instead.

"That's crazy talk. You're as smart as anyone I know." When he makes another one of those scoffing sounds, I jab him in the arm with my elbow. "You *are*. Going back to school as an adult while working a full-time job is no joke. Having a hard time with it doesn't mean you're not smart. College isn't supposed to be easy. That's why writing labs, tutors, and study groups exist."

"Do you really think you can help me?" He turns to look at me finally, his expression so full of doubt I get a sympathetic pain in my chest.

"Absolutely positive." My arms ache to hug him, but now I'm worried it'll seem like pity, which I don't think he'll appreciate. "I'll have you acing that English lit class in no time."

He doesn't seem convinced. "I just got back an essay that I need to rewrite by Monday."

"What's the topic?"

"*Great Expectations*."

This is my time to shine. Dickens happens to be one of my favorite authors. "No problem. We can get to work on it first thing tomorrow."

"Thank you." Gareth offers a faint smile. "Then I guess we have a deal."

I nod. "I tutor you in English, and you tutor me in making love."

He winces. "Can we not call it that?"

"I didn't mean *love* love. It's a figure of speech."

"Yeah, I know. I've just always hated that particular expression." He shudders slightly. "It creeps me out."

"Okay, we can call it whatever you want."

"How about we just call it sex? It's short and sweet and doesn't make me cringe."

"Great. I look forward to doing business with you."

He stares at me.

"I meant—"

"I know what you meant." Amusement tugs at the corner of his mouth.

My pulse quickens as I stare at his lips, remembering what it felt like to kiss them.

I'm going to get to do it again. That and a whole lot more, apparently.

I feel my face warm and bite the inside of my cheek. "So we're really doing this?"

His smile deepens, unleashing a flurry of butterflies in my stomach. "Yeah, I guess we are."

CASEY

I'm going to have sex with Gareth.

That's my first thought when I wake up in the morning. We're starting my sex lessons next weekend, after my brother leaves for his camping trip on Friday night.

I still can't quite believe it, but the empty bottle of Gatorade on my nightstand proves Gareth was in my room last night. It wasn't a dream.

He made me drink the entire bottle of Gatorade before he'd let me go to sleep, so I only feel like I got run over by a compact SUV instead of an Amtrak train. On the downside, I have to pee so badly I'm worried I might actually burst on the way to the bathroom. There's always a price to pay.

A long, hot shower takes care of most of my aches and leaves me feeling a lot more cheerful. Not only do I have sex with Gareth to look forward to next weekend, but I get to spend today helping him with his Dickens essay.

Best. Sunday. Ever.

And that's before I step into the kitchen, where I'm greeted by the delicious aroma of bacon and the sight of Gareth flipping pancakes at the stove. The day just got infinitely better.

He glances over his shoulder and flashes a smile. "Morning, sunshine. How's the hangover?"

I'm going to have sex with him.

My knees turn jelly-like at the thought, and I grip the edge of the counter to steady myself. "Not too bad."

"Good. My special hangover-busting breakfast should take care of any lingering ill effects." His big body moves around the kitchen with practiced ease, looking like a fantasy in faded jeans and a threadbare heather gray T-shirt.

"Are those chocolate chip pancakes?" I ask, venturing closer to peek at the pan.

"Yep. Served with sliced bananas and a side of bacon. Guaranteed to have you feeling good as new." He gives me a wink. "I need that brain of yours in tip-top shape."

"Don't worry, I'll be able to put my thinking cap on as soon as I ingest some coffee."

"Go sit. I'll get it." He gives me a gentle push toward the breakfast table as he crosses to the coffeemaker.

A girl could get seriously used to being pampered like this. Not that Gareth doesn't cook for us all the time, but he doesn't usually play waiter. Not unless I'm sick or feeling down and he's trying to cheer me up.

I slide into a seat at the table in the breakfast nook off the kitchen. At the seat across from me, Gareth's laptop sits beside a dog-eared copy of *Great Expectations*. I reach for the paperback and thumb through it. The pages are full of highlights and scrawled notes in the margin. Whatever problems he's having with the class aren't for lack of doing the reading, that's for sure.

"Here." His forearm brushes mine as he sets a steaming cup of coffee next to me.

I smile my thanks up at him. "Why does it feel like you're trying to butter me up?"

"Because I want you in a good mood before you have to read my essay."

"I'm pretty sure I'm the one who should be waiting on you hand and foot since you're doing me the way bigger favor." I take a cautious sip of the hot coffee. Cream with two sugars, the way I like it. He even put it in my favorite "Puffins of the World" mug.

His mouth twists. "You haven't seen my essay yet."

"Is it on your laptop? Pull it up."

Gareth shakes his head as he unlocks his laptop and slides it toward me. "Don't say I didn't warn you."

"Will you stop being so hard on yourself? I'm sure it's not that bad."

While he goes back to tending the pancakes, I settle in to read his essay. It's only a five-page paper, so it doesn't take long. And I was right. It's not that bad.

The major problems jump out right away, and reading the instructor's comments confirm my initial impressions. Gareth shows a decent mastery of the material, but his engagement with it is superficial. His professor's looking for a critical analysis of the text rather than a summary, which is something a lot of first-year students struggle with.

The essay also lacks coherent structure. Instead of starting off with a thesis statement followed by supporting evidence, it meanders around the topic in a chaotic and sometimes circular fashion. But that's easy enough to fix with a refresher on essay structure.

His grammar and sentence structure could also use some work. Unfortunately for Gareth, his instructor is a stickler about it who takes off ten points for every single grammar error. It only takes ten minor mistakes to earn him a zero on the assignment. No wonder he was so disheartened.

Back when I was in high school, some of the teachers would try to scare us with tales of college professors who'd give you an automatic F if you turned in a paper with even one small typo. But when I got to college I quickly learned that most professors aren't nearly as concerned with the minutia as they are with your critical thinking skills and grasp of the larger concepts. Furthermore, not that many professors could meet such a rigorous standard themselves because they're only human and make mistakes like everyone else. Also, some of them happen to have a terrible grasp of grammar.

The fact that Gareth's professor is such a zealot about it makes him seem like a jerk, given that he's teaching an online course in a continuing education program aimed at working adults. He must get lots of students with rusty writing skills or gaps in their education. Failing them over a few misplaced commas and apostrophes will only discourage them, just like it discouraged Gareth.

I move the laptop aside as Gareth sets the table. "I hate your instructor."

"That makes two of us. But I'd love to hear why you hate him."

"He's a grammar bully."

Gareth deposits a mountain of chocolate chip pancakes and a slightly smaller mountain of bacon in the middle of the table. He's made enough food to feed an army. "I figured that was standard operating procedure for English professors."

I shrug as I pile my plate with pancakes. "It's highly dependent on the professor. Some couldn't care less. Most will take a limited number of points off for overall poor grammar, but they don't generally consider it their jobs to be the grammar police like your instructor. This grading rubric he uses is excessively harsh."

Gareth drops into the seat across from me. "That makes me feel a hell of a lot better. You have no idea."

"Any linguist will tell you there's no such thing as perfect grammar," I say as I butter my pancakes. "It's a framework that facilitates communication, but it's not meant to be immutable. Look at Charles Dickens—he played fast and loose with grammar rules all the time. You know the opening sentence of *A Tale of Two Cities*?"

Gareth gives me a blank look.

"It was the best of times, it was the worst of times..."

"Oh yeah, I've heard that." He picks up the bowl of bananas and reaches across the table to spoon them onto my pancakes. "Don't forget to replenish your potassium."

I pick up a banana slice and pop it into my mouth. "It's one of the most famous sentences in literature, and it's a massive run-on. No one loved a run-on sentence like Dickens."

Gareth's jaw drops. "Holy shit, is that why I keep getting lost in the middle of his sentences?"

"He's notorious for it. You should try reading *Bleak House* sometime."

He makes a face. "No thanks."

See, this is exactly why I don't like Gareth's instructor. Instead of teaching him to appreciate great literature, he's teaching him to loathe and fear it. It's like the PE teachers who used to make us play dodgeball. Getting pummeled by the stronger kids didn't make me more athletic. It made me feel like a loser and taught me to hate sports.

"I find it kind of rich that your instructor has such a strict attitude about grammar when Charles Dickens wouldn't even pass his grading rubric."

Gareth shakes his head as he drowns his pancakes in syrup. "And here I was thinking I just sucked."

"That's why I called him a grammar bully, because this rubric makes his students feel that way. I promise you don't suck."

He glances up, and a tender pang shoots through my heart as our eyes meet. "That's nice to hear."

"The bad news is, you'll still have to learn the grammar in order to pass the class."

"But you can help me with that, right?"

"Absolutely."

He looks almost boyish as he ducks his head. "Fuck, I should have asked for your help weeks ago."

Two hours later, we're both full of pancakes and sitting side by side, going through Gareth's essay. The remnants of breakfast still litter the table around us, and I'm holding Mr. Twinkletoes in my lap feeding him leftover banana slices.

"What the fuck is a comma splice?" Gareth complains. "That just sounds made up."

"I'm sorry to tell you this, but all grammar is made up."

He slumps over with a groan and bangs his forehead against the laminate table. "Then why did they have to go and make it so fucking complicated?"

Mr. Twinkletoes nuzzles his arm in sympathy. Or maybe he's hoping for more food.

I pat Gareth on the back and give the rabbit another slice of banana. "That is a question for the ages, my friend. Believe me, you are not alone in your frustration with the English language and all its stupid, arbitrary rules."

"And yet you don't seem to have any problem understanding it."

"I didn't just pick it up out of thin air. I had to work for years to learn all the rules."

Although, I guess to an extent I did pick a lot of it up from being a voracious reader growing up. By the time we learned the formal rules of grammar in school, I already had an innate understanding that made the lessons easier. I don't think it would make Gareth feel better to point that out though.

He's already admitted he wasn't the kind of kid who read for fun. He was out having an actual social life and playing sports instead of at home living vicariously through books. He wasn't a nerd like me who did more than the required reading, asked the teachers for extra assignments, and crushed the library's summer reading challenge every year.

"I'm never going to learn all these stupid grammar rules," he says, pressing his fingers to his temples.

"What are the symptoms of a severe allergic reaction?"

His brow furrows. "Why?"

"Just answer the question."

"Edema, hives, severe dyspnea, wheezing, cyanosis, unstable blood pressure," he rattles off automatically.

"Exactly."

"Exactly what?"

"I don't even know what half of those words mean, much less what to do about them. But you do, because you studied and learned it so you can save people's lives. That's way harder and more important than knowing what a stupid comma splice is."

He reaches over to scratch Mr. Twinkletoes between the ears. "Can you tell my professor that?"

"He's not going to listen to me. But if you can learn all those much more impressive lifesaving skills to pass your EMT certification, you can learn this too."

Darius wanders into the kitchen and stops mid-yawn when he sees us at the table.

Gareth slams the laptop shut. Super low-key and not suspicious at all.

"Morning!" I say cheerfully as Mr. Twinkletoes springs off my lap and hops over to nuzzle Darius's ankle.

Darius grunts and shuffles over to the coffeemaker.

He's not a morning person. Not that he's much more talkative later in the day, but his grunts and silences have a slightly less grumpy vibe after he's had his coffee.

"There are still plenty of pancakes left," Gareth says, discreetly sliding *Great Expectations* into his lap. "Although they're kind of cold by now."

Darius grunts in thanks as he pours a cup of coffee.

"Do I smell bacon?" Footsteps pound down the stairs, and Ozzy saunters into the kitchen in a black T-shirt with *MAN MEAT* printed across the chest. "What's all this?"

"Gareth made breakfast," I explain.

"Yeah, I can see that." Ozzy drops into a chair and shoves an entire piece of bacon into his mouth. He jerks his chin at Gareth's laptop. "What are y'all doing?"

I glance at Gareth. It's not my place to share his secret. But I'm not going to lie for him either.

Gareth smiles tightly. "Nothing."

"Are you planning my birthday party?" Ozzy asks as he rolls a cold pancake up like a taquito. "If so, I want one of those bouncy castles. And a stripper. A bouncy castle full of strippers. That's what I want."

"Your birthday was two months ago," I remind him.

"It's never too early to start planning for next year." He bites off a mouthful of pancake and stares back and forth between us while he chews. "Seriously, why do you two look like you're planning a heist?"

Gareth stares at the table. "I guess I might as well fess up."

Darius leans against the counter, sipping his coffee.

Ozzy's eyebrows shoot up. "Shit, *are* you planning a heist? Can I help? What are we heisting? Is it the Mona Lisa? I've always wanted to go to Paris."

Gareth sets *Great Expectations* on the table next to his laptop.

"You're stealing books from the library?" Ozzy looks at me. "Don't tell me you're okay with this."

"I didn't steal it," Gareth says. "I bought it for class. I've been taking online classes for an emergency management administration degree."

"Oh, cool," Ozzy says and stuffs the rest of the pancake taquito in his mouth.

Darius sets two more plates on the table and claps Gareth on the shoulder. "Good for you."

"I've been struggling with English lit," Gareth admits. "So Casey's helping me out."

"Smart move," Ozzy says as he forks pancakes onto a plate. "Put the nerd brain to work for you."

Gareth smiles at me. I smile back.

"That explains why you've been such a homebody lately. I was starting to think you'd lost your taste for fun." Ozzy dumps the last of the syrup on his pancakes and shoves his chair back. "Do we have any more syrup?"

"In the pantry," Gareth says.

Ozzy opens the pantry door and shrieks so loud Mr. Twinkletoes bolts upstairs.

Pennywise leers evilly inside the pantry.

"Motherfucking clown!" Ozzy wheezes as he clutches his chest. "Which one of you assholes put that there?"

Gareth and I grin at each other and double over laughing.

12

GARETH

"Pick up your feet," McCafferty bellows. "You're not getting tired are you, princess?"

I shoot him an irritated look as I adjust the forty-pound high-rise pack balanced on my shoulder.

For some reason the lieutenant singled me out for weighted agility ladder drills in the yard behind the firehouse while the rest of the company gets to do their workout in the exercise room. Lucky bastards. I must be in trouble for McCafferty to inflict his favorite punishment on me, but I'll be damned if I know what I did wrong.

My lungs are on fire, but if I step on the agility ladder, I know he'll make me start the whole fucking drill over again. So I concentrate on picking up my feet and pray for a swift end to this hell.

"All right, you're done," McCafferty says after I complete a few more runs. "Good work."

I'm done, all right. I drop the pack to the ground and collapse onto my back, panting for air.

Darkness falls across my closed eyelids as McCafferty looms over me, his six-foot-five-inch frame blotting out the sun. I squint one eye open and scowl at him. "Respectfully, Lieutenant, I hate your guts right now."

He laughs and extends one of his big bear paws to help me up. "You love me because you know it's good for you."

I let him haul me off the ground. "Did I do something to piss you off?"

"Maybe I just enjoy your company." He tosses me my water bottle and cocks his head at the picnic table by the grill. "Let's sit a spell."

I drop onto the bench and use the bottom of my T-shirt to wipe the sweat off my face. The wood lets out a groan of protest when McCafferty settles down next to me. He stretches his long legs out in front of him and lounges back against the table.

I endure his silent scrutiny for ten full seconds before I snap. "Christ, what is it? Just say it and put me out of my misery."

McCafferty smiles. "Now that I've got you all tuckered out with your defenses down, I figured you might be willing to tell me what's had you so distracted lately."

I tip my head back and guzzle down some water to hide my grimace. I should have seen this coming. McCafferty's got a sixth sense for picking up on the mood of his crew, and between school stress and this stuff with Casey, I've definitely had more shit on my mind than usual.

"It's nothing," I mutter, swiping my hand across my mouth.

"Maybe I should have you do some carry drills with me on your shoulders. What do you think?"

I'm no slouch, but Ryan McCafferty is a walking mountain. The dude's got at least a hundred pounds on me. Not that I couldn't carry him if I had to, but I'd be hurting for days afterward, and I really don't fucking want to. I also know he's not going to let up unless I give him something to appease him.

"It's just roommate trouble. Nothing serious."

"I'm listening."

I don't like talking about myself or my problems, but the truth is I could use a gut check on this Casey situation. And if there's anyone I'm willing to ask for advice, it's the lieutenant.

A firehouse is like a surrogate family. We don't just work together, we live together for twenty-four-hour stretches, cook and eat our meals together, laugh together, get on each other's nerves, and watch each other's backs. Captain Ortiz is the intimidating father figure, and Lieutenant McCafferty is our older, wiser brother. He's the guy you go to when you're in a jam or need a sympathetic ear, the guy we all know would drop everything to help us if we asked.

"This stays between you and me?"

He gives me a solemn nod. "The cone of silence is in effect. Nothing leaves the vault."

Casey would absolutely kill me for telling Ryan about this. But I trust him to keep a tight lid on it. The only problem is I don't know where to start.

"You ever been in a friends with benefits situation?" I ask him, feeling awkward as hell.

I can tell by the way he blinks that I've surprised him. But he recovers quickly.

"This is about Casey, I'm guessing, and not Ozzy or Darius?"

I give a brief nod. "Have you ever tried it?"

"Once."

"How'd it work out?"

He tips his head and winces. "Honestly? Not all that great."

Not what I was hoping to hear.

"Did it ruin the friendship?" That's what I'm most afraid of. I don't want to lose Casey over this. But I also can't stand by and not try to help.

McCafferty studies me. "Something going on between you two? Or are you thinking about starting something up?"

"Not exactly." I rub my forehead. "She asked me to take her virginity."

There's an extended silence after I drop that bomb, and I'm afraid to see what kind of expression is on McCafferty's face.

He clears his throat. "Huh."

I exhale heavily. "She's got it in her head that she's defective or something because she's never had sex. I tried to tell her there was nothing wrong with her, but she's dead set on losing her virginity. And if I won't do it, she's determined to go out and let some random creep deflower her. So tell me, Big Red, what am I supposed to do here?"

"Well..." His brow furrows as he scratches his jaw. "When it comes down to it, it's her body and her choice, isn't it? There's no reason she can't go out and have a one-night stand if that's what she wants."

"Even if she's not thinking clearly?"

"Is she really not thinking clearly? Or are you just afraid she might be making a mistake?"

I ponder that. "The second one, I guess."

"You want to protect her so she doesn't get hurt. But sometimes you have to let people make their own mistakes."

I don't like the sound of that. Theoretically, I get what he's saying and I sort of agree. But it goes against every instinct I've got. "What if I agreed to do it? Does that make me an asshole?"

"You're both consenting adults, G. That means you've got a free choice to make as much as she does. The question is, do you want to sleep with her?"

"She's my friend. I don't want her to be unhappy."

"So she'd be some kind of charity project you're volunteering to take on? I'm not sure how happy it'll make her knowing that's how you see it."

"It's not like that. Jesus."

"Isn't that what you said?"

"Fuck no." Except it sort of was, wasn't it? Shit. Put like that, it does sound shitty.

"Are you attracted to her?"

Yes. If we weren't friends, I'd sleep with her in a heartbeat.

I take a drink of water and frown into the distance. "It feels wrong to think about Casey like that."

"Why?"

"She's my roommate. I thought I was supposed to think of her as a sister."

"*Do* you think of her as a sister?"

"I've never had a sister, but I'm guessing you're probably not supposed to get hard because you can see your sister's nipples through her shirt."

"Definitely fucking not."

"So I guess I don't think of Casey as a sister, then."

McCafferty gives me a long, considering look. "Do you have feelings for her?"

I squeeze the back of my neck. "I care about her, sure. She's one of my best friends. But I'm not looking to make her my girl-friend or anything, if that's what you're asking."

"Because you don't want a girlfriend, right?"

"Exactly."

We've talked about my stance on relationships before, which McCafferty used to share with me. Until he met Maggie. Now he's gone over to the dark side, leaving me the lone bachelor on the crew.

"Casey's important to me. I don't want to mess up the good thing we've got going by bringing sex into it."

"Hmmm." McCafferty nods as he sips his water. "It's a real quandary, all right."

"That's all you've got? It's a quandary? I could have gotten more than that out of a fucking Magic 8 Ball."

He shrugs. "I'm not sure it's the kind of situation where

someone else can tell you what to do, G. I think you need to trust your own conscience on this one."

"Fucking excellent. Thanks a lot."

"Happy to help." He grins at me and arches an eyebrow. "Are you gonna do it?"

"I already told her I would."

"Figured as much."

"I'm that predictable, am I?"

He shrugs again. "Have you ever slept with a virgin before?"

I nod, wincing at the memory. It was a long time ago, and I didn't have all that much experience myself at that point. I'd tried to be considerate, but I'm pretty sure I came off as a clumsy oaf. I'd like to think I could do a better job of it now. Make it a good memory for Casey instead of a cringey one.

"So you know to take it slow?"

"Yeah, I know to take it slow. Christ." I lean over and rub my forehead. "I can't afford to fuck this up. Not only will I never forgive myself, but Ozzy will flip his shit, Darius will glower me to death, and everyone else will join the 'Gareth sucks' brigade."

McCafferty grunts. "Can I ask you something?"

"Is there any way I can stop you?"

"How come you don't want a girlfriend? Really?"

"It's just not for me." I cut him a sidelong glance. "It wasn't so long ago that you felt the same."

His answering grin is a little bit wry and a lot sappy. "Yeah, well. That's what happens when you meet the woman of your dreams. Love has a way of changing your perspective on things. I'm curious though—which part of having a girlfriend is it exactly that puts you off? The companionship and moral support? Or is it the regular sex with a woman you adore?"

I roll my eyes. "It's the sense of obligation, actually."

"Ah, I see." He nods sagely. "You're afraid of commitment."

"I'm not afraid. I'm realistic. The average relationship is far more likely to end in abject misery than happily ever after. I don't believe in making bad bets."

"What about Jamal and Ayesha? They seem miserable to you?"

Our apparatus operator Jamal Allen married his high school sweetheart last year, and they've recently started trying to get pregnant. Which means Ayesha shows up at the firehouse sometimes during her ovulation window, and we all pretend not to notice when she drags Jamal off for a babymaking quickie.

"They're still in the honeymoon period when everything's all rainbows and hot sex," I say. "Give it a few more years, and we'll see how happy they still are."

McCafferty's eyebrows lift. "That's a gloomy fucking outlook you've got there. I suppose you think Maggie and I are a bad bet too."

I shake my head. "I don't think anything. Honestly, I hope you and Jamal are the lucky ones who beat the odds. It's just not a gamble I'm personally looking to take."

I could tell him that I've seen what happens when relationships go bad. That I had a front-row seat to the slow death of my parents' marriage. I watched them tear each other down and make each other's lives and mine a misery for years before they split up. And then I watched the whole cycle play out again after my mom remarried.

Both my parents' lives were better when they were single, and so was mine. So why would I want to risk my happiness on someone else when I'm perfectly content on my own? Same as my dad was happier alone. Like he used to say, attachment leads to suffering.

But I don't talk about my past or my parents, not beyond the sparest, most basic facts. Not with anyone. Not even Ryan McCafferty.

It's too painful. Too messy. And too tangled up with my own shameful mistakes.

Better to leave it all in the past where it belongs than dredge up all those unpleasant feelings. I'm a different person now. I've moved on. Grown up. Made a new life here, in a place where no one knows anything about all of that.

That's how I prefer it, so I clamp my mouth shut and keep my thoughts to myself.

13

CASEY

I don't understand why anyone would want to go camping at all, much less in a swamp filled with alligators. But apparently that's my brother's idea of a good time because he and some of his high school friends are camping at Brazos Bend State Park all weekend.

More importantly, he left this afternoon and won't be back until Sunday. Which means Gareth and I will have the house to ourselves tonight *and* tomorrow night while Darius is at work.

Operation Sex Lessons can finally commence.

I raced home from work today to get ready for my "date" with Gareth. I've exfoliated, shaved, moisturized, polished, and perfumed myself from head to toe. There's nothing left to do now but wait for Darius to leave.

I wasn't sure what to wear tonight. It feels weird to go to so much effort only to put on casual clothes. But this doesn't seem like a dress-up occasion. It's not a real date, and I don't want Gareth to think I'm confused about that.

In the end I went with jeans and a tank top. With my new bra and thong underneath, of course. Just because it's not a real date doesn't mean I can't try to make a good impression.

Speaking of which, my room doesn't exactly resemble the sort of sophisticated love nest where grown-ups have sex. My floral quilt looks like it belongs on someone's grandmother's bed, and all the stuffed animals make it seem like a kid's room. Even if I put them away, there's still the rest of my puffin collection sitting on top of my bookcases like a little seabird audience, watching everything that happens with their adorable puffin eyes.

I'm in the middle of hiding my stuffed animals a few minutes later when there's a knock on my bedroom door.

I freeze with my arms full of puffin stuffies. "Yeah?"

The door opens, and Gareth leans against the frame. His lips twitch as I fling the stuffies into the closet and pull the door closed. "He's gone. Finally."

"Oh." My mouth seems to have forgotten how to produce saliva. It's literally never been this dry before.

"You still want to do this?"

I nod. "Definitely."

He crosses his arms as he studies me from the doorway. "If you're having second thoughts, it's okay to say so."

"Are you trying to get out of it?" I won't hold him to our arrangement if he's changed his mind. But I will be deeply disappointed.

"Not at all. I'm just checking in with you, like we agreed."

"I'm good," I assure him, although my wildly thumping heart isn't quite so certain. "Thank you for doing this. I know it's a lot to ask."

"Are you kidding me? It's a fucking privilege."

I let out an unsexy snort of disbelief.

Gareth shakes his head as he moves into the room. "You need to stop acting like having sex with you is some kind of terrible burden."

While I appreciate that he's trying to make me feel better, I know he's only doing this out of pity. The sooner we get it done, the sooner he'll be off the hook. Then things can go back to being normal and comfortable between us again without this big sex elephant in the room making it weird.

"Did you bring a condom?" I ask. "I'm on the pill, but you can't be too safe, right? I went and bought some condoms, but I wasn't sure if you have a certain type you prefer. Who knew there were so many different options? They have these ones that claim to get both hot and cold, but I don't understand how that would feel good because it seems like—"

"Casey."

My mouth snaps shut when Gareth rests his hands on my shoulders.

"Take a breath."

I make myself draw air into my lungs as heat radiates from his palms and spirals through me, all the way down to the soles of my feet like a grounding charge. "Sorry. I'm babbling, I know."

"It's okay." His lips press together to hide his smile, but it leaks out through his twinkling eyes.

It's like standing in a ray of sunshine. I have to remind myself that this is just the Gareth Effect. It's the same radiance he projects at every woman he smiles at. I'm supposed to be immune to it.

I try to relax, but it's pretty much impossible. I feel like a baby deer trapped in the headlights of an oncoming eighteen-wheeler.

"Should I take my clothes off?" I blurt in a panicked attempt to fill the silence.

Gareth's eyebrows raise. "Are you in a rush or something?"

"The sooner we get it over with, the sooner we'll be done, right?"

"Wow. That's got to be the most romantic thing a woman's ever said to me. You sure know how to make a moment special."

"I only meant—"

"I know what you meant." His fingers squeeze my shoulders. "Sex is supposed to be fun. *Get it over with* is never something I want to feel about it, and it's not how I want you feeling about it either—especially not when you're having it with me. Okay?"

"Okay." I swallow, and it sounds so loud in my ears he has to be able to hear it too. "What did you have in mind?"

"We're going to take it nice and slow." As if to illustrate, Gareth's hands smooth slowly down my arms. "That's lesson number one. Don't be in too big of a hurry to get to the main event. It's better to take your time and let the anticipation grow. Enjoy the build-up."

I try to ignore the tingling buzz of sensation as his hands slide over my skin. It definitely feels like it's building to something good, but if I let myself think about it, I'm afraid I'll sneeze.

"I thought men were always eager to get right to it."

"It depends on the man, but most of us like a little encouragement." His fingers curl around mine and give a gentle squeeze.

Now we're just holding hands, which is easier somehow. I can handle holding hands.

Although I don't think I've ever held hands with someone like this, not because they were leading me somewhere, but just to enjoy the sensation. I'm pretty sure this is a first. I like it. Holding hands is nice. Especially holding Gareth's hands, which are big and warm and a lot rougher than mine.

"I think that might be part of my problem," I admit, relaxing a little. "I don't know how to be encouraging. There are probably things I should be doing to show when I'm interested in someone, but I don't know what they are."

"I can help you with that."

Gareth's thumbs stroke over my palms. I think he might be showing me what he means by encouragement. I certainly feel encouraged. All the parts of my body not being touched by his thumbs are living vicariously through my palms and rapidly melting to the consistency of warm butter. How is he doing all that with such a minuscule movement that it's barely a movement at all?

"Can you help with my awkward babbling too? Because I'm thinking that probably drives a lot of guys away."

He shakes his head, frowning as if I've said something wrong. "Your babbling is fucking adorable, and any guy in his right mind would agree with me on that."

"What? No. Pfft." I wrinkle my nose. "That's crazy."

Gareth tilts his head back briefly, as if he's asking the ceiling to lend him patience. "We are definitely going to work on taking compliments. But what you don't need to do is change who you are. That's only going to attract someone who's all wrong for you."

"I'm really just focused on attracting *anyone* right now. I don't care if they're right for me or not."

"Don't sell yourself short like that. Once you get comfortable putting yourself out there, dudes are going to be tripping over each other for your attention. You'll be able to take your pick."

"Uh huh," I say dubiously.

"I'm sensing a lack of faith on your part."

"You're good at a lot of things, but you're not a miracle worker." The palms he's stroking would like to register their disagreement with that statement, but the rest of me stands by it.

"It's not going to take a miracle. Just a little confidence. Sex appeal is all about how you carry yourself. When you act like you know your own value, other people will see it too."

"Is that really true?"

"Hundred percent."

Maybe he's right. Assuming I can refrain from sneezing on everyone who tries to get near me. But I'm hoping the sneezing will resolve itself once I get enough experience that I don't feel like a clueless newb.

"Okay," I say. "Tell me what to do."

"You can start by looking at me."

"I am looking at you."

"No you're not. You're looking past my ear." He touches my chin and turns my head so I'm staring directly into his eyes. "Hey, there you are."

The smile that breaks across his face is dazzling. I swear I can see glitter and rainbows and cartoon musical notes dancing in my vision.

"You almost never look directly at me, did you know that?"

"I wouldn't want you to think I was ogling you." It's so hard not to look away. I'm practically trembling with the effort of holding his gaze.

"Yeah, I really hate being admired. It sucks to know people like looking at me."

"You're saying ogling is good? I thought staring was rude."

"Does the way I'm looking at you right now feel rude?"

It feels like a physical touch, like fingers stroking over my skin. "Extremely."

He laughs. "Yeah, but in a good way, right?"

"Well..." I don't want to admit how good it feels, although he can probably tell it's making my face flush, along with several other parts of my body.

"How is anyone going to know you're interested if you never look at them?"

"What if they don't want me to be interested?" That's the part that scares me, putting myself out on a limb without knowing if it's going to snap and send me crashing to the ground.

"Then they won't show interest back, and you'll leave it at that." He shrugs as if it's no big deal and not the worst feeling I can imagine. "There's nothing wrong with finding someone attractive. It's only persisting when the interest isn't reciprocated that gets you in trouble."

"But how do you know if it's reciprocated?"

"It's usually pretty obvious. Like if you smile and they smile back. Or if they blush and look away, that's a good sign. But if they frown or clench their jaw as they look away, that's a no. You'll be able to tell from watching how they react. That's all flirting is—showing someone you're attracted to them and letting them show you whether they're attracted back. You can do it with your eyes or with your words. A combination of both is ideal, but you should feel free to play to your strengths."

"What if I don't have any strengths?"

"I'd say your eyes are a definite strength."

"They are?"

"The way you're looking at me right now is making my heart race. Feel." Gareth presses my hand flat against his chest.

I'm basically groping his pec now, but since he's the one making me do it I try not to worry he'll be bothered. I even manage to relax my hand enough to appreciate the firm muscle beneath it. When I press a little harder and hold very still, I detect the faint flutter of his heartbeat. I can't tell if it's actually racing, but it does seem to be beating awfully fast.

As fast as my own, in fact.

"You've got gorgeous eyes," he says, smiling at me. "They're like a treasure chest full of hidden riches."

It's the kind of line Gareth uses on women all the time. He's got a million like it, and they're so cheesy-sounding I always have to roll my eyes.

But he's never used one of his lines on me while gazing into my eyes and holding my hand against his chest. It doesn't sound so cheesy anymore. My brain might know better than to fall for it, but my insides buy it hook, line, and sinker.

An unfamiliar fizzing sensation swarms over my stomach

and swells up through me. It's giddiness. I'm so giddy, I damn near giggle and bat my eyelashes.

Not that I know how to bat my eyelashes.

Gareth's not looking at my eyes now anyway. He's staring at my mouth, and when I lick my dry lips his gaze seems to darken, which makes my body feel too tight but also like it's made of syrup.

We're standing close enough that I can hear the slight hitch in his breathing before he lifts his hand to cup my jaw. His eyelids lower as he strokes his thumb across my cheek.

It's just a small movement, so subtle it could be the brush of a feather, but it's the sexiest touch I've ever felt.

Is he closer now, or am I imagining it?

No, he's definitely leaning in.

I'm frozen in place, and I've forgotten how to breathe. He's moving in for a kiss that I should have expected but somehow didn't, and oh my Lord, he's actually going to kiss me.

Oh shoot.

No no no no no no—

Ahh-CHOO!

14

CASEY

G areth must have been ready for it because he moves out of the line of fire before the sneeze explodes out of me. So at least there's that. I didn't sneeze all over him or do either of us bodily injury.

This time.

"Well, damn," he says, sounding amused. "I really thought you were going to make it there for a second."

I cover my face. "I'm sorry. I'm so sorry."

"It's okay."

"It's not." I sniffle, hanging my head. "It's the worst."

"Nah, that was nothing compared to the time a girl accidentally kneed me in the junk when we were fooling around. *That* was the worst." He gives the back of my neck a squeeze. "You okay? You need a tissue?"

I wriggle my nose to make sure there aren't any more sneezes on the way and shake my head. "I'm sorry. It was going so well, and I ruined it."

"Nope. None of that. No more apologizing."

"But—"

Before I can get the rest of my sentence out, Gareth picks me up.

I cling to him in surprise when my feet leave the floor. But unlike the other night when he slung me over his shoulders like a caveman —or like a firefighter, I guess—now he's cradling me against his chest with one arm around my back and the other under my knees. It's not nearly as uncomfortable. In fact, it's kind of wonderful.

"What are you doing?" I ask as he carries me across the room.

"We're cuddling."

I squeak in surprise when he tosses me onto the bed.

Before I can scramble away, he flops down next to me. The impact of his weight hitting the mattress causes me to roll into the depression made by his body. His arms wrap around me, and he hauls me onto his chest, so I'm half splayed across him.

The impulse to protest his manhandling dies on my tongue. It'd be silly to complain about something that feels this incredible.

"There," he says, letting out a long, satisfied breath once he's arranged me to his liking. "That's better, isn't it?"

It is. It really is.

All this up close and personal contact should be intimidating, but instead it's soothing. The solid warmth of Gareth's body and his clean, spicy scent have an instant calming effect. It's like sinking into a hot bath after being out in the cold for years.

"You still feeling nervous?" Gareth asks.

"No, this is nice."

"Good." He tugs my hand onto his stomach and interlaces our fingers together.

The house is silent and peaceful for once. It's just the two of us, alone in the quiet. Lying in the soft glow of my bedside lamp with our bodies plastered together like it's perfectly normal for us to be lounging all over each other. The only thing weird about it is how right it feels.

"Are you comfortable?" I ask him.

"I may never move again. Why is your bed so much better than mine?"

"Probably because I didn't find my mattress by the side of the road."

"I'll have you know I bought that mattress from my previous roommate's roommate. It didn't come from the side of any road."

"That you know of. But where did your previous roommate's roommate get it from?"

"Shit, you're right. I hope you don't mind having a big, dumb oaf in your bed because this is where I live now."

"You're not a dumb oaf." Since I've been helping him with his schoolwork, I've started to notice how many offhand cracks he makes about his intelligence, and I don't like it.

"But you do agree I'm big." He lets go of my hand to flex his biceps.

I laugh and push his arm back down. His skin is warm and smooth, and if I take the opportunity to feel up that rock-hard biceps he was showing off, well who can blame me?

Apparently not Gareth.

"Better enjoy those muscles while you can. It's gonna be hard to keep this awesome body in tip-top shape without ever leaving your bed." He tests the softness of the mattress. "I could probably do push-ups and crunches from here though."

"What about work?"

"I'll have to quit my job, obviously."

"So you're planning to freeload in my bed all day like Charlie Bucket's grandparents while I go off to work and toil my fingers to the bone for food and rent money? That's nice."

"Oh no, did I not make myself clear? You're not allowed to move from this spot either." Gareth's arms tighten around me, hard enough to force a *whuff* of air from my lungs. "Sorry, but your presence is required for cuddling."

"I didn't realize you were such a cuddler."

"Neither did I," he says as if he's surprised himself. "Why haven't we been doing this all along? What a fucking waste."

I try not to think too hard about that *we* in there. Teasing me with jokey pretend scenarios doesn't mean he's seriously proposing we should have regular cuddling sessions from now on. Although if he was...I'd be okay with that.

He reaches down and hauls my leg across his. So now I'm sort of straddling him. Or at least straddling one of his legs.

This all felt more innocent before I could feel his big, meaty thigh pressing between my legs. I have to concentrate on holding still, because I'm suddenly, incredibly, embarrassingly aware of what part of me is touching him.

If I move even a little, I might accidentally *rub* myself against him, which is all I can think about now.

That and the fact that Gareth's hand is still on my thigh. He even drags my leg up higher, and surely it must be close to his crotch by now. I almost think I might feel something brush against the top of my thigh. I'm afraid if I move a fraction of an inch, I'll be actively touching his penis.

Is that why he put my leg there? Does he want me to feel it?

I can't be sure. If it's meant to be an invitation, I'm not confident enough to take him up on it.

Although I really want to.

There are definitely things happening in my lower regions. I'm having certain...sensations. And urges. It's making my pulse pound and my breathing shaky.

And apparently Gareth can tell.

"You okay?" he asks quietly. There's a huskiness to his voice that reverberates through my lower belly, making it even harder to stay still.

"Fine." I'm proud of myself for managing to sound almost normal when my whole body feels electrified like there's a current running through it.

And that's before Gareth starts to stroke my leg.

His palm drags over my jeans as it travels down my thigh and *whoa*.

I actually let out a gasp when his fingers reach the back of my knee. Who knew that was an erogenous zone? Not me, that's for sure.

"Ticklish?"

"A little," I lie, embarrassed to admit the truth.

I shouldn't be, I know. Getting turned on ought to be a good thing. It's kind of the whole point of what we're doing here. But too many years of hiding my perpetually unrequited feelings have created defensive instincts that aren't so easy to undo. I'm having a hard time letting go of the idea that I'm not supposed to let it show when I'm attracted to someone.

My efforts to hold still fall apart completely when Gareth zeroes in on the sensitive spot behind my knee, stroking his fingers over it in a way that makes me twitch involuntarily and squirm against him.

I'm thinking that might be his intent, to make me wriggle and rub against him. Because when I do it, he makes a noise in the back of his throat. I think it might be a good noise.

I'm pretty sure it is.

But he takes pity on me and reverses course, sliding his hand back up my thigh.

He's approaching another erogenous zone now, one that's much more obvious. I go still as every nerve in my body jangles a red alert, and although I try to stay relaxed, I know he can feel me tense because he pauses with his hand just below my hip.

"Still comfortable?"

"Uh huh." I don't sound so normal anymore. It's an effort to speak. But I'm afraid he'll stop if I don't show any encouragement, and I don't want him to stop. So I add a squeaky, "Very."

Gareth's hand resumes its travels, smoothing over my hip to my waist, where his fingers dig into my flesh ever so slightly before spreading out over my lower back.

And then they slip under the hem of my T-shirt.

My stomach flips over at the first exquisite skin-to-skin touch. I forget how to breathe as his fingers stroke an unhurried, deliberate path along the waistband of my jeans. He knows exactly what he's doing. This is a move. He's making a move on me. I can suss that much out, even though no one but Seth Bumgarner has ever done it before, and his move was way less smooth.

Gareth's hand travels higher, skimming up my back as his fingers trace teasing loops and swirls over my bare skin. My breath hitches when one of his caresses nears my breast, but he veers away. I'm disappointed. But he does it again. And again. Getting closer each time. Teasing me with the promise of his touch.

There's a pulsing ache between my legs. Everything feels swollen and too tight. I'm shaking with the urge to grab his hand and put it where I'm dying to feel his touch, but I can't make myself do it, so I impotently grip his shirt in a clenched fist.

His other hand, the one that's not moving under my shirt, massages the back of my neck. "Still with me?"

I answer with a jerky nod.

"Want me to keep going?"

"Yes," I whisper. "So much yes."

"You're fucking gorgeous, you know that?"

I feel the tingle in my nose right as Gareth's palm slides around my rib cage to cup my breast. I bite down on my lip and scrunch my face up, trying to hold it in.

Ah—

I fight to clamp it down. I am *not* going to ruin this by sneezing. I won't.

Ah—

I will not sneeze. I refuse.

CHOO!

Dammit.

15

CASEY

"**S**o close." Gareth's voice is full of suppressed laughter. So glad he's able to find this amusing. But I guess it's good that he's not annoyed with me. *Yet*.

"Sorry, sorry, sorry." I roll onto my back and rub my cursed itchy nose.

"You say sorry too much, you know that?" Before I can apologize for apologizing, he covers my mouth with his hand. "You better not be about to say sorry again." His eyes narrow. "You were, weren't you?"

I'm forced to take the Fifth because I totally was. Also because he's still got his hand clamped over my mouth, so I couldn't speak if I wanted to. The childish impulse to lick his palm is strong, but I manage to resist. Barely.

He removes his hand from my mouth to wag a chiding finger at me. "You need to stop apologizing for being yourself. Yourself is awesome. It's not something you should apologize for, ever."

I wrinkle my nose.

"Really? I tell you that I think you're awesome, and your response is to make a face like you just smelled dog shit?"

I open my mouth to apologize but snap it shut again at Gareth's warning eyebrow raise.

"So was it me touching your boob that made you sneeze?" he asks, propping his head on his hand. "Or was it because I called you gorgeous?"

I frown as I consider the question. "I'm not actually sure. They both happened at the same time."

He touches my cheek to turn my face toward his. "I do think you're gorgeous, you know. I didn't just say that so you'd let me touch you. I said it because it's true."

My throat goes dry, and I swallow thickly, feeling my face heat.

But I don't sneeze.

A smile crinkles the corners of Gareth's eyes. "So it wasn't the compliment that made you sneeze."

"Guess not."

"But it does make you uncomfortable, doesn't it? I want to know why."

The urge to look anywhere but at him is so strong it's painful. I'm not used to being stared at so intently. It's even harder to take than his compliments. But he's still cradling my face in his hand, holding me hostage in his gaze.

"I don't know," I mumble, fighting the urge to fidget. "I suppose I'm not used to it."

He continues to study me, his expression thoughtful. Pondering. "What would you do if I said you're the smartest person I know?"

"Say thank you?" There, see. I can take a compliment.

"And what if I told you you're the most beautiful woman I know?"

I let out a snort and roll my eyes.

Gareth's frown grows mighty. "So you're fine when I compliment your brains. It's when I say you're beautiful that you get uncomfortable. Why is that?"

I know the answer, but I don't want to say it. The best option is to say nothing at all, which is what I do.

"Is it because you don't believe me when I say you're beautiful?"

"Maybe," I confess in a whisper. My face is on fire. I feel exposed. Naked, even though I'm fully clothed.

Something twists through Gareth's expression, darkening his eyes to storm clouds. "It breaks my fucking heart to hear you say that."

I close my eyes, unable to bear his pity.

"Well I guess I know what I need to do." His voice has gone soft and sort of smoky.

"What?" I'm afraid to ask, and yet every atom in my body is straining toward him. I can't help it. I'm practically twitching with the need to know.

"I'm simply going to have to show you how beautiful I think you are over and over again until you believe it."

My eyes fly open, and my breath catches at Gareth's expression. It's more than just seductive. It's downright covetous.

"I just need to figure out how to do it without kissing you or doing anything else that makes you sneeze."

I grimace. "Yeah, good luck with that."

When he touches the pad of his thumb to the corner of my mouth. I can't help flinching.

"What exactly is it about kissing that makes you so nervous?" he asks with a frown. "Did you have a bad experience in the past?"

I shake my head. Seth Bumgarner may have been a jerk, but I can't lay all my problems at his feet. It's the ten-plus-year dry spell after him that really did a number on me. "I think it's my lack of practice. It'd be one thing if I was still sixteen, when nobody expects anyone to be good at this stuff. But by the time you're nearing thirty, it's generally assumed everyone's acquired a certain level of skill. Only I haven't, and I'm scared I'm going to be an awful kisser."

"Having actually kissed you, I can say with absolute authority that you are not an awful kisser."

"Is that why you were so traumatized you bolted across the room? Because it was such a great kiss?"

"You thought I freaked out because the kiss was bad?"

He looks so dismayed I immediately try to take it back. "No, of course not. I was only giving you a hard time." I attempt a smile as proof of how totally nonserious I was.

"I told you it was only because—"

"I know. It's fine. We don't need to go over it again." My throat's tightening, and I want to hide from those eyes that feel like they're trying to swallow me whole.

But the second I think about moving, Gareth's hand slips around the nape of my neck so I can't go anywhere. He'd let me go if I pulled away hard enough, but doing that would only confirm I'm trying to hide my feelings and make everything worse. I'm stuck.

"Casey." He sighs as he rests his forehead against mine. Strong, gentle fingers knead the back of my neck. "That was an amazing fucking kiss, okay? I haven't been able to stop thinking about it and how much I want to kiss you again."

"Really?" I have to pull back to search his expression. I need to know if he's telling the truth.

"Really," he says, solemn and by all appearances sincere. No lies detected. "If you want the god's honest truth, it's been keeping me awake every night, thinking about you and all the things I want to do to you."

I'm stunned into silence. No one's ever said anything like

that to me. And I sure never expected Gareth to be the one to say it.

"Honestly, I feel like I'm going to die if I don't get to kiss you again." His gaze bores into me, and I feel it between my legs like a slow, hot caress. "Do you want to kiss me?"

A flush swarms my cheeks, but I can't look away. I can't lie to him either. Not when he's saying things like that. "Yes."

His lips curve with a smile. "You know, it occurs to me...you didn't sneeze the first time, when you kissed me."

It's true. I didn't. And I'm not sure why. I assumed it was because we were friends that I felt comfortable enough to kiss Gareth. But tonight's sneezes have put the lie to that hypothesis.

"Maybe you need to be the one to initiate it," he suggests. "Maybe that's the key—you need to feel like you're the one in control instead of passively waiting for someone else to make a move on you."

I've never considered that possibility before. My brow scrunches as I mull it over. "You think?"

"I think you should kiss me and find out." Every husky word sends a soft gust of warmth over me.

"What if it doesn't work? I'm afraid I'll sneeze in your face."

I'm afraid of more than failure, if I'm being honest. After the way our last kiss ended, I'm afraid of putting myself out there and being rejected again. It's irrational, I know. But the feeling stubbornly remains nonetheless.

"Only one way to find out." A challenge gleams in Gareth's eyes as his gaze drops to my mouth. "Kiss me, Casey. Come on."

It's not just an invitation. He's daring me. Because he knows exactly how to provoke me into doing what he wants.

But it's what I want too, so much I'm practically shaking. If it's what we both want, there's no reason not to take him up on the challenge.

I swallow hard and watch his Adam's apple move as he swallows too. When his lips part, mine do the same automatically. They're so beautiful. Lushly curved and exactly the right amount of full. I want to touch them. So I do.

My hand trembles as I lift it to his face. I can hear his breathing change when I press my fingers to his cheek, but he remains motionless. Even the hand curled around the back of my neck stays perfectly still, exerting no pressure.

I stroke the line of his jaw. The short layer of golden stubble is nearly invisible against his tanned skin, but it's prickly under my fingertips. It's like touching a live wire, the way it sends sparks shooting up my arm and through my whole body. I run the pad of my thumb along the edge of his bottom lip, which is unbelievably soft by comparison. Just the way I remember from our last kiss.

The contrast between rough and smooth fascinates me. I remember that from kissing him too, the exciting pins and needles sting of his stubble alongside the silky softness of his lips.

I follow the line of his bristles and rub my thumb over the two bare patches of skin below the corners of his mouth. Shivers of pleasure travel down my spine, pooling in my stomach as I trace the perfect curve of his upper lip.

All the while, Gareth watches me. Waiting. Letting me take my time and explore his face as much as I want. But I can hear his breathing quicken and grow less steady with every passing second. Just like mine.

Maybe he's right about letting me take control because there's something exhilarating about this feeling. Knowing that the way I'm touching him is having an effect on him gives me an unbelievable thrill.

I want more.

Emboldened, I lean in and touch my mouth to Gareth's. A light, experimental brush. Nothing more.

At his sharp intake of breath, I draw back again to observe his reaction. His eyes are heavy-lidded, soft, and hazy. A smile plays over his lips as the fingers on the back of my neck flex in encouragement, so I do it again.

This time I allow myself to linger, soaking up the sensation. His lips are warm. Pillowy soft. But also firm as they move against mine in a gentle caress. He follows my lead, matching my movements. It's like a slow dance. A sensual tease. But I can tell from the way his muscles tremble that he's fighting to hold himself back.

I take my time scouting the landscape of his lips. Traversing their supple hills and valleys. Experimenting with different angles. God. It's so good. I don't mean to suck on his lower lip, but it's like my mouth has a mind of its own.

Gareth signals his approval with a raspy groan. So I do it again, sucking harder this time and even using a little teeth.

His answering growl vibrates through my whole body. He angles his head and teases his tongue along the seam of my lips. They part for him automatically, issuing an invitation that he accepts with gusto.

We both moan when his tongue slides into my mouth. Now I'm the one following Gareth's lead as he deepens the kiss. His tongue strokes greedily over mine, showing me how much he wants this. I shiver with pleasure as pulsing waves of heat ripple through me.

But then he eases off. Softening the kiss again. His lips brush slowly over mine, unhurried and purposeful.

"I love the way you taste," he whispers into my mouth. His tongue darts against mine before retreating again.

It's a skillful, seductive tease, and it drives me wild. My hands wander over his chest. I need to be closer to him, to feel his skin against mine. I pluck at his T-shirt, trying to find the bottom, but it's twisted around his torso and doesn't want to move.

"Take this off?" I mumble in between kisses as I give it another impatient tug.

He sits up and yanks it over his head.

Sweet baby Jesus.

It's not like it's a surprise how hot his body is. I've seen his bare chest plenty of times. But I've always tried not to look. I've never had it offered up on a platter for me before. I stare hungrily as he kneels on the bed.

The sculpted muscles, taut stomach, and sun-kissed skin are like something out of a magazine. The only difference between Gareth and your average model is the sparse layer of chest hair he doesn't bother to wax. It's darker than the hair on his head, and instead of forming the happy trail I've read about in so many romance novels, it spreads out over his abs, growing in thicker around his belly button before disappearing into the jeans slung low on his hips.

I lift my hand, then hesitate. "Can I touch?"

He grants permission with a nod.

His stomach muscles twitch when I press my fingertips to them. They're flexed and hard, his skin so hot it feels like it could burn me. I slide my hand up, stroking over his chest, and he draws a shuddery breath when my finger brushes his nipple. I make a note of that as I move on, journeying back down to trace the lines between his abs. Truly, his body is a thing of wonder.

The lower my fingers go, the heavier Gareth's breathing gets. There's a bulge in the front of his jeans that's impossible to ignore. It's undeniable proof of his arousal.

I did that to him. *Me*.

I can't take my eyes off it. When I graze his waistband, he makes a tortured sound and grabs my hand.

"Kiss me," he rasps, leaning over me.

It's a request I'm only too happy to grant, twining my arms around his neck.

"Is this okay?" he asks as he rests his hand on my waist.

Is it ever.

I answer with an eager nod and tug him toward me.

His lips pull into a smile as he kisses me again. I feel dizzy as he lavishes me with long, languid, steamy kisses that seem to go on forever. My hand explores his broad, muscled back, stroking over his smooth, warm flesh as he kisses me senseless.

I want him to touch me too, but the hand on my waist hasn't moved an inch. His thumb rubs little circles above my hipbone, but that's it. That's all I get.

He's waiting for me to make the next move. To show him what I want.

Pushing aside the fear of rejection trying to rear its ugly head in the back of my mind, I cover his hand with mine and slide it up under my shirt to my breast. He makes a low, husky sound as he palms my bra cup and gives it a gentle squeeze. When his thumb drags across my nipple, I let out a whimper at the unexpected zing of pleasure.

"Feel good?"

My answer is an incoherent string of mumbled syllables. It feels *amazing*. As he can no doubt tell from the way I'm shamelessly arching my back to push my boob against his hand.

His mouth locks onto mine again as he plays with my nipple, rubbing it between his fingers. God, why was I so afraid of this? I love the way he kisses me. I love the feel of his touch and the heavy weight of his body, the way he's lying half on top of me.

I meet him kiss for kiss, lightheaded and aching for more. But when my exploring hand moves to the front of his jeans, he grunts and captures it in his.

"I meant it when I said we're taking it slow. No going past second base tonight."

"No! But we're on a roll." I don't even try to hide my disappointment. "I think we should just go with it."

"Nope." He smiles and taps my nose with his finger. "I'm not rushing this."

"But why?" My lower lip pushes out in a pout, and he leans in to give it a gentle nip.

"Because I'm taking this responsibility seriously." He pulls back again and props his head on his hand, gazing down at me. "We've made some great progress tonight, but I want to be certain you're really over your anxiety before we take the next step, okay?"

I sigh, knowing he's probably right. "Fine."

He leans in to kiss me again, a soft, tender nuzzle of lips that's both soothing and full of promises. "I want your first time to feel special," he whispers as he rubs our noses together. "You deserve a lot better than a quick fuck."

And then he gets up and walks out of my room without a look back.

GARETH

I'm up early the next morning. I try to get up early most mornings because it makes the early start on shift days easier. But this morning it's restless energy rather than force of habit that drives me from my bed.

If self-control was an Olympic event, I'd deserve to win the gold for leaving Casey's bed last night. God, how I wanted to stay. I could have held her in my arms all night long. I could have lost myself in that sweet mouth of hers and given her everything she wanted and then some.

But taking it slow is the right move. I'm more certain of that than ever after getting up close and personal with her apprehension last night.

Casey's sensitive. Shy. *Special*. She's not someone who can dive headfirst into physical intimacy. I need to find a way to make her more comfortable. Build up her confidence. That means crossing one intimacy bridge at a time instead of rushing for a touchdown.

I have to do this right. Casey means too much to me.

So much it freaks me out.

I've generally avoided getting too close to anyone. I only ever fool around with women I can keep at a distance. Sex is just fucking. A purely physical act. I'm not looking for intimacy or meaning. Just some temporary, insignificant fun.

But Casey's not temporary or insignificant.

She's my friend. She doesn't just know me, she *gets* me. I'm more than a hot body to her. She's the only woman who sees past the surface and actually likes what's underneath. I can relax and be myself around her without having to put on a show, which is refreshing but also fucking terrifying.

Sleeping with someone I care about is unfamiliar territory for me. The stakes are higher than I'm used to. For the first time in a long while, I've got something to lose. One wrong move could ruin everything. And I can't fucking stand the thought of losing her.

"No pancakes this morning?"

I startle so badly at the sound of Casey's voice I almost knock over my coffee.

She covers a yawn as she wanders into the kitchen in a tight gray tank top and black pajama pants with planets on them. They're glow-in-the-dark. I know this because she wears them all the time. It's not the first time I've seen her in that tank top without a bra. But it's the first time since I held her soft breast in my hand and stroked the nipple I can see beneath the thin cotton. It's the first time since I heard her breathy moans and felt her arch into my touch.

My groin tightens with want, and I have the craziest urge to pull her into my lap and kiss her senseless. But that's not part of our arrangement. It's the sort of thing a boyfriend would do, and I'm not Casey's boyfriend.

I clear my throat and tilt my head at the bakery box on the counter. "No, but I did go out for kolaches."

A smile lights her face. "You're seriously the best roommate in the world. If there was a Nobel Prize for roommates, you'd win hands down."

As she opens the box I stare at her lips, which are pink and swollen from kissing me last night.

"Did you get any strawberry?"

"As if I'd forget your favorite." I tear my gaze away from her and focus on my laptop. I planned to get some work done on my next essay this morning, but I've been so distracted I haven't managed to write a word.

Casey pours a cup of coffee and brings it over to the breakfast table with her kolaches. Her hip brushes my arm as she slides into the seat next to me, and a shiver of awareness runs over my skin. When she leans in for a look at my screen, I catch the fragrant scent of her hair. "Is that your *Scarlet Letter* essay? How's it going?"

"All right," I lie.

Her whiskey-brown eyes see right through me. "I can help you work on it today."

"No can do, unfortunately."

Her disappointed expression fills my chest with liquid warmth. It's bonkers how much she actually *likes* helping me with my schoolwork. Just as much as I like doing pretty much anything with her.

"We've got other plans today, as it happens."

That brings her smile back. "We do?"

"We do," I confirm, shutting my laptop.

"Care to tell me what they are?"

"That would spoil the surprise."

"Is it a good surprise?"

Slugging down the last of my coffee, I get to my feet. "Guess you'll find out when we get there."

Believe it or not, I have a plan. It came to me last night after seeing how self-conscious she was. I don't know if it will help at all, but I figure it's worth a shot. If nothing else, it'll be fun. For me, anyway.

While Casey's getting changed, I pack a picnic lunch and load everything we'll need into my truck. By the time I get back inside, she's ready to go. I told her to dress for doing something active outdoors, which she wasn't too pleased about. I didn't expect her to be. The whole point of today's field trip is to take her out of her comfort zone.

"Is this okay?" She shifts uneasily in her red Converse and plucks at her *It's a Good Day to Read Banned Books* T-shirt. In deference to the warm weather, her legs are bare beneath a pair of hip-hugging jeans shorts, and her pouf of curly brown hair is held back with a fabric scrunchie.

"You look great." Ideally, she should be wearing shoes with treads for better traction, but for our purposes today she'll be fine. "Let's roll."

On the way, she fiddles with the radio in my truck, making herself at home. Our musical tastes are similar, so I don't mind. After stopping on an old Robert Earl Keen song, she sits back in her seat and twists a loose lock of hair around her finger.

"You don't have to be nervous," I tell her.

"Maybe if you'd tell me where we're going."

"You'll find out soon enough."

I take us to Lovett Park. Casey casts a curious look around as she climbs out of the truck. The sounds of a little league game drift over from the baseball field by the community center, but it's quieter at this end of the green space under a shady canopy of live oaks.

"Can I carry something?" she offers as I lower the tailgate and shoulder the cooler.

"Here, take this." I shove a woven blanket at her.

Her expression grows wary when I grab the sheaf and pitchfork from the bed of my truck. "Why do we need those? Are you practicing?"

"Nope," I say as I slam the tailgate shut. "You are."

"Gareth."

"Casey."

"I don't do Highland Games."

"I'm aware." Taking her hand, I twine our fingers together and tug her away from the truck. There's an open clearing beyond the trees, and that's where I lead her.

"I don't *want* to do Highland Games," she says, dragging her feet.

I give her hand a squeeze. It's slender and delicate in mine. And soft. I swallow hard, remembering the feel of her hands on my body. "I just want you to try the sheaf toss. That's all."

"Why?"

I shake my head at the unhappy whine in her voice. "It'll be fun."

"It's not my idea of fun."

"Why not? What do you have against it?" As we wend through the trees, I keep an eye on the ground, watching out for roots hidden in the spongy layer of leaves and catkins underfoot.

"I don't like sports."

"Why is that?" I ask even though I can guess the answer.

"Because I suck at them."

"So? You don't have to be good at something to enjoy it."

She makes a scoffing sound. "Name one thing you're bad at that you enjoy doing."

"Bowling," I say cheerfully. "I absolutely suck ass at bowling."

We reach the edge of the clearing, and I let go of Casey's hand to swing the cooler to the ground. The new spring grass is a bright emerald green and dotted with patches of clover.

"Yeah? When's the last time you went bowling?"

"I don't remember, but I'm happy to go bowling with you anytime. Just say the word." I take the blanket from her and drop it beside the cooler as I hand her the pitchfork. "This is yours."

You'd think it was a stick of dynamite from the face she makes and the way she holds it at arm's length. "Why are you making me do this?"

"Because." Resting the sheaf on my hip, I drape my other arm around her shoulders. I lean in, catching another fragrant whiff of her hair, and lower my voice. "You said last night you were worried about being bad at sex."

She draws back, her gaze jumping anxiously to mine. "And?"

Letting go of her, I take a step back to toss the sheaf from one hand to the other. "And I want you to get more comfortable being bad at something in front of me."

"How is embarrassing myself going to help?"

"Because you'll see that it's not the end of the world. You can still have fun even when you don't know what the hell you're doing."

"Then why don't we go bowling instead, and you can show me how much fun you have being bad at it," she grumbles.

I give her a long look. "We've been doing something I'm bad at all week. It's your turn now."

Her shoulders sink in resignation because I've got her there and she knows it.

"Humor me, okay?" I touch her cheek, brushing back a stray wisp of hair. "It's only you and me here, and I promise I won't make fun of you. We're just goofing around and having some fun. No one's going to judge you, least of all me."

She looks like she wants to shrivel into the grass. But she gives me a nod, willing to try. Because I asked her to.

"Come on." Pressing my hand against her back, I guide her to the middle of the clearing.

She goes voluntarily but without enthusiasm. When we're

far enough from the trees, I drag a line in the grass with my foot to stand in for the upright we'd be trying to clear if this was a competition. From there I measure out my steps and drop the sheaf.

It's the lightest practice sheaf we have, a Frankenstein-looking burlap cube stuffed with straw that I made myself. In competition, the women usually toss a ten- or twelve-pound sheaf. This one's closer to sixteen pounds, which will make it even harder for someone as small and inexperienced as Casey to get much lift. But I figure that'll actually work for our purposes today since the point isn't for her to be good at it.

I beckon her over. "Stand here and face that way."

She follows my instructions, and I step up behind her. Heat floods my gut at her proximity as I reach around her to move her hands in the right positions on the pitchfork handle.

"Spread your legs more and bend your knees. Now lean over for me just a little." My chest nudges against her back to urge her forward.

"Are you sure this isn't all an excuse for you to issue a bunch of sexually suggestive instructions?" she mutters.

We're practically cheek to cheek, so I only have to turn my head to nuzzle her ear. "That's just a happy bonus," I murmur and hear her breath hitch. My pulse thrums beneath my skin as I place my hands on her waist. "Now you'll want to keep your hips nice and loose."

"Seriously?" she says with a huff of laughter.

"Trust me, your hips are very important." As I move her into the right position, I fight the urge to press my straining erection against her. Part of me desperately wants to find out how she'd respond to the feel of my cock, but we're in a public park so now's probably not the time or the place.

I grip the pitchfork again, bracketing her hands with mine. "Keep your arms straight and swing in a smooth arc like this." I demonstrate the motion a few times, showing her how far to extend the arc and letting her get a feel for it. "Right around here is where you want the sheaf to release. Let it go too soon, and it'll sail out in front of you. Release too late, and it'll land behind you. This is the sweet spot, okay?"

She nods, her brow wrinkled in concentration.

Next I show her where to stab the tines through the sheaf to pick it up, and we go through the motion of the swing a few more times with the sheaf in place.

"It's heavy," she complains.

"I know. But it's more about using the momentum than using your strength. You can do it."

"I highly doubt that."

I brush my lips against her cheek. "I believe in you."

She shivers in my arms. "If you're trying to distract me, it's working."

"Good." I fight a grin as I step back to give her room. "It's all you now. Give it a few test swings before you let 'er rip."

The sun tinges Casey's hair and skin with a golden glow as she makes a few tentative arcs with the pitchfork.

"This is going to suck," she says, shaking her head.

"Probably, but everyone messes up their first throws. Don't be afraid to suck."

A smile quirks the corner of her mouth. "There you go with the innuendo again."

I laugh. "Quit trying to make me horny and take the throw."

She digs in and gives it her best effort. The sheaf flies off the pitchfork too soon and travels about ten feet out in front of her before dropping into the grass.

"See?" She scowls, jabbing the pitchfork into the ground in frustration. "Told you I'd suck."

I toss her a grin as I retrieve the sheaf. "Yeah, but you looked super hot doing it."

"Meh."

"Hey." I drop the sheaf at her feet and cup her face in my hands. "We talked about this. If I say you're hot, I mean it."

Casey blinks up at me, her eyes glinting like amber in the sunlight. A flush spreads over her already-pink cheeks as she purses her lips.

I've wanted to kiss those lips all morning, and it's more than I can take. I lean in closer, breathing the warm scent of her skin. "Do I need to prove it?"

"We're in the middle of a park."

After a glance around to make sure no one we know is strolling by, I refocus my attention on her plump, enticing lips. "Does that mean I can't kiss you?"

"I..." She swallows thickly enough for me to hear. "I guess it's okay."

"Are you going to sneeze on me if I do?"

"You'll have to try it to find out." The heat in her gaze licks down my spine, going straight to my hard-on.

I bend my head, hesitating when my mouth is a hairbreadth from hers. My heart pounds as I hover, waiting. I hear her draw in a breath, but she doesn't sneeze.

"Do it," she whispers.

When my lips touch hers, she sighs with relief.

I sweep my thumbs over her cheeks as I take her breath into me. She tastes like strawberries and sugar. "You're crazy beautiful." I kiss her again and again, soft, reverent, exploratory. "I've been dying to kiss you since I woke up."

"You have?"

The surprise in her voice makes my heart squeeze. I shift my hips, letting the hard bulge in my shorts press against her stomach. "Does it feel like I'm lying?"

Her eyes widen, and she lets the pitchfork fall to clutch at my arms, pulling me closer.

I swallow a groan and kiss her again, sucking at her lower lip as my dick throbs between us. Fortunately, part of my brain manages to remember we're in a public park with children around. We need to keep this scene PG.

I make myself draw back. "Time for your next throw."

"Hmmm?" Casey's teeth sink into her lip as she stares at my mouth.

Fuck, this is going to be harder than I expected. I adjust myself as I stoop to retrieve the pitchfork. "No more stalling."

"Can't we call that good enough? It seems to have worked. Mission accomplished." She gives me big doe eyes.

"Nice try, but no. I brought you here to practice, and that's what you're going to do."

Her lip juts out in a pout I want to devour. "Have you always been this mean?"

"Mean, am I?" Smiling, I shake my head. "Okay, I'll make you a deal."

She leans into me, arching a brow. "I'm listening."

"You wanted kissing practice, right? For every throw you make, you get one kiss."

"Really?" The way she lights up does all kinds of things to my insides.

"Really." I run a heavy gaze over her, taking in the swell of her breasts beneath her cotton T-shirt. "But we have to keep it chaste."

Her lips quirk. "Chaste isn't exactly the kind of experience I was hoping for."

"I'm not getting arrested for public indecency." Grinning, I lean in to murmur in her ear. "The other plans I've got for you require privacy. So they'll have to wait until tonight."

17

CASEY

Reluctant as I am to admit it, Gareth was right. I do have fun trying the sheaf toss even though I suck at it.

The kissing definitely helps.

After every throw he dutifully trots over and delivers the promised kiss. Even if we do have to exercise restraint and keep it family-friendly, it more than makes up for being dragged out here and forced to do sports. If PE class had been like this, I would have liked it a lot more.

Aside from the kisses, the throwing itself is surprisingly fun. I put myself in Gareth's extremely capable hands, listening to his pointers, and with every toss I get a little better. It becomes strangely addictive once I start to get the hang of it. Before long, I'm the one who's raring to try my next toss.

We laugh together over some of my more dramatic failures, but there's no mockery in Gareth's amusement. His face beams with pride at every single one of my attempts, no matter how far off the mark it goes. When I eventually pull off a perfect release that sends the sheaf sailing a good ten feet into the air, right over the line Gareth made in the grass, he runs out and sweeps me up in his arms, whooping as he spins me around.

He's the one who eventually insists we stop, saying he doesn't want my arms to be too sore tomorrow. I hadn't thought about that, but as soon as he mentions it, I realize how tired my muscles are from the unfamiliar workout.

"Will they get as big as yours if I keep it up?" I ask, flexing my nonexistent biceps.

"No, but they could get as big as Kenzie's if you want to start doing this regularly."

Much as I wouldn't mind having Kenzie's muscles, I don't see myself taking this up as a regular hobby. It's one thing to get private lessons from Gareth, but making my puny throws in front of all our athlete friends isn't as appealing.

"Your turn," I say, handing him the pitchfork. "Show me how it's supposed to be done."

"You've seen me toss the sheaf hundreds of times."

True, but I've never seen him do it purely for my benefit, and that's what I want. "Come on, show off for me. I want to see how good you are."

The man loves attention, so it doesn't take much to convince him.

It's a gorgeous throw. He's so graceful he makes it look effortless. But now that I've tried it myself, I can truly appreciate how impressive a feat it is. The command Gareth has of his body is a thing of beauty. *He's* a thing a beauty. In the bright sunshine he's golden, the perfectly proportioned muscles of his arms and legs bunching beneath his smooth skin like a bronze sculpture come to life.

"Happy?" he asks after he retrieves the sheaf from the grass.

"I'll say." There's a dopey grin on my face. I might even be drooling.

Gareth's mouth curls into a smirk as he stands in front of me. "You like what you see, do you?"

My gaze travels over his body, and I lick my suddenly dry lips. "God, yes."

"Christ," he mutters, taking me by the arm and leading me over to the cooler. "You have to stop looking at me like that."

"Why?"

"Because I'm about five seconds away from laying you down in the grass and despoiling you right fucking here, that's why."

The roughness of his voice makes my heart stutter. He sounds like he's in actual pain from wanting me.

Gareth Kelly.

Wants *me*.

It's possibly the first time I've truly believed it. I probably should have believed it before now, but I have too many pesky insecurities whispering in my ear that someone like him could never want someone like me. They kept insisting he was just pretending. Going through the motions to be nice.

They're not whispering that now. They've all gone quiet. Even *they* know that the way Gareth's been looking at me all day, the way he's been kissing me and touching me, it's not pretend. It's real attraction.

My cheeks heat, but not from embarrassment. It's lust. And for once in my life I don't feel the need to hide it. I'm not ashamed to let Gareth see my attraction because I know he likes it.

What a rush.

We unfold the blanket on a soft patch of grass in the shade and sit down to share the lunch he packed—chicken salad sandwiches, chips, and leftover kolaches. While we eat, he entertains me with a funny story about one of the calls on his last shift, and I fill him in on the latest interpersonal drama unfolding at the gym.

It's nice to hang out like this, just the two of us talking and laughing. We do it a lot at home, but I can't recall ever going out anywhere alone with Gareth before. It almost feels like we're on a date. But of course it's not a date. It would be dangerous to think of it that way.

When I can't eat any more, I lie back on the blanket and interlace my hands behind my head. Gareth stretches out next to me, and for a while we lie there in tranquil silence, gazing up at the sky.

"How did you get into doing Highland Games?" I ask him, realizing I have no idea.

It's not exactly a popular sport. The only reason our town has such a high concentration of throwers is because of the Crowder Scottish Festival and Highland Games held here every year. But Gareth's not from Crowder. He grew up in Lubbock, near the panhandle, and only moved here a few years ago to take a job with the fire department.

"McCafferty," he says with an easy chuckle. "He took one look at me when I reported for my first day on the job and announced I needed to start doing Highland Games. I had no idea what it was, but he kept hassling me until I agreed to come to a practice session at his house to shut him up."

"And then you were hooked?"

"Yeah, I suppose I was. I hadn't done any sports since high school, and I realized that I missed it." A cocky grin spreads over Gareth's face as he swivels his head toward me. "Plus girls seriously dig the kilt. Once I figured that out, I was in with both feet."

"Of course you were." I roll my eyes, but the reminder of how popular he is with women sits in my stomach like sour milk. It's not even all the women he's slept with that bothers me, so much as the way he moves from one to the next. I can't help thinking how much it would hurt to be dismissed from Gareth's life so easily.

"To be honest, it was the people I met at McCafferty's place that hooked me more than the sport itself," he says. "I was the new guy in town and didn't have any friends."

"What about the people at the firehouse? I thought you said they were like family?"

"They are, but that doesn't necessarily make it easy to fit in. When you're the new kid, you have to prove yourself and go through a certain amount of hazing before you're accepted. It's a little like being the stepkid foisted on a tight-knit pack of siblings. Especially when you're an outsider who isn't from here like everybody else. I think McCafferty knew that, and that's why he nagged me into joining the Highland Games club."

"And that's how you ended up friends with Ozzy and Darius."

"And you." A smile lights Gareth's eyes as he threads our fingers together. "I owe McCafferty big-time for bringing you into my life."

I'm not sure if that second *you* is meant to be collective or singular—if he's saying he's grateful to have all of us in his life or if he's referring to me specifically. But the way he's holding my hand and looking at me makes it feel like the latter. It feels like the kind of thing you'd say to someone special. Not just special like a friend—someone who's more than that.

And suddenly I can understand why Gareth was reluctant to mix sex with friendship. When you add sexual attraction to friendly affection, all those feelings are easy to get confused. It's tempting to read more into them than you should.

Especially when he says what he says next.

"I think I was searching for something back then and didn't even know it."

"What were you searching for?" I ask around the growing lump in my throat.

He stares past me, his expression growing distant. "A place to belong. Or maybe not so much a place, as people I felt like I belonged with. I never had that before."

"Not even growing up?"

He's quiet for so long I start to think he's not going to answer. Gareth doesn't talk much about his family or his life before he came here. I know he's an only child and his dad was a firefighter too. I know he has a mother back home who he doesn't have much to do with, but he's never said why. And I know he lost his father at some point, but I don't know how he died or when.

That's as much as I've managed to glean in three years of being roommates. Gareth tends to shut down or change the subject whenever his family comes up, so I've learned to avoid pressing him on it. But I can't help being curious about his past and why it's such a sore subject.

"I guess I did have a place I belonged for a while," he says finally. "But I lost it when my dad died." Shaking off the memories, he stands and brushes himself off. "It's getting hot. Let's head back to the house."

And apparently we're done talking about his past.

Gareth's chatty and full of smiles on the drive home. But I get the sense it's a show he's putting on to distract from the dangerous conversational territory we almost ventured into.

When we get to the house, Darius is folding laundry at the kitchen table.

"Hey." He raises an eyebrow at the cooler Gareth sets on the counter. "You two go on a picnic?"

Beside me, I feel Gareth stiffen.

"Gareth took me to the park to try the sheaf toss," I answer, hoping Darius didn't notice Gareth's reaction.

"Yeah?" Darius's gaze flicks to me in surprise. "You thinking of joining us at the next practice?"

I shake my head as I help Gareth unload the cooler. "I just wanted to see what it was like. And now I can say with authority that it's not for me."

"She's a natural," Gareth tells Darius. "She'd fucking crush it if she decided she wanted to."

I hide my blush by carrying the unopened drinks to the fridge.

"Doesn't surprise me," Darius says. "She's got the perfect proportions for it. And discipline coming out of her ears. Just needs a little strength training."

"It's too bad she doesn't have free access to a gym or any friends who'd be willing to help her with a training program," Gareth says.

Darius grunts as he matches socks. "Yeah, it's a real pity she's so disadvantaged."

"Ha ha," I say sourly. "Sarcasm doesn't look good on either of you."

"I'll have you know I make everything look good," Gareth replies with a wink.

I roll my eyes despite the tummy flutters his wink inspires. "Whatever. You still can't make me like exercise."

"Wanna bet?" He wags his brows. "That sounds like a challenge I'm willing to take."

"Not interested," I say, conscious of Darius watching our interaction.

Gareth shrugs. "Your loss."

"What do y'all think about ordering a pizza for dinner?" I ask, turning to Darius. "We could call it in early so you can have some before you leave for work."

He shakes his head as he stacks his folded laundry in the

basket. "I'm planning to hit the gym before work. I'll grab something later."

"I'm up for pizza," Gareth says, lounging against the counter all casual-like.

"You're not going out tonight?" I ask as if it's a normal day around the house like any other day, and we're just ordinary roommates who don't have plans to fool around as soon as we're alone.

"I'm on shift tomorrow. I should probably hit the sack early and catch up on my sleep." Gareth watches Darius head upstairs with his laundry basket before letting his gaze drift back to me. "I'm in the mood for a movie marathon. Wanna join me?"

His tone is carefree and light, but his expression is anything but. It's heavy with suggestion, reminding me of what he promised earlier.

The plans I've got for you require privacy.

"Do I get a say in the movies?" I ask as my pulse jumps.

"Maybe," he says. "If you're a good girl."

Holy smokes. It's handy he's a firefighter because I'm about to spontaneously combust.

"I can be good."

"Don't I know it."

The molten heat in his eyes makes me ache all over, especially in the places Gareth didn't touch me last night. And I know he can tell by the way he smiles.

"I'm gonna grab a quick shower." He pushes off the counter and strides toward me. After darting a glance at the stairs, he leans in and presses his lips to mine.

My knees go weak as his tongue slides into my mouth, but the kiss ends almost as quickly as it started.

"Meet you in the living room in fifteen?"

I nod mutely because it's all I can manage.

18

CASEY

When Gareth rejoins me downstairs, he's changed into gray knit gym shorts and a white tank top. But I catch a subtle hint of cologne as he sprawls on the couch next to me.

I took a hasty shower as well, and it's possible I sprayed a tiny bit of perfume into my cleavage. I also elected not to wear a bra underneath my baggy T-shirt, figuring there was no upside to putting extra layers between us.

But we have to wait for Darius to leave before we can start our next sex lesson, which means we'll need to stay on our good behavior until then.

"What do you say to a horror marathon?" Gareth asks, taking the remote out of my hand.

I wrinkle my nose. "I was thinking of something more fun, like a comedy."

"Horror movies can be fun."

"Being scared isn't my idea of fun."

He slants a suggestive glance my way. "Not even when you've got a big, strong dude to grab on to during the scary parts? Sounds pretty fun to me."

I hadn't considered that. A scary movie would give us an excuse to sit close together without raising suspicion.

"Here." Gareth reaches behind him for the blanket on the back of the couch and tosses it into my lap. "If it gets too scary, you can hide behind this and hold on to me."

"All right."

I spread the blanket over my legs while Gareth searches for a movie.

"Want to watch *It*?" he asks, shooting me a smirk.

The image of Pennywise on the screen provokes a full-body shudder. "Absolutely not."

He laughs and slings an arm around me. "Don't worry, babe. I'll protect you from the big bad clown."

The word *babe* does something funny to my insides. Gareth's never called me that before. Or any pet name for that matter. When his gaze meets mine I can tell he's thinking the same thing. His playful swagger shifts into something more intense that makes my stomach flip.

He returns his attention to the TV but leaves his arm around me. "Yeah, I didn't think you'd be up for that one. What about a *Stranger Things* rewatch? It's scary but also fun."

I agree, and Gareth settles back and presses play on episode one.

Of course the first episode starts off with a scary Demogorgon attack in the creepy military lab. By the time the title card appears, I'm holding Gareth's hand over my eyes and watching the screen through his fingers. There's not another scary scene for a while after that, so I relax and lean my head on Gareth's shoulder. His hand rests on my leg under the blanket, his fingers tracing idle patterns as he focuses on the show, making occasional jokes and comments.

It's sublime, being nestled against him. I'm not sure how I'm supposed to go back to watching TV the old way. It seems a waste to ever sit by ourselves when we could be snuggled up like this.

When he twitches the blanket over his lap, I slide closer to make it easier to share. The next time things in the episode get scary, I bury my face in Gareth's chest, and he strokes his hand over my hair. His warm, delicious scent fills my nose, a mix of his spicy cologne, soap, and the familiar smell of his skin. I breathe it in, forgetting all about what's on the screen.

He presses his nose into my hair, inhaling deep and letting out a long, slow exhale. "You smell so fucking good, it's making me crazy."

His whisper shivers over my skin and throbs between my thighs.

"You smell good too," I whisper back.

Gareth's fingers stroke a path down my back, a slow, leisurely exploration that consumes my full attention. His hand spreads over my hip beneath the blanket and slips under my shirt. It ventures upward ever so slowly, searing every atom of skin it touches. When his thumb grazes the side of my breast, I gasp.

"Shh," he murmurs. "Don't move."

I hold still as his hand strokes down my ribs before sliding up again to palm my breast. His fingers press into the tender flesh, then skim over it in tantalizing circles, teasing and playing.

I'm trembling by the time his finger finally finds my nipple. He toys with the stiff peak, gently at first. But the more my breathing speeds up, the bolder his touch grows, rubbing and pinching until I find it almost impossible to hold still.

I want to kiss him. But we can't. We shouldn't even be doing what we're doing. Not with Darius in the house. He could come downstairs any second, and I'm so distracted I'm not sure I'd hear his footsteps.

I'm not sure Gareth would either. His muscles twitch as if he's fighting to hold himself back, and his heart thumps loudly beneath my ear. We're both lost in a fog of lust, whatever's happening on the TV blurring to background static.

"I wish I could put my mouth right here," he whispers, rolling my achy nipple between his fingers. "Do you think I could make you come just by sucking on your pretty tits?"

God, I don't know. But I want to find out. So badly that the only answer I can manage is a moan. I no longer remember how to talk. What even are words anymore?

"Fuck," he hisses. "Hang on."

I tense as Gareth drags his arm out from behind me, thinking he's heard Darius on the stairs. But no, he's only rearranging himself. And me.

"Lean back," he murmurs. "Slide down a little more." When I do, he slips his hand under the blanket and drags my leg over his.

To look at us, you'd think we were innocently sitting side by side, watching TV. But under the cover of the blanket, my legs are splayed wide and Gareth's hand is on my inner thigh.

Not just *on* my thigh. It's sliding up the inside of my leg.

His gaze stays firmly locked on the TV as his hand moves steadily higher at a snail's pace that's utterly divine torture. He hasn't even reached the good part yet and it's already the hottest, horniest thing that's ever happened to me.

I'm practically panting by the time his fingers slide inside my shorts. Thank god I had the foresight to change into a pair of loose, stretchy sleep shorts. *Way to go, past me. For once, your chronic overthinking has actually paid off.*

At the moment, I'm not doing any thinking, however. My cognitive function has short-circuited. I can't even see what's on the TV screen in front of me. Unspeakable horrors are happening in the town of Hawkins, but all my awareness is on Gareth's hand, which is so close to giving me what I want that I've stopped breathing.

When his fingertips brush the edge of my underwear, my whole body jerks as the contact shoots through me like an electric current.

"I need you to be still and very, very quiet," he says in a low, rough voice. "Can you do that for me?"

Probably not. But I nod my agreement anyway.

I wore my only pair of sexy underwear last night, so I'm back to my normal cotton boy briefs today and they're completely soaked with arousal. I can feel the wetness press against my throbbing pussy as Gareth lightly strokes his fingers over the damp fabric.

It's not enough. I need more. My hips arch involuntarily, seeking the pressure I want to feel.

"You like that?" he mutters, and I'm pretty sure it's a rhetorical question because it must be obvious how much I like it. "Feels good, doesn't it?"

So good. I bite my lip to keep from moaning as his fingers rub my clit.

"You want me inside?"

I assume it's another rhetorical question. But apparently not because he cruelly takes his hand away when I don't answer.

"Yes or no, Casey. You have to tell me."

He actually expects me to speak. The note of sexy command in his voice sparks along my spine and jump-starts my brain enough to force out a single breathy syllable.

"Please."

He makes a noise in the back of his throat and eases inside my underwear, his big hand stretching the elastic to its limit. The world tilts off its axis as his fingers slide through my wanting sex. I've been waiting my whole life to feel a man's touch there, and the sensation is so intense, sparks explode across my vision.

I must make some kind of noise because Gareth shushes me

softly as he circles my clit with a teasing finger. "If you can't be quiet, I'll have to stop."

I'll die if he does. Literally expire on the spot.

Rolling my lips between my teeth, I vow not to make another sound.

It's so much better than when I touch myself. Not knowing what he's going to do next adds an element of excitement and anticipation that can't be replicated by a solo session. Not to mention, his fingers are so much bigger than mine and so wonderfully callused.

"I want to lick you here," he rasps, so quiet I almost can't hear him over the eerie synth music and monster noises coming from the TV. "I can't wait to taste you later."

Waves of pleasure spiral through me, building in strength as he works me over with his exploratory, methodical caresses. I have no awareness of time passing. I'm too swept up in the moment, too lost in the dizzying sensations as he drives me closer and closer to that distant, enticing edge.

The sound of a door opening upstairs causes us both to freeze. As heavy footsteps make their way down the stairs, Gareth slips his hand out of my underwear and rests it on top of my thigh. Darius's tennis shoes squeak on the tile floor behind us as he heads into the kitchen, and we pretend to be riveted by the TV as he putters around filling his water bottle.

"I'm out," he announces, passing through the living room again on his way to the front door. "Enjoy your night."

My eyes meet Gareth's, and our lips curl with matching smiles.

"You too," Gareth calls back.

"Yeah, have a good night," I chime in. "Be careful at work."

"Always am," Darius replies on his way out.

Gareth and I stare at each other, neither of us moving a

muscle as we listen to the slide of the deadbolt as Darius locks it behind him.

As soon as his heavy footfalls fade away, Gareth flicks the blanket aside, curls his hand around the back of my neck, and hauls me toward him.

Our mouths meet in a hungry crush, his tongue thrusting deep to claim me with a hot, demanding kiss. It's nothing at all like any of our previous kisses, which were tentative and tender. He kisses me like a man who's greedy for it. A growl rumbles through his chest as he guides me back onto the couch. He hovers above me, his broad shoulders filling my view as he devours me with his bruising kisses.

My fingers curl in his hair, pulling him down, wanting everything he's got. A needy moan claws its way out of my throat when his hand strokes down my side and slides under my shirt.

Abruptly tearing his mouth away, he sits back and repositions my legs so he's kneeling between them. His gaze smolders as it falls on my chest. "I need to see you."

A flicker of insecurity has me tensing. I've never been naked in front of a man before.

Understanding softens Gareth's eyes as they search mine, seeking permission. His hands stroke gently over my stomach, all his former impatience gone as he waits for my answer.

I close my eyes and nod.

Slowly, he pushes my shirt up, and I shiver as the cool air hits my skin. His satisfied hum tempts me to peek through my eyelashes. The solemn, reverent way he's staring at me makes my heart flip over.

"So beautiful," he murmurs as his warm hands smooth up my stomach and over my chest, exploring every bare inch. His tongue slides across his upper lip as his thumb circles my stiff nipple. "Just as gorgeous as I imagined."

The words are barely out of his mouth before he's bending

down and flicking his tongue over me. My back arches, thrusting my breast against his lips, and he takes the opportunity to draw my whole nipple into his mouth.

I've never thought my breasts were all that sensitive, but the feel of Gareth's mouth on them has every nerve ending crackling to life. I whimper as he sucks and tugs, kneading them with his big hands.

"You can be as loud as you want now, honey." His hot breath sets my skin on fire. "Don't hold back, okay? I want to hear how much you like it."

I moan, writhing beneath him as he spoils me with his mouth. My hands smooth over his bare shoulders, savoring the way his muscles shift and flex. Curling my fingers in his tank top, I give it an impatient tug.

Sensing my need, he sits back and yanks it off. As soon as his chest is bare, I have to touch him. He's too beautiful.

"Your body is unreal," I murmur as my hands smooth over his torso.

A pleased grin quirks his lips. "You can touch it as much as you want."

"I can?"

He gives a distracted nod as his gaze lowers to my chest. "God, you look so pretty all pink and flushed like this."

Before I can feel self-conscious, he takes my mouth again, claiming it with deep, rhythmic thrusts of his tongue. His delicious weight presses me into the couch as he settles his rock-hard body in the cradle of my hips.

Oh wow, oh wow. That's his cock I can feel between us. When it pulses against my pussy, I can't help arching into it. Gareth grunts and rocks his hips, grinding against me.

It's the most incredible feeling. I almost think I'm about to come. Maybe I am, but I don't get to find out.

"Fuck," he rasps as he tears his body from mine with a shudder.

My whimper of protest dies in my throat when he drags my shorts and underwear down my legs. He usually does everything with such confidence and skill that it's a little shocking to realize his hands are shaking. His movements are almost clumsy as he fumbles with my clothes before finally getting them off. Casting them over his shoulder, he slides his palms up the insides of my thighs, opening them wider.

A guttural sound rumbles in his throat as he stares at me with unblinking eyes. I've never felt so exposed before. I should be embarrassed, but his rapt, worshipful expression leaves no room for doubting that he likes what he sees.

My whole body is a ball of anticipation. When my hips try to lift off the couch, Gareth spreads a hand over my stomach and leans over to kiss me. I moan into his mouth as his hand slides down to cup my sex.

He picks up where he left off before we were interrupted. But this time his mouth can get in on the action, sucking at my neck and my breasts as his fingers stroke between my legs, driving me wild with pleasure.

"Casey," he whispers against my skin as I gasp and writhe beneath him. "That's it, honey. Give it up for me."

I'm already so worked up, I'm coming before I know it, making more noise than I ever imagined I would as the orgasm pulses through me in wave after wave.

Holy shit!

I just had sex.

Not intercourse, but I'd say my first orgasm with another human being qualifies as sex.

"You okay?" Gareth asks.

I blink, and his face comes into focus. So handsome.

Nodding, I reach out to run my fingers over his jaw. "Yeah, I'm good."

His mouth quirks. "Good, huh? That's all? It didn't even rate a great?"

"No, it was awesome. I swear. I thought you were asking if I was—"

He stops me with a kiss. "I can do better. I'm just getting warmed up."

"No, you don't have to—" I break off with a gasp when his thumb grazes my oversensitive clit.

"I'm not even close to finished with you," he says with a wink.

Just before he buries his face between my legs.

My body jerks so hard I nearly punch through the sofa. I'd be halfway across the room right now if he wasn't holding me so tightly. The way his hands are gripping my hips, it's almost as if he knew how I'd react and wanted to make sure I didn't launch myself through the wall.

No, not almost like that. It's *exactly* like that, based on the grin he flashes when he glances up at me.

"Sensitive, aren't you? That's the way it is right after an orgasm. All the nerve endings are overexcited, so even the barest touch can feel like a nuclear explosion."

To demonstrate, he touches the tip of his tongue ever so gently to my clit, and I gasp at the shock wave of sensation.

"Women are lucky like that," he says, and the feel of his breath is almost more than I can take. "You can have one orgasm right on top of another that way. It can be easier for you to get off again right after you've come."

After delivering this lesson on the female orgasm, he buries his face between my legs again, devouring me with his greedy mouth. The sound I make is like some kind of dying whale noise, because *oh my god, it's so incredible.*

"I fucking love the way you taste," he murmurs, holding me still with his strong arms as his tongue works me over. "Such a sweet, juicy pussy."

I never imagined I'd enjoy dirty talk. It always makes me cringe a little to read it in books, so I figured it wasn't my cup of tea. But when Gareth says things like that to me? It is *so very much* my cup of tea. I will take all the cups of dirty-talk tea, please and thank you.

Also my cup of tea? Oral sex. Holy wow. It's everything I imagined it would be and so much more. God, his tongue. It's so hot and slick and dexterous as it slides all around like he's licking batter off a mixer blade. He's not even going near my clit, and my head's about to spin around *Exorcist*-style. Possibly because of the sounds Gareth's making as he does it. He's moaning, just like I am, and I can feel his moans vibrating through *everything* down there, including the hypersensitive bud he's not touching.

I'm fairly certain he's avoiding it on purpose. Building up to it. If the things he's doing with his tongue right now are just the opening act, I don't know how I'm going to survive the rest. It seems impossible for this experience to get any more intense than it already is.

But I'm wrong about that, as I find out when he rubs two of his fingers over my swollen folds to spread them wider. Wide enough for him to kiss that tiny, hypersensitive bud.

It's like sticking a fork in a light socket. It makes my whole body shake and judder, and I escalate from dying whale noises to something that sounds more like a deranged peacock wail.

Gareth glances up at me, and god, the sight of those gorgeous blue eyes burns right through me. They're so dark and *intense*. Part of me wants to look away, but I can't. I'm held in his tractor-beam gaze as he speaks.

"You like that, don't you? Look how worked up you are. It's

such a fucking turn-on when you roll your hips to rub yourself against me like you can't get enough of my mouth."

Was I doing that? I don't remember doing that. Then again, I can barely remember my own name, so maybe I was.

"You want to come again, don't you? You think I should let you?"

I really think he should. I can feel another orgasm hovering just out of reach, and I don't just want it, I *need* it. I've never needed anything this much.

He teases a blunt finger over my entrance before pushing it slowly inside me.

My whole body trembles at the delicious sensation.

"That okay?" he asks, watching me closely.

"More like incredible."

He smiles as he pumps his finger in and out. "Fucking hell, you feel so good. You ever found your G-spot before?"

I thought I had. I've used sex toys that claim to reach the G-spot. But they never felt anything like the sizzle of pleasure I get when Gareth crooks his fingers inside me just right.

"Jesus, honey, you look so good like this. Pull your shirt up higher so I can see your gorgeous tits while I get you off."

I do, shivering when the cold air hits my overheated skin.

"Fuck yeah," he rasps as his gaze rakes over me. "Good girl."

It shouldn't turn me on so much to hear him say that, but it does, oh god it does. I love it as much as I love the feel of his eyes on me and that greedy expression on his face.

He makes another noise in his throat and lowers his mouth to me. My hips buck when he latches onto my clit, and I'm coming again.

It's even more powerful than the last one, more powerful than any orgasm I've had before on my own. Gareth caresses me through it until I disintegrate into a limp, breathless heap.

"I'm dead," I mumble. "You killed me."

"Then how come I can see you breathing?" He places a tender kiss between my breasts before gently tugging my shirt back down.

When his lips brush mine, I wrap my arms around his neck to keep him there. "That was amazing."

He smiles against my mouth as he peppers it with tiny, gentle kisses. "Amazing is much better than good."

"The first one was pretty amazing too."

"Yeah, but the second one was much better, wasn't it? Tell the truth."

"I want to go all the way tonight," I say, feeling braver than I ever have, as if those orgasms flooded my brain with courage instead of oxytocin.

Forget going slow. I want fast. And rough. And hard.

I want *everything*.

And I want it with Gareth.

19

GARETH

"I don't think that's a good idea," I hear myself say.

What the fuck is wrong with me?

Oh, right. I'm trying to be a good guy.

I tuck my face into Casey's neck, so she won't see how torn I am, but also because I want to touch my lips to her tender skin. "We agreed to take it slow, remember?"

"What if I'm tired of taking it slow?" She slides her hand down my stomach, and my brain shorts out.

I will not fuck Casey tonight.

I will not fuck Casey tonight.

I will *not*.

God, but I want to so goddamn bad my dick might actually explode.

Doesn't matter. I'm not doing it. We're taking it slow. That's the plan. Tonight's third base. That's as far as I go. No stealing home plate.

I just need to remember there are very good reasons for the multistep plan.

Like—

Shit, what are the reasons again? I'm so hard I can't think straight.

Right. Taking time to make sure Casey's comfortable with everything we're doing. That's important. And there was also something about anticipation and giving her the full first-time experience. Trying to make it special for her by replicating the slow buildup she'd get with a real boyfriend.

Not that I know the first thing about being anyone's boyfriend. I'm a "get in, get out" kind of guy. Flirt, fuck, move on, that's my M.O. Taking things slowly isn't my strong suit and neither is sticking around afterward. So I'm basically winging it here.

But I'm pretty sure the fact that I *want* to fuck Casey so bad right now means I shouldn't. It makes me doubt my motives when all I can think about is how hot it was to spread her legs and feel her come on my tongue. I'm not supposed to be in this for my own gratification. This is about Casey and giving her what she needs. She deserves to be happy, to fall in love, to have a rich, full sex life with a man who'll take good care of her. As her friend, I want that for her.

That's why I'm doing this—to help her find someone who can give her all the things I can't.

It takes every bit of my willpower to grab her hand before it reaches my aching hard-on. "I don't think we should push it." I swallow as I bring her knuckles to my lips. "Let's stick with the plan. One step at a time."

My dick officially hates me.

Casey's lower lip juts out. "Why do you have to be so responsible?"

I want to kiss her disappointment away. But I can't risk it. If I start kissing her again right now, I won't be able to stop.

So instead I give her a big, fake-ass smile and snag her shorts and underwear off the back of the couch. "Pout all you want, but it's not getting you laid tonight, honey."

And Jesus, where did that come from? I've never called anyone "honey" before. Not in bed or anywhere else. *Sweetheart* and *babe* are my usual go-tos for flirting, so why does *honey* keep slipping out with Casey?

I said a whole bunch of shit just now that I didn't plan to say. I couldn't seem to help myself. Seeing her let go like that did something to me. The sounds she made, the greedy way she responded to my touch, it unleashed a flood of lust so powerful that I lost my head like some sort of teenager at the mercy of his hormones.

I've had sex with lots of women—not as many as people assume—but it's always been an orchestrated performance. A little give here and a little take there. Whatever's needed to get us both over the finish line. I've never lost myself in the sheer pleasure of getting a woman off before. I've never been so ravenous to watch her fall apart that I lost control.

And now Casey's gazing at me like I'm exactly what she wants. There's no hesitation, no fear or self-doubt in her anymore. The way she looks right now, with her untamed hair slipping free of its tie, her body open and flushed with wanting, it makes me want to grant every wish she's ever had.

I nearly cave, but I'm saved by the fucking rabbit.

Mr. Twinkletoes pops his head up beside us and noses Casey's bare hip. She squeaks and levitates off the couch, and then we're both laughing and wriggling back into our clothes.

We order pizza and watch a couple more episodes of *Stranger Things*. Casey snuggles up against me, and I hold her tight during the scary scenes, but other than stroking her hair or toying with her fingers, I manage to keep my hands mostly to myself. And it's nice, just being close and enjoying each other's company, even without the sex. It's better than nice. It's one of the best times I've had in ages.

Eventually we switch over to a nature documentary, so Casey won't have nightmares when she goes to bed. Sometime between the sea lions and the cormorants, she falls asleep with her head pillowed on my chest.

It's getting late, and I'm on shift tomorrow. I should put her to bed and take myself upstairs to my own lonely, uncomfortable mattress. But instead I tuck the blanket around her and settle my hand on her back, feeling it rise and fall with each of her soft breaths.

I'm not ready for tonight to end yet. I don't know how many more moments I'll get like this.

It's not lost on me that I'm teaching Casey to be confident enough to go out and have sex with other people. I'm definitely not having any mixed feelings about that at all.

Except for the part where I'm having a lot of mixed feelings about it.

I hate the idea of her with someone else. Every time I think about it I get this possessive knot in my gut. I suppose I'm over-protective of her. That must be it, because I've never gotten jealous over a woman before. I'm just worried about some dick-head not treating my friend right. That's all.

It could be that's why I'm putting off the big event. The longer I can drag our arrangement out, the longer it'll be before Casey's ready to go looking for another partner.

And the longer I can have her for myself.

Once Casey gets what she wants from me, there won't be any reason for us to keep fooling around. No more kissing, no more touching, no more cuddling on the couch like this.

The truth is I don't want to give it up yet.

But I will. Soon.

I just want to enjoy it for a little longer first.

20

GARETH

I don't know who was in charge of the decorating here at the Cedar Creek resort, but they were clearly deranged. The carpet that lines the corridors of the resort's hotel is a garish cartoon collage of every stereotypical Texan thing you can imagine: cowboy boots and hats, wagon wheels, horseshoes, rope, steer skulls, and Texas flags. It's so butt-ugly it gives me a headache. As a native Texan, the fact that this carpet even exists makes me embarrassed on behalf of the entire state.

Then again, it's probably the vibe most of their customers expect. The resort trades mostly in corporate retreats and conventions—out-of-state business customers wanting a getaway in the picturesque Texas Hill Country that's an hour from the Austin airport and has all the amenities of a nice hotel —along with all the upcharges that come with them.

We get a good number of callouts to the resort. Rogue fire alarms and medical emergencies mostly, but today we're here for a hotel guest stuck in a stalled elevator car.

As Lieutenant McCafferty paces in the ugly hotel corridor behind me, I lean my forehead against the closed hoistway door to talk to the woman who's been trapped inside the car alone for the better part of an hour now. "How you doing in there, Ashley?"

She's an ultrasound technician from Milwaukee who's here for a biotech conference and has a touch of claustrophobia, so I've been talking to her to keep her calm. So far we've discussed her labradoodle Sparky, her annoying boss with bad breath, and her fuckup younger brother who's sponging off her parents while he tries to monetize his fitspo TikTok account.

"I'm really, really ready to get out of here." Her voice sounds shaky and a little breathless.

McCafferty and I exchange a glance, and I can tell he's thinking the same thing I am—she's heading for a panic attack if we don't get her out of there soon.

He walks a few steps away and reaches for his radio to check in with Jamal Allen, our ladder company's elevator expert. "Einstein, how's that system check coming? Any luck yet?"

While the lieutenant's doing that, I press my forehead against the door again. "Do me a favor, Ashley. I want you to sit down on the floor and take a few deep breaths from your diaphragm. Can you do that for me? In and out, nice and slow."

Jamal's voice crackles over the radio from the elevator machine room where he and our apparatus operator, Erica Quincy, have been running through the troubleshooting checklist, trying to get the car moving again. "Negative. System reboot was a bust."

"Okay, it's time to open these doors and get her out of there," McCafferty says into the radio. "Terminate elevator power."

"You're doing great, Ashley," I call through the doors. "Sit tight. We'll have you out soon, okay?"

Once Jamal confirms the power's shut off and the elevator car's secure, McCafferty steps up next to me and inserts his drop key into the locking mechanism on the outer elevator door. Using my pike pole to trip the rollers, I shove the hoistway door open and chock it with a wedge. The elevator car is stalled between the second and third floors, but it's only about eighteen inches below the opening on this floor, so we won't need to use a ladder to bring Ashley out.

She scrambles to her feet as I force the inner door open. She's younger than I expected—in her twenties by my estimate —and dressed for the gym in black leggings and an orange yoga top. "Oh my god, are you a sight for sore eyes!"

"Told you we'd get you out." I chock the inner door with another wedge and gesture for her to exit the elevator car. "There's just a little step up. Think you can make it?"

"Is it safe?" she asks, eying the opening warily. "It's not going to start moving and chop me in half, is it?"

"Not to worry, ma'am. We've shut off power to the elevators so it can't go anywhere."

"You promise?"

"Absolutely." I give her an encouraging smile and bend down, extending my arm. "Give me your hand. I'll help you up."

After a brief hesitation, she grabs hold of me and steps up out of the elevator. "Whew! It feels good to be out of there."

"I'll bet," I say as I guide her toward the paramedics waiting to check her out. "Aren't you glad you came to Texas?"

She seeks me out again a few minutes later as we're getting ready to leave and asks if I'd mind taking a picture with her for her Instagram. We get that kind of thing a lot, so I agree and Quincy offers to take the pic.

"Thank you so much!" Ashley says afterward, giving me a grateful hug. "You're a real-life hero."

"We're just doing our jobs, ma'am. Happy to help." I gently disentangle myself and head downstairs with the rest of the crew.

"Oh, Firefighter Kelly, you're so handsome and brave! How

will I ever thank you?" Jamal mocks in a falsetto as soon as we're out of the lobby.

Quincy shakes her head. "Another rescue, another straight woman smitten by the G-Man. I wish I knew your secret."

"It's the turnout pants and suspenders," I say. "I don't know why, but women go nuts for them."

Quincy frowns down at her pants and twists around like she's trying to check out her own ass. "You think?"

"Yeah, right," Jamal says with a roll of his eyes as we load our gear back on the truck. "I'm sure your pretty face and muscles have nothing at all to do with it."

"How come we never get to rescue any hot lesbians, is what I want to know," Quincy complains.

I lean against the truck while we wait for the lieutenant to finish talking to the hotel manager. "You already have a girl-friend, Quincy. What do you need with another hot lesbian?"

"I just want to bask in some hot girl gratitude is all. There's nothing wrong with that."

Jamal leans around Quincy to wag his eyebrows at me. "Did you get her number, pretty boy?"

"I did not." I'm not saying I've never hooked up with a woman I met on the job, but I try not to make a habit of it. Sometimes people can get overly attached to the firefighters who help them, which is exactly the type of complication I prefer to avoid.

"Why the hell not? She was obviously into you."

I definitely picked up on her interest. But I didn't feel the slightest temptation to encourage it, which is unusual for me. I usually enjoy a little flirting even when I don't plan to follow through. "She wasn't my type, I guess."

Jamal snorts. "Since when is young and cute not your type?"

"Was she cute?" I shrug. "I didn't notice.

Quincy presses her hand to my forehead. "Are you feeling okay?"

"Yeah." I wave her away, wishing the lieutenant would hurry up. "Why?"

"A cute girl was flirting with you and you didn't even notice, so I assume you must be dying," she says, and Jamal hoots with laughter.

"You're hilarious," I mutter, pushing off the truck as the lieutenant starts heading our way.

"Come on," McCafferty says, pounding me on the back before climbing into the officer's seat. "Let's get back to the house so our local superhero can make us all dinner."

———

THE KITCHEN at Crowder's Fire Station 1 is designed for utility rather than aesthetics: plain white cupboards, stainless steel prep counters, a big gas range, and an easy-to-clean concrete floor. Next to it is our laminate-top dining table, and beyond that a grouping of black recliners are arranged around the common room TV.

Quincy and Jamal are in there watching an NCAA women's basketball game while I throw together a peach cobbler to go with tonight's dinner. I don't usually bother with dessert, but on Sunday shifts I like to make dinner a little more special. My traditional Sunday pot roast is cooking in the Instant Pot, filling the common room with mouthwatering smells, which leaves me more than enough time to whip up a simple dessert.

Before I joined the firehouse, they used to rotate chow duty. But it didn't take long for them to realize I was the best chef on B shift and ask if I'd mind taking over the job on a permanent basis. Fine by me. Cooking gets me out of some other chores that I'm more than happy to miss. Like cleaning. I fucking hate cleaning. I'll cook all day as long as I don't have to clean the bathroom or mop the apparatus floor.

McCafferty's a decent hand in the kitchen, and sometimes he'll still bring in his smoker and smoke us up some brisket or homemade sausages out back. But Jamal's an indifferent cook at best, and Quincy's fucking horrible. Her version of a tuna casserole should be prosecuted as a federal hate crime. She's also currently banned from setting foot in my kitchen after I caught her trying to sneak cumin into my Bolognese last shift. Like, who the fuck puts cumin in Bolognese? The woman's a goddamn menace.

Aside from Quincy's barbarous attempts to sabotage my recipes, I find cooking a relaxing way to pass the downtime between calls. My dad used to be his firehouse cook too, and he taught me everything he knew. He's been dead for thirteen years, but I always feel closer to him when I'm cooking. I can still hear his voice in my head, telling me how to chop an onion, how to take care of a cast iron pan, how to make food go further on a tight budget.

A lot of the recipes I make are his. He never wrote anything down, but I've got them all stored away in my head. Like the Sunday pot roast I adapted for the Instant Pot I donated to the firehouse last year. Dad would have fucking loved this Instant Pot. It's a damn shame he didn't live long enough to have one.

McCafferty wanders into the kitchen while I'm slicing peaches. "How long until dinner, G-Man?"

"Another half an hour."

He grabs an apple from the fruit bowl and polishes it on his CFD polo shirt as he leans his hip against the counter. "Hey, so how's everything with you and Casey?"

I glance toward the common room to make sure Jamal and Quincy aren't paying attention to us before shooting him an *I don't want to talk about this here* frown. "Fine."

"You do that thing we talked about last shift?"

"No." It's not exactly a lie. Technically, Casey's still a virgin. But I'm sure as shit not giving McCafferty a detailed play-by-play. Especially not where everyone else can overhear. The last thing I need is Frick and Frack on my case about this. My arrangement with Casey is private, and not something I want put up for public heckling.

McCafferty's gaze lingers on me as he bites into his apple, and I get the unsettling sense he can see right through me. He *knows*. Not just about the sex we're not quite having yet, but that the whole situation is already starting to feel a lot more complicated than I bargained for.

Mind-reading bastard.

"What are you two broody hens gossiping about over here?" Quincy asks, wandering into the kitchen with Jamal.

"Big Red's having some plumbing issues," I say while he's still got his mouth full of apple. "Major blockage."

"Sorry I asked."

McCafferty's scowl says he'll be getting me back for that later, but I'm okay with doing some extra drills next shift. I shoot him a grin as I set the skillet of melted butter on a hot pad.

"Artichokes are good for promoting gut health," Jamal says. "Also chia seeds. Did you know a single chia seed can hold twelve times its weight in water?"

And that's why he's got the nickname Einstein. The only other person I know who reads as much as Jamal is Casey.

"You know what would be good in that cobbler?" Quincy pipes up as she digs into a box of Cheez-Its. "Paprika."

"Come anywhere near my batter, and you'd better be prepared to lose a finger," I growl.

Quincy gasps.

I'm pretty sure she's just enjoying fucking with me at this

point. She can't seriously be advocating for paprika peach cobbler. But I'm not willing to risk it.

The lieutenant stifles a laugh and clears his throat. "Hey, so I was talking to my brother Tanner yesterday, and he's looking to hire an assistant manager to help him out at the bookstore."

McCafferty has the unlikely distinction of being the stepson of George King, owner of the second-best-selling ice cream brand in the country and Crowder's largest employer. Between King's Creamery's corporate headquarters, the manufacturing plant, and the amusement park, this town basically owes its existence to the King family and their money. George King's been married a few times, and McCafferty's mother was one of his wives for a while before she died. The lieutenant doesn't talk about his rich stepfather much, but he's close to his two half-brothers and a bunch of his stepsiblings, most of whom I met last year when McCafferty was in the hospital with a concussion.

"I don't suppose any of y'all know someone who'd be interested in the job?" he tosses out.

I open my mouth, but Quincy beats me to it.

"What about Casey? She'd be perfect for something like that, don't you think?"

"She *would* be perfect for it," I agree.

"Funny, that's exactly what I was thinking," McCafferty says, watching me pour the cobbler batter into the cast iron skillet.

"How happy is she working at the gym?" Jamal asks. "Is she looking for another job?"

I shrug. "She's not *un*happy there, but she might be open to a better opportunity if one came along."

"You think she'd consider coming to work at the bookstore?" McCafferty asks.

I have a feeling Casey would sell one of her organs to work at that bookstore. Two, if she could convince someone to buy a slightly used appendix.

When she found out the old guy who owned the town's one and only bookstore was planning to retire and sell the place last year, she went into a weeklong funk. But then McCafferty's brother swooped in to buy it and save the day. Apparently he's made a bunch of improvements since he took it over, including adding a coffee bar, which a lot of people in town have been excited about—including Casey. There was a light in her eyes when she was telling me all about it that isn't there when she talks about her job at the gym.

But it's not my place to commit her to considering anything, much less a job change, so all I say is, "You'd have to ask her that question."

"You could call her right now and ask," Jamal suggests.

"Yeah, where's your phone?" Quincy starts to frisk me while I'm spooning the sliced peaches over the batter.

I elbow her away when she tries to shove her hand in my pocket. "Would you get out of my pants?"

"That's got to be the first time Kelly's ever said that to a woman," Jamal wisecracks.

Quincy and I both throw Cheez-Its at him. He plucks them off the counter and pops them in his mouth.

"You children are gonna spoil your appetites with all that snacking," I point out.

"Spoil away," McCafferty says as he tosses his apple core into the trash. "More Sunday roast for me."

"Call Casey," Quincy wheedles at my elbow.

"Hold your horses," I say. "Damn. Let me put the cobbler in the oven first."

"I'll do it." Jamal grabs the oven mitts away from me and sweeps the skillet off the counter.

"In the middle rack," I order as I pull up Casey's number. "And set the timer for thirty-five minutes."

"Hey!" Casey answers cheerfully, and my smile grows at the sound of her voice. "How's your shift going?"

I catch Quincy and McCafferty sharing a look, and now I'm wondering what that's about. I know better than to think McCafferty would blab about a confidential conversation, which means Quincy thinks she's figured something out all on her own. Shit.

"Not too bad," I tell Casey, turning my back on my nosy coworkers. "So listen, you know McCafferty's brother who bought the bookstore? He's hiring an assistant manager, and we were wondering if you'd be interested in applying for the job."

I have to hold the phone away from my ear to protect it from Casey's high-pitched squeal.

"*Ohmygodohmygodohmygod, are you serious?*" she shrieks.

I'll take that as a yes.

21

CASEY

I t's not so bad, working in a gym. It has its advantages. Like, for instance, I get to see my friends all the time when they come to work out. And then there's the upbeat music they play over the speakers, even if it is all ten to twenty years past its prime. Who needs new, fresh music when you could listen to "Mr. Brightside" twice a day? Not me.

The gym's owner, Dennis, is pretty hands-off these days, so I've got a lot of freedom as long as I keep everything running smoothly. The longer I've worked here, the more responsibility he's handed off to me and the more he's cut back his own hours.

I also get to watch a lot of hot, muscular people work out, which isn't too bad. But it's not all eye candy all the time. There are quite a few wrinkly old men who insist on taking their shirts off. Like Mr. Luedeker, a Korean war vet with an impressive bench press for an eighty-seven-year-old, who's currently standing in front of my desk.

"One of the commodes in the men's room is clogged," Mr. Luedeker announces.

I try not to make eye contact with his hairy nipples as I

glance up from my computer. "Thank you for letting me know, Mr. Luedeker. I'll make sure it gets taken care of."

Which probably means doing it myself unless Dennis decides to come in before noon.

"I'm not naming names," Mr. Luedeker says, raising his voice to carry across the gym, "but I'm pretty sure it was Bruno. Saw him coming out of the john earlier with a guilty look on his face."

"He who smelt it, dealt it," Mr. Bruno shouts back between dumbbell curls. He's a retired mailman close to Mr. Luedeker's age, and the two of them have been gym-buddies-slash-frenemies for decades.

I shake my head at Mr. Luedeker, used to their mostly good-natured squabbling and one-upmanship. "I thought you weren't naming names."

"Where's the fun in that?" Mr. Luedeker winks and wanders off to heckle Mr. Bruno about his curls.

Connor Autry pushes through the front door with his gym bag slung over his shoulder and gives me one of those cool-dude head nods on his way past the front desk. "Morning."

The old me would have mumbled a reply while keeping my eyes lowered. But this morning I remember all the things Gareth said about flirting and eye contact. I guess the lessons he's been giving me are working because I'm feeling confident enough to look Connor Autry right in the eye and smile. "Morning, Connor."

He returns my smile, and instead of heading straight for the office in the back, he comes over to lean on the reception desk. "How was your weekend?"

"Really great." I can't help the blush that rises to my cheeks at the memory of everything I did with Gareth this weekend. Which, of course, Connor notices.

"That good, huh?" His eyebrows raise with a sly grin. "Who should I be jealous of?"

Whoa. I think Connor Autry might be flirting with me.

I guess Gareth did know what he was talking about. I can't believe it was that easy. And here I am, totally taking it in stride with nary a nose itch or tingle.

By rights I should be swooning with delight, but that swirling in my stomach isn't glee—it's guilt. With the memory of Gareth's kisses and caresses fresh in my mind, it feels wrong to be flirting with Connor.

On the other hand, it's not as if Gareth and I are dating. We were very explicit about that not being what this is. If we're only friends, presumably we're both free to pursue other options. I don't doubt that Gareth still flirts with pretty much every woman he talks to, so why should I feel bad? Shouldn't I enjoy the prospect of having something else after our arrangement ends?

"How about you?" I say to Connor. "How was your weekend?"

He starts telling me how he drove to Austin to see some friends, and they went to this place called Donut Taco Palace, where apparently you can get donuts, tacos, or a donut taco, which sounds messy and sort of gross to me, but I'll bet my brother would love it. And the whole time Connor's talking, I'm trying my best to seem interested, but my heart's not in it.

I've had a crush on him forever, but there's no trace of the butterflies I usually get in his presence. When I look at his face, all I can think about is how he's not as handsome as Gareth, and what I used to see as quiet intensity now feels like blandness. I also can't help noticing that the hair I used to fantasize about touching has too much product in it. I'll bet it doesn't feel nearly as soft as Gareth's hair does when I run my fingers through it.

"You know what?" Connor says, resting his forearms on the counter in front of my desk. "Maybe sometime we should—"

"Casey!"

I break into a smile as Gareth saunters in the door holding two paper coffee cups, and suddenly those missing butterflies are back in full force, throwing a celebration in my tummy.

Which is not good. I'm not supposed to be crushing on Gareth, who doesn't date and doesn't want to be my boyfriend. I need to get these unauthorized feelings in check.

"Hey! How was the rest of your shift?"

"Good." Gareth's smile fades when he sees Connor, but he quickly pastes it back in place as he sets one of the cups in front of me. "I brought you a coffee."

"Thanks! That's sweet."

Gareth nods a greeting at Connor. "Sorry I didn't bring you one, Autry."

"No worries." A frown thins Connor's mouth as he glances back and forth between us. "I better get ready for my first client."

"You two seemed chummy," Gareth comments as he watches Connor walk away. "Did I interrupt something?"

"Nope." I study his expression as I sip my coffee. Is that a hint of jealousy I'm detecting? Or just his usual dislike of Connor? It's hard to tell what he's thinking. "Where'd you get the coffee from?"

Gareth cocks a grin at me. "Misfit Books. Thought I'd do a little reconnaissance."

"Oh! That reminds me—" I stop and shake my head because my big news can wait. "No, first I want to know if you got your essay back yet."

His smile disappears as his jaw goes rigid. "Sure did."

My heart sinks at his expression. "And?"

"See for yourself." Gareth passes his phone over, stone-faced. Anxiously, I scan the email on the screen. I swear, I will haunt that lit instructor to his pedantic grave if he didn't like Gareth's essay after he worked so hard revising it.

My mouth falls open when I see the new grade. "You got a ninety???"

"Yep." Gareth's broken into another grin.

"You butthead!" I reach across the counter and smack his arm. "You had me worried! I was all prepared to hunt down your instructor and give him a piece of my mind."

Gareth laughs as he shoves his phone back in his pocket. "No need, although I would love to see that. You really pulled my ass out of the fire."

"You did that yourself. So this puts you back on track to pass the class, right?"

He nods. "If I can do this well on the Hawthorne essay due next week, it'll pull my overall grade up into the seventies."

"You will. You've got this in the bag."

His gaze holds mine. "Because of you. I owe you big-time for all your help."

"You don't owe me anything." The butterflies are back, fluttering around my heart this time, and I smile down at my coffee. "So what did you think of the bookstore?"

"It seems great. I can totally see you working there. Have you heard anything from Tanner yet?"

"Yeah, actually. He emailed me this morning."

After I got off the phone with Gareth last night, I updated my résumé and emailed it to Ryan before I went to bed. By the time I woke up today, there was already an email from Tanner in my inbox.

"And?" Gareth prompted. "What'd he say?"

I glance around before whispering, "I've got an interview on Wednesday at noon."

"Hey, that's awesome! Are you excited?"

"Excited and nervous. And frazzled. And jittery. It's possible

I'm freaking out a tiny bit." I really, really want this job. It's been hard to think about anything else since Gareth told me about it last night.

Being the assistant manager at a bookstore is basically my dream job. Which is funny, because if you'd asked me yesterday, I would have said I didn't have a dream job.

Some people know exactly what they want to do. They have a calling, like Gareth and being a firefighter, or Kenzie and being a vet. Or they have a passion, like my politician mother or my artist father. Or they have the inspiration to start up their own business, like my brother did.

And then there's me. Aimlessly drifting through my life with no real idea what I want to do. Nothing's ever called to me or inflamed me or inspired me. Not enough to try and make it my career.

I was excellent at being in school. School comes with rules and clear paths to follow. Lesson plans, rubrics, syllabi. I'm great at following rules and paths. Give me a goal, and I can get myself across that finish line with maximum efficiency and minimal fuss.

The problem is that once you finish school, there's no one telling you what your goal should be anymore. You have to choose your own adventure.

I never liked those Choose Your Own Adventure books. I'd read them straight through from cover to cover because I was afraid of making the wrong choice. I wanted to know what all the possibilities were before I chose so I could decide which path was the *best* one.

I'm not adventurous. I don't like taking risks or going it on my own. I've never wanted anything badly enough to leave my family and friends and the town I grew up in. I like it here. It's familiar. Comfortable. Safe.

But staying here means my job opportunities are limited. It's never bothered me that much since I didn't have any particular career ambitions anyway. I was okay with whatever job happened to come along.

Until I heard about this job at the bookstore. And now I've gone and made the fatal mistake of getting my hopes up. Like, really far up. *Way* up there.

"Sounds like coffee's exactly what you need," Gareth quips, and I laugh. "Don't stress. You're going to impress the hell out of Tanner at the interview."

"I hope so."

Opportunities like this don't come around that often in a town this size. If I blow this shot, there might not be another one.

22

CASEY

I don't know Tanner King personally. He was far enough ahead of me in school that our paths never crossed, but everyone in Crowder knows who all the Kings are.

Tanner's great-grandfather started the creamery that put Crowder on the map, and his family has more money than god —or at least more money than anyone else in the county, which is saying something since this is oil and cattle ranch country. My mom might hold the office of mayor, but Tanner's father, George King, is the one who holds the power in this town.

Tanner is generally known as the quiet, slightly nerdy King brother, so it makes sense that he was the one to buy the bookstore. I keep telling myself he's simply Ryan's brother, but I'm still nervous to meet him. But more than that, I'm nervous about this job interview.

It's ten minutes to noon when I pull into the parking lot of Misfit Books on Wednesday, so I sit in the car for a few minutes and try to find my calm before I go inside.

I've been coming to this bookstore ever since I can remember. My dad used to bring me here whenever I got straight As on my report card. He'd let me pick out two books as a reward—any two books I wanted because he didn't believe in censoring my reading. We'd end up spending the whole afternoon there, him talking to Seamus Hill behind the counter and me sitting on the floor in some quiet, hidden-away aisle, engrossed in whatever books I'd found.

The thought of getting to come to work here every day fills me with giddy excitement. I'm not used to wanting things this much. I think I've spent so long trying to be happy with my safe little life that I forgot what it feels like to want things.

The only other thing that's come close to this feeling lately is my arrangement with Gareth. But my feelings about him and what we're doing are tempered by the knowledge that it's only temporary, which makes it all a little bittersweet. I'm trying hard not to let myself want it too much.

That's the whole problem, right there. There's not a lot that I've let myself want in my life. I don't tend to aim high for fear of being shot down. Better to set realistic expectations and only try for things that are easy to get—or at least things I don't want all that badly, so I won't be disappointed if I don't get them.

But this? Working at Misfit Books? That's something I want. If this job doesn't pan out for whatever reason—whether I screw up the interview or Tanner happens to find someone better—I'm going to be devastated.

It's scary, knowing that. Scary enough that I can feel my fight-or-flight reflex stirring in the pit of my stomach, tempting me to do a runner. But it's too late to bail on the interview, and not just because there's a chance Tanner King has already seen me out here in the parking lot.

I can't bail because running won't make anything better. I'll still be devastated to lose this opportunity even if I'm the one who shuts the door on it.

I'm probably going to sneeze when I go in there and meet Tanner King, who holds all my hopes and dreams in the palm of his hand. But there's nothing I can do about that. So I force myself to get out of the car.

The store lives in an old Queen Anne-style house two blocks off Main Street. Since Tanner took it over, it's gotten a fresh coat of paint and most of the wraparound porches have been enclosed to make more room for the new café and gift shop he added.

It already seems to be doing a brisk business in coffee if nothing else. On my way in, I hold the door for a woman balancing a tray of to-go coffees and a paper bag that I'm guessing is full of the pastries they sell in the café. I've only been here once since the bookstore changed hands, during the grand reopening weekend, and I'm glad to see there's a short line at the café counter in addition to the smattering of people who've posted up with their laptops in the small seating area. There are a few people browsing the bookstore too, mostly kids and moms in the newly expanded children's section at the back.

Other than that, the place looks remarkably unchanged. The front of the store is a bit more organized and spread out, with several tables of featured new releases and curated recommendations positioned to catch the eye when customers first walk in. But the rest of it feels the same as ever, a wondrous labyrinth of narrow aisles and towering bookcases stuffed into every room of the old two-story house. It's the kind of place where you wouldn't be all that surprised to find a hidden door or secret passageway to a storybook fantasyland. Or at least that was what I used to think when I was a kid.

"Are you Casey?"

A short blonde woman smiles at me from behind the counter. She's outfitted in stylish business clothes that seem awfully dressy for a bookstore sales clerk and make me worry the assistant manager job I'm here for has already been claimed.

"That's right," I say, returning her smile. "I'm here for an interview?" I hate that question mark I put at the end, as if I don't know whether I'm here for an interview or not. Already I'm failing at the confident competence vibe I wanted to project.

"I know," she says cheerfully. "I'm Lucy. Let me go grab Tanner. Hang on a sec."

Everything about her is bright and sunny, and she's got the confident competence thing down pat. If I were hiring an assistant manager, she's exactly who I'd want, which makes me wonder why I'm here.

Surely they'd have called me if the job was no longer available? I cling to the thought like a security blanket while I wait.

"You need help?" a male voice says behind me.

I spin around and find myself face-to-face with Tanner's younger brother, Wyatt King. He's widely considered the hottest of the King brothers and also happens to be the lead singer of Crowder's most popular local band, Shiny Heathens—two facts that are almost certainly related.

I recognize him right away, not only because I've seen him onstage at the Rusty Spoke, but also because he was a senior when I was a freshman in high school. Not that we ever interacted. Back then he had a reputation as a rebellious stoner who was always getting into trouble of one type or another and was therefore way too cool and dangerous for the likes of me. And now he's standing right in front of me in all his tattooed, shaggy-haired, hot musician glory.

"I'm good, thanks. Lucy's getting Tanner."

"Cool." His smile is incandescent. "You're here for the interview, right? Ryan's friend Casey?"

The formerly long-buried part of me that's still a fifteen-year-old girl squeals *Wyatt King knows my name!* and faints dead away.

But since I'm not actually a teenager anymore, I manage to

return his smile with one that hopefully doesn't look too deranged and say, "That's right. I am."

"I'm Wyatt." He shifts the toolbox he's holding to his left hand as he steps forward to extend his right, grinning in a way that makes me think he knows exactly what effect he's having on me.

It reminds me a lot of Gareth, which gives me a hard pang of the bittersweet feeling I've been getting whenever I think about him lately. It also helps me find my cool, even when Wyatt King wraps his guitar-callused fingers around my hand and flashes his dimples at me.

"Casey Goodrich," I say as I slip my hand back out of his.

For some reason this seems to delight him even more. "Oh wow, your mom's the mayor, right? I love those dogs of hers. She's a real hoot."

I cringe slightly at the mention of my mom, which makes Wyatt laugh.

"Aw, come on now, don't tell me that having a locally infamous parent isn't always all it's cracked up to be."

Even though he's still chuckling, it's a dark kind of amusement that makes me feel a kinship with him. As uncomfortable as my mom's notoriety sometimes makes me, it's small potatoes compared to growing up as the troublemaker son of the most prominent man in town.

"I guess you'd know all about that," I say, offering a commiserating smile.

"I guess I would," he agrees.

"Wyatt, you'd better not be scaring off a prospective employee."

Tanner King has appeared, with the wee Lucy at his side. Even if I hadn't seen him around town before, he's got the signature King good looks. In fact, he's nearly a copy of his younger brother—or I guess his younger brother is a copy of him. Except where Wyatt oozes slacker bad boy coolness, Tanner is clean-cut and stiff. He's sporting a short beard, but it's neatly groomed just like his hair. His jeans are neat too, as are his shoes and the T-shirt he's wearing with the store's logo splashed across the chest. At first glance he doesn't look much like the nerd he's alleged to be, but there's a wry edginess in his expression that stands apart from his brother's cheeky nonchalance.

"I'll have you know I was making her feel welcome, which is supposed to be your job." Wyatt flourishes his arm in an exaggerated gesture of introduction. "Casey Goodrich, allow me to present my brother Tanner, the owner of this fine establishment you're standing in. And I believe you've already met his better half, Lucy."

Lucy gives me a small wave, which is when I notice the engagement ring on her left hand.

Tanner steps forward to offer a businesslike handshake. "Thanks for coming in, Casey. Ryan speaks highly of you."

I feel my cheeks flush. If I was going to sneeze, this is probably the moment it would happen. But miraculously I don't feel anything coming on. "Nice to meet you."

"Don't let Tanner's serious demeanor intimidate you," Wyatt drawls. "He's a big softie underneath that frowny face."

Tanner shoots his brother an irritated look. "Don't you have a sink to fix?"

"Yeah, yeah, I know my place," Wyatt says, rolling his eyes. "Casey, it's been a pleasure. I hope you get the job 'cause this guy's in desperate need of some help around here."

"I love all the updates you've made to the old place," I tell Tanner as Wyatt disappears into the back with his toolbox. "I especially like how you've made the front of the store feel more spacious and welcoming while keeping the essential character of the bookstore intact."

Tanner's mouth quirks. "I have to give Wyatt most of the credit for that. He handled all the renovations for me."

"Based on *your* vision," Lucy adds loyally, and Tanner's ears go slightly pink.

"The café addition was a great idea," I tell him. "It seems to be bringing a lot of people into the store."

"Yeah, I don't know how many of them are sticking around to buy books, but I guess we'll see. It's been a steep learning curve, adding the food service component into the retail mix, but hopefully we've made it past the worst bumps in the road." Tanner looks at Lucy. "Would you mind holding down the register while Casey and I talk in my office?"

"That's why I'm here on my lunch break, isn't it?" she replies with a smile. "That and because I'm nosy and wanted to meet Casey."

"Thanks, babe." Since she's more than half a foot shorter than him, he has to stoop to kiss the top of her head. They are without a doubt the cutest couple I've ever seen.

Lucy slips behind the counter while I follow Tanner into a small, cramped office that's doubling as a stockroom, with towering piles of books and boxes stacked all over the floor around the single desk against the wall. Beyond an open doorway is the bathroom with the broken sink Wyatt's working on, judging from the sounds coming from it.

"Hey, Wyatt, can you shut that door?" Tanner calls out as he shifts a stack of books off a chair and gestures for me to sit.

"Yep," Wyatt answers, and the door slams shut, leaving us effectively alone.

"So," Tanner says as he takes his own seat in a rickety rolling desk chair that looks like it's been here as long as the bookstore. He flashes a hesitant, strained smile that puts me oddly at ease because he's obviously as nervous about interviewing me as I am about being interviewed.

When he doesn't follow up that *so* with anything, it's surprisingly easy for me to take the baton and run with it. I've spent most of my adult life working customer service jobs, so putting other people at ease is something I know how to do. "Could you tell me a little more about the job?" I prompt gently. "Ryan only gave me the bare bones."

Relief blooms across Tanner's face at my suggestion. He just needed a little nudge to get him going, and he looks so grateful for it that I can't help thinking this is going to work out perfectly. How could it not, when I'm already starting to figure out what sort of help he needs? I'm absolutely positive that I'm the perfect person for this job.

Now I just need to convince him of that.

———

WHEN I EMERGE from Tanner's office forty-five minutes later, it's with a job offer I've already accepted. I follow him to the register, where Wyatt's loitering with Lucy, having long since finished repairing the sink. When he came back through the office, Tanner and I were so absorbed in our conversation about twentieth century feminist literature we'd barely noticed him.

Tanner tells them I'll be coming on board after I give my notice at the gym, and I accept their enthusiastic congratulations. The four of us stand around for another few minutes talking about the store and Tanner's vision for it. As I listen to him describe the things he hopes to do now that he has someone to help with the day-to-day work that's been overwhelming him, I can't stop gazing around in wonder.

This is about to be my life now. Instead of spending my days in a gym that smells like sweat and protein farts, soon I'll be coming to work in this beautiful old house that smells like fresh coffee and books, the two most wonderful smells in the world.

It's a dream come true. Today is officially the greatest day ever.

I could easily stand here all afternoon chatting with these people I've just met but already like. Sadly, I need to get back to work. Wyatt offers to walk out with me since he's got another job to get to, and we bid Tanner and Lucy goodbye.

But when we step out into the parking lot, we both come to an abrupt halt.

There's a huge plume of black smoke rising into the sky on the other side of downtown. In the distance, I hear the wail of sirens. I think I might smell smoke on the breeze, but maybe that's just my overactive imagination.

"That looks like a really big fire," I say, stating the obvious.

"Yeah," Wyatt agrees, not smiling anymore. "That's too big to be a routine farm burn."

"Where do you think it is?"

"Hard to say. Maybe out close to the highway?"

As we stand there staring at the smoke and listening to the sirens, I can guess that Wyatt's thinking about Ryan, just like I'm thinking about Gareth.

One of those sirens is probably their truck. They're probably headed to the fire right now, if they're not already there.

I know I shouldn't worry. They've trained for this. They know what they're doing and how to stay safe.

But none of that is enough to stop me from worrying anyway.

23

GARETH

The funny thing about being a firefighter is that very little of your time is spent putting out fires. Most of our calls are either false alarms or medical emergencies—motor vehicle accidents, heart attacks, that sort of thing. The ambulance service is handled by the county EMS, but the city fire department gets dispatched to medical calls too since we're often closer and all of us are certified EMTs. We can't transport patients, but we can help evaluate and stabilize them until the paramedics arrive.

Today was different. Today's fire was one of the biggest structure fires the town has seen in a while. It's the biggest fire I've seen in the four years I've lived here, not counting the wildfires that we get sent to help contain around the state every summer.

Fortunately, the old motel was vacant and undergoing renovations that may or may not have had something to do with the fire. But the size of the structure means there's plenty of work for our ladder company to do. While the engine companies are pulling handlines and focusing on fire attack, we're kept busy forcing entry and conducting a primary search of the forty guest rooms, venting the building, and throwing ground ladders to facilitate access to the second floor rooms.

Because of the construction, there's a lot of flammable materials being stored on site, and it takes the rest of the day and the help of some extra engine companies from neighboring counties to get the blaze under control. Once the main body of the fire's been knocked down, we do a secondary search and then assist with salvage and overhaul.

It's well past dark before I get enough of a breather to sit down for a few minutes and check my phone.

There's a voicemail from Casey, which surprises me until I remember that she had her job interview today. Shit, I totally forgot.

Only when I listen to the message, I realize that's not why she called at all.

Hey, Gareth, it's me. I know you're busy right now and probably won't see this message. I just...I saw the smoke and I've been following the fire on the news and...well I guess I just wanted to check in with you. Maybe when you get this, if you have a minute, you could send me a quick text to let me know you're okay.

Of course she saw the smoke, along with everyone else in a twenty-mile radius. Even if she hadn't, there are news crews here from Austin and San Antonio filming our efforts to put out the fire. It's probably the only thing anyone in town is talking about today. But it hadn't occurred to me until just now that Casey might be worried.

Guilt pools in my stomach, along with a nameless unpleasant feeling. Gulping down some water to wash the smoke out of my throat, I tap the phone icon to return her call.

She answers on the first ring. "Gareth?"

"Hey," I say as something loosens in my chest at the sound of her voice. "I'm fine."

"Oh good," she breathes. "I knew you would be, I just..."

"You were worried about me."

It's been so long since I've had anyone to worry over me that I've forgotten what it's like. I'm not entirely comfortable with it, to tell the truth. This phone call right here is exactly the sort of complication I've spent my adult life trying to avoid.

Back when my parents were still married, they used to fight constantly about Dad's job and how much my mom worried when he was at work. That and how much more of my dad's focus he gave to his job than he gave to her. But it was all interrelated. His job made her miserable, and it killed any love there might once have been between them.

That's why I've always avoided attachments. If I have to choose between being a firefighter and being in a relationship, I'll choose the job, no hesitation.

Attachment leads to suffering, my Dad always used to say.

On the other hand, it doesn't feel completely terrible to know someone cares about me enough to worry. It feels even better that it's Casey who cares. I can't deny that, even if it triggers some alarm bells in my head.

"It was a big fire," she says, and I can picture her twisting a lock of hair around her finger the way she does when she's anxious. "It looked pretty scary from downtown."

It looked pretty scary from where I was standing too. But it won't make her feel better to hear that, so I keep it to myself.

"We had it under control. You didn't need to worry." It comes out more brusque than I mean it to, and Casey goes quiet for a second.

"I'm sorry," she says, her voice sounding small enough to make me hate myself. "I probably shouldn't have bothered you at work. It's not like we're—"

"Hey." I don't let her finish that sentence because I can't bear to hear where it's going. Never mind that it's the truth and what I'm supposed to want. "You're not bothering me. You can call me whenever you want, okay? I'm always happy to hear from you."

That's just as true as what she was about to say. We may not be a couple, but she's still my favorite person in the whole damn world. I can't pretend otherwise anymore. That thing in my chest that loosened at the sound of her voice is still loose, even now. Even though this conversation feels like stumbling through a minefield, I still feel better having it than I did before I talked to her.

"Okay." She doesn't sound entirely convinced.

"I'm really glad you called," I tell her, hoping she can hear how much I mean it. "It's good to hear your voice."

"Really?" she says, a little happier, which makes me feel happier too. But then she goes and says, "Are you sure you're all right?"

I blow out a breath and rub my face. "Yeah, I'm just beat, is all. It's been a long day, and it's going to be an even longer night. But it's nothing I can't handle."

"It's good to hear your voice too."

My heart swells so much it aches, and I have to take a second and rub my chest. "How'd your interview go? I thought you were going to text me."

"Oh! My gosh, I totally forgot after I came out of the book-store and saw the smoke."

"Well? Don't keep me in suspense."

"He offered me the job on the spot! And I accepted!"

I smile at how excited she sounds. I can't just hear the grin in her voice, I can feel it warming me from the inside out, washing away some of the soot and exhaustion weighing me down. "Hey, that's great. Congratulations."

"I was super nervous, but I guess he liked me. And I didn't even sneeze once!"

"Did you like him? Does he seem like he'll be a good boss?"

"Yeah, he seems nice. I think I'm going to love working there. I still can't quite believe it's real, you know?"

"I'm really happy for you. We'll celebrate when I'm home, okay?" I wish I was with her now, seeing the grin on her face and hearing all about her new job and what they talked about in the interview. I wish I could give her a hug and tell her how proud I am and how great it is that she's found something she's so enthusiastic about. But that'll all have to wait another twenty-four hours, until she gets home from work tomorrow night.

Speaking of work, I need to get back to mine, so we say our goodbyes and I force myself to my feet.

Salvage and overhaul takes us most of the night. After we return to quarters, cleaning our PPE gear and apparatus keeps us at the house past shift change, so it's later than usual by the time I make it home, where I immediately fall into bed.

As exhausted as I am, it's a while before my mind quiets enough that I can fall asleep. When I finally do, I sleep hard and long.

It's getting dark outside when I wake up. I'm sore all over and stiff as fuck as I pull on a pair of sweats and make my way downstairs. The house is full of delicious cooking smells, and I find my roommates in the kitchen, halfway through eating dinner.

It's not that often we all sit down and eat a meal together. What with everyone's different schedules, you never know who's going to be home when. Most nights everyone fends for themselves, trickling in to grab something whenever they feel like it. But tonight they're all sitting around the table together, which means someone other than me must have cooked for everyone.

Ozzy's chattering away, telling some story about a runaway chicken, Darius is listening silently as usual, and Casey's rolling her eyes at her brother's story. Her curly hair is piled up in a messy bunch on top of her head with stray wisps sticking out around her face. She's still in the branded polo shirt and black pants she wears for work, her eye makeup slightly smudged like it always is at the end of the day, and she's such a familiar, welcome sight that I pause to silently soak it in.

Casey's the first to notice me standing there, and she breaks into a smile that loosens that thing in my chest again and triggers a spark of longing. I want to walk straight into her arms. But I can't. Not in front of everyone when we're supposed to be acting like we're friends and nothing more.

You aren't *anything more than friends*, a voice whispers in my head. *Isn't that the deal you agreed to?*

"You're up!" Casey announces brightly, and Darius greets me with a nod while Ozzy makes a crack about how long I slept.

"What smells so good?" I ask as I shuffle toward the fridge in desperate need of a beer.

"I made lasagna," Casey says. "Here, I'll dish you up a plate."

When I drop into the empty seat across the table from her, she sets a heaping serving in front of me.

"What's the occasion?" I ask as I reach for the fork she's set out for me.

She shrugs. "Just had a craving for lasagna tonight."

I'm pretty sure that's a lie. I suspect she made it for me because she knew I had an exhausting shift and guessed I'd be too tired to cook tonight.

Her lasagna's fucking delicious. I slept through lunch, so I'm half starved. The cheese and carbs and red sauce are like a religious experience in my stomach. While I hoover it up, Ozzy asks me about the fire yesterday, and I give him vague answers until he changes the subject.

I don't like to talk about what I do at work. Most of it is either boring and technical or too upsetting for dinner table talk. After a shift, I'd rather leave it all behind and think about almost anything else for the next forty-eight hours.

Ozzy tells me about this job he has tomorrow—window and

gutter cleaning plus an exterior power wash on one of the big old Victorian houses near the university. He's already recruited Darius to help and wants to know if I'd be up for coming along as well.

"Sure," I agree, knowing it'll go pretty fast with three of us. And I'm never opposed to picking up some extra cash. I let Ozzy go on about the job for a little longer before I change the subject to Casey's new job offer.

When she starts telling me about her interview, Ozzy and Darius carry their empty plates to the dishwasher and wander off to other parts of the house since they already heard it all last night while I was on shift.

I help myself to another piece of lasagna, and in between bites I steal glances at Casey. The more she talks about her new job, the more animated she gets, and the more I forget about the aches and pains I woke up with. She looks so pretty with her big smile, pink cheeks, and bright eyes. Her voice sounds like a song I could listen to all night.

I'm thinking about how sappy that is and wondering where a thought like that even came from, considering I've never been the least bit sentimental, when I realize the voice I was waxing poetical about has stopped talking.

"What?" I ask when I catch her staring at me with a different type of smile on her pretty face—sort of subdued, sort of thoughtful.

She shakes her head. "Nothing."

I reach across the table for her hand and press her soft, slender fingers between mine. "Tell me."

"I'm just happy you're home. I missed you." As soon as she says the words, she blushes and ducks her head. "I don't know if I'm allowed to say that or not."

"I missed you too." The words spill out of me of their own

will. My chest feels like an accordion that's been squeezed, forcing out an unintentional confession. "It's good to be home."

But what I mean is that it's good to be with *her*. When I came home to an empty house this morning, it didn't feel the same as this. It didn't feel like coming home until I saw Casey. Without her in it, this is just a house.

I don't tell her that though. It feels too reckless. Too big. Too complicated. These aren't regular friend feelings, and it feels like a violation of our arrangement. I'm guessing that's what she meant by "I don't know if I'm allowed to say that or not."

We're both feeling things we shouldn't be feeling. Which means this situation is heading into dangerous territory.

We should pull the plug right now. Call off our deal before we break something that can't be unbroken. That would be the safe thing to do.

But if I wanted to play it safe, I wouldn't have agreed to the deal in the first place, would I?

Apparently I'm still not interested in playing it safe because instead of steering us away from the edge of the oncoming cliff, I stand up from the table and pull Casey into my arms the way I wanted to when I first came downstairs and saw her.

24

CASEY

When Gareth stands, I think he's getting up to carry his plate to the sink—but really I think he's doing it to put some distance between us and the things we just said.

It feels like we've both crossed an invisible line. Or at least we're treading dangerously close to crossing over into...*something*.

I don't know what exactly, but it's something that's more than just the friends we're supposed to be.

It's not the words themselves, which were relatively innocuous. *I missed you. I'm glad you're home.* They're the kinds of things friends *could* say to each other. But they feel more like the kinds of things couples say. And they're not words Gareth and I have ever said to each other before, which makes them feel precariously weighted. More couple-y than friend-y.

I'm afraid it might be too much. That we've gone too far and now he's going to retreat.

Instead, he pulls me out of my chair and into a big bear hug. My nose presses into the groove between his pecs, and the irresistible scent of Gareth's skin floods my senses.

He holds me like he *needs* me, like I'm the happy end of a long, hard day. It catches me off guard, after I'd braced myself for distance, to feel him clinging to me like this. Instead of putting up walls between us, he's letting down the drawbridge and inviting me in.

If saying *I missed you* felt like a big declaration, this hug feels monumental. It feels like saying *I missed you* times a thousand. It feels like a confession.

I close my eyes as my heart sticks in my throat. After I spent so much of yesterday afraid for him and missing him more than I've ever missed him before—so much that it scares me even now to think about it—it's such a relief to hold him that I do some clinging of my own.

But when my arms tighten around him, Gareth flinches and emits a sharp hiss of pain.

"What's wrong?" I ask as he sets me back on my feet.

"Nothing." He takes his plate to the sink, putting that distance between us after all. "I'm a little sore, that's all."

I'm not letting him put me off that easily. Not after the way he just hugged me. It's too late for distance. We've already stepped over the line into something more.

I follow him to the sink and push up the back of his T-shirt.

"Hey," he protests and tries to twist away, but I've already caught a glimpse of what he's hiding under there.

"Stop that," I snap, refusing to let go as I spin along with him, the two of us locked in some sort of awkward back-to-front dance while I wrestle his shirt up to expose the giant bruise on his back. "Oh my god, what happened to you?"

"Ceiling collapse," he mutters. "Took a glancing hit. It's nothing."

It's *not* nothing. The bruise covers half his back and the top of one shoulder, mottling his skin with an angry mix of blue and deep purple.

He stiffens when I gently brush my fingertips over the darkest part.

Darius clears his throat behind us. "Sorry. Didn't mean to interrupt."

Gareth tries to jerk away, but I don't let go.

"Look at this," I say to Darius as I hold Gareth's T-shirt up to show off the bruise.

Darius moves closer, cradling Mr. Twinkletoes in his arms like a baby as he frowns at Gareth's bruised back. "Looks painful."

"I'm fine." Gareth twists away, and this time I let him go.

Darius opens the fridge and gets a carrot from the vegetable drawer. "You should soak that with Epsom salts," he tosses over his shoulder as he carries Mr. Twinkletoes and the carrot back upstairs.

"That's a good idea," I say.

Gareth snorts as he covers the leftover lasagna. "I'm almost positive Ozzy pees in our shower, so I'd rather die than soak in that bathtub."

"He definitely does," I agree. "You should use mine."

Unlike the upstairs bathroom with its combo shower-tub, mine has a big separate corner tub that my brother has never besmirched. To my knowledge, anyway. If he has, I do not want to know.

I go into my room and turn on the bathtub faucet. While I wait for the water to get hot, I search the cabinet under the sink. I'm pretty sure I remember buying some scented Epsom salt a while back, thinking I'd indulge myself with an at-home spa experience, and never followed through... *Yes!* I seize the bag in triumph.

"Damn, that's a hell of a nice view," Gareth says from the doorway behind me.

"Here, open this." I thrust the bag at him and go to check the temperature of the water.

"This isn't Epsom salt. This is froufrou girly bath salts."

"It's both." I reclaim the bag, tear it open, and dump what I guesstimate to be two cups worth into the steamy water. Then I pour in some more for good measure. Those bruises are *really* dark, and he's been moving awfully stiffly.

As the bathroom fills with the smell of rosemary and peppermint, I study Gareth from my perch on the edge of the tub. To anyone else, he probably looks the same as always. But I can see the difference in him, the strain around his eyes and the way the perfect lines of his face stand out in sharp relief.

"Why didn't you tell me you'd been hurt?"

"I didn't want you worrying about me." His rigid jaw and the way he's closed himself off by folding his arms across his chest remind me how snappish he sounded on the phone yesterday when he told me I didn't need to worry.

I cross the bathroom and put myself right in front of him so I can look into his eyes. "Was it on fire?"

"What?"

"When the ceiling fell on you, was it on fire?" I'm trying to sound very matter-of-fact, like an insurance adjuster collecting information for a report—*And can you tell me exactly how close you came to death or dismemberment, Mr. Kelly, so I can fill out the appropriate form?* But it's hard not to picture it: the motel I saw on the news yesterday engulfed in flames, Gareth blindly stumbling around inside that smoky inferno, an avalanche of burning ceiling collapsing on top of him.

I suspect I don't sound very matter-of-fact.

He drags his teeth over his lower lip. "No, it wasn't on fire."

"Really?" I search his face, trying to decide if he's telling me the truth or shielding me from it, but it's like studying a blank slate.

"It was long after the fire was out." He pulls me against him, and I sink into the shelter of his body. "I don't want you worrying about that sort of stuff, okay?"

"Do you think I can't handle it?"

"Whether you can or not, you shouldn't have to."

I'm not sure if he's saying that because worrying is what a girlfriend would do, or if he's simply trying to protect me from the scary reality of his job. "Friends are allowed to worry about each other."

"I know," he says, but it sounds like he's still wrestling with some lingering dissatisfaction.

When he kisses my forehead, it's not exactly forgiveness or permission, but it feels a little like both. It's an acknowledgement that I'm going to worry and he's going to let me even though he doesn't like it. Which is good enough for now.

Dropping the subject, I take a step backward, out of his arms. "Time for you to get naked."

The corner of Gareth's mouth kicks up.

"So you can get in the tub," I clarify, smiling as I shake my head. "I'll be in the other room."

"Where's the fun in that?" He blocks the doorway with his arm when I try to leave. "You could get in the tub with me."

It's not that I don't want that. I do. Very much. But I can't stop seeing that bruise on his back and the way his big body flinched in pain. I'm not going to risk hurting him by getting in that hard-sided tub with him.

"Not a chance," I say and duck under his arm.

Backing toward the tub with a grin, he drags his T-shirt off and tosses it to the floor. "You sure you don't want to reconsider?"

The man really knows how to fight dirty. I bite my lip as I stare at the flat planes of his broad chest stacked above the heavenly ridges of his abs.

When he hooks his thumbs under the band of his sweat-pants, I pull the bathroom door shut between us. Because I'm the one who needs walls and distance now.

"No coming out until you've soaked for at least ten minutes," I call through the door. "I'm timing you."

I hear him chuckle and try not to think about him naked only a few feet away. Or how easy it would be to open the door again and join him. I wouldn't even have to get in the tub. I could just watch...

No. Ozzy and Darius are right upstairs.

Not to mention Gareth is hurt. It's not a good idea.

I can be strong for both of us. Although I do go close and lock my bedroom door. Not that we're doing anything untoward in here—it's all perfectly innocent roommate stuff!—but just to be on the safe side. I don't need Ozzy wandering in and hearing Gareth splashing around in my tub. I'd have to explain why he's in there, and my brother would demand the right to use my tub too, and it would turn into a whole annoyance I don't need.

While Gareth soaks, I flop down on my bed and try to read the new Alexis Hall historical romance I started last night. But it's impossible to concentrate when I can hear every little sound on the other side of the bathroom door, every single splash and contented sigh and groan. The walls in this house are disconcertingly thin.

After thirteen minutes—yes, I did time him—I hear the tub start to empty and the louder splooshing sounds of Gareth standing up and stepping onto the bath mat. In my mind's eye I can see the droplets of water beading on his skin as he reaches for the clean towel I set out for him. I can see him rubbing that towel—*my* towel—all over his body, and all I can think about is how much I would like to trade places with that towel.

I'm still thinking about it when the bathroom door opens a

minute later, and Gareth comes out with that very same towel tied around his hips.

I swallow, trying to remember how to speak as I drink in the sight of him. Before I figure it out, he's on the bed, lowering himself over me.

My pulse leaps as he kisses me, his mouth hot and open, taking what he wants, and I lose myself in him, savoring the slightly salty taste of his lips, the warmth of his faintly damp skin, the solid weight of his body pressing down on me.

He makes a humming sound and nips at my lower lip. "It was lonely in that big, cold bathroom all by myself."

"You're injured," I remind him. Or perhaps it's me I'm reminding.

"I'm fine." He licks into my mouth, taking a long, leisurely taste of me before kissing his way down my neck. "I've spent the last few days thinking about all the things I'd like to do to you. All the ways I want to have you."

I shiver at the word *have*. Like I'm some sort of decadent dessert he's been saving for himself. The way he says it, *have* sounds like the sexiest word in the entire English language.

"Does that mean you want to—"

"Yes." His voice is husky and hot on my skin.

"No more going slow?"

He raises his head, his vivid blue gaze tangling with mine. "Not unless you need to."

I don't. I'm long past needing slow. When he looks at me, I don't feel the least bit self-conscious. Not when I can see how much he wants me and feel it in the way his body reacts to mine.

I want him just as much. But I'm not convinced this is the right moment for it, with our roommates upstairs and that pinched, worn-out look on Gareth's face.

To prove the point, I slide my hands around his rib cage and feel him suck in a breath and see his expression pinch even more when I touch his back.

"When you're feeling better." I can't believe I'm saying no. But when I finally get to have him, I want him at full strength, not wincing with fresh aches and pains. "Maybe tomorrow. But not tonight."

There's something else making me hesitate as well—a nagging sense that Gareth's using sex to distract me from things he doesn't want to talk about.

He grunts unhappily and rolls off me onto his back. The stiff, gingerly way he does it makes me certain I did the right thing.

"I'm sorry," I say anyway. I hate denying him anything, even if it's for his own good.

"Come here." He stretches his arm out, inviting me to snuggle up against him.

I don't hesitate to take him up on the offer, although I do it carefully, afraid of accidentally hurting him.

"I'm not that fragile," he grumbles, tugging my leg over his the same way he did the first time we cuddled.

"I know." I touch my fingers to his brow, tracing the too-pronounced lines there. His eyelids flutter, and I feel his body relax. I smooth my fingertips along his hairline and down to his jaw. "I know you're tough. But you're not immune to pain. And when you hurt, I hurt."

The way he looks at me, I think I might have said too much. But then his hand slides into my hair, and he pulls me close to press his lips against my temple. "I don't like you hurting."

"So you know exactly how I feel."

He makes a noise that's half a laugh and half a discontented grunt. "I hate knowing you're hurting because of me."

"Get over it," I murmur. "That's what friends do."

We both fall quiet as the word *friends* hangs over us. It gets bigger and heavier the longer the silence goes on, expanding until it feels like it's stolen all the air in the room.

"Is that what we are?" he asks, barely above a whisper.

"Aren't we?"

He doesn't answer, which feels like an answer of some kind, but I'm afraid to think too much about it.

Gareth's fingers toy with my hair while I lightly stroke his stomach, well above that cruelly taunting towel around his hips. It's barely holding on, mere millimeters from coming undone. I'm frankly amazed it's stayed in place this long, through all his crawling on the bed and rolling over.

"I couldn't wait to get home to you. I feel better like this."

"Like what?" I ask, my heart in my throat.

"When you're touching me."

I press my lips to his chest and feel a tremor go through him. He cradles my face and brings my mouth to his for a kiss so slow, deep, and tender it makes incautious words flit through my brain. Words like *mine* and *keep* that I don't dare say aloud and shouldn't even be thinking.

"I could take care of you," I hear myself say.

"You already did." Gareth's lips pull at my lower one in a soft suckle. "You are."

"No, I mean I could...do things to you."

He goes stock-still. Except for his breathing, which seems to have gotten louder and harsher all of a sudden. "What sort of things?"

"I don't know." That's a lie. I know exactly what sort of things I want to do. "You can tell me what you like, and I'll do it."

As long as I do all the work, that should be okay. It shouldn't hurt him.

"You can do anything you want to me and I'll like it."

"Anything?" My fingers skim along the edge of the towel around his waist, toying with the material that's so close to coming off on its own. It'd only take the tiniest flick to get it out of the way.

"Fuck, yes." His voice sounds strained, probably because of the way his stomach muscles are quivering under my hand.

"So you'd be okay if I wanted to do this..." I push up and touch my lips to the center of his chest.

"I'm absolutely okay with that," he says as he tugs the scrunchie out of my hair to let it spill over his skin.

Smiling, I pepper Gareth's chest with kisses, working my way over to one of his nipples. It's as stiff as mine, and when I circle my tongue around it, his breath makes this lovely hitching sound.

Once I've done that, it's easy to keep going, tasting different parts of his skin, licking and sucking and even biting a little. I don't know what I'm doing. I'm making it up as I go along, experimenting with my hands and teeth and tongue.

As I feel Gareth's body react to everything I do, it dawns on me how silly it was to be so worried about my lack of experience. It's not as if everyone likes exactly the same things done in the exact same way. There's no one universal sex formula to learn because everybody has their own individual tastes and preferences. Whenever you're with someone new, you have to learn them and adapt the way I'm learning Gareth now.

It's easy to tell what he likes best because his reaction gets much bigger. His chest heaves and he makes these sort of choking noises that make me wonder what type of noises he'd make if he wasn't trying so hard to be quiet.

I almost find out when I dip my tongue into his belly button, and he arches off the bed with a gasp loud enough to make me repeat the threat he used on me last weekend: "If you can't be quiet, I'll have to stop."

Ozzy and Darius are home, and the walls are *very* thin.

"Don't you dare stop," Gareth hisses. "I swear to god..."

He doesn't finish, because my mouth is on him again. I'm straddling his thighs, my hands planted on either side of his waist as I tongue his navel. When I lick a wet path down to his hip bone, he bites off a whispered curse. His whole body is shaking, beads of sweat clinging to his clean skin as his muscles contract and quiver, and I love that it's because of what I'm doing to him. It makes me feel unbelievably powerful.

But I think I've teased him long enough. It's time for the thing I've been slowly working my way up to. Gareth watches with a heated gaze as I tug the towel off his hips.

It's not as if I've never seen him naked before. Obviously. But I've never been this close or felt permitted to stare. I've certainly never had an explicit invitation to touch him the way I do now.

I want to be sexy and confident, but I lose my nerve a little. Stomachs and chests are one thing, but I don't know how to handle this unfamiliar appendage. I know it's supposed to be sensitive, which means if I do something wrong I could hurt it. I could hurt *him*.

"Please," he groans, his expression a mixture of torture and ecstasy. "I need you to touch me. I think I might die if you don't."

I like the sound of the word *need* on his lips, especially followed by the word *you*. It gives me the push I need to wrap my fingers around his shaft. It jumps at my touch, pulsing in my hand like it's got a mind of its own. The skin feels shockingly soft and delicate as I glide my fingers along its length experimentally.

Gareth holds himself still, letting me play, but hisses when I graze the underside of the flared head.

"Show me," I say. "Teach me how you like to be touched."

He swallows hard and wraps his big hand around mine. He squeezes, demonstrating how much pressure he likes—more than I would have expected!—then guides my hand up and down, showing me how to pump from root to tip with a little bit of a twist.

"Right here," he says, guiding my thumb to that sensitive spot on the underside. "Ohhhh yeah, just like that."

It makes him crazy when I rub that spot. He fists the sheets, biting his lower lip as his hips jerk beneath me. It's something else, seeing this big, strong guy rendered completely helpless by a single touch of my finger. So I decide to find out what happens when I rub that spot with my tongue.

What happens is that a ragged moan tears out of Gareth's throat as his back jolts off the bed. "Jesus, honey...ahh...keep doing that...just...fuck, do whatever you want."

What I want is to see him lose it completely. I'm so turned on right now my thighs are quivering almost as much as his. I love the feel of him in my mouth, the touch of that silky skin against my tongue, and the taste of the salty liquid leaking from the tip.

I take him as deep as I can, which isn't all that deep, I'm disappointed to say. But Gareth doesn't seem disappointed at all.

"Oh fuck yeah, honey. That's so good." His fingers tangle in my hair, clenching and releasing, but he's careful not to pull my head down or thrust into my mouth. "It's so fucking good."

My jaw aches and it's a little hard to breathe, but I don't care. I'm happy to do this for as long as he'll let me. I take my time, running the flat of my tongue over every glorious inch of him, watching his reactions as I do. When I cup his balls in my palm, his whole body shudders. And then he reaches down to guide my hand again, pressing two of my fingers against the strip of skin behind them.

It makes him grunt like an animal. "Fuck. Fuck. Fuck. I'm gonna...I'm gonna come, honey."

I want him to. I can't wait to see it. But it seems to freak him out a little.

"Seriously, you need to stop or I'm gonna do it in your mouth. Please, honey."

I don't want to stop, and I don't think he wants me to either. I think he's asking for permission. Our eyes lock as his fingers touch my cheek, and he's so exposed, so vulnerable, so breath-takingly lovely.

His cock swells as his body goes stiff, and then he floods my mouth. Thick spurts of liquid fill the back of my throat, and even though it's all I can do not to choke, it's such a thrill to feel him juddering and groaning as his hands spasm in my hair.

Even better is the look of wonder on his face afterward. And the way he pulls me into his arms.

And the tenderness of his kisses as he holds me close and whispers sweet words like *beautiful* and *sexy* and *perfect* that imprint themselves on the surface of my skin, leaving perma-nent marks behind.

25

GARETH

Lying in Casey's bed with her wild curls spread over my chest and her soft, perfect curves pressed against me, I feel oddly at ease. It's a novel experience for me, lingering in someone's bed like this. Simply being together. It feels a lot more intimate than sex.

Usually I'd be itching to get up and find my clothes by now. That's what I probably should do. But I'm way too comfortable to move. A forklift couldn't shift me from this spot.

All the aches and worries that were filling my head have gone quiet, their grating noise replaced by something soothing and completely new. Everything feels new, like a breath of early morning air at the start of a spring day. Like the clouds and shadows have been chased away by Casey's bright presence at my side.

Maybe it has something to do with the earth-shattering orgasm she just gave me, but I suspect it's more than that. Something much bigger. Something important that I'm afraid to name.

"Did you always want to be a fireman?" she asks, running her fingertips over my arm.

The question's treading on the edge of risky territory, and I hide my unease with a chuckle. "No. I wanted to be a dinosaur hunter."

Her soft laugh vibrates through my chest. "Not a lot of opportunities for that these days."

"You can imagine how crushed I was when I found out all the dinosaurs were already dead."

"When did you realize you wanted to be a firefighter like your dad?"

It's an obvious question, and one I always dread. I brace for a surge of grief, that hollow pit that always opens up in my stomach when I talk about my father, the one that used to be my constant companion in those terrible years after his death.

But it doesn't come. The sense of loss is still there, but it's muted, no longer as raw as it used to be. Maybe enough time has passed that I can talk about him without feeling bereft.

Or maybe it's that it's Casey asking. I find myself wanting to tell her things. Important, painful things I've never talked about with anyone else. Because I want her to know me, which means knowing about the past that made me who I am.

I shift my jaw to unclench my teeth. "Not until after he'd died."

Casey stills, her beat of silence letting me know she recognizes how hard this is for me, how huge it is that I'm answering instead of shutting down. "How old were you?"

"Sixteen."

"That's too young."

Too young for what? I'm tempted to ask, but I bite back the snarky, defensive reflex. I know what she means, even if I sometimes think I would have been better off if I'd been a lot younger and not so close to legal adulthood when I lost him.

"How did he die?" she asks, stroking my chest. "Was it...on the job?"

There's a tremor in her voice that sits in my stomach like a rock because I know she's thinking about the fire yesterday and that bruise on my back.

"It was a heart attack."

She looks relieved, although she probably shouldn't. Cardio-vascular events are the number one cause of firefighter fatalities, accounting for fully half of all line-of-duty deaths. My dad was just another medical data point. A forty-five-year-old seemingly healthy guy who came home from an uneventful shift and had a heart attack in his favorite recliner.

I don't tell Casey any of that because it would only scare her more. I also don't tell her that I was the one who found my dad on the living room floor with the TV still on when I came home that night after football practice.

"My parents were divorced," I say instead. "They split up when I was ten. My mom remarried, and I'd had some...issues with my stepfather, so I'd been living with my dad for a couple of years."

"What sort of issues?"

I can tell what she's thinking, but it wasn't like that. Not exactly like that, anyway. My stepfather never laid a hand on me. I can say that much for him at least.

"It wasn't all his fault." With the benefit of maturity and hindsight, I can admit to my share of the blame. I'm not proud of the way I picked fights and provoked Craig until he couldn't do anything but blow up. How I refused to show him any respect, in part because I'd been influenced by the things my dad said about him. "I was a mouthy, defiant little prick who made it my life's mission to push his buttons."

"In other words, you were a typical teenage boy."

I'm not going to argue with her. While I can acknowledge it's not really fair to expect a man with no parenting experience to expertly handle a fourteen-year-old with a chip on his shoulder,

I still carry hatred in my heart for some of the things Craig said to me, not to mention some of the things I've heard him say to my mom. The truth is he's not a kind or loving man, and he hasn't treated my mother all that much better than he treated me.

"He had a lot of rules and rigid ideas about how a kid should behave. And I resented him for marrying my mom and for thinking he had the right to lay down the law with me in his own house. I think I wanted him to kick me out so my mom would have to let me live with my dad."

Which was exactly what happened. Even though my dad worked the same twenty-four-hour shifts I work now, my parents decided I was old enough at fifteen to spend one night out of every three on my own, that it was better for everyone that way than having me and my stepfather at each other's throats.

At the time, I thought I was in hog heaven, getting to live with my dad, with his lax rules and regular overnight absences. He never got on me about my homework or grades, never nagged me to do chores, didn't complain about my language or enforce a curfew. But I can see now how it wasn't the best, at the peak of my rebellious teens, to be left so much to my own devices without enough supervision or structure. Looking back on it, that was really when things first started to go off the rails with me.

"After my dad died, I had to move back in with my mom and stepdad, and I didn't deal with it well. There was already bad blood between us, and I was in a pretty dark place. I was so angry all the time, about everything, and I took it out on everyone around me."

Casey takes my hand and threads our fingers together. It's the sort of comfort I wouldn't let anyone give me back then, and I don't exactly know what to do with it now. But the steady pressure of her fingers helps anchor me while I tell the rest of the story.

"I quit football, started skipping school and getting into trouble. Eventually I dropped out of school altogether. As things at home got worse, I stayed away more, crashing with friends as much as I could. I didn't so much move out as just stop going back."

"That's why you never mention your family or go home for the holidays."

"Pretty much." There's more to it than that. I haven't even gotten to the parts I'm most ashamed of yet.

"Do you talk to your mom at all?"

"The last time I called her was right after I moved here." I pause, shutting my eyes against the memory. "She told me she didn't ever want to hear from me again."

"Oh Gareth," Casey whispers. "That's an awful thing for a mother to do to her son. You don't deserve that."

"You haven't heard the whole story yet. She's got her reasons."

"I doubt it."

She says it with such unshakable faith, it makes my heart do something funny. She doesn't know how misplaced that faith in me is. She won't understand until I tell her.

I have to tell her.

I don't want to. But also I kind of do. There's this self-destructive part of me that wants her to know everything. Not just to prove how wrong she is, but to see if she can be pushed away.

"If you knew what I was like back then, you wouldn't even recognize me. I was an irresponsible, reckless fuckup who didn't give a shit about anyone or anything. Trust me, you wouldn't have wanted to know me."

"You were grieving," she says. "You weren't yourself."

Or maybe who I am now is the one who isn't really me.

Maybe I'm only pretending to be this upstanding guy, desperately trying to convince everyone I'm not still that waste of space I used to be.

I have to clear my throat before I can continue. "When I turned eighteen, I came into the money from my dad's firefighter death benefits. My mom and I fought over it. She didn't think I was mature enough to handle it responsibly, and I accused her of trying to get her hands on it for herself."

"Was she?"

I shrug. "Maybe. I know my stepfather was on her about it because he felt like he was owed something for putting up with me—besides the stipend they'd been getting for being my legal guardians. But she wasn't wrong about me not being mature enough. We had a big blowup, and I said some pretty awful stuff to my mom."

"You didn't mean it. People say things in the heat of—"

"I meant enough of it," I interrupt. "I told you, I wasn't someone you'd recognize."

Casey falls silent, but she keeps gripping my hand. Stubbornly refusing to let go.

"As soon as I got access to the money, I bought myself a new car, a stupidly expensive one, and got the hell out of Lubbock. I set out for the West Coast, traveled around for a while, and eventually ended up renting a place on the beach in San Diego."

"That sounds nice, after everything you'd been through."

It's hard to hear the hopeful note in her voice. She wants so much for it to have been nice for me, for this to be the part of the story where everything starts to get better. She's probably picturing it a lot like I did at the time: relaxing walks along the beach, learning to surf, making new friends in a new place, getting my head on straight.

I wish to hell that was true.

"It wasn't," I say with a grimace. "It was pretty much the

worst thing I could have done. I didn't get a job or go to grief counseling or make any plans for the future. I didn't have anyone telling me what to do anymore, so I was partying every night, drunk or high most of the time, spending money on stupid shit. I was hanging out with these losers I bought weed from who weren't my friends, they were just parasites who'd attached themselves to me because I was flush. But I couldn't see that at the time. I was too busy numbing myself, convinced I was having the time of my life."

I pause and take a breath, girding myself to confess the next part. "I lived like that for three years. Until the money ran out. I blew all of my dad's death benefit like a fucking idiot, and I can't even tell you where the money went."

Casey's smile is unbearably gentle as she brings my hand to her lips. "Did you know the part of the human brain responsible for rational thinking and our awareness of long-term consequences doesn't fully develop until the age of twenty-five? That's why adolescents react to things emotionally and make decisions without thinking. They literally can't help it."

I know she's trying to make me feel better by absolving me of responsibility for my mistakes, but it doesn't undo what I did. There's no excusing it.

"Casey, it was five hundred thousand dollars."

It's all I can do to say the number aloud without choking. The enormity of the figure still haunts me, keeping me up at night sometimes. I'll never stop feeling sick over it.

"Whoa," she breathes, and I know I've finally shocked her.

"Do you know what I could have done with that much money?" My voice is shaking with anger, but it's all self-directed and weighted with shame. "If I'd invested it and exercised a little restraint, I could have lived comfortably for the rest of my life. Or I could have given it all away to charity and done some fucking good in the world. It was my dad's legacy, and I threw it all away on takeout and bar tabs and a bunch of worthless crap I don't even remember anymore."

"Gareth." Casey's voice is soft with sympathy I don't deserve.

"No," I say, shaking my head. "I fucked up. I have to own it."

"Tell me the rest. What did you do after the money ran out?"

"I sold off everything I had—except my car, which I needed to get out of San Diego and go somewhere cheaper where I could afford to live. I drifted around for a bit, taking jobs for food and gas money wherever I could find them. Eventually I got steady work installing appliances in Tucson. The job was miserable, but one of the guys there needed a roommate, so I had a decent place to sleep. That was when I decided I needed to come back to Texas. As part of my dad's death benefits, I get free tuition at any state school here. So I worked until I'd saved up some money, got my GED online, and applied to the fire academy at Texas A&M. And, well...here I am."

"You pulled yourself together and built a whole new life for yourself."

"Yeah, I guess." After I hit rock bottom and didn't have any other choice.

"Look at me." Casey cups my cheek, forcing my gaze to her. "I'm proud of you."

"How can you say that after everything I did?"

"What did you do? You spent some money that belonged to you."

"It wasn't just *some* money."

"You didn't hurt anyone except yourself."

"I think my mom would disagree with you there."

"I don't give a crap what she thinks. You were a child in pain, and she wasn't there for you the way you needed."

"It wasn't her fault."

"It wasn't your fault either."

My throat thickens. No one who knows the whole story has

ever said those words to me. I don't know if I believe it, but it feels good to hear it nonetheless.

Casey leans in and kisses me. "All that story proves is how incredibly strong you are. That money wasn't your father's legacy, Gareth. *You* are. The man you became, the one I'm looking at right now who's kind and caring and works hard helping others—*that's* your father's legacy."

"How do you do that?"

"Do what?"

"Make everything better?"

I'm supposed to be the strong one. The protector. But she's the one defending me. Easing my pain. Holding me close and murmuring soothing words against my skin.

And for the first time since my dad died, I don't feel all alone in the world.

It should make me feel more secure, but it brings a flicker of unease. *Attachment leads to suffering.* The more you allow yourself to need something—or some*one*—the more you have to lose.

And I know better than anyone how easily the things that matter can slip away.

26

CASEY

F*riends.*

I've been thinking about that word a lot today.

What does it mean to be friends? Where exactly is the line between friends and more-than-friends? Because it feels like I've crossed that line with Gareth. After last night, it feels like that line is a dot receding in the rearview mirror.

But I'm not sure he feels the same.

My gut says yes, but I can't trust my gut. My gut told me to go to Sonic and get Frito pie for lunch, and now my gut doesn't feel so great. So clearly my gut doesn't know what's good for either of us.

Halfway through the afternoon I text Gareth to ask how his back is feeling. What I really want to know is if he's feeling well enough for us to have sex tonight. But that doesn't seem like something I should put in a text, especially when he's out on a job with my brother and Darius today. I'm hoping Gareth will know why I'm asking without me having to explicitly say it.

He answers with a thumbs-up emoji.

I feel like he could have been a little more expansive there, but I'll take what I can get.

It occurs to me that *I'll take what I can get* more or less sums up my whole relationship with Gareth, which isn't a particularly nice thought.

A few minutes later, he sends another text.

GARETH

> See you after work? The usual time?

I take a page from his playbook and reply with a thumbs-up. It seems like the way someone who's just a friend would answer.

Is that what we are?

It's the question Gareth whispered in my bed last night, and it keeps playing on repeat in my head, along with his deafening silence after I replied with *Aren't we?*

What am I supposed to make of that silence? Especially considering everything else that came after. How he opened up to me about his past, and I held him in my arms with so much fierce affection, wishing I could build a protective wall around him while my heart wept for everything he'd been through.

It feels like something has definitely changed between us. Something big.

And tonight we're going to have sex. All-the-way sex, that is. If you subscribe to the patriarchal concept of female virginity, I'm about to give him mine.

Rationally, I know sex doesn't have to mean anything we don't want it to mean. But it means something to me, no matter how much I've tried to pretend it doesn't.

I have a sneaking suspicion it might mean something to Gareth too, but I can't take my hinky gut's word for it.

What I do know is that there's no one else I'd rather have my first time with. There's no one else in the world I trust as much as I trust Gareth. It's the only thing about all of this I'm absolutely certain of.

———

TODAY IS the longest Friday in the history of Fridays. It takes forever for five o'clock to roll around. When it finally does, I'm out the door of the gym like a shot.

I haven't seen Gareth since he snuck out of my room last night. He was still in his own bed when I left for work this morning, which was a little disappointing. It would have been nice to see him. Which is not a very *friends* thing to be feeling.

Neither is the way my heart leaps when I get home and find Gareth in the kitchen. Or the urge I have to walk straight into his arms and set my mouth against his.

But Darius and my brother are in the kitchen too, helping Gareth make dinner. So I keep my hands and my mouth to myself, even when Gareth smiles at me and my stomach does a cartwheel.

I'm so, so glad to see him. But now that we're together, I want us to be together the way we are when we're alone, the way we were together last night in my room.

It drives home how very much my reaction to Gareth is not a *friends* kind of reaction. Because Darius is my friend, and I don't have any urge to put my hands or my mouth on him. I don't sit around at work and think about him all day long.

"What are we making?" I ask, keeping a careful distance from Gareth.

"Nacho pizza." He's wearing the apron my brother gave him for Christmas, the one with a drawing of a woman's naked torso on the front so it looks like he has boobs. It was supposed to be a prank gift, but Gareth loves it. He claims it helps him get in touch with his feminine side, but I'm pretty sure he just thinks it's hilarious.

When I reach out to steal a slice of olive, Ozzy tries to smack my hand. "Didn't you hear him? It's *not yo pizza*."

I groan and roll my eyes as I pop my pilfered olive in my mouth. "Awful. That's the worst dad joke I've ever heard."

He only looks more pleased with himself as he goes back to dicing tomatoes. "Dad jokes are supposed to be awful, so what you're saying is that it's the *best* dad joke you've ever heard."

"Jesus, dude. You want to cut your fingers off?" Gareth commandeers the chef's knife from Ozzy and proceeds to give him a lecture on the proper way to dice a tomato.

The guys like to joke about me being the house mom, but Gareth's pretty mom-ish himself. I might be more organized when it comes to making rules and keeping the house clean, but Gareth's the one who's always cooking for us and making sure there's food in the house. He's the one who keeps the first aid supplies stocked and knows how to treat a cold, wrap a sprained ankle, and what to do when Ozzy gets his hand stuck in the hazelnut butter jar. *Again.*

Maybe it's because Gareth's a firefighter, so he's used to cooking for the people on his shift and dealing with medical emergencies. But after what he told me last night, I have to wonder if it has something to do with losing his dad and being forced to fend for himself at such a young age. Maybe he's trying to recreate the sense of family he lost. The thought makes my throat thicken.

Ozzy and Gareth are still bickering over the proper way to dice a tomato, and Darius is wearing a rare smile on his face as he grates a block of cheddar-jack cheese. They're all in a good mood after spending the day together.

The kitchen is a mess. Ingredients, dishes, and cutting boards litter the counter, along with half-consumed beer bottles. It's chaos, but it's the good kind of chaos. The kind that feels like home. Like family.

It makes me feel guilty for being disappointed to find Ozzy and Darius here. I like it when we all hang out together like this.

It's the kind of evening Gareth probably needs a lot more than he needs to be alone with me.

My gaze drifts over to him as he and Ozzy continue trading verbal jabs. Gareth's kneading pizza dough, which isn't something I would have expected to find sexy, but the sight of his long fingers working and stretching the dough has me oddly mesmerized. And that's before he tosses it into the air and casually catches the spinning disc of floppy dough with a dexterity I'll never have.

"Where'd you learn to do that?" I ask.

He grins and tosses the dough into the air again. "Worked at a pizzeria one summer in high school. Girls used to come in every day just to watch me do this."

"I'll bet they did." I probably would have been one of them if I'd lived in Lubbock where Gareth grew up.

"I want to try," Ozzy says. "I'll bet I can do it."

"Fuck no," Gareth says, warding him off with an elbow. "You think I'm letting you drop our dinner on the floor?"

Once Gareth's got the pizzas assembled and in the oven, we all pitch in to clean the kitchen. When the pizzas are ready, we crowd around our small dinner table, trading jokes and laughter while we eat. Gareth is a warm presence at my side, but aside from an occasional brush of elbows we keep a careful distance between us.

By the time we've polished off the pizza, it's almost time for Darius to leave for work. I don't know what Ozzy's Friday night plans are, and I'm afraid to ask, afraid that everyone will see through me and guess that I want to be alone with Gareth. So when the cleanup's done, I leave the guys chatting in the kitchen and go to take a shower.

It's nice to get out of my work clothes and wash the lingering smell of the gym out of my hair. I consider changing into a sundress to look nice for Gareth, but I don't know. We're supposed to be keeping this casual, and I don't want to seem like I'm making a big deal out of it. Even if it feels like a big deal to me.

It's not a date, I tell myself. Gareth and I are not dating. Which means I shouldn't be dressing up for him.

I don't even know for sure that anything is happening tonight. It's possible Gareth's made plans with Ozzy instead.

Playing it safe, I stick with more typical comfy evening attire —a tank top and a pair of cut-off shorts. I don't think to check my phone until I've finished drying my hair. That's when I see the text from Gareth.

GARETH

They're gone. Meet me in my room?

27

GARETH

I'm a nervous wreck. I'm not the one who's supposed to be nervous, but I'm a fucking mess. I don't know how to do this with a woman who knows me. I can't hide from Casey. She breaks down all my barriers.

My hands shake as I fumble with the lighter. It takes multiple tries before the flame sparks to life.

As much as I've been anticipating this moment—impatient for it, even—the truth is I've been dreading it a little too. Not because I don't want to have sex with Casey. But because I'm afraid of how much I want it. And more afraid of what it will do to me.

After that blow job last night I nearly threw myself at her feet and confessed my never-ending devotion. If that's what her mouth does to me, what's going to happen when I finally sink myself inside her? It makes me weak just thinking about it. I've never wanted anyone as much as I want Casey. It makes it difficult to keep myself under control.

No, not just difficult.

Impossible.

After I finish lighting the candles, I stand back to survey the room. The bed made up with freshly laundered sheets, the candles flickering on every flat surface, the rose petals I stole from our neighbor's yard to scatter on the floor.

It would have been nicer if we could have had a quiet candlelit dinner beforehand, just the two of us. But I couldn't figure out how to get rid of Ozzy and Darius. Maybe I should have offered to take Casey out, but people might have seen us, and that would have raised questions neither of us wants to answer. So I did what seemed like the next best thing.

But now, as I'm looking at everything, I'm wondering if it's too much. *Too* romantic.

Not that Casey doesn't deserve romance. But I'm not sure I'm the guy she should be getting it from. I don't know if she wants it from me.

It's unfamiliar, this sort of uncertainty. Being too romantic isn't a problem I've ever had before.

There's a soft knock on the door, which means it's too late to change my mind about the candles and rose petals. I'm in it now.

I drop the lighter into my bedside table drawer and say, "Come in."

Casey pushes the door open and freezes, drawing in a breath. The flickering flames dance in the pools of her wide brown eyes as she takes in the room. "Oh wow. You did all of this for me?"

"Too much?" I ask, shifting on my feet.

She bites her lip and shakes her head. "No, it's..." Her eyes find mine as she breaks into a smile. "Amazing."

A punch of giddy pleasure hits me square in the chest, and I grin so wide my cheeks hurt. Fuck, I'm such a goner. She's turned me into someone who makes cheesy romantic gestures, and I don't even care.

Her gaze skates down my body, taking in the button-down

shirt and jeans I changed into. "I should've dressed up. I almost did, but then I thought—"

"You look perfect exactly the way you are."

She does. I wouldn't change a fucking thing about those shorts that show off her legs and that thin tank top that drives me wild. She's so gorgeous, so lovely, my chest feels like it might cave in.

I'm not conscious of moving, but I've crossed the room to bury my nose in her hair. My arms wrap around her as I breathe her scent deep into my lungs. No one on earth smells like Casey.

A fierce surge of lust goes through me, but I don't kiss her yet. Once I start, I'm not sure I'll be able to stop. Instead I cup her cheek and gaze into her eyes. "Are you still sure this is what you want?"

I have to stop and check. To make sure she feels safe and in control. It's important.

She leans into my touch and smiles. It might be the best smile I've ever seen. There's nothing tentative or nervous about it. It's a smile that says she knows exactly what she wants. And what she wants is me.

"Yes," she whispers. Then says it again, louder and more insistent, as she rises on her toes. *"Yes."*

Casey's lips touch mine, and then we're kissing like we need each other's oxygen to breathe. It's hunger and heat, seeking tongues, and warm, wet mouths.

God, she's delicious. I can't get enough of kissing her. Can't get enough of *her*.

I clutch at her in barely restrained desperation, my fingers digging into her hips and fisting in her hair. *Too rough*, I warn myself. *Too frantic*. But she's almost as frantic, pushing her hands up under my shirt and pulling me against her rocking hips.

Her breathy whimpers push all thoughts of going slow from my head. With a grunt, I grip her ass and walk us toward the bed. We're all clumsy scrabbling hands as we undress each other in between kisses. She undoes my shirt buttons while I slide down the zipper of her shorts. When my questing fingers slip inside to rub over the already-damp fabric between her legs, she drops her head back with a moan. I run my tongue up her neck, then I'm dragging her top off and pushing her back onto the bed. Her skin is so soft and smooth I can't stop touching it. I can't stop tasting it either, stroking my tongue over her pillowy breasts and sucking at the rosy tips of her nipples.

Mine, I think with every pounding beat of my heart. *Mine, mine, mine.*

That's what I'm thinking as I pull her shorts and underwear off, spread her thighs, and press my face between them. *Mine, mine, mine.*

My name spills from her lips as she rocks beneath my tongue. Her hands sink into my hair, putting me where she wants me, as greedy for it as I am for her. Damn, I love the sounds she makes and the way she pushes into me. I sink a finger inside her tight channel, pumping in and out, then adding a second one as I rub my tongue over the place she's most sensitive. When she comes, it's loud and uninhibited, and all I can think is what a privilege it is to see her like this, to know I'm the only one who ever has.

After the pulsing around my fingers fades, I ease them out and kiss the inside of her thigh and her stomach. She watches me with her lower lip caught between her teeth.

Mine, I think again as I kiss my way up her beautiful body. When I reach her mouth, I dip my tongue in for a taste, and she moans, sucking at it hungrily.

"Now," she says, stroking her fingers over the bulge in my pants. "I want you now."

I drop my head to the mattress with a groan and move her hand, because I won't last long if she keeps touching me.

Standing, I shed the rest of my clothes. Casey scoots into the middle of the bed, watching me with eager eyes. She keeps watching as I grab a condom out of the nightstand, and as I roll it on. I should probably have let her do it. I'm supposed to be teaching her how to do things like that. But I don't think I could stand it. It's already so fucking arousing, the way she's watching me, my hands fumble like it's my first time instead of hers.

I'm shaking like a leaf as I lower myself over her. Dipping my head to kiss her, I settle my hips between her legs. My cock is so hard it hurts. When I rub it against her slick, wet heat, she sighs into my mouth and strokes her hands over the curve of my ass.

Focus, I order myself, clenching my jaw. I need to do right by her.

"Still good?" I ask, watching her closely.

She nods and squeezes my glute, urging me to move.

Canting my hips, I notch myself against her entrance. God, it's so warm and tight, I can't wait to sink inside her. But there's no way in hell I'm rushing this part. My lips press against her temple as I cautiously nudge forward.

Almost immediately, I feel Casey tense beneath me.

"Does it hurt?" I ask, stilling.

"No, it's just a lot bigger than your fingers."

"Do you want to stop?"

"No, keep going."

I push in a little more but don't get far before I encounter resistance. "You okay?"

She nods, but her jaw's set like a vise.

"Honey, take a breath. You've got to relax."

"I know. I'm trying." She's the opposite of relaxed, her eyes squeezed shut and her body rigid.

"Casey," I say softly, reaching up to cup her cheek. "Look at me."

She does, and something in my chest pulls tight at the trepidation in her eyes. She looks so fragile beneath me. A primal, caveman need to protect her ignites in me, burning away everything else.

"You know I love you, right? I'd never do anything to hurt you." The words spill out, impulsive and unguarded. I'm barely aware of what I'm saying, only of the need to make her feel safe, to be strong for her and take care of her.

"I know," she whispers, her expression softening. "I know that."

"You're the one in control here. We can stop anytime you want."

"I don't want to stop. It's just so hard not to tense up."

"That's all right. We'll go nice and slow." I kiss her, gently at first, then deeper and harder as her mouth softens, opening for me.

The more we kiss, the more her body relaxes beneath me. When I reach between us to stroke her clit, she gasps and I slip farther inside.

"You okay?" My arms shake as I hold myself still above her.

"More," she says, tilting her hips. "Give me more."

Holy fuck. Her movement makes me slide in deeper, and a ragged groan tears out of my throat. I've died and gone to heaven. She's squeezing my dick so hard, I think I actually black out for a second.

"Still good?" I rasp, fighting the urge to thrust into her like a fucking beast.

"Yeah. God, it's so..." The look of wonder on her face steals my breath. Her eyelashes flutter as she rocks against me. "So good."

Jesus Christ. I'm seated deep in her slick, snug heat, and good doesn't begin to cover it. Electric shocks of pleasure lick down my spine as my dick throbs inside her. I hold still for a few seconds, giving her time to adjust to the intrusion before I withdraw a little and slowly glide back in, going even deeper.

"Oh!" Her eyes widen with her breathy gasp. "That's nice. Do that again."

On the next stroke of my hips her body welcomes me, and she moans as I sink all the way home, burying myself deep inside her. I think I probably moan too, but I'm barely aware of it. The sensation is out of this world. It's like nothing I've ever felt before, this perfect fitting together.

"Yes," Casey says before I can check in with her. "More of that."

I give her what she wants, slowly, carefully, straining for self-control as I feel her clench around me. Watching her face with every stroke. She's too fucking beautiful like this. Pink and dewy, flushed with pleasure. I have to dip my head to steal a taste of her luscious mouth.

There's a sharp pang growing inside me, something unruly and so fierce it burns me from the inside out. When Casey's eyes lock with mine, it cracks my chest wide open.

I've never had sex with someone who matters to me this much. It makes this as much a first for me as it is for her. Because it's the first time sex has ever meant anything. The feeling hits me so strongly it's painful, but it's the good kind of pain, like loosening up a knotted muscle.

My thrusts grow faster as I give myself over to the need roiling inside me. I'm losing control, but Casey's losing it right along with me, taking her own pleasure with a wild abandon that sweeps me along with her. She urges me on with her nails raking my back, with her rolling hips, and with her words.

"More," she pleads, begging for relief. "Gareth, please."

The way she gasps my name is the most erotic sound I've ever heard. The way her pussy clamps around my cock lights my whole body on fire. We both cry out as I pound into her. *Too hard, too rough.* But she's meeting me thrust for thrust, locking her legs around my hips to take me deeper, welcoming everything I'm giving her.

Nothing exists except her. Right now. This moment. Us.

She utters a cry as her body stiffens against mine. Her climax shudders through her, tugging at my dick in dizzying pulses. Somehow I manage to hold it together long enough to see her all the way through it. Only when her moans have quieted do I fall over the edge, burying my face in her neck as I groan and shake with the intensity of my own release.

We clutch at each other in the trembling aftermath, neither of us speaking as the reality of what we've done settles over us. My chest hurts like there's something inside me trying to claw its way out, but I can't find the words I want to say.

So instead I tip her face up and set my mouth against hers, so soft and sweet. I could kiss her like this forever, hold her in my arms forever, keep her close forever.

28

CASEY

I wake up in my own bed. Alone.

I have a foggy memory of Gareth kissing me goodbye in the pre-dawn dark when he left for his shift. I vaguely remember scooting into the warm spot he'd recently vacated and slipping back into a boneless sleep, enveloped by the lingering scent of him on the pillow.

We'd ended up falling asleep in my bed last night. Eventually. After he'd blown out all the candles in his room, I'd admitted to being a little sore from our activities. Whereupon Gareth had carried me downstairs and insisted on running a bath for me. Then he'd insisted on getting into said bath with me, and we'd engaged in further activities that had probably canceled out any restorative benefits of the bath. Not that I was complaining. I also hadn't complained when we moved our activities to my bed, where Gareth continued my sex education.

Those memories aren't foggy like this morning's goodbye kiss. I remember every detail of last night—the feel of Gareth's hands on my hips as he moved inside me, the taste of his skin all dewy with sweat, the sound he made when he came. I remember the way he tucked himself against my back when we'd finally exhausted ourselves, the weight of his arm curled around my waist, the occasional twitch of his muscles as he drifted off to sleep.

You know I love you, right?

I remember those words most of all. I wasn't sure what to make of them at the time, and I'm still not sure now. It didn't feel like a declaration of romantic love. There was too much offhandedness in the way he phrased it, as if he didn't consider it much of a revelation. *Of course I love you*, he seemed to be saying. *You already know that, don't you?*

He might as well have tacked a *buddy* or a *pal* onto the end. The fact that he hadn't repeated the sentiment supports the theory that it was a purely platonic pronouncement of love. Between two friends. Who just happened to be having sex.

I shouldn't attach too much meaning to it. It would be a mistake to read too much into it or anything else we did last night.

I know that.

But it doesn't stop the word *love* from bouncing around in my head the whole rest of the day.

———

"SOMETHING'S DIFFERENT ABOUT YOU," Kenzie says, studying me over the rim of her coffee mug.

It's Sunday, the morning after the morning after I lost my virginity, and we're catching up over breakfast at Bluebonnet Kitchen. Kenzie's been extra busy with work and stuff lately, and I've been busy with...well, Gareth mostly, so it's the first time in almost two weeks that we've been able to get together.

It's nice to get some girl time in. I spend way too much of my life around men who make fart and penis jokes all day long. Not that Kenzie doesn't also make fart and penis jokes, but she does it with a voice in a higher register.

"I'm pretty sure I look the same as always," I say as I watch Kenzie's grandmother bark at one of Kenzie's teenage cousins for being too slow with his tables' coffee refills. The McKenzie family has been running Bluebonnet Kitchen for longer than I've been alive, and Granny Rose rules the place with an iron hand. Kenzie did her time working here too, all through high school and college until she got out of it by going to vet school.

Kenzie's eyes narrow. "Something's changed. Don't tell me— I'll figure it out."

She can't possibly tell I've had sex from looking at my face.

Can she?

No way. Impossible.

"Maybe it's the new job?" I suggest.

"I don't think so. But congrats on that, by the way. When do you start?"

"I talked to Dennis and my last day is Friday. I start at the bookstore the very next day."

"Are you excited?"

"*So* excited."

My life feels like it's finally coming together. Ever since I graduated from college, I've felt like I was stuck in a holding pattern, lagging farther behind with each passing year. But now I have a sex life and I'm about to have a job I actually care about, like a real adult. I don't know if working in the bookstore is meant to be my calling, but it's a project I'm invested in. I can't wait to get started and throw myself into it.

"I know what it is!" Kenzie snaps her fingers and leans across the table to whisper, "You had sex, didn't you?"

Okay, maybe she *can* tell from my face.

I gape in dismay. "Is it really that obvious?"

"Only to me. It's not like anyone else can tell. Well, maybe Granny, but that's because she's got a touch of the second sight."

Lord, I hope not. I adore Granny Rose, but she also scares me a little, and not just because Kenzie claims she can give people the evil eye.

"Tell me everything," Kenzie says. "Leave nothing out."

I press my lips together. Everything that's transpired between Gareth and me feels too personal to share with anyone else, even my best friend. Talking about it would turn it into something trivial and superficial. It's too big, too important to offer up as fodder for discussion or to satisfy Kenzie's well-meaning curiosity.

Ever since Gareth left my bed early yesterday to go to his shift, I've been in a strangely pensive mood. The sex was obviously incredible, but there's that same bittersweetness threading through the memories that keep intruding on my thoughts.

"Okay, then just give me the highlight reel," Kenzie says at my reticence. "You owe me at least that much since I'm the one who gave you the initial push in Gareth's direction. I need to know if he did right by you, or if I'm going to have to make his life a living hell until the day he takes his last breath."

I smile, touched and amused at Kenzie's loyal pit bull energy. "You can let him live out his life in peace. He behaved like a perfect gentleman."

"God, I hope not."

I clamp my mouth shut as Granny Rose bustles up to the table with half a dozen plates balanced on her meaty arms.

"Two of my special breakfasts for my wee Rosie and her best pal," Granny announces as she sets more food in front of us than even my brother could eat—eggs, bacon, sausage, hash browns, grits, biscuits, and pancakes.

Kenzie enjoys the privileges of favorite grandchild status, both because she was named after Granny Rose—although she doesn't let anyone outside her family call her by her real first name—and because she's the first doctor in the family.

"Thank you, Granny," Kenzie says as her grandma bends down to smack a kiss on her cheek.

"Yes, thank you very much, Granny," I chime in.

Granny Rose cocks a hand on her hip and squints at me. "Everything all right, love? You look like you're not quite yourself this morning."

I stammer something about being hungry but otherwise perfectly fine while Kenzie tries and fails to keep a straight face.

Granny's look says she's not buying any of what I'm selling, but she promises to send over a couple of cinnamon rolls from the tray about to come out of the oven, as if we didn't already have enough food to feed an entire team of powerlifters. Then she hustles off to the kitchen and I can breathe easy again.

"Don't worry about Granny," Kenzie says as she slathers butter on her pancakes. "She could tell the moment I had sex for the first time too."

"God, what ever happened to Brian Urquhart," I muse, recalling the boy Kenzie lost her virginity with in a short-lived ninth grade dalliance. "I haven't thought of him in ages."

"He went to clown college after graduation."

I pause in the middle of dowsing my eggs with hot sauce. "You're joking."

"I wish I was. Waiting until you're twenty-eight doesn't seem so bad compared to having a literal clown in your sexual history, now does it?"

"Okay, but he was cute in high school. You can't deny that."

"I can barely remember, honestly. So do you feel any different now that you've cleaned the cobwebs out of the womb room?"

"Not really," I say, even though a lot feels different now. But the things that feel different have more to do with my heart than my hymen.

"Told you. The whole virginity thing is a lot of hullabaloo over nothing."

"Well," I demur, "I wouldn't say it was *nothing*."

Kenzie breaks into a grin. "Are you saying our Gareth lives up to the hype?"

"And then some."

"Look at you, your face is bright red."

"I put too much hot sauce on my eggs."

"Uh huh." Her eyebrows waggle. "I hope that means he took the *Enterprise* to warp speed."

"Very much so. Several times, in fact."

"Hell yeah, girl. Fist bump."

I can't help my smile as I touch my knuckles to hers.

"And are you two still just friends or...?"

That bittersweet feeling washes over me again, and I focus on my pancakes. "Still just friends."

"Things aren't weird between you now that you've done the no-pants dance?"

"No. I mean, I'm sure they won't be. He had a shift yesterday, so I haven't actually seen him since we...you know."

"Put a hole in your welcome mat?"

I huff a laugh. "I'm sure it'll be fine."

I'm not sure of any such thing, but I need it to be fine, so I'm going to eat my weight in breakfast foods and pretend it will be.

Kenzie studies me as she chews a piece of bacon. "So you're really sticking with this whole just friends thing? Are you sure all this extracurricular activity hasn't awakened any previously repressed feelings?"

I shove a giant bite of pancakes into my mouth, keeping my gaze superglued to my plate.

"Ruh roh," Kenzie says, watching me.

I swallow. "It doesn't matter."

We agreed to sex and nothing more. Only in secret and only temporarily. I have to abide by the terms of the deal.

Even if I've already violated it in my heart.

I promised not to fall for Gareth, but that's exactly what I've done.

It's too late to do anything about it now. These feelings are too far gone. I've been too far gone for a while, even if I didn't want to admit it.

I love Gareth, and not in a platonic *of course I love you, old buddy, old pal-o-mine* kind of way. I love him in a bone-shaking, heart-stopping, *stay with me forever* kind of way.

That's what I really want. Not just *stay with me tonight*, but *stay with me always. Keep me, love me, let me be yours and say you'll be mine.*

But I'm too afraid to ask for what I really want. Afraid to put him into the position of having to say no. Afraid to put myself in the position of having to hear his no.

It feels like the sort of thing that might be hard to move past. And he made me swear we wouldn't let sex ruin our friendship.

I'll never forgive myself, he'd said.

My feelings are a problem for me, but they don't have to become a problem for Gareth. For us. I can hold up that much of our bargain at least. I promised nothing would change between us, and so it won't.

What does it matter, when it comes down to it, what kind of love I feel for him? He's still my friend, and he's still not interested in being my boyfriend. That's how it is.

I got everything I needed out of our deal. Experience. Self-confidence. Some excellent memories to keep me warm at night. That'll have to be enough.

Kenzie frowns across the table at me. "Your feelings absolutely matter."

I slug down a mouthful of coffee. "Gareth doesn't do girl-friends. You know that as well as I do."

"That doesn't mean he can't. It's not like an immutable law of physics."

"But he doesn't want to. That's the reality and hoping other-wise won't change it."

"I think you should talk to him about it."

"Why? What good will that do?"

She gives me a pointed look, like I'm being particularly obtuse. "Honesty is generally considered a good thing between friends."

I know she's right, but the thought of admitting how I feel to Gareth makes my stomach churn. I may not be the same meek wallflower I was a few weeks ago, but that doesn't mean I'm ready to go around making romantic confessions to people who are unlikely to welcome them. That's advanced-level confidence, and I'm not there yet.

"If I developed romantic feelings for you, would you want me to tell you?" I ask Kenzie.

"You bet your ass I would. First of all, it's a huge compliment, and I *love* compliments. Secondly, I'd want us to talk that shit out. I'd hate for you to keep something like that from me. Because then things would be all weird between us and I wouldn't know why."

"But it would just be a different kind of weird if I confessed my feelings, because then you'd have to tell me you don't return them."

"Unless I *do* return your feelings." She lifts a brow. "I'm curious why you're discounting that possibility."

"Because you're straight?"

Kenzie makes a noise of frustration. "Okay, but we're not actually talking about me here. We're talking about Gareth, who is very much attracted to women in general and presumably to you in particular, or he wouldn't have slept with you."

"Yeah, but—"

She holds up a hand, stopping me. "How will you ever get what you want if you don't ask for it?"

"Sometimes asking isn't enough."

"Maybe not. But it's a start. You'll never win the game if you refuse to even step onto the field."

"You can't lose a game you're not playing," I point out stubbornly.

"That's not true. An automatic forfeit is still a loss. And that's what you're doing—conceding without a fight." Kenzie leans back in the booth and folds her arms. "You need to tell Gareth how you feel. Maybe he'll surprise you and rise to the occasion."

29

GARETH

I only meant to take a short nap when I got home after shift this morning. It was a relatively quiet night without any callouts after one a.m., so I actually managed to catch a little sleep in my bunk. Not a lot, since our mattresses aren't much more comfortable than sleeping on a bag of sand, and Quincy snores like a jet engine. But I got enough sleep that I figured I could take a quick power nap while Casey was still sleeping in this morning.

Apparently my internal sleep clock didn't agree because it's past noon when I wake up. I curse myself when I see the time. Those four hours I just frittered away could have been spent with Casey.

Leaving her bed yesterday morning was the hardest time I've had dragging myself to a shift since I was a brand-new probationary candidate. I've been missing the feel of her body ever since, carrying a sense of incompleteness around with me that throbbed through the whole shift like a phantom pain.

The house is oddly quiet as I pad down the hall to the bathroom. Ozzy and Darius's bedroom doors are wide open, and there's no sign of them upstairs. That might be why I slept so long. Usually one or the other of them wakes me up with their stomping around.

When I wander downstairs after brushing my teeth, I find Casey on the couch in front of the TV. There's a nature doc on the screen, and she's got the sound turned down with the closed captions on.

"You could have turned the volume up."

She startles at the sound of my voice before flashing a quick smile. "I didn't want to wake you up."

"I wish you had." I walk around the couch and sink down next to her.

She scoots farther away, giving me extra space I don't want. "How was your shift?"

"Nice and uneventful." I rest my hand palm-up on the couch between us, and she lays her hand in mine. "I didn't mean to sleep so long."

Her shoulder twitches. "I went to Bluebonnet Kitchen with Kenzie this morning."

"Nice." I can't stop staring at Casey's legs. In particular, I'm staring at the hem of her shorts where it's gapping wide enough to tease me with the riches hidden within.

"I brought back a ton of leftovers if you want them."

My dick twitches at the same time as my stomach gurgles. I'm starving, but for a lot more than just breakfast. "Where's everyone else?"

"Darius is helping Ozzy with a job."

In other words, they'll probably be gone for most of the day. That's excellent news because I need to put my hands all over Casey. I want to taste her mouth and then her pussy. I want to wrap her legs around my hips and bury myself inside her. On this couch, but also in her shower and again later in her bed.

Tonight, tomorrow, and every day, as much as she'll let me.

Now that I've experienced the slick pulse of her pleasure

clenching around my dick, I'll never be able to get enough. I don't want to give this up. I can barely remember what life was like before Casey was mine, but I don't want to go back there.

I lean over to kiss her, cupping my hand around the nape of her neck, feel her mouth soften under mine, and plunge my tongue in deep as her lips part for me. I'm dizzy with the taste of her, with how much I missed her the last twenty-four hours, with how good it feels to be with her again.

"Gareth," she breathes as I slide my hand inside her shorts. "We shouldn't be doing this."

I squeeze the back of her neck. "It's fine. They'll be gone for hours."

"No, that's not—" She pulls away, and I let her go.

I don't want to, but I do.

"What's wrong?" I search her face, but she ducks her head, avoiding my eyes as she twists a strand of hair around her finger. "Casey?"

Something's shifted, and I don't know what it is.

"We should talk about...this." She flaps her hand in the space between us.

Well, fuck. That can't be good.

I sit back and drag a hand through my hair, waiting for her to say whatever it is she wants to say.

Casey clears her throat, still not looking at me, but I can feel the tension radiating off her. "First of all, I need to thank you."

I choke back a humorless laugh. Because what the shit? She's fucking *thanking* me? As if she still thinks I've been doing her a favor? As if she hasn't figured out by now that she's the one giving me a gift.

"You've been wonderful," she goes on. "Everything you've done for me, it's meant more than I can tell you. But you've officially fulfilled your end of the bargain, so consider yourself off the hook."

Off the hook? Is she serious with this? I don't want to be off the hook.

"That doesn't mean we have to stop." I reach for her hand, and it's a relief when she lets me take it. "We're good together."

Her expression softens as I rub my thumb over her knuckles. "We are. That's the problem."

"I don't see how that's a problem."

"You're too hard to resist."

"So don't resist me." I lean in to kiss her neck, but she shrinks back, slipping her hand out of mine and pressing it against her stomach.

"That would be beyond the scope of our arrangement."

"Fuck the arrangement."

"Which part of the arrangement?" she asks, watching me closely. "The part where we keep it a secret? The part where we're not supposed to get attached? Or the part where we don't let it change our friendship? What are you envisioning for us exactly? A short-term fling? An open-ended friends with benefits situation? Or are you proposing we start dating?"

I don't know what I'm proposing. I haven't thought that far ahead, so I don't have an answer ready. I just wanted more time with her. More of that feeling I have when we're together. I want to hold her. Kiss her. Lose myself in her for a little longer.

I didn't think beyond that to what I was really asking or whether it's what Casey needs. Or what she wants.

Reckless, a voice whispers in my head. *Selfish.*

"That's what I figured," she says at my silence, as if she already knows what I want even if I don't.

I've ended up in one of those state-of-the relationship conversations I've always avoided like the plague, and now it feels like I'm trapped in a trash compactor with the walls closing in around me. I bring my hand to the back of my neck where I can feel the prickle of my fight-or-flight reflex trying to kick in. "What are you asking for?"

"Nothing at all," Casey says. "I know you're not a relationship type of guy. I don't expect anything from you."

I don't think she means those words to wound. But hearing them from the woman who knows me better than anyone else coats my insides with a cold, oily feeling.

She rises to pace across the room, leaving me to stare at the back of her head. "This is entirely a me problem. Because I'm a relationship type of girl. I want a lot more than just no-strings sex. Which is why, as much as I've enjoyed everything we've done, I think it's best if we end it cleanly now." When she turns around, her eyes are regretful. "The whole point of this was to help me find a boyfriend, right? So that's what I should probably do."

What if I wanted to be your boyfriend?

The words are right on the tip of my tongue. I even open my mouth to say them...

But nothing comes out.

How can I ask Casey to take a chance on me with my track record? I'm the worst kind of bad bet.

I wish I hadn't told her all those things about my past, because now she knows who I really am. I'm the irresponsible, unreliable fuckup who makes all the wrong choices. I mess things up and then I bounce. Why would she ever put her faith in me?

I'd never be able to stick it out. I don't even believe in true love or happily ever after. I'm not the right man to give Casey what she needs. Christ, I've never even wanted to be in a relationship.

Until now.

But is that what I *really* want?

Or do I only think that because I'm selfishly trying to hold on to something I never deserved in the first place?

"So," Casey says after a lengthy silence.

I have a feeling she was waiting to see if I'd step up.

But I don't.

I can't.

Because she's right. I need to let her go be happy with someone worthy of her, someone who's capable of giving her everything she wants. A better bet than me. I care about her too much to try and keep her for myself when I know I'd only end up hurting her.

"Okay," I tell her like a fucking grown-up. "If that's what you want."

I don't feel like a grown-up. I feel like shit, but I'm trying to do the right thing.

Casey stares at the floor. "I think it's best if we go back to being just friends."

All I can do is nod. It's too hard to speak around the lead balloon lodged in my throat.

Her brown eyes seek out mine. "We're still good, right?"

It feels like I'm wading through deep water as I force myself to my feet and move toward her. I'm afraid she'll shrink away again. But she doesn't. Not even when I pull her into a hug. A breath shudders out of her as she settles her head against my chest.

"Of course we are," I mutter into her hair.

God, it fucking hurts to think this might be the last time I get to hold her close like this. But somehow I make myself let her go after only a few seconds. It's not nearly long enough. There's no such thing as enough of her. But I numb my reckless heart and make my body move as if I'm fine with all of this.

We don't look at each other when we step back. I try to tell myself this isn't disappointment coiling through me as she walks away. I tell myself that I'm relieved, that it's better this way.

But it doesn't feel like we're good. It feels like everything's wrong.

Casey stops at the threshold of her room and clutches the doorframe. "Here's the thing," she says with her back to me and her voice so soft I have to strain to hear it. "I know we said this wasn't supposed to change anything between us, and I know I promised I wouldn't get clingy. But you also told me I should ask for what I want..."

I hold my breath, rooted in place, as she turns around.

"I've been too afraid to admit that I have feelings for you, but if there's anyone I trust enough to be honest with, it's you." Her eyes are shiny when they lift to mine. "So this is me being honest and saying that I don't want to give you up."

She's standing there offering me her heart. Even though she knows it might get broken, she thinks it's worth the risk. She thinks *I'm* worth the risk.

I can't repay her faith in me with anything less than the same courage she's shown. "I don't want to be off the hook. I like being on your hook."

Casey's chin wobbles. She starts to take a step toward me but stops herself. "I can't just be your friend with benefits or secret booty call. I want to be more to you than that. I know you don't date—"

"I could," I say, stepping forward. "I could try dating."

The smile that lights up her face is a beautiful thing to see. "Would you want to try dating me?"

"Fuck yes. If you'll let me."

She blinks at me like I'm out of my mind. "*Let you?* Do you actually think there's a chance I wouldn't?"

"I don't know. You probably shouldn't. I'll probably be terrible at it."

I'm still not convinced I'm doing the right thing. This feels like something the old me would do—thoughtless, rash, selfish. Jumping into dangerous waters without a life jacket or any consideration of the consequences. But it also feels right in a way that all those bad choices never did. It feels like something's finally clicking into place. The last time I felt like this was my first day at the fire academy.

Casey crosses the room to me and lays a hand on my chest. Her eyes are soft with understanding, and I know she can feel my heart pounding. "I seriously doubt that."

"I've never been anyone's boyfriend before. You know that, right?"

"That's okay. I've never been anyone's girlfriend before. We can figure it out together."

I pull her against my body. "I like the sound of that. You being my girlfriend."

This is what I want. More of this feeling. More of Casey. I'm certain of that much at least.

I want to make her laugh as much as I want to make her come. I want to cook her dinner and watch nature documentaries together snuggled under a blanket on the couch. I want to curl my body around hers and fall asleep to the sound of her breathing. I want her face to be the first thing I see in the morning and the last thing I see at night.

I've never felt this way about anyone before. All the women I've been with, and not once have I been able to see a future with any of them. But with Casey, I can't imagine my future without her.

"I like the sound of it too," she says.

I tip her face up to mine and trace my fingertips over her cheek. "I'm warning you now, I'll probably screw up. No, not probably. Definitely."

"You don't have to be perfect for me."

That settles it. I'm going to hold on to this woman with both hands and do my damnedest to deserve her. Maybe it won't be good enough, but it won't be for lack of trying.

I bend my head, and she rises up, meeting me halfway. I'm smiling as I kiss her, but I'm also making a promise. I'm pouring my heart into this, giving Casey everything I've got.

No more shields between us. No boundaries. No holding back. No running.

My hands tangle in her hair as I devour her mouth, kissing her like it's the first time and I'm learning her all over again. Her hands slide under my shirt, stroking, urging. Our breaths grow ragged as our kisses turn messy. I'm so hot I can barely get enough oxygen. My achingly hard dick is suffocating between us.

I back Casey toward the couch and we fall onto it, fumbling with each other's clothes.

"Mine," I murmur, dipping my tongue into her cleavage.

She's fucking *mine*.

Her legs loop around my waist, and she moans as my hips rock against her. God, she's so fucking perfect. I can't get enough. I'm utterly lost in the taste of her skin and the beautiful sound of her breathy gasps.

Which is probably why I don't hear the front door open.

I don't realize we're not alone anymore until Ozzy's anguished shriek cuts through my consciousness like a gunshot.

"Arrgh! What the fuck? *That's my sister!*"

30

CASEY

Gareth jumps to his feet so fast it makes me dizzy.

I wrestle my shirt down before I peer over the back of the couch.

Yep, that's my older brother standing there in a state of shock. And just behind him is a stone-faced Darius.

Well, this is fantastic.

Gareth's a disheveled mess, his hair wild from me running my hands through it, his shirt hiked up, and his sweatpants conspicuously tented. I doubt I look much better. It couldn't be more obvious what we've been up to, even if they hadn't caught us in the middle of a hot and heavy make-out session.

I'm just glad it hadn't progressed any further. The thought of what they might have seen if they'd walked in five minutes later makes me shudder.

"Dude!" Ozzy chokes out, looking faintly green. "You're defiling my sister!"

"He's not defiling me," I snap, getting to my feet. "I'm a consenting adult whose personhood isn't defined by my sexual activities."

"Yeah, well, in my head you'll always be five years old, so

you'll have to excuse me if I don't want to see my best friend plowing my baby sister." Ozzy presses his fists against his eyes. "Christ on a motorboat! You know I've got a sensitive gag reflex."

Gareth finally finds his voice. "Ozzy, man. Look, I—"

I swivel my head, cutting him off. "Don't you dare apologize to him. My brother gets no say in what you and I choose to do."

He wisely shuts his mouth again.

"Unbelievable," Ozzy moans, clutching his head. "On the TV couch, for fuck's sake! I watch *Bluey* on that couch! That's a sacred space you've besmirched with your love juices!"

I turn to Darius, who still hasn't uttered a word, although he's doing plenty of looming and glowering. "Do you have anything you want to say about it?"

His head jerks from side to side. "Definitely not."

"I need a drink," Ozzy mutters, stalking to the fridge. He twists the cap off a beer and drains half of it in one long guzzle.

I glance at Gareth again, not liking the deep furrow in his brow. He just agreed to something that I know he's a little skittish about, and I'm afraid he'll use my brother as an excuse to change his mind.

"So what is this, exactly?" Ozzy asks. "Are you two just fucking or are you actually, like, dating or something?"

Gareth swallows as his gaze darts to me.

My heart starts to sink.

But then he moves to my side and takes my hand, squeezing it tight in his. "Casey and I are dating."

The breath I was holding rushes out of me.

"For real?" Ozzy says, dumbfounded. "How long has this been going on?"

"It's new," I mumble at the same time as Darius says, "At least a week."

My mouth falls open. So does Gareth's.

"You *knew*?" Ozzy squawks like an indignant chicken.

Darius shrugs.

"How did you know?" I ask him.

"It was obvious," he says. "Were you actually trying to hide it?"

"Why didn't you say anything?" Ozzy demands.

Darius gives him a long look. "If people want to keep their love lives to themselves, it's none of my business. Is it?"

Ozzy snaps his mouth shut with an audible click.

My sister senses start to tingle, and I narrow my eyes at my brother.

"New house rule," he announces before I can ask what that look Darius gave him meant. "No rumpy pumpy in the living room. I don't care what nasty business you two get up to, as long as I don't have to see it or hear it or know it's happening. Allow me the grace of plausible deniability when it comes to my sister's sex life."

"You're not pissed at me?" Gareth asks.

"Dude. As if I'd think my best friend isn't good enough for my sister. I mean, come on. I've been waiting for you two idiots to figure out your shit for years. I can't believe it took this long."

"Wait, what?" I say.

"Everyone knows you two have hot pants for each other," Ozzy replies.

"Define everyone."

Before he can answer, the front door opens, and it sounds like our house is being invaded by congested orcs.

"Toodle-oo!" my mother trills over the cacophony of snorting and scuffling. "Can we come in?"

My blood runs cold, and not because of the imminent orc invasion. I'd take a whole army of phlegmy orcs over a visit from my mother on a good day, and this is definitely not a good day for it.

Gareth's already jumped away from me and is frantically

trying to smooth his hair down into something that looks less like sex hair. At least the tentpole in his sweatpants has deflated. His poor penis has probably retracted all the way inside his body by now.

"It's Mom and Dad," my father calls out. "Don't bother hiding the weed if you've got any. Remember, it's rude not to share."

Dad's an artist who thinks he's also a comedian. He has an online store where he sells prints of his original paintings of cats doing human things like sitting on the toilet, playing Scrabble, and doing yoga. His series of popular boy bands reimagined as cats went viral on social media and are selling so fast he can't keep them in stock.

"Sorry, we're all out of weed," Ozzy calls back before giving me an evil grin. "Oh, shoot, did I forget to mention Mom and Dad were on their way over? I guess I got distracted by the sight of you two getting your—"

"Hi, Mom! Hi, Dad!" I shout over him in a panic. "Come on in!"

Gareth looks like he's seriously considering throwing himself out a window.

I don't blame him. In fact, I may follow suit.

As if getting walked in on by my brother and Darius wasn't uncomfortable enough, now my parents are here to complicate an uncomfortable situation even more.

Seeing how Gareth's never had a girlfriend before, I'm guessing he's not real keen on the whole meet-the-parents thing. Not that he hasn't met my parents plenty of times, but that was when he was just one of their son's friends. He wasn't meeting them as *their only daughter's very first boyfriend*, which is some advanced-level parent interaction I doubt he's ready for. Talk about a trial by fire.

I know I'm not ready for it. Not when Gareth and I have been officially dating for all of five minutes. I need more time to prep. Preferably with alcohol. Or Xanax.

But there's no reason we have to tell my parents yet. As long as we act normal and keep my brother from spilling the beans, everything will be fine.

The orc sounds get louder as my mother's dragged into the living room by two snorting French bulldogs straining against their rhinestone leashes. Both dogs are wearing clothes, one in a yellow satin dress and the other in a blue velvet jacket with a lace cravat.

It takes a second to click that they're dressed as Belle and the Beast from *Beauty and the Beast*. Because of course they are. In addition to being the mayor, my mother is Instagram-famous for dressing up her two prized Frenchies, Popcorn and Milk Dud, and posting pictures of them reenacting famous scenes from movies.

And no, I'm not jealous that her Dogstagram account has five hundred thousand more followers than my humble Book-stagram.

Except maybe I am a little jealous.

Mom teeters on her heels as she bends over to unclip the dogs' leashes. "Be free, my babies."

It's Sunday, so she's dressed for church. Mom believes in dressing her best everywhere she goes, so her church clothes aren't much different from her everyday wardrobe, which consists mainly of pastel-colored skirt suits that look like she's perpetually headed to a bridal luncheon. But on Sundays she pairs them with a hat. Today's hat is lavender like her suit, with two gargantuan purple silk mums on the brim.

My dad, on the other hand, doesn't believe in either going to church or dressing up if he can help it, and Mom gave up trying to reform him years ago. This morning he's in his usual tie-dyed T-shirt, plaid shorts, and Birkenstocks.

"Hello, pumpkin." Dad ambles over to plant a kiss on my cheek while Popcorn and Milk Dud zoom around the living room like goblins hopped up on cocaine.

"Ow," Gareth says when Popcorn crashes face first into his shin, leaving a wet eyeball print behind.

Mom swans over to beam a smile up at Darius. "Hello, dear. Your hair is looking absolutely luxurious today."

Mom's always adored Darius, who weirdly seems to tolerate her too-muchness a lot better than he tolerates most other people.

"Thanks, Mrs. G. I've been using a new conditioner." He dutifully stoops so she can give him a double cheek kiss, because my mom likes to pretend she's Princess Margaret instead of the mayor of a rural Texas town.

When Mom turns to hug Ozzy, Darius drops down to the floor where he's immediately mobbed by Popcorn and Milk Dud, who scramble into his lap and try to lick his beard.

"What are y'all doing here?" I ask when Mom comes over to hug me next.

"Surprise inspection!" Dad chirps.

He's kidding.

Mostly.

They don't actually conduct surprise house inspections. Although they do like to stop by occasionally just to "check in with our offspring." Which I suspect is both them wanting to see their kids and wanting to make sure we haven't significantly lowered the value of their rental property.

Mom grasps my chin and frowns at me. "Sweetheart, have you been sick? You look like you've just rolled out of bed, and your face is all pink and blotchy."

Ozzy lets out a loud snort, and I shoot him a death glare while Mom checks my forehead for a fever.

"I'm fine. This is just what my natural complexion looks like."

"Are you drinking enough water? Hydration is so important for your skin, and it keeps you regular. You're not stopped up, are you? I think I've got some magnesium in my bag."

Ozzy's doubled over clutching his stomach now, and I can't even look at Gareth.

Dad plops onto the couch and starts flipping through the channels. "Keep talking about her bowel movements, Jeannette. That'll definitely make your daughter's face less pink."

While I appreciate that he's trying to stick up for me, saying the words "bowel movements" out loud isn't helping as much as he thinks it is.

Popcorn and Milk Dud spot Mr. Twinkletoes hopping down the stairs and race over to greet him. The rabbit loudly thumps his back feet, and the snorting dogs both come to a screeching halt in front of him, wagging their tail-less butts.

"Aww, did you find your best friend?" Mom coos. "You love your bunny-wunny buddy, don't you sweet babies?"

The dogs' eyes bulge with barely contained excitement as Mr. Twinkletoes gingerly sniffs each of their noses. Because they know who's boss, and it's absolutely the rabbit. When Mr. Twinkletoes is satisfied by their subservience, he flops onto his side. Popcorn and Milk Dud gleefully flop down next to him, and the three animals lose their minds rolling around together on the floor.

I tense when Mom sets her sights on Gareth.

He manages to find his smile as she delivers the requisite cheek kisses. "Nice to see you, Mrs. G."

"Gareth, dear. Such a handsome young man."

I wince as she pinches both of his cheeks, but he doesn't appear to mind. Like Darius, he actually seems to enjoy being fussed over by my mom. Which makes a lot more sense now that I know about his family history.

For all their eccentricities, my parents are pretty cool as parents go. I should probably try to appreciate them more, even when they insist on talking about my bowel movements in mixed company.

"You're much too good a catch to still be single," my mother says to Gareth. "When are you finally going to let some nice young woman lock you down?"

Gareth's smile freezes in place.

"Well, actually," Ozzy says, breaking into another evil grin, "Casey and Gareth were just—*mummph*."

He doesn't finish that sentence because I've hurtled myself at him and slapped my hand over his mouth to shut him up. Ozzy tries to shake me off, but I cling to him like a monkey while Popcorn and Milk Dud run in circles around us, yapping and play growling. Darius watches from the floor in amused silence.

I only release my brother when something slimy and warm swirls over my palm. "Ugh! You *licked* me, you filthy animal!"

"Play stupid games, win stupid prizes," Ozzy retorts.

"Now, now, children," Dad says without looking away from the TV.

"Casey has some news to share," my brother announces with a foolhardy lack of fear for his life.

"Oh?" my mother says, turning to me expectantly.

"Ozzy borrowed Dad's Firebird without asking when he was fifteen!" I shout in desperation. "He's the one who put the ding in the door!" If he didn't want to be thrown under the bus, he should have kept his dumb mouth shut.

"Casey and Gareth are dating!" Ozzy hollers before our parents can react.

I'm going to eviscerate the rat fink with a rusty garden trowel. Just as soon as I can get my hands on one.

Mom's eyes go round as they snap to me. "Is that true?"

"Um," I say, casting a *help me* look at Gareth.

Who calmly walks over and slips his arm around me.

"Yes, ma'am," he says, tugging me firmly against his side. "Your daughter owns the one and only key to my heart." He's wearing his charming, cocky smile, but his eyes are soft and earnest as he gazes at me, telling me that he's still all in, no matter how awkward the situation is.

All I can do is smile back at him, utterly smitten.

"I knew it!" my mom shrieks, loud enough that Popcorn and Milk Dud put their heads down and cover their ears with their paws. "Didn't I tell you, Wayne? *I knew it!*"

"What do you mean you knew?" I choke out as Mom pulls me and Gareth into a strangling three-way neck hug.

"Oh please, sweetheart. You two have been making soppy eyes at each other for as long as I've known Gareth. Eeeeee!" She squeezes us again, briefly cutting off my airway. "I'm so happy!"

"I hope you're treating my daughter well," Dad says from the couch.

I think he's trying to look threatening, but he's not really the threatening type, especially with Mr. Twinkletoes sitting in his lap.

"Like the queen she is," Gareth answers solemnly.

"Oh, but sweetheart, couldn't you at least brush your hair for your new beau?" Mom despairs, ruining my good mood.

"Brushing curly hair makes it frizzier," I answer with a sigh.

"If you'd only let me take you for a Brazilian blowout."

"I like her hair exactly the way it is," Gareth says, reaching up to touch one of my messy curls, and I fall in love with him all over again.

My mom sniffles. "Goodness, he's charming."

Milk Dud tries to hump Gareth's leg, but I nudge him away because *that's my man* and no one gets to hump him but me.

Dad moves Mr. Twinkletoes off his lap and rises from the couch. "I think this news calls for celebratory tacos."

My dad likes to celebrate everything with tacos—graduations, birthdays, local elections, the garbage being picked up on the designated garbage pickup day. As far as he's concerned, there's no event too big or too small to commemorate with tacos.

While Dad's out getting tacos for everyone, I whip up a batch of margaritas, because today requires tequila. Darius helps me squeeze the limes while Gareth salts the rims and somehow manages to remain utterly charming as he deftly deflects my mom's incessant and intrusive third degree about our relationship. Whatever his trick is, I need to get him to teach it to me.

"I'm glad you finally got laid," Ozzy whispers to me at one point while Gareth's busy talking to my mom.

I can't decide if I should kick him in the shin or hug him.

Until he adds, "If he ever hurts you, let me know. Friend or no friend, I'll make him wish he'd never been born."

That settles it. My brother gets a hug.

Dad comes back with approximately a million tacos, and we eat them standing around the kitchen island since we only have four dining chairs. Popcorn, Milk Dud, and Mr. Twinkletoes snuffle around our feet hopefully in case anyone drops a taco on the floor. No one does, but Darius slips some chicken to the dogs and a piece of lettuce to the rabbit. Gareth stands beside me, unobtrusively stroking my back whenever my mom says something to annoy me, and refilling my margarita glass until I don't even mind that she keeps dropping references to all her friends' kids' weddings.

I thought it would be stressful and terrible, making him hang out with my family now that we're a couple, but it turns out to be kind of great. Gareth looks happy—not like he's pretending to be happy for my benefit, but like he's actually having a good time. Watching him clown around with my brother, laugh at my dad's dumb jokes, and smile at my mom's not-so-veiled hints drives home how lucky I am. To have him. To have the family I do. And to have all of us together like this.

Still, I can't help apologizing to Gareth later, after my parents leave. Because maybe he's just good at pretending, and he's actually been miserable and annoyed all day. I might know him better than anyone else does, but there are some things he keeps locked up tight, even from me.

"I'm sorry about my parents," I say as we're cleaning up the kitchen. "I didn't mean for you to get thrown into the deep end like that with no warning."

Gareth pulls me into his arms, and it's like sinking into a warm bath. Cozy. Soothing. Exactly what I need.

"It was fine," he murmurs into my hair as his hands smooth over my back. "The only bad part was not being able to touch you like I wanted."

Ozzy makes a gagging noise, and Darius takes him by the scruff of the neck and marches him upstairs, leaving us alone. God bless Darius. As soon as I start my job at the bookstore, I'm going to buy him a whole sackful of romance novels.

"You weren't freaked out?" I ask, watching Gareth's face for hidden signs of tension. "Because I definitely was."

He cups my jaw in a hand that's still damp from rinsing margarita glasses. "I know your mom pushes your buttons, but I thought it all went fine, considering."

"It did," I agree. "My parents adore you. I was just afraid it might have been a lot of pressure to put on you so soon."

"I like being around your family. But even if I didn't, that's what boyfriends do, right?"

My heart fills with that same feeling I get when I think about my new job, like my life is coming together. That path I've been trying to find? Being with Gareth feels like a key part of it. It's like something sliding into place that I didn't know was missing.

To think he was right here in front of me all this time, and I never even suspected he might be meant for me.

"I mean, I assume," he adds with a goofy grin that matches mine. "I seriously have no idea how to do this boyfriend thing. I'm just faking it here."

"You're doing A-plus work so far," I say, rising on my toes to kiss him.

He backs me up against the counter as he slants his mouth over mine.

This is what I've always wanted. Not just *a* man but *this* man.

It took me a stupidly long time to figure it out. But now that I have him, I'm holding on with both hands and I'm not letting go.

31

GARETH

It's still sinking in that I've got a girlfriend, but the more I get used to the feeling, the more I like it.

Gotta say, I was not expecting that at all.

I actually caught myself *humming* yesterday at the firehouse. I am not someone who ordinarily hums, but there I was, thinking of Casey and humming Taylor Swift's "How You Get the Girl."

Thank god no one heard me, or I'd never live it down.

The strange part isn't that Casey and I are together, but how easy it is. In a lot of ways, it's like nothing between us has changed. We're still friends, we still make each other laugh, and we still have as much fun hanging out as we always did. Only now with lots of hot, sweaty sex added to the mix. Not to mention all the kissing, touching, and cuddling, which is new for me, but I like it as much as I like the sex.

I love being able to run my hands over Casey's body and hold her close as much as I want. When we're in the kitchen, I can brush aside her hair and press my lips to the back of her neck. When we're watching TV, I can pull her into my lap and breathe in her scent. When we're out together, I can put my arm around her, and she'll fit herself against me like there's nowhere else she'd rather be.

Like she's doing right now. We're on our first "official" public outing as a couple tonight, meeting up with some friends at King's Palace to celebrate Casey's last day at the gym yesterday and her first shift working at the bookstore today. It's not the first time we've been here together, but it's the first time we've been here *together* together, not as two individuals who are part of the same group but as a paired-off unit.

There's something oddly satisfying about that. I love knowing that I'm her guy and she's my girl, and I love that everyone else knows it too. Every time she smiles at me or I slip my arm around her, my chest fills with pride that she's all mine. But also relief. It's nice not having to be "on" anymore. I don't need to pay attention to any of the women around us or play along with their flirting. I can relax and just *be*, knowing the only woman who matters likes me for who I am and not how charming I can be.

I never really understood what it means to be part of a couple. I always assumed relationships came with lots of murky rules and expectations, and that I'd chafe under all that pressure. But it's not like that at all. There's no pressure with Casey. The only thing I have to do is try and make her happy, which isn't a chore at all. It's a pleasure and a privilege because seeing her happy makes me happy.

There are other benefits I didn't fully appreciate. We're not just a couple, we're a team. Partners. I've been on my own for so long, I forgot what it means to have someone who's always in your corner, always there to offer support, leap to your defense, or step in to provide whatever you need—sometimes before you even know you need it. Sure, it means compromising, but that's what teams do. They look out for each other and take turns being the one who gets leaned on and the one doing the leaning.

Casey's leaning on me pretty hard at the moment. Quite literally. She's tucked up against me with her head resting on my shoulder. Even though she's been trying to power through, she's exhausted after a long day on her feet learning the ropes at her new job. But she's happy too. When she got home tonight she was bursting with stories about her first day, her face lit up and animated even through her yawns. After I ran her a bubble bath and rubbed her aching feet and back, she got a second wind, but now that she's eaten and had most of a beer, she's starting to fade again.

In fact, I think she might be asleep on my shoulder.

When I squeeze her hip and kiss the top of her head, Casey stirs and makes a happy sound.

"How you doing?" I murmur. "You want to go home?"

"Nooo." The hand she's resting in my lap squeezes my thigh. "I'm having a good time."

"Really? Because it seemed like you might be taking a little bit of a nap on me."

"Napping on you is a good time."

I catch Connor Autry watching us from farther down the table. As soon as he catches me catching him, he yanks his gaze away and tips back his beer.

Funny thing is, I don't feel any resentment toward him anymore. Because I'm the one who got the girl. I guess maybe some of my irrational anger was jealousy that Casey was so hung up on him, but she's with me now. I don't have any reason to be jealous of Connor. If anything, I feel sorry for the guy. He looks like he might be having some regrets over letting her slip through his fingers.

Lucky for me he did.

I stroke my hand over Casey's back. "You can nap on me as much as you want, honey. I just thought you might be more comfortable doing it at home in bed."

We've only been together a week, and I've already started thinking of Casey's bed as *our* bed. How wild is that? I've spent every night I'm not on shift in her bed, and I can't see myself wanting to sleep in my own room ever again. The nights I am on shift, the awful twin bunk at the firehouse feels even more uncomfortable than usual without Casey's body next to mine and the sound of her breathing to lull me to sleep. Yesterday I even brought one of the pillowcases off her bed to work, just to have her scent with me in my bunk.

Jesus, I've turned into such a fucking sap.

"We can't leave," she says. "We haven't gotten to dance yet."

The live music doesn't start for another twenty minutes, so we're all camped out at one of the long wooden tables at the back of the old country-western dance hall. King's Palace is a local landmark that goes back to the late eighteen hundreds when it served as a community center for German immigrants who used to hold Saturday night dances and Sunday morning sermons here. The King family bought it back in the fifties to convert into a dance hall, and people still flock from Austin and San Antonio for the live music on Friday and Saturday nights.

The smell of pit smoke drifts in through the open hangar-style door from the food truck in the parking lot that sells the best barbecue in town. Seriously, their brisket is some of the moistest I've ever had, and don't get me started on the wonders of the German sausage. The remnants of everyone's dinners litter our end of the table, along with several buckets of beer and a whole lot of empty bottles.

I dip a waffle fry in ketchup and hand it to Casey. If she wants to do any dancing she'll need the carbs for energy. "You want another beer?"

"Yeah," she says, lifting her head from my shoulder. "I do, actually."

When I reach my hand out, Darius snags a bottle of Shiner

Bock from the bucket in front of him and passes it to me. I dry it on my shirt and twist the cap off before giving it to Casey.

"Hey, do you get an employee discount?" Kenzie asks her, leaning on the table across from us.

Casey swallows down a mouthful of beer and nods. "Fifty percent off at the café and twenty-five percent at the bookstore."

Kenzie whistles. "You know that means you're buying all my books for me from now on?"

"I figured," Casey says.

I rub the back of her neck. "I'm going to need to build you some more bookcases, aren't I?"

"Maybe." A smile spreads across her face, and fuck, she's so pretty. My heart can't take it when she smiles at me like that—without holding back, her big brown eyes all warm and soft. She's so much more than pretty. She's fucking perfect.

My hand lifts of its own accord to wind one of her curls around my finger.

"God, you two are so fucking cute, making heart-eyes at each other," Kenzie says.

Weirdly, everyone took the news of our change in relationship status in stride. The distrust and reproach I expected to encounter, given my manwhore reputation, never materialized. All our friends seemed both happy to see us together and completely unsurprised. I still don't understand what they thought they saw, but apparently everyone else knew how we felt about each other long before we did. Go figure.

"Aren't we though," Casey murmurs and fists her hand in the front of my shirt to pull my mouth against hers. I suckle her lower lip, and her fingers tighten in my hair as she angles her head to deepen the kiss.

"Quit tongue-fucking my sister, or my dinner is gonna come back up all over the both of you!" Ozzy hollers as he chucks a handful of french fries at us.

Kenzie elbows him sharply in the ribs.

"Ow!" he yelps, rubbing his side. "Motherfucker."

Quincy shakes her head in bemusement. "That's not what tongue-fucking means, dipshit."

I untangle a fry caught in Casey's hair and wing it across the table at Ozzy, hitting him square in the forehead.

"Don't be an asshole," Darius growls at Ozzy. "Let them enjoy being happy."

"God knows it took them long enough to get here," Jamal says. "Anyone know who won the pool?"

Casey's jaw drops. "There was a *pool*? Whose idea was that?"

Everyone looks at McCafferty, who offers a sheepish shrug. "I'll have to double-check my spreadsheet, but I think Ayesha came the closest."

"Hell yeah!" Jamal high-fives his wife. "Well done, baby."

"Has everyone really been waiting for us to get together all this time?" Casey asks.

Kenzie cups her hands around her mouth to shout down the table. "Everyone who knew all along that G and Casey had it bad for each other, raise your hand."

Every single one of our friends smugly puts a hand in the air. Even Connor Autry. The fucker.

"Wait, so what's tongue-fucking, then?" Ozzy asks.

I cut a sly look at Casey, who turns bright pink and rolls her lips together.

Kenzie sighs loudly and massages her forehead. "I'll explain it to you later, dum-dum."

"Not a day goes by that I don't feel genuinely sorry for straight women," Quincy's girlfriend Jordan says.

"I'll have you know some of us are *very* well taken care of," McCafferty's girlfriend Maggie replies with a Cheshire cat smile.

The lieutenant's ears go red, and he takes a slug of beer.

"I'm not a great aural learner," Ozzy tells Kenzie. "I think I might need a live demonstration to understand the concept."

Kenzie shoves him off the end of the bench and sends him sprawling on the weathered wood floor.

McCafferty clears his throat and lifts his beer in a toast. "To Casey—the woman who tamed the savage G-Man."

"Hear, hear," everyone chimes in as they raise their bottles.

"You know you can do better than this guy though, right?" Quincy says.

"He's always leaving his wet clothes in the washing machine," Jamal points out.

"That's true, he does," Darius agrees.

"I'm aware," Casey says, patting my cheek fondly.

"And his sleep farts could wake the dead," Quincy adds.

"Only when I have to eat your cooking," I shoot back.

"We all know Casey's a saint," Kenzie says. "I'm just glad our boy G finally found someone who's willing to tolerate him."

"We've got some very nice single lesbian friends I think you'd really hit it off with," Quincy whispers loudly to Casey. "Just so you know."

"Quit trying to set my girlfriend up," I say as I tug Casey against me. "I licked her, so she's mine now."

"Dude," Ozzy says. "Seriously gross."

Ayesha urges Jamal to his feet as the band launches into their first song of the night on the stage at the far end of the hall. "Come on, babycakes. Let's dance."

"Still want to dance?" I ask Casey.

"I do," she says, her lower lip jutting out in a cute little pout, "but I don't think my poor feet are up to two-stepping tonight. Can we wait for a slow song?"

"We can do whatever you want," I tell her, leaning in to claim a soft kiss.

The other couples at the table peel off to follow Jamal and Ayesha to the dance floor, and I ply Casey with more waffle fries while Kenzie and Ozzy argue about whether a hot dog counts as a sandwich. Personally, I'm on the fence, since I don't see how they're that different from a sub or po' boy, but Casey joins Kenzie in the not-a-sandwich camp and wins me over to their side when she points out that people never cut a hot dog in half to eat it like they do with subs.

By the time the band slows things down with a cover of Tim McGraw's "My Best Friend," Casey's most of the way through her second beer and riding a happy buzz. I lead her to the dance floor and slip my arms around her waist to pull her close. We sway together, and I find myself blinking rapidly as she sings the lyrics into the crook of my neck.

I don't think I've ever been this happy my entire fucking life.

And it's all down to Casey. She's my peace, hope, and shelter. The connection I feel with her, it's so much bigger than anything I've ever experienced before. It's so strong it's overwhelming. So strong it scares the shit out of me.

It's not just that I can see myself with her for a lifetime. It's that I can't picture my future without her in it.

When your life gets smashed to pieces by loss, it leaves permanent scars behind. Too much of who I am has been shaped by the fear of being left behind again with nothing to hold on to for support. It's hard to feel safe when you know how fragile life is.

So all this happiness makes me a little uneasy. Because it depends entirely on one person. What if Casey gets tired of me? What if I fuck this up and lose her? What if she finds someone better? Or what if—god forbid—something happens to her?

She's my lifeline. If she ever lets me go, it'll smash me to pieces all over again.

Even though part of me is convinced this happiness can't last, at least I've got this moment right now. All I can do is keep holding on to Casey as tight as I can.

32

CASEY

The last month has been a crazy, hectic, thrilling ride, between training my replacement at the gym, learning the ropes at the bookstore, getting to know my new coworkers, and adjusting to my new schedule, which varies from week to week and day to day.

And of course, on top of all that, trying to squeeze in as much time as I can with Gareth.

Is it normal to think about sex, like, *constantly* when you have a boyfriend? Is everyone else who's in a relationship thinking about sex this much? Are they really all out there going through their daily lives horny on main all the time? Because I sure am.

Not that I'm complaining. I've lost count of how many orgasms I've had in the last four weeks. You'd think after a while I'd get tired of having so much sex, but nope. I still can't seem to get enough. Fortunately, neither can Gareth, which works out nicely for both of us.

Having a boyfriend is awesome.

The sex is out of this world, but so is everything else. Coming home to Gareth's kisses. Stealing touches as we make dinner together. Going out on dates. Reading beside him while he works on his English lit assignments. Falling asleep with his body curled around mine.

After living most of my life with a persistent feeling of discontent, I finally know what it feels like to have everything I want. A month ago I didn't even know *what* I wanted, and now look at me—I've got a super hot, thoughtful, amazing boyfriend *and* a new job that feels like it was made specifically for me.

I didn't expect any of this, but now I can't imagine going back to the way my life was before. Part of me is afraid I'm going to wake up and find out it was all just a dream.

A really, *really* great dream.

I absolutely adore working at the bookstore. Every other job I've ever had, I've compulsively watched the clock all day, counting down the hours and minutes until I could leave. Now the days pass so quickly I sometimes don't even notice when it's time to go home.

Tanner King is a great boss. He's patient, polite, welcomes all my suggestions, and loves what I've been doing with the store's social media, which he was only too happy to hand off to me. I've also been getting to know his fiancée Lucy, who works in marketing at King's Creamery and has been giving me tips to take my social media game to the next level.

I've liked everyone I've met at the bookstore, both the other employees and the customers. Well, except that one guy who tried to shoplift a copy of *Ice Planet Barbarians* by shoving it down the front of his pants. He was icky, but everyone else has been great. I feel as if I've found a place where I fit in, where I'm not just tagging along with my brother's friend group. Not that I don't love my brother's friends—obviously, since my boyfriend is one of them—but it's been nice to spend my days around fellow book nerds instead of listening to jocks talk about deadlift form and SLAP tears.

"We're getting low on napkins," Megan says, interrupting my wandering thoughts. "And stirring sticks."

She's the bookstore's only other full-time employee, a barista friend of Wyatt King's who runs the café for Tanner and supervises the other two part-time baristas she trained.

"Napkins and stirring sticks," I repeat as I make a note. "Check and check. Anything else I need to reorder?"

Megan's bright pink hair emerges from the cabinet underneath the counter. "Paper bags," she says as she straightens and glances around with her hands on her hips. "And what do you think about getting some pastry boxes for larger orders?"

"That's a great idea." I add it to my list as Megan grabs a towel to wipe down the empty tables.

It's near closing, and café traffic has mostly wound down for the day. There are only two people quietly working on their laptops, both of them regulars whose faces are familiar to me now.

While I'm here, I take a mental inventory of the remaining items in the pastry case, noting what sold out and what didn't so I can adjust our next order. We get them fresh daily from Leshikar's Bakery, which closes at noon, and people in town are gradually figuring out that they can get their favorite Leshikar's treats here later in the day.

My phone buzzes in my pocket, and my belly flutters when I see it's a new text from Gareth.

GARETH

Just saved a litter of kittens from a storm drain.

It's accompanied by a photo of him turned out in his firefighting gear holding three tiny gray kittens in his arms.

Be still my heart.

"Based on that dreamy sigh, I'm guessing that must be a text from your super-cute boyfriend," Megan says, shooting me a grin.

Gareth brings me lunch sometimes on his days off, so he's become a familiar face around the bookstore. Last week he even showed up in his fire truck with Ryan and the rest of the crew to pick up coffees on their way back to the firehouse. Let me tell you, they turned quite a few of our customers' heads as they came through the door in their firefighter uniforms, and I'm not too proud to admit I enjoyed the envious looks I got when Gareth greeted me with a kiss.

"You guessed right." I hold my phone out so Megan can see the photo he sent me.

"Holy ovary explosion. You are one lucky girl."

Don't I know it.

CASEY

It's mean to send a pic like this when I'm at work. How am I supposed to concentrate now?

GARETH

You can get me back by sending a sexy pic of you.

I take a selfie posing in front of the bakery case and send it to him.

GARETH

Mmmmm tasty

CASEY

Are you referring to me or the pastries?

GARETH

Both?

Kidding. I've only got eyes for your pretty face.

It's gonna be a long, lonely night in my bunk
with only this picture to keep me company.

"You guys seem pretty serious," Megan says.

Are we? We're serious compared to all of Gareth's previous no-strings hookups. Or compared to my nonexistent love life before him. But are we *serious* serious?

It's hard to say with no basis for comparison. It feels serious to me. There's no doubting how I feel about Gareth. Every day I fall a little more in love with him. But I'm not convinced we're both on the same page yet.

He hasn't told me he loves me other than the one time that I don't think counts. I haven't explicitly told him how I feel either because I don't want to put any pressure on him. For now, I'm trying to just enjoy what we have and let things run their course naturally.

"We've barely been together a month," I hedge.

Twenty-six days, to be exact, but who's counting?

Megan looks surprised. "Could have fooled me. I would have guessed that man was seconds away from going down on one knee and popping the question."

I don't know how to feel about that. It'd be nice to think so—not that I'm looking to get married *anytime* soon. But it would at least be confirmation that Gareth loves me as much as I love him.

I'm just not sure Megan's right. She's a bit of a romantic, so it's possible she's seeing what she wants to see instead of what's actually there.

"We've been friends for a while, so maybe that's why we seem so close."

"Ah, the old friends-to-lovers trope," she says with a smile. "One of my favorites."

"What are you two grinning about?" Lucy plops her laptop

bag on an empty table and sinks into a chair. She hangs out at the store most days after she gets off work until Tanner's ready to go home.

"Casey's dreamy fireman boyfriend," Megan says. "Show her the pic he sent."

I carry my phone over to Lucy, who lets out a squeal.

"Oh my god, that's the most adorable thing ever!"

"You're just looking at the kittens, aren't you?" Megan says.

"I mean, they're *kittens*. But your boyfriend is cute too." Lucy hands me back my phone. "Does that mean he's working tonight?"

"Unfortunately, yes."

Gareth's shift schedule is a bummer sometimes. Now that I'm used to sharing a bed with him, having to sleep alone one night out of every three sucks pretty hard. There are advantages though. Like that he's basically got the equivalent of a weekend off between every shift. Which is especially nice now that I work retail hours instead of a regular nine-to-five.

"We should all go out tonight," Lucy proposes. "It's been a long week, and I could definitely use a drink."

"I'm game," Megan answers.

"Yeah, okay," I say with a smile. "Sounds like fun."

Look at me, going out for drinks with my coworkers and making my own new friends!

After Lucy goes to tell Tanner about the after-work drinks plan, my phone lights up with another text.

GARETH

I miss the hell out of you when I'm on shift. I can't sleep unless I'm next to you.

The flutters in my belly bubble up into my chest. Because that sounds an awful lot like we *are* on the same page.

My fingers itch to type the words *I love you*. But I stop myself from doing it. The first time I tell him, I don't want it to be over text. I want to be looking at Gareth when I say it.

I'm going to tell him though. Tomorrow morning, as soon as he comes home from his shift. I've decided.

I love him and I want him to know. Even if he's not ready to say it back.

I'm done being afraid.

33

GARETH

"**D**amn, G-Man. Are these homemade biscuits?" Jamal rubs his hands together as I set the baking sheet on the counter. "What's the occasion?"

The occasion is that I had a crazy hot dream last night about licking honey off Casey's naked body. Which is now a fantasy I plan to make a reality at the first available opportunity. In the meantime, it left me craving biscuits, because nothing tastes better on a warm biscuit than honey. So for chow tonight I went the extra mile and whipped up some homemade biscuits to go with the buttermilk roasted chicken.

"Guess I felt like spoiling you bums," I say as everyone grabs a plate.

Captain Ortiz shoots me an odd look as we take our seats around the table. "Are you *humming*, Kelly?"

Shit. Didn't realize I was doing it again.

Guess I'm in a good mood. Aside from the kitten rescue this afternoon, it's been a quiet shift. Although I doubt that will last. Friday nights tend to get busy. But I don't mind busy. It makes the time pass more quickly. The sooner the end of shift comes, the sooner I get to see Casey again.

"He's been doing that a lot lately," McCafferty says, crooking a grin. "Can't imagine what's got him so chipper."

"I know that tune," Jamal says, narrowing his eyes. "You were humming a Taylor Swift song!"

"Dude," Quincy says with a snort. "You've got it bad."

I shrug as I butter my biscuit. "So what if I do?"

The bells go off and everyone falls silent as the firehouse intercom system dispatches Ladder 1 to a motor vehicle accident. So much for dinner.

"I'll put your leftovers in the fridge," the captain says as we shove our chairs back.

I cram my biscuit in my mouth and head out to the apparatus floor where our turnout gear is waiting by the rig. Focused and steady, we step out of our shoes and into the boots that are sitting inside our pants, then pull up the suspenders and haul on our coats. In less than sixty seconds we're all buckled into our seats on the truck as Quincy pulls out of the house with lights and sirens going.

The MVA is on Route 105, a ranch road on the outskirts of town. There's not a lot out that way except a large animal vet, a farm equipment supplier, and the Pumpjack, a local craft brewery that took over an old hay and grain warehouse a couple of years back.

"Hope it's not another DWI," Jamal says as we rumble toward the address dispatch gave us.

I grunt my agreement and peer out the side window. It's a narrow, windy stretch of road, and there's been an uptick in accidents out here since the Pumpjack opened.

"Oh fuck," Quincy says as we pull up on the scene.

"What is it?" I can't see out the front windshield from my seat in the rear, but something in her voice sends a trickle of icy dread down my spine.

In the officer's seat beside the driver, McCafferty turns

around to look at me, and the icy trickle of dread turns into a glacier at his grim expression. "It's Casey's car."

I'm flying out the door before we've finished rolling to a stop. As soon as my boots hit the pavement, I see it.

Casey's bright green hatchback.

Sitting in the road with its front half folded up like an accordion.

Christ, it's bad.

Suddenly, I can't move. The others jump into action around me. McCafferty barks orders as he and Jamal sprint toward Casey's car, but I can't hear a word he's saying over the buzz of white noise in my head. I'm frozen in place with my heart in my throat, staring at that crumpled hunk of green metal up ahead.

The one that's got my girlfriend inside it.

I've seen some horrific accidents in my time as a firefighter, a few so bad they gave me nightmares, but I've never frozen up like this before. Not even as a green candidate fresh out of the academy. Fire, heights, carnage—whatever the job throws at me, I've always been able to handle it. For better or worse, I've got enough of a daredevil streak that I can charge into dangerous or difficult situations without thinking about it too much. That's what the training's for. It's supposed to kick in automatically so I can do my job.

But that's not some stranger inside that twisted wreck.

It's the woman I love.

She's my whole fucking world. I can't live without her.

If she's in there—

"Gareth." Quincy gives my shoulder a hard shake, but her voice is gentle. "Come on, let's go."

Somehow, my feet start moving at her prompting. Not fast. It feels like I'm wading through concrete as Quincy guides me toward Casey's car like I'm a fucking victim instead of an experienced first responder.

McCafferty yanks on the handle of the driver's door, but it doesn't budge. Jamal doesn't appear to be having any better luck with the passenger door. Numbly, I register that the steering wheel airbag's deployed, and Casey's windshield is intact.

When I spot the blood smear on the driver's side window, an anguished sound tears out of my throat.

Quincy grabs my arm to keep me from getting any closer. "Lieutenant?"

She's strong, but not strong enough to stop me if I decide I want to go somewhere. I don't want to get any closer though. I'm too afraid of what I'll see.

What if Casey's dead?

I can't lose her.

I can't.

My stomach lurches as the ground beneath me tilts. I think I'm going to be sick. If it wasn't for Quincy's vise grip on my arm, I'd be on my hands and knees right now.

McCafferty motions us over as he bends down to peer in the side window. "Close your eyes for me, Casey. I'm gonna break the glass."

If he's talking to her, that means she's conscious.

Thank fucking god.

The realization lights a fire under my feet, and I surge forward, wrenching out of Quincy's grip as McCafferty's window punch shatters the bloodstained glass.

He squeezes my shoulder and steps back, giving me room.

"Casey," I croak, crouching beside the car.

Jesus. There's blood all over the side of her face. In her hair. Running down her neck and staining her shirt. The sight of it hits me in the chest hard enough that I have to clutch the door handle to steady myself.

"Gareth?" She tries to turn toward me and winces.

"I'm here." I reach inside the car and gently touch her shoulder. "Don't try to move, honey. I'm right here."

"Casey, can you tell me what hurts?" McCafferty says behind me.

"My neck. And my...my head."

She seems dazed but not disoriented, which is a good sign. But there's no telling how serious that head laceration is under all that blood.

"Yeah, looks like you've got a little cut there on your head," McCafferty says in the genial, *everything's just fine* voice he uses with victims to keep them calm. "Do you think you lost consciousness?"

"I don't think so."

"We're gonna get you out," I tell her. "We've got you, honey."

McCafferty passes me a C-collar. "Stabilize her neck."

"There was a deer," Casey says as I put the collar on her. "It ran out right in front of my car and...and I did what you always say to do. I swear, I—I didn't swerve or slam the brakes, just like you told me. But there wasn't time to slow down much and...I hit it." Her lip wobbles, and my heart caves in on itself. "I couldn't help it."

"It's okay, baby." I blink as my vision blurs. "You did great. I'm so proud of you."

"Can you see it anywhere? Is it dead? I killed it, didn't I?"

Jesus ever-loving Christ, she could have *died*, and she's worried about the fucking deer.

"I don't know, honey. Don't worry about that now. It wasn't your fault."

Quincy crouches beside me with a blanket. "Casey, we're gonna drape this over you to keep you safe while we get your door open, okay?"

I help her get Casey covered, and Jamal arrives with the Jaws of Life. We step back while McCafferty uses the hydraulic spreader to force the door open. The county ambulance pulls up as the four of us are lifting Casey out of the car and onto the backboard.

"Go with her," McCafferty tells me as the paramedics load her into the ambo. "We'll meet you at the hospital after we finish up here."

"Thanks, Lieutenant," I mumble and climb into the back.

My fingers are like ice as I hold Casey's hand on the way to the emergency room.

She's okay, I tell myself over and over again. *She's going to be okay.*

I need her to be okay.

She *has* to be.

34

GARETH

"She's okay," I tell Ozzy when he shows up at the hospital, wild-eyed with panic. "She's fine."

I tried not to alarm him too much with my text, but it's hard to downplay *your sister was in a car accident.*

He sags with relief and scrubs his hands over his face. "What the fuck happened?"

"She was on her way to the Pumpjack to meet up with some people from work, and a deer ran out in front of her car."

"Jesus." He looks like he's going to be sick.

"We had to use the Jaws to extricate her, but her injuries are minor—mostly just bruises and a cut on her forehead that needs a couple of stitches. She's sore and shaken up, but otherwise she's fine."

Me? Not so much. I've been putting on a decent show for Casey's benefit, but on the inside I'm a fucking mess.

"Thank god," Ozzy breathes, and pulls me into a hug. "And thank god you were there for her, man."

My throat closes as guilt swarms over my insides. I didn't do a fucking thing to help. All I did was go to pieces when Casey needed me.

"Where is she? Can I see her?"

"They took her for a CT scan, but you can see her as soon as she gets back."

Ozzy nods and stares around the waiting room like he doesn't know what to do. "I called our parents. They're on their way."

"Here, let's sit down." I lead him to an empty chair and sink down next to him. It guts me to see my best friend looking so lost. I can keep shoving my own shit down a little longer to be there for him.

A few minutes later, Mayor Goodrich flies through the automatic doors with her husband in her wake. It's the first time I've ever seen her without her dogs in tow. "Where's my daughter? Is she all right?"

Everyone in the ER waiting room does a double take of recognition, then politely looks away as Ozzy falls into her arms.

I explain what happened and try to reassure Casey's parents that she's going to be just fine.

Mrs. Goodrich wraps her arms around me. "Oh, Gareth, we're so lucky you were there to save our baby girl."

"I really didn't do anything," I say as guilt burns in my gut like battery acid.

I'm no kind of hero. I'm a fucking useless coward is what I am.

The doors slide open again and Kenzie rushes in. "How is she?"

I start over at the beginning and go through the whole story again for her benefit.

I'm barely holding my shit together at this point. I don't know how many more times I can do this, describing Casey's accident over and over. Every time I do, the images of her bloody face inside that crumpled car come rushing back and try to choke me.

It's hard to stand here and assure everyone that Casey's okay when I still haven't processed it myself. It's hard to project comforting calm when I'm in pieces on the inside.

I fucking hate hospitals. I can't be in one without reliving the worst night of my life, when I came home and found my dad unresponsive on the floor. I rode with him in the back of the ambulance just like I rode here with Casey tonight, and then I spent hours sitting in an ER waiting room a lot like this one, scared, in shock, and all alone.

Unlike my dad, Casey's going to be fine. But I can't climb out from under the crush of emotions. The fear. The despair. The guilt. I'm drowning in it.

Over the next half hour, more people trickle into the waiting room. Some of Casey's extended family, including her cousin Kaylee, and the coworkers from the bookstore who she was on her way to meet at the Pumpjack tonight.

Finally, McCafferty walks in, flanked by Quincy and Jamal. They came straight over after cleaning up the scene, so they're still in their turnout pants like me and wearing their radios in case they get another call. After I update them on Casey's condition, I introduce them to her parents as the *real* heroes who rescued Casey.

Because it sure as fuck wasn't me.

Casey's doctor comes out, and I introduce him to Casey's parents too. Apparently he knows McCafferty because they greet each other by their first names with a friendly handshake. Dr. Bayliss tells the Goodriches that Casey's CT scan was clear, and she can go home as soon as they can get someone from plastics to come down and do her facial stitches.

They'll only allow four people back into the treatment room to see her. Obviously Casey's parents and Ozzy should go. They try to get me to come with them, but I insist that Kenzie should go instead. I've already seen Casey, I tell them. It should be

Kenzie, not me. She's Casey's best friend. Casey'll want to see her. And I know she'll be better at cheering Casey up than I will.

If I go back there again, I'm afraid I'll lose it.

While we're arguing about it, McCafferty wanders over to talk to his brother Tanner, who was one of the people Casey was meeting at the Pumpjack, along with Tanner's fiancée. I can't remember her name, even though I've met her before. I can't remember any of the bookstore people's names, even though Casey talks about them all the time. I can barely remember my own name right now. I don't know how I'm still managing to go through the motions of being fine. It's amazing no one's noticed what a wreck I am.

After Dr. Bayliss takes Kenzie and Casey's family into the back, McCafferty breaks off his conversation with Tanner and pulls me aside.

"You okay, Kelly?"

I nod stiffly. "I'm ready to go whenever you are, Lieutenant."

He gives me a long, measured look. "Captain gave the okay if you want to take the rest of shift off."

"Not necessary," I say too quickly, earning another, harder look.

"Gareth," McCafferty says quietly. "Stay. You should be with her."

I can't.

I've got to get out of this place.

I can't talk about the accident anymore.

I can't keep accepting thanks for something I didn't do.

And I can't face Casey right now. Not like this. I won't be able to hold myself together, and I can't afford to fall apart.

Not again.

It's taken me years to get my life back on track. Everything was finally going okay, and then I had to go and let my walls down. I should have known better than to pin so much of my happiness on someone else. Because the only thing that's ever permanent is death. If you let yourself *need* someone, then when something eventually comes along to take them away, your whole world gets blown apart.

I've lived through it once already. I can't do it a second time.

I *can't*.

I'm the fucking worst. I know it.

But I can't be here another minute longer.

I swallow the bile rising in my throat and shake my head, refusing to look McCafferty in the eye. "Casey has plenty of people here for her, and I've still got a shift to finish."

Before he can say anything more, I grab my turnout coat and head outside to wait by the truck.

———

I'M the last one off the rig when we get back to the house. I take my time putting back my gear, letting everyone else go inside ahead of me.

They must guess I need a minute because no one hangs back or tries to talk to me. Thank god.

A couple of the guys from the engine company are talking to Quincy and Jamal when I walk through the common room.

"Hey, Kelly," one of them calls out as I pass by. "Your dinner's in the fridge."

"Thanks," I say without pausing. "I'll get it later."

I head straight for the bathroom, grateful to find it empty, and lock myself in a stall. There's an iron vise around my chest, and I can't fucking breathe. I bend over the toilet, brace my hands on my knees, and try to take long, slow breaths.

But when I close my eyes, all I can see is Casey in that smashed-up car with blood pouring down her face.

All I can smell is the hospital.

All I can hear is a doctor telling me the person I love most in the world is gone.

Breathe. Breathe.

It's not real. Casey's fine.

Everything's fine.

But I'm not.

35

CASEY

Every muscle in my body hurts. Dr. Bayliss said to expect it, that I'd probably hurt worse today, and boy, was he right.

The pain wakes me up midmorning. I lie in my bed, groggily taking stock of all the new aches that have cropped up while I was sleeping off the last of the good hospital pain meds. My wrists and knees are throbbing. My elbows too. My calves hurt. So do my shoulders and my back. Pretty much everything. If it's a muscle, it hurts. Even my freaking *butt* muscles.

On the bright side, my neck and head actually hurt a little *less* than they did last night. Or maybe it's that everything else hurts so much more it's drowning them out.

Even though there was nothing seriously wrong with me, it took forever to get discharged from the ER. It was almost two a.m. by the time my parents drove me home, and I could fall into bed.

It's after ten in the morning now. Gareth should be home. That's enough reason to haul my aching body out of bed.

I'm not hurt he didn't stay with me at the hospital. It's not his fault he was still on shift and had to get back to work. Although it might have been nice if he'd said goodbye before he left. But I had my parents with me, so it's not like I *needed* him to stay. Even if I would have liked to have him there to hold my hand while I was getting my stitches and run interference with my mother.

I sort of hoped he might get into bed with me this morning when he came home, but he was probably trying to let me rest. I'm only a little disappointed that I woke up alone.

When I shuffle out of my room, Darius and my brother are having a whispered conversation in the kitchen.

"You're up!" Ozzy chirps, quickly replacing his frown with a smile when he sees me. "How's the patient?"

"Achy," I mumble, setting my sights on the coffeemaker.

Darius steps into my path and envelops me in a very careful, very gentle hug. "I'm glad you're okay."

"Me too." I lean against him, needing a hug more than I realized.

"I'm sorry I couldn't come to the hospital last night," he says gruffly.

"It's okay, you were working. I had more people there than I needed anyway."

"Still." He releases me and frowns at the bandage on my forehead. "I don't like getting a text that you're in the ER."

"I'm fine," I tell him, pressing my fingers to the edge of the bandage. "I just need some coffee and ibuprofen."

"I'll get the coffee," Ozzy volunteers.

"I'll get the ibuprofen," Darius says.

"Are you hungry?" Ozzy asks as he fills my favorite mug with coffee. "I could make you some breakfast."

"Only if you want to kill me."

Darius snorts as he hands me two ibuprofen and a glass of water.

Ozzy opens his mouth to retort and shuts it again. "Since you were in an accident, I'll pretend not to be hurt by your disparagement of my cooking skills, and instead offer you a choice between frozen waffles, toaster pastries, and pizza rolls. Basically, anything your heart desires that can be heated in the toaster oven."

It freaks me out that my brother's being so nice to me. I mean, it's sweet, but it also makes me feel like there's something really wrong, like I'm secretly dying and no one wants to tell me. I sort of wish he'd go back to being a pill like normal.

"Or I can get donuts," Darius offers.

"Is Gareth upstairs?" I ask, because everything hurts and I could really use a hug from *him*, and it's hard not to be disappointed that he's not down here offering to make me breakfast instead of my brother. He's probably sleeping off his shift, but I'm hoping he won't mind if I wake him up for some cuddling.

Ozzy and Darius exchange a look.

"What?" Now they're *both* acting weird, and I don't like it.

"He's, uh, not here," Ozzy says, not meeting my gaze as he hands me my coffee.

I set it down on the counter too hard and it sloshes over the rim. "Where is he?"

Ozzy's jaw clenches. "We don't know."

"But his shift ended hours ago."

"He hasn't come home yet," Darius says as he wipes up the coffee I spilled.

"What do you mean he hasn't come home? Have you tried calling him?" My voice is creeping into a dangerously high register.

"He's not answering," Ozzy says.

"Either of us," Darius adds.

I fumble my phone out of the pocket of my pajamas and double-check my texts in case I missed one from Gareth.

Nothing. Not a word since yesterday evening.

It's alarming that he hasn't texted at all. Last he saw me, I was in the emergency room. Why hasn't he checked in to see how I'm doing? Or to find out if I got home okay? Or to ask if I need anything? Why isn't he *here*?

This isn't like him.

I knew something felt off with him at the hospital last night. I *knew* it. The way he left without a word was so odd. Even before that, he'd had this strained, vacant look, but I told myself it was only because he was worried.

I should have listened to my gut because now I'm certain something's not right.

I call Gareth's number, hoping I'm wrong. Praying he'll pick up for me even if he didn't pick up for Ozzy or Darius.

It goes straight to voicemail.

I leave a message. "Gareth, it's me. You haven't come home yet, and I'm worried about you. Please call me back and tell me you're okay."

Then I send him a text: *Where are you? Are you OK??? I'm worried. Please call me.*

"I'm sure he's fine," Ozzy tries to reassure me, but he's not very convincing.

Gareth's not fine. I know it, Ozzy knows it, and Darius knows it. That's why they were in a frowning huddle when I came out of my room.

I text Ryan McCafferty next: *Do you know where Gareth is? He's not home from shift yet.*

There's a good chance Ryan's asleep and won't see my text for hours. I resign myself to waiting and nearly jump out of my skin when my phone rings in my hand a few seconds later.

It's Ryan, calling me back already.

"Gareth didn't come home?" he says when I answer.

"I don't suppose he stayed late at the firehouse this morning?"

"He was the first one out the door."

I don't like the sound of that at all. "Do you have any idea where he might be? Did he mention stopping off anywhere on his way home or having something to do today?"

"No, nothing. I assumed he was headed straight home to you."

"Oh." I swallow and blink, trying not to cry. I'm probably overreacting. It's probably nothing, and Gareth will be home soon and everything will be fine.

"I just tried calling him, but it went to voicemail."

"Yeah, same with us." I hesitate, biting my lip. "Can I ask— did Gareth seem all right to you last night?"

There's a pause before Ryan answers. "No, not really. He seemed pretty shaken up, to tell the truth. I tried to talk to him, but he insisted he was fine."

Of course he did. That's so Gareth. I sniffle and rub my nose. "He never wants to admit when something's wrong."

"I know," Ryan says gently. "He's a lot like me that way. I think he might just need some space right now."

"Space for what?"

"You have to understand, Casey. Doing what we do, you see a lot of bad things on the job, and the only way to get through it is to keep yourself emotionally distant. But when the bad things happen to someone we care about, that's basically our worst nightmare. So when Gareth rolled up on that accident and saw that it was your car...well, let's just say it hit him hard."

As Ryan speaks, a bell starts ringing in my brain. All I can think about is sixteen-year-old Gareth losing his father, and how that loss shattered his whole life. He didn't just lose a parent he loved, he lost his home, any semblance of stability, and the only place he'd felt truly wanted. And when I think about all that pain Gareth keeps buried deep inside, it's easy to imagine how traumatizing last night would have been, and there's no doubt in my mind that he's trying to deal with it alone. Because being alone is all he knows how to do.

"How do we help him?" I ask, my voice wavering under the weight of my sadness. "What do I do?"

"Try not to panic. Gareth's got a good head on his shoulders, and my gut tells me he's not in any danger. I suspect he needed some time to work through some things. But I'll see what I can do to track him down, okay?"

"How much time do I have to give him before I'm allowed to panic?"

"If he hasn't checked in by tonight, I'll organize a full-blown search party. But I have a feeling he'll turn up before then."

"You really think he's going to be all right?" I ask, twisting a strand of hair around my finger.

"I really do. He probably just went somewhere he could be alone to get his head on straight. Try to take it easy and get some rest, okay? Do you have people looking after you? I can ask Maggie to sit with you if it'll help."

"Thanks, but I'm all right. Ozzy and Darius are here."

"Hand your brother the phone. I want to talk to him."

I pass my phone to Ozzy, who's been watching me through the whole conversation.

He presses it to his ear and paces away from me. "Hey, Big Red."

I can't hear what Ryan says to him, but Ozzy tugs on his hair as he listens, nodding and occasionally replying with an "uh huh" or a "yeah." After a minute, Ozzy thanks Ryan and hands me back my phone.

"He says not to worry, he'll find Gareth."

"I'm having donuts delivered," Darius announces, pulling out his phone.

"Get her chocolate-filled," Ozzy says. "*Lots* of chocolate-filled."

I remind my aching heart how lucky I am to have people who love me and are here for me. Even if Gareth isn't. He'll come back. I know he will. I have to believe that. I refuse to lose faith in him.

But that doesn't keep it from hurting that the person I love the most is missing.

36

GARETH

I get all the way to Austin before it occurs to me to wonder what the fuck I'm doing. I don't know where I thought I was headed when I got on the highway, or what I thought I was going to do when I got there.

I wasn't thinking, that's the problem. I was running away in a mindless panic. Because I'm too chickenshit to face my problems.

Except I can't get away from my problems when *I'm* the problem. You can't run away from yourself. I tried that already and it spectacularly didn't work.

What have I done?

My girlfriend was in a car accident last night, and I fucking ran away.

What kind of man does that? Not a good one, that's for sure.

I left her. I ran.

And I'm still running now.

After shift change this morning, I got into my car and started driving. All the way out of town. And past the next town. And the next. For seventy miles. *What the hell?*

When I see the exit for South Congress, I get off Highway 71 and drive toward the big pink dome of the capitol. I used to come to Austin a lot when I first took the job in Crowder. I didn't know anyone in town back then, so I'd drive up here on my days off for lack of anything better to do. I spent a lot of time driving around aimlessly, like I'm doing now. Seeing the sights. People watching. When the weather was nice, I'd go to a park or do some hiking on one of the trails around town. Occasionally, I'd check out a cool-looking restaurant or a bar, but I didn't have a lot of money for things like that in those days.

Today, I've got a little more money in my bank account, but no desire to be around people. I end up heading west on 35th Street, past MoPac and Camp Mabry, up to Mount Bonnell.

I used to come up here a lot to enjoy the view. It's usually crowded on the weekends, but it's raining today. Not hard, but enough to keep people inside.

I don't pass anyone on the stairs up to the summit. When I reach the pavilion at the top, I've got it all to myself. I'm also thoroughly wet, but I don't care. The gloomy, overcast weather matches my mood.

It's peaceful and quiet up here in the rain. A good place for some serious introspection. I find a flat rock overlooking Lake Austin and sit my ass down to contemplate how badly I've fucked up.

Epically, is my conclusion.

Casey needed me, and I fell apart. Not just at the hospital, but before that at the accident scene. I froze up in the middle of an emergency because I couldn't face the possibility of losing her. I'm trained to help people, and I couldn't help the one person who means more to me than anyone else in the world.

Because I got scared.

Casey was scared too. Injured. In pain. And I wasn't strong enough to help her.

If I can't be there for the woman I love when she needs me,

what fucking use am I? What business do I have being in a relationship?

None at all.

God only knows how long I sit there wallowing in my shame before I remember I forgot to take my phone off Do Not Disturb this morning.

Shit.

I have dozens of new notifications. There are texts, missed calls, and voicemails from a bunch of my closest friends, including Casey. Ignoring everyone else, I pull up her texts and my heart crumbles to a pile of dust and throws itself into Lake Austin.

Dear god, I really am the world's worst boyfriend. I've been so busy spinning out I didn't even consider how worried Casey would be when I didn't come home this morning.

What the fuck am I doing? I should be home taking care of her. Making her favorite foods and bringing her tea and ice packs. I should be running bubble baths and rubbing her feet and making sure she remembers to take her pain meds. Not sitting on a fucking rock in Austin in the rain like a one-person chapter of the broody emo losers club.

I don't deserve Casey.

I always knew it, but this is the proof. I was fooling myself to think otherwise. Peter Pan doesn't get to keep Wendy. He has to let her go so she can have the normal, happy life she deserves, with someone who isn't in a state of arrested emotional development.

While I'm still trying to work up the nerve to listen to Casey's voicemail, my screen lights up with an incoming call from Ryan McCafferty.

Calling to read me the riot act, no doubt.

I accept the call, prepared to take my medicine. "Hey."

McCafferty's deep voice rumbles in my ear. "Finally decided to answer your phone, huh?"

"Sorry, I've been...hiding, I guess."

"I figured as much. How's that working out for you?"

I snort. "Well, I'm sitting on a rock in the rain, contemplating my own breathtaking stupidity, so not great at the moment."

"Sorry to hear that."

"Is Casey all right?" I can't imagine what she must be thinking of me right now. It can't be anything good, that's for sure. I wouldn't blame her if she never wanted to see me again.

The long pause he takes before answering feels like a punishment, but it's one I've earned. "She's okay. Worried about you though."

I blow out a breath and lean forward, grinding the heel of my hand against my forehead. "I really fucked up, Big Red."

There's another long silence, and I figure he's about to launch into the lecture I so richly deserve. Which would be great, actually, because I could use some McCafferty wisdom right about now.

But all he says is, "Want to talk about it?"

Guess I haven't earned the lecture yet.

I stare through the mist at the gray water below. "Casey needed me, and I ran away."

"Yeah, you did." He's using his genial, *everything's just fine* voice on me like he's handling a shell-shocked victim.

"I don't deserve her."

He barks a laugh. "That's the dumbest thing I've ever heard you say, and you once tried to claim the best Indiana Jones movie was the fourth one."

"I'm serious, man."

"Don't you think Casey should get to decide who deserves her?"

I swipe the rain off my face. "I completely froze up last night when I saw her car. I took one look at all that twisted metal and the—the blood smear on the window, and I lost it. I couldn't do my job. If you hadn't been there—"

"But I was. That's why we work in teams. So none of us has to do it alone."

"I couldn't do it at all!" The words burst out past the constriction in my throat. "I locked up. I couldn't even move. What kind of man does that when his girlfriend's hurt?"

"A human one."

Why is he being so fucking *nice* to me? I want him to kick my ass, not tell me that what I did was okay. "Maybe she's better off without me."

"Why? Because you love her so much you're scared of losing her? If you're trying to convince me that makes you a villain, you're not gonna get me to agree."

"Because I can't be what she needs me to be."

"There's no shame in being scared, Gareth. If that had been Maggie's car last night, I'd be a total fucking head case right now, and you'd be the one trying to talk me off the ledge."

"You wouldn't have left Maggie at the hospital."

McCafferty's the strongest, most stand-up guy I've ever met. There's a zero percent chance he'd bail on the woman he loves.

"You don't know that, and neither do I. Until it happens, no one can know how they'll react. Last night knocked you for a loop. I get it. And now I bet you're trying to tell yourself it'll be easier to give Casey up on your own terms than lose her against your will. I've been there, brother. Believe me. But I've got bad news for you. You can't just wish away all these feelings you have for her. They're not going anywhere, whether you're with her or not. It's scary as hell, loving someone, but putting up walls won't keep you safe. And anyway, what would you rather have, a good life or a safe life?"

Well I got my lecture. And it's just the thorough ass-kicking I was looking for. Every one of McCafferty's words burns in my chest because he's right on the money about all of it. I don't know how he knows exactly what's going through my head, but it's like he's in there hearing the ugly voices whispering at me.

How much energy have I spent over the years telling myself that needing anyone was a bad idea? And for what? So I could live a small, lonely, self-contained life? I wasn't happy like that. I wasn't really living at all. I didn't feel alive until I lowered my guard and let myself love Casey.

And god, I do love her. So fucking much it feels like my heart's going to tear itself apart. She's made me soft and fragile by peeling back my armor to expose the raw skin underneath.

I thought the old wounds had healed, but they were smoldering inside me all this time like a hidden pocket of embers, waiting for an influx of oxygen to reignite the pain. Instead of letting Casey quench it with her cooling touch, I did the worst possible thing I could do—I ran away.

I get that now, but the damage is already done. I don't know how to undo this mess I've made. How am I supposed to face Casey after walking out on her? What if she doesn't want me back?

A lump of pain the size of a softball sticks in my throat, pressing hot tears to my eyes. "I let her down," I force out in a surge of shame, not hiding the wetness choking my voice.

"You made a mistake. It won't be the last."

I laugh-sob. "No shit."

"So fix it, Romeo."

"I don't know how."

"Well, the first thing you do is let Casey know you're alive. And then you apologize for disappearing without a word this morning and giving her a panic attack. After you've done that, I recommend you throw yourself on her mercy and beg her to take you back."

"Christ," I mutter, scraping my thumbnail over my eyebrow. "How did I fuck everything up this bad?"

"You've got issues. We all do. So talk to Casey. Tell her everything you're feeling. Be honest with her and with yourself."

A weak laugh bubbles out of me. "That's all?"

"It's harder than it sounds."

I grunt in acknowledgement. I don't need him to tell me that.

"If Casey knows you even half as well as I do, she'll understand."

Fuck, I miss her. I'd give anything to be with her right now instead of sitting on this godforsaken rock in the pissing-down rain. I can't remember anymore why I thought this would be better than going home to her.

I swipe at my eyes. "You really think she'll be able to forgive me?"

"If you want forgiveness, you have to ask for it."

Then that's what I'll do. I can't give Casey up without a fight.

I've been letting fear call the shots since I was sixteen years old. But I'm not going to let it destroy the best thing that's ever happened to me.

I'm still fucking terrified. Love is the biggest risk there is. But I don't want to be miserable and alone anymore.

I'm ready to look that fear in the eye and tell it to fuck off instead of letting it rule me. Loving Casey is a risk worth taking. If she'll let me, I'm going to love her the way she deserves to be loved. Wholeheartedly and forever.

37

CASEY

GARETH

I'm so sorry for making you worry.

I'll be home later today. I promise.

That's all I get from Gareth when he finally texts me. There's no explanation of where he's been or why he disappeared. I don't even get a concrete ETA, just a vague twelve-hour window. Sometime between noon and midnight.

"You should call him," Ozzy says when I show him Gareth's text.

"No," I say, struggling against the urge to do exactly that and demand an explanation. "If he wanted to talk to me on the phone, he would have called."

"Fuck that." Ozzy digs his phone out of his pocket. "I'll call him if you won't."

"Don't." I put my hand over his screen. "I'm asking you not to."

If Gareth needs space, he should have it. I owe him that

much. Yes, I want him here, but I want him to come back because he wants to, not because my brother guilted him into it.

Ozzy throws Darius a *help me out here* look, but Darius only frowns and shakes his head.

"Fine, whatever," Ozzy grumbles. "But I wish I understood what the fuck's going on."

I think I've got an idea. But Ozzy doesn't know as much about Gareth's past as I do, and it's not my place to tell him. He doesn't know how Gareth lost his father when he was a teenager, or that Gareth was the one who found his body. He doesn't know about Gareth's bullying stepfather, and how his mother turned her back on him and left him all alone in the world. How Gareth ran away and drifted around in a cloud of grief for years, trying to numb himself.

Knowing everything I do, it's not hard to imagine how my car accident must have forced him to relive those old traumas, breathing new life into half-healed hurts.

I'm not surprised he chose to run and hide rather than admit he might be struggling. I know him too well to expect anything different. I don't blame him, but it hurts to know he's hurting because of me. It hurts that I can't fix it. And it hurts that he turned away from me instead of turning *to* me.

I want to protect him. Take care of him. *Fix* him. But I can't. I can't undo the losses he's suffered, and I can't make him stop beating himself up over ancient mistakes.

I just wish he could see all the good in him that I can see. I wish he didn't feel the need to hide his pain from everyone. From *me*. I wish he trusted me as much as I trust him.

I don't know how to make him stop running from his feelings. I don't know if he'll ever be able to let down the walls he's put up. I don't know if he'll ever love me enough to want to let me in.

And that really sucks. For both of us.

Ryan calls a few minutes later to let me know he's heard from Gareth, and I don't need to worry. I thank him for calling, but I keep worrying anyway.

It's a relief to know Gareth's coming back. But I don't know what he's going to say when he gets here. I don't know that he's coming back to *me*. Maybe he's coming back to tell me he needs space. Not just today but on an ongoing basis.

He didn't want to be in a relationship. I basically pressured him into it. What if he's decided it's not worth it?

I want him to try, to choose to stay and love me, but I can't make him do it.

The day drags by at an excruciating pace. Every passing minute feels like an hour and carves a little more out of the growing hollow in my heart. I'm achy, sad, and listless. My bruises throb, my stitches itch, and I can't concentrate on anything except how much I wish Gareth was here to hold me in his arms. I keep staring toward the door, listening for the sound of his key in the lock.

"You want another slice?" Ozzy asks me, reaching for the pizza box on the coffee table next to the Settlers of Catan board.

My appetite's abandoned me, so I shake my head.

Ozzy's still being overly solicitous, and it's still unsettling. Whatever Ryan said to him on the phone this morning only made it worse. He and Darius have both been glued to my side all day, waiting on me hand and foot, ordering all my favorite takeout and trying to distract me with board games and nature documentaries.

I love them dearly for it, but it's Gareth I want sitting beside me. If I can't have him, I'd rather be alone so I can curl up in a ball and cry. Maybe that's why I understand Gareth so well. Because we're alike that way.

Ozzy sinks back onto the couch and focuses on the TV again.

"That mongoose is a goner. No way something that small and cute is taking out a black mamba."

"Twenty bucks says the mongoose eats that mamba for lunch," Darius says.

"You're on." Ozzy reaches around me to seal the bet with a fist bump. "I can see why you like these nature shows so much. This shit is hard-core as fuck."

We all freeze at the sound of the front door opening. Ozzy and Darius rocket to their feet, but I stay where I am. I don't entirely trust my legs to hold me up right now.

My stomach flips over when Gareth walks into the room. He's damp and bedraggled, clutching a brown paper shopping bag as tension rides his stiff shoulders, and the haunted look on his face does nothing to put my fears to rest.

"Dude, what the actual fuck?" Ozzy yells while Darius silently crosses his arms and looms.

Gareth darts an edgy glance at both of them before his gaze finally seeks me out. My heart trips and does an ungainly belly flop. He looks as miserable as I feel.

"Where've you been?" Ozzy demands. "Casey's been a basket case worrying about you all day. Did you forget she was in a car accident last night, or did you just not give a damn that she might have needed you today?"

"Oswald Theodore Goodrich," I snap as I get to my feet. "I don't require you to speak on my behalf."

My outburst draws three startled stares. Pulling out full names is the equivalent of DEFCON 2.

"Can't I even yell at him a little bit?" Ozzy pouts. "At least let me punch him in the balls for you."

"I want to talk to Gareth alone."

Darius starts corralling my brother toward the door. "Let's you and me go get a beer."

Ozzy gives a huff of defiance but lets Darius manhandle him out of the house without putting up a fight.

Gareth's shoulders hunch when the door slams behind them. His bloodshot blue eyes stare at me, but he doesn't come any closer.

It's not the joyful reunion I was hoping for. He's here, but he still feels far away. I want to throw myself into his arms, but he looks as if a touch will shatter him.

"Hey," he says in a voice that's a shadow of its usual self.

"You came back."

He takes a half step and stops, looking pained. "Did you think I wouldn't?"

"I hoped you would."

"I'm sorry, I didn't mean to make you worry. How are you feeling? How's your neck?"

"Just a little sore." I shrug carefully, because shrugging is one of the movements that hurts. "I'm lucky."

His lips pinch together as he sets the paper bag next to the pizza box on the coffee table. "I brought you some stuff from Austin. Sort of a get-well present."

I stare at the bag and then at him, my brow furrowing in confusion. "Is that where you've been? Getting me a present?"

"No—I mean, yes, I went to Austin, but that's not why." He shakes his head at the floor.

I don't say anything. Just wait to see if he wants to tell me why.

He does, it seems, although it takes him a few seconds to work up to it.

"I guess I've been spinning out a little since last night. And this morning I got in my car and—" He cuts himself off with another head shake and squeezes the back of his neck. "I needed to clear my head, I guess, and figure out some things."

I swallow with difficulty. "And did you?"

"Well, I figured out that I've been a shitty boyfriend."

"Don't say that."

His brow knits. "You're supposed to be mad at me."

"Would it make you feel better if I was?"

"You were hurt, and I left." The words lash out of him like a whip. "You deserve a hell of a lot better than that, Casey. So yeah, you should be angry. You should be fucking livid."

My arms ache to pull him into a hug, but I only allow myself to take a single step toward him. I still don't know how much space he needs. "You really think I'd get mad at you for being afraid? You don't think I understand what that's like?"

He shakes his head. "You needed me and I couldn't help you."

"What are you talking about? You're the one who rescued me."

"I didn't. That wasn't me."

"Gareth, you were right there. I remember every second of it. You talked to me and helped get me out of the car and—"

"You don't understand." His throat works on a swallow. "I'm trained to run toward an emergency and spring into action. But when I saw your car all smashed up at the side of the road, I couldn't move. I just stood there paralyzed. Quincy had to bodily move me toward the scene. You were hurt, and I didn't run to help you because—" His chest heaves with a strangled sob. "I was afraid to find out how bad it was. Because what if it was too late to save you? What if it was just like when I found my dad, and I couldn't save him?"

"Come here." I close the space between us and wrap my arms around him.

He shudders, then sags, dropping his head to my shoulder. Cold wetness from his shirt soaks into my pajamas as he clutches my waist like a life preserver.

"God, Casey." A ragged breath gusts out of him. "I

completely lost my shit. The thought of losing you—I couldn't stand it. I can't go through that again."

Guilt pulls at my heart as I stroke his damp hair and the taut muscles of his neck and shoulders. I hate that I put him through this and made him relive the worst experience of his life. "I'm okay. It's okay."

"It's not fucking okay. You *needed* me, and I failed you." His arms tremble as they tighten around me. Arms so thick and strong they feel like they're made of granite instead of muscle. The same arms that lifted me out of the wreck of my car last night and helped carry me to safety. The arms that gently cradled me against his body at the hospital while we were waiting for the doctor. Arms that have held me, comforted me, sheltered me more times than I can count.

My own arms seem weak and ineffectual by comparison, but they're all I have, and I hold on to Gareth with everything I've got, trying to give him back some of the strength he's given me.

"Listen to me. You may have hesitated for a moment, but you did everything I needed you to do last night. You talked to me and kept me calm and held my hand in the ambulance. There were other people there who could pry the car door open and take my blood pressure. I only needed you to comfort me, Gareth, and that's exactly what you did. You didn't fail me."

"I should have stayed with you at the hospital last night. McCafferty offered to let me stay, but I left. Just like I left this morning. I didn't want you to see me fall apart. That's why I ran. I knew I wouldn't be able to hide it from you." He lifts his head to look at me with brimming eyes. "I've never let anyone else get close enough to really know me. But you look at me, and it's like you see *everything*, even the broken mess I try to hide."

A smile pulls at my lips as I run my fingers over his rough, stubbly jaw. "Vulnerability is scary, isn't it?"

The corners of his eyes crinkle as he huffs a wry laugh.

"Yeah, no shit. I'm not exactly good at opening up. Or dealing with my feelings."

"Me neither."

"You're better than me." His smile fades as he touches his fingertips to the bandage on my forehead. "In so many ways."

"Gareth—"

"No, listen. I know I don't deserve you, and I can't guarantee I won't ever lose my shit again, but if you'll give me another chance, I promise I'll try my damnedest to keep you safe and happy from now on."

"You already make me happy. You always have."

He releases a breath, as if he really thought there was a chance I'd turn him away. Silly, beautiful man.

The lines in his face soften as his gaze roams over me. "Do you have any idea how much I love you?"

I make an incoherent sound as my heart leaps into my throat.

A smile lights his bright blue eyes, and he takes my face in his hands. "I love you, Casey. So much."

Relief and joy surge through me as Gareth touches his lips to my temple, my cheek, and finally my mouth, each tender kiss feeling like both a promise and an apology.

I tunnel my hands in his hair, pulling him against me, holding him close. "I love you too."

He tightens his grip and buries his face in the crook of my neck with a muffled sigh. "I'm so fucking relieved to hear you say that. I know I've got some things I need to work on so I can love you the way you deserve, but I swear to god, I'm gonna get better at this. Starting right now. There are some things I want to tell you."

"Okay," I whisper. It's such a relief he's not putting distance between us anymore—both physical and emotional—that my eyes blur with tears.

He lifts his head to look down at me, his expression serious, and clears his throat. "When my dad died, I went into free fall and let my life spin out of control. It changed me, made me afraid to let myself need anyone else. I'm guessing you probably figured that out already."

"I sort of had an idea."

His mouth quirks with a soft smile, and he presses his palm to the side of my neck. "I've worked pretty hard to keep a certain distance from people so it couldn't hurt me if they disappeared. But falling in love with you was so easy, I didn't even realize it was happening until I was in too deep to stop it. When you got in that accident, I had to confront the possibility of losing you, and it scared me so bad I panicked. It felt like I was spinning out of control all over again, but I'm such a stupid motherfucker that I ran away from you when I should have been holding you even tighter."

I squeeze him hard enough to let him know I'm willing to hold on for both of us, so hard I hear his breath leave him with an *oof*.

"I'm sorry for that," he says, stroking his thumb along the line of my jaw. "I'm sorry for not believing in us. I want you to know it was never about you. It was my fear and my past making me doubt myself. It took me some time to figure that out though. I got all the way to Austin before I realized I'd run away from the best thing that ever happened to me."

A tear slips down my cheek, and he swipes it away with the pad of his thumb.

"All those years, I was keeping my life small and controlled and telling myself it was safer that way. But that wasn't me taking control, it was letting my fear control me. I just didn't realize how lonely and cold my world was until you showed me what I'd been missing. I don't want to go back to that."

"Good." I reach up to cover his hand with mine, holding it against my wet cheek.

He bends his head and kisses me once, lightly. "The way I love you is too big to run away from. You're my center of gravity. So from now on, I'm going to run toward you instead of away."

I grasp the back of his neck to pull his mouth against mine again. It's a slow, heartbreakingly tender, perfect kiss. At the end of it, his gaze finds mine, and he smiles.

"You're going to be the one for me forever. No matter how long our forever is, I'll be grateful for every second I get to love you."

My hands cradle his face, reacquainting themselves with the familiar planes and prickly texture. "You're the best thing that ever happened to me too. I hope you know that."

His smile shines even brighter. "Feel free to keep telling me that until it sinks in."

"I will."

He pulls me against him in a possessive hug. I lose track of how long we stand there holding each other, enjoying in the feeling of closeness, before he lets me go.

"Don't you want to see your presents?"

I'd forgotten all about them. I don't need presents when I've got Gareth, but he looks so eager that I nod and hold out my hand.

He snags the bag off the coffee table and guides me to the couch, sitting down next to me as he sets it on my lap.

I reach inside the slightly damp and surprisingly heavy paper bag and come out with a small box wrapped in a plastic bag. Inside that is my favorite pomegranate green tea.

"Please tell me you didn't drive all the way to Austin just to get me tea."

He shakes his head with a laugh. "I wish I had, but that's just where I happened to be when I came to my senses. And since I was there, I figured I better come back with a peace offering."

"You didn't need to do that," I say, stroking his face as I touch my lips to his. "You could have come straight home, and I would have been just as overjoyed to see you. But thank you. This is very sweet."

"I got you something else," he says, nodding at the bag.

Whatever it is, it's heavy and square, and fills up the whole bottom of the bag. It's hard to slip my fingers around it to maneuver it out, but Gareth helps by pulling the paper bag away.

Leaving me holding a boxed set of the Penguin Classics clothbound editions of Jane Austen's complete works.

"Oh my god," I whisper. They're so beautiful, all I can do is stare in awe. These foil-stamped clothbound editions are the ultimate indulgence coveted by Bookstagrammers everywhere. "How did you even know I wanted these?"

He shrugs like it was nothing. "I heard you talking to Kenzie about them once."

"And you remembered?" I don't even remember it, so it must have been ages ago, long before we started dating, back when he wouldn't have had any reason to pay attention to something like that.

"I always listen to everything you say. I want to know about all the stuff you like."

I set the books and tea safely on the coffee table before I throw my arms around Gareth's neck and kiss him hard on the mouth. "I love you. I really do. So much."

He laughs as he carefully lifts me into his lap, cautious of my aches and bruises. "I guess that means you like the books."

"You really, really did not have to get them for me, just so we're clear. But yes, I love them." My fingers thread into his hair as I kiss him again. "Not as much as I love you though, obviously."

His hand smooths over my hip. "I'm glad I didn't completely fuck this up."

I cup his rough cheek and press my mouth to his. His lips part, and I feel him tremble as he kisses me back, deep and needy, as if we've been apart for years instead of hours. I'm light-headed by the time we part for breath, and my heart's so full, it feels like it's going to burst.

"I love you," Gareth whispers, nuzzling my cheek. "I'm never going to let you forget it."

"Surprising me with the clothbound Austen set officially makes you the best boyfriend in the entire world, for the record."

He lets out a husky laugh. "Good to know."

I sigh happily, wrapped up in his arms and his love. It's all I need in the world. Just him. Nothing else.

"Tell me the truth," he murmurs, stroking the side of my neck. "Weren't you even a little bit mad that I ran off?"

"You won't like my answer," I say, toying with his shirt.

"Tell me anyway."

"I wasn't mad. I was sad."

He groans and drops his head back against the couch. "God, that's so much worse."

"I know." My palm presses against his cheek. "I'm sorry."

His brow knits as he captures my fingers and brings them to his lips. "Don't ever be sorry for telling me how you feel."

"You either."

"I'll try," he vows solemnly. "I'll really try. For you."

"That's all I ask." My lips curve into a smile as we kiss again.

I'm overwhelmed with how much I love this man. He's a survivor. Wounded, but still fighting. So brave it blows my mind. So thoughtful, loyal, and protective, it's a privilege to be his friend. He's smart, loving, and the sexiest, most generous man I've ever known.

But best of all?

He's mine. And I'm his.

What a beautiful, perfectly imperfect miracle that is.

EPILOGUE
GARETH

> *It was the best of times, it was the worst of times, it was the age of wisdom, it was the age of foolishness, it was the epoch of belief, it was the epoch of incredulity, it was the season of Light, it was the season of Darkness, it was the spring of hope, it was the winter of despair, we had everything before us, we had nothing before us, we were all going direct to Heaven, we were all going direct the other way...*

I shake my head as I sip my coffee. Casey was not wrong about Charles Dickens's fondness for a run-on sentence. That one's a real whopper, but I'm pleased to find that I can follow it without as much trouble as I once would have had. Thanks to my English lit class—which I passed with a solid B-minus, thank you very much—and Casey's enthusiastic encouragement and influence, I'm no longer intimidated by the meandering, antiquated writing style.

I doubt I'll ever grow to love Dickens as much as Casey does, but I can read a sentence like that and appreciate what it's saying. Hell, I'm actually sitting in a bookstore reading nineteenth-century English literature for fun right now. I've come a long way the last few months.

"You good?" Megan asks, pausing next to my table. "Want another coffee?"

I look up from my book with a smile. "Thanks, but I'm all set."

I'm just hanging out, waiting to give Casey a ride home from work. The insurance payout for the totaled Picklemobile wasn't a lot, so Casey's saving up to buy a Picklemobile 2.0. In the meantime, we've been sharing my truck. The bookstore doesn't close for another hour, but I was already out running errands and figured I'd chill here in the café until she's ready to go.

"Just let me know if you change your mind."

As Megan walks away, I catch the woman sitting at the table across from mine eyeing me over her laptop. She smiles in a way I recognize as a hopeful invitation, but I don't feel the slightest temptation to flirt back. There's only one woman I want to flirt with anymore. I don't get a rush from other women's attention. Now it just makes me uncomfortable. I can't fucking wait until the day I've got a wedding ring on my finger to let everyone know my heart already belongs to someone else.

Casey doesn't know it, but while she's been saving for a car, I've been saving for an engagement ring. I've got it picked out and the proposal planned and everything. We're taking a trip to Scotland next year—another thing we're saving money for—and that's when I'm going to do it. I'll have finished my degree by then, which is what the trip's supposed to be celebrating. We're going for a Highland Games in Loch Lomond, but after that we're spending a few nights in Edinburgh, then going to Fife and taking a boat out to the wildlife reserve on the Isle of May to see the puffins that nest there every summer.

That's where I'm going to pop the question and slip a ring on Casey's finger.

I hate that it's so far away, but it'll be worth it to make a memory she'll never forget. Otherwise I'd elope with her tomorrow. And I have to admit, as ready as I am to be married, I'm not in a big rush to change the way things are right now.

We've been so happy together these last few months. I love our lives, and I love living with our friends in the house where Casey and I fell in love. They're more than just friends to me. They're family. Part of me doesn't want anything to change, even while another part of me can't wait to start a new chapter of my life with Casey in our own place.

Speaking of family...I glance at my phone when it lights up with a text from my mom.

She called me out of the blue last month to tell me she left my stepfather. She actually apologized to me, if you can believe it, and said she wants to get to know me and be part of my life again.

Initially, I wasn't sure how I felt about that. I admit to being skeptical. But we've been talking and tentatively trying to rebuild our relationship. It hasn't been all sunshine and rainbows, but it's getting a little better. I have to give her credit for making an effort, and I'm trying to meet her halfway. I'm not sure we'll ever be truly close, but it's kind of nice to feel like I have a mom again instead of a painful, hollow place where she used to be.

I'm five chapters into *A Tale of Two Cities* when Casey comes into the café. As soon as she spots me, a smile overtakes her face, transforming it from beautiful to utterly stunning. "Hey there."

"Hey," I murmur as she bends down to kiss me. "Mmm, you taste like honey."

Her cheeks go red. "It must be the tea I was drinking."

That sex dream I had featuring Casey and honey? Yeah, we made that dream come true, and the reality was even better than the fantasy. Her blush tells me she's thinking about it right now just like I am. Tonight's looking like a good night for a repeat.

"Hey Gareth," Tanner says, which is the first I notice him standing there with Casey.

What can I say? I've only got eyes for my girl.

He flashes a knowing smile as I stand to greet him. "She's all yours. Sorry for keeping her late."

I was so caught up in the political intrigues of the French Revolution, I hadn't even noticed it was past six.

"Do we have anything planned tonight?" Casey asks me.

"Lucy and I are going to the Rusty Spoke later to see Wyatt's band, if y'all feel like joining us," Tanner says. "We could all grab dinner first."

"It's entirely up to you," I say, slipping my arm around Casey's waist. "What do you think, honey?"

"I think I could murder a burrito bowl." She smiles up at me before turning to Tanner. "What about Groovy's for dinner?"

"Sounds good to me," Tanner says. "You're welcome to come too, Megan."

"Thanks, but I've already got plans," the pink-haired barista says as she ties up the trash bag.

"She's got a hot date tonight," Casey says, and Megan laughs.

"I don't know about hot, but I've got my fingers crossed."

The bell on the shop's front door rings, and Tanner breaks into a smile. "There's my hot date now. I'll go ask her how she feels about burritos."

"You sure you don't mind?" Casey murmurs after Tanner walks off to greet his fiancée. "We don't have to go out."

"I'm game for whatever, as long as I'm with you," I say and brush a light kiss to her lips.

Would I rather take her home right now, drizzle honey on her naked body, and give her orgasms for as long as she'll let me? Hell yes. I want her all the time. Every delicious inch of her.

Always. But there'll be plenty of time for orgasms later, and the anticipation will only make it that much sweeter when I eventually take Casey to bed.

I reach up to remove a large binder clip from her bun. "You might want to leave this here."

She takes it from me with a sheepish smile. "I hope you weren't too bored waiting on me."

"It's a bookstore. There's plenty of entertainment to pass the time."

Casey notices the book lying on the table. "You're reading *A Tale of Two Cities*?"

"It's your favorite Dickens, so I thought I'd check it out. You said it's a love story, right?"

"It's a love story, but it's not a romance. If you want a happy ending, you should read Jane Austen. Her books are a lot less tragic."

"I'll give her a try one day too, but I can handle a little tragedy. I don't need to read a happy ending when I've already got a real-life one of my own."

"I love you," Casey whispers, stroking her fingers along my jaw. "Have I told you that recently?"

"Only every day."

I still can't believe how lucky I am to have her. I never expected to experience this kind of happiness. It's not something I'll ever take for granted.

I finally found myself.

With her.

I'm exactly where I belong.

ABOUT THE AUTHOR

SUSANNAH NIX is a RITA® Award-winning and *USA Today* bestselling author of rom-coms and contemporary romances who lives in Texas with her husband. On the rare occasions she's not writing, she can be found reading, knitting, lifting weights, drinking wine, or obsessively watching *Ted Lasso* on repeat to stave off existential angst.

———

To learn more about Susannah Nix, visit:

susannahnix.com

Or follow her on social media:

facebook.com/SusannahNix

twitter.com/Susannah_Nix

instagram.com/susannahnixauthor

bookbub.com/profile/susannah-nix

goodreads.com/susannah_nix

Made in United States
North Haven, CT
24 August 2023

40694485R00203